Sunstroke

Marc Blake

FLAME
Hodder & Stoughton

First published in 1998 by Hodder and Stoughton
First published in paperback in 1999 by Hodder and Stoughton
A division of Hodder Headline PLC
A Flame Paperback

10 9 8 7 6 5 4 3 2 1

A CIP catalogue record for this title is available
from the British Library

ISBN 0 340 75048 0

Typeset by Palimpsest Book Production Limited,
Polmont, Stirlingshire
Printed and bound in Great Britain by
Mackays of Chatham PLC, Chatham, Kent

Hodder and Stoughton
A division of Hodder Headline PLC
338 Euston Road
London NW1 3BH

To Claire

PROLOGUE

The Brit stood on the balcony of the old villa and gazed at the morning mist settling in the valley. Taking a final drag on his cigarette, he ground it under his trainer and put his hands on the railing. The metal was already warm to the touch. He let out a sigh, thinking of how the harsh Spanish sun would soon be baking his belly, frying his fading tattoos and roasting his bald head to a violent crimson. It hadn't been a good year so far. He'd been given the prognosis, the diagnosis, the second and the third opinions and now the truth was undeniable: he was dying. Not slowly, basting in sun and Sangria like the other expats, but fast, eaten up inside. He spat out a bolus of phlegm. It was going to be his last summer in the Costa del Sol and he intended to make it count.

A pair of flip-flops smacked on the tiles and a dark Andalucian youth appeared at his side.

'Venga, Señor! Aquí, ahora.'

The boy scuttled through to the bedroom and hovered by the doorway. As the Brit padded inside, he saw that the youth was pointing a trembling finger at the bed. A naked girl lay twisted on the sweat-stained sheets. Removing the gag from her mouth, he slapped her across the face. Nothing. He stood back and stared at her, hearing only the faint clunk of a goat's bell in the distance as the herd returned from milking. The youth's eyes were on him now, willing him to magic her back to life.

'Fuck it,' he said.

He strolled through to the kitchen, the boy watching as he sprung open the fridge, fished out a cool San Miguel and drained it in one. Tossing the bottle aside, he wiped the froth from his lips and crooked a gold-encrusted finger to summon the youth closer.

'*¿Qué vamos a hacer, Señor?*'

He put a fatherly arm around the boy's shoulders and the youth melted into his chest. Tears dampened his shirt front. He began to smooth the boy's hair, stroking and preening and then twining a clump of it around his fist. Another whimper, softer this time. The Brit slowly shuffled across to the fridge. Without warning, he gripped the youth by the neck and rammed his head against the freezer door. He pulled back and, with all his strength, hit home again and again until red tears of blood ran down the white metal surface. Grunting with the effort, he gave a final thrust and the door buckled inwards. The youth folded on to the filthy tiles and lay still.

The refrigerator shuddered. Wiping trickles of sweat from his temples, the Brit leaned forward, wrenched the door open against the body and groped inside for another beer.

'Gonna be a scorcher today,' he muttered.

PAI

A disco beat murmured in the midnight air as Mike Trent slipped into the deserted pool. Above him, blue television strobes played on the hotel balconies. He swam a length, stopping short of the filter which was fizzing away like a giant aspirin. Treading water now, he relaxed as the smooth liquid licked his shoulders and caressed his hair. He peddled his legs to the surface, spread his arms wide and prepared to float. Gazing up at the sky, he smiled at the stars. They were bright and in sharp focus. Better than London, he thought. It never really gets dark there, just shades of plum and dirty orange like rotten fruit. He kicked back and sculled to the centre of the pool.

'This is the life,' he said aloud.

The body plummeted into the water from three storeys above him.

As the wash dragged him under, it occurred to Mike that perhaps the holiday hadn't started so well after all.

That morning as they were packing, he'd failed to prevent Nicola from forcing the contents of her wardrobe into two cases.

'You won't need all that stuff,' he'd said, waving a hand at the battered suitcase he'd borrowed from his mother. 'See? That's all I'm taking.'

He stuffed in a shirt and took inventory. T-shirts, jeans, trunks, a crumpled jacket and several books he'd always meant to get round to reading and probably still wouldn't.

Nicola ignored him and crammed in another pair of sandals.

Arriving at Gatwick too late to get smoking seats, Nicola stared doe-eyed at the check-in clerk and invented a number of medical reasons why she had to sit at the rear. When this didn't work, she strode off in her new white platforms and sulked until take-off. Her mood improved only when the plane punctured England's perennial grey blanket. However, it nose-dived again at the arrivals lounge in Malaga when one of her bags emerged leaking moisturiser on to the carousel. Leaving her to mop up in the restroom, Mike heaved the other cases on to a trolley and wheeled off to find the rep.

Sarah Rutherford's bright uniform was more a cry for help than a fashion statement. She was standing in the epicentre of the hurricane of tired holiday-makers and ticking off names on her clipboard. Her dark curls were thrust into a wiry bun and her pretty, elfin face was lightly tanned. It was enough to make Mike tuck in his shirt and feign the nonchalance of a more experienced traveller. He'd almost reached her when Nicola clopped up alongside. He averted his eyes and fell into step as they followed the others on to the coach bound for Fuengirola.

The coastal strip of the motorway which stretches between Malaga and Gibraltar is known as the road of death. One reason for this is tourists who, new to driving on the right, swerve on to the busy carriageways with the caution of teenagers let loose on the dodgems; another reason is the local coach drivers. Mike and Nicola had been unlucky enough to get Pepe, a man who wore sunglasses day and night in the mistaken belief he was a South American despot. Consequently, he drove like one. As he wrenched the silver juggernaut into the teeming lanes, Mike clung to his seat and shuffled through his passport to check the 'next of kin' section.

After half an hour of crazed slaloming, their speed decreased as they approached the suburbs of Torremolinos. The Tannoy crackled as Sarah began to recite her rehearsed speech. The passengers showed no interest when she explained that the town had once been a tiny fishing village, they failed to react when she informed them that Ernest Hemingway had spent time in Ronda and they ignored her suggestion to visit the *pueblos blancos* up in the Sierras. However, when she pointed out that Sean Connery lived off the *autovía*, their heads whiplashed back and forth like wipers in a hail storm.

Nicola shuffled beside him as she dug into her bag for her

lighter. Mike reached between his feet for the carton of duty-free cigarettes and, snapping open the cellophane, handed her a fresh pack. She lit one, revolved the cassette in her Walkman and settled back with her eyes shut and her chin raised. He smiled at this habit of hers. It wasn't that she was scared of getting a double chin: quite the reverse, her chin was tiny and it barely cupped her face. She was sensitive about it and constantly pulled at the skin or stretched out her neck in an attempt to firm up her jaw. This often had the effect of causing people to think she'd spotted someone more interesting across the room.

Mike gazed out at the dark hills and rewound their relationship. They had met when she came to *Sorted!* magazine as a temp. Although her arrival had led to a marked improvement in grooming amongst the staffers, Mike's only concession had been to rake a comb through his tangled brush of hair. He hadn't thought he stood a chance with this effervescent blonde. After all, who'd want a sub-editor twelve years past his sexual peak? He'd immersed himself in his copy-editing and had studiously ignored her.

Opportunity came by default. One slack day in February, the staff drew up a list of her more visible attributes and held a sweepstake on who'd be first past the bedpost. Mike, having arrived late due to a dose of flu, found her weeping at the word processor. Apparently, she'd found the list and had called them all animals. Someone had then corrected her by saying 'Mammals'. Her response was to start lobbing potted plants as they retreated to the pub to re-evaluate their attitudes. Mike discovered she was on the rebound. Her ex, Gavin, was a car salesman whose hobbies were his Maserati, other women and his Maserati. He slipped into the role of transitional man with a mixture of gratitude and ill-concealed glee.

The following month was a sexual marathon which culminated in pet-names and thrush. Come April, they had stopped writing weekly love-notes to each other. Soon after that, their differences emerged. She was twenty-two; he was thirty-one. She was a compulsive clubber who wanted to be out six nights a week; he wanted to sit at home, watch the telly and gripe. It was around this time that she had suggested the holiday.

Mike thought she was being ironic. Two weeks in the Costa

del Sol? 'I learn it from a *boook,*' he'd joked in a passable imitation of Manuel from *Fawlty Towers*. Nicola explained that her family alternated holidays between southern Spain and Ibiza. However, this year they had chosen Disneyland, which she didn't much fancy because it sounded childish. He'd considered it. On the plus side, it was an affordable and stress-free way of spending a fortnight. On the negative, he preferred the kind of holidays where you avoid other English people, the sort where you find struggling with foreign languages and customs exhilarating; not that he'd been on one, of course, but he had been to Norfolk. In the end, he agreed to go.

Now he wondered if he would regret it. Still fresh in their minds was a row along the lines of the classic 'move in or break up' argument. They had parted for a week and really only got back together because of the unrefundable deposit.

'We are now arriving in Fuengirola so those of you who are staying at the Hotel del Playa please remain in your seats.'

Mike gazed at Sarah. She looked like she wanted to be elsewhere. She made no eye contact with her charges and wasn't bothering to maintain even a superficial smile. In fact, she didn't seem like your typical tour rep at all.

'If you're at the Hotel Bella Vista, we'll be dropping you first, so—'

The coach became a jungle of grabbing, stretching limbs.

'—please wait until the coach has stopped,' she added with an exasperated sigh.

He chuckled.

'What's up?' asked Nicola, plucking out her earphones.

'We're nearly there.'

'What were you staring at?' She craned round a shuffling blouson jacket to get a better view. 'Oh, I see. Pretty, isn't she?'

'Is she?'

'Course she is,' she said, shooting him a mean look.

Concealment wasn't Mike's thing. His sole game of office poker had resulted in the loss of a week's wages and the suggestion that should he wish to take it up professionally, he should consider playing in a mask.

* * *

PROLOGUE

The Brit stood on the balcony of the old villa and gazed at the morning mist settling in the valley. Taking a final drag on his cigarette, he ground it under his trainer and put his hands on the railing. The metal was already warm to the touch. He let out a sigh, thinking of how the harsh Spanish sun would soon be baking his belly, frying his fading tattoos and roasting his bald head to a violent crimson. It hadn't been a good year so far. He'd been given the prognosis, the diagnosis, the second and the third opinions and now the truth was undeniable: he was dying. Not slowly, basting in sun and Sangria like the other expats, but fast, eaten up inside. He spat out a bolus of phlegm. It was going to be his last summer in the Costa del Sol and he intended to make it count.

A pair of flip-flops smacked on the tiles and a dark Andalucian youth appeared at his side.

'*Venga, Señor! Aquí, ahora.*'

The boy scuttled through to the bedroom and hovered by the doorway. As the Brit padded inside, he saw that the youth was pointing a trembling finger at the bed. A naked girl lay twisted on the sweat-stained sheets. Removing the gag from her mouth, he slapped her across the face. Nothing. He stood back and stared at her, hearing only the faint clunk of a goat's bell in the distance as the herd returned from milking. The youth's eyes were on him now, willing him to magic her back to life.

'Fuck it,' he said.

He strolled through to the kitchen, the boy watching as he sprung open the fridge, fished out a cool San Miguel and drained it in one. Tossing the bottle aside, he wiped the froth from his lips and crooked a gold-encrusted finger to summon the youth closer.

'*¿Qué vamos a hacer, Señor?*'

He put a fatherly arm around the boy's shoulders and the youth melted into his chest. Tears dampened his shirt front. He began to smooth the boy's hair, stroking and preening and then twining a clump of it around his fist. Another whimper, softer this time. The Brit slowly shuffled across to the fridge. Without warning, he gripped the youth by the neck and rammed his head against the freezer door. He pulled back and, with all his strength, hit home again and again until red tears of blood ran down the white metal surface. Grunting with the effort, he gave a final thrust and the door buckled inwards. The youth folded on to the filthy tiles and lay still.

The refrigerator shuddered. Wiping trickles of sweat from his temples, the Brit leaned forward, wrenched the door open against the body and groped inside for another beer.

'Gonna be a scorcher today,' he muttered.

PART ONE

A disco beat murmured in the midnight air as Mike Trent slipped into the deserted pool. Above him, blue television strobes played on the hotel balconies. He swam a length, stopping short of the filter which was fizzing away like a giant aspirin. Treading water now, he relaxed as the smooth liquid licked his shoulders and caressed his hair. He peddled his legs to the surface, spread his arms wide and prepared to float. Gazing up at the sky, he smiled at the stars. They were bright and in sharp focus. Better than London, he thought. It never really gets dark there, just shades of plum and dirty orange like rotten fruit. He kicked back and sculled to the centre of the pool.

'This is the life,' he said aloud.

The body plummeted into the water from three storeys above him.

As the wash dragged him under, it occurred to Mike that perhaps the holiday hadn't started so well after all.

That morning as they were packing, he'd failed to prevent Nicola from forcing the contents of her wardrobe into two cases.

'You won't need all that stuff,' he'd said, waving a hand at the battered suitcase he'd borrowed from his mother. 'See? That's all I'm taking.'

He stuffed in a shirt and took inventory. T-shirts, jeans, trunks, a crumpled jacket and several books he'd always meant to get round to reading and probably still wouldn't.

Nicola ignored him and crammed in another pair of sandals.

Arriving at Gatwick too late to get smoking seats, Nicola stared doe-eyed at the check-in clerk and invented a number of medical reasons why she had to sit at the rear. When this didn't work, she strode off in her new white platforms and sulked until take-off. Her mood improved only when the plane punctured England's perennial grey blanket. However, it nose-dived again at the arrivals lounge in Malaga when one of her bags emerged leaking moisturiser on to the carousel. Leaving her to mop up in the restroom, Mike heaved the other cases on to a trolley and wheeled off to find the rep.

Sarah Rutherford's bright uniform was more a cry for help than a fashion statement. She was standing in the epicentre of the hurricane of tired holiday-makers and ticking off names on her clipboard. Her dark curls were thrust into a wiry bun and her pretty, elfin face was lightly tanned. It was enough to make Mike tuck in his shirt and feign the nonchalance of a more experienced traveller. He'd almost reached her when Nicola clopped up alongside. He averted his eyes and fell into step as they followed the others on to the coach bound for Fuengirola.

The coastal strip of the motorway which stretches between Malaga and Gibraltar is known as the road of death. One reason for this is tourists who, new to driving on the right, swerve on to the busy carriageways with the caution of teenagers let loose on the dodgems; another reason is the local coach drivers. Mike and Nicola had been unlucky enough to get Pepe, a man who wore sunglasses day and night in the mistaken belief he was a South American despot. Consequently, he drove like one. As he wrenched the silver juggernaut into the teeming lanes, Mike clung to his seat and shuffled through his passport to check the 'next of kin' section.

After half an hour of crazed slaloming, their speed decreased as they approached the suburbs of Torremolinos. The Tannoy crackled as Sarah began to recite her rehearsed speech. The passengers showed no interest when she explained that the town had once been a tiny fishing village, they failed to react when she informed them that Ernest Hemingway had spent time in Ronda and they ignored her suggestion to visit the *pueblos blancos* up in the Sierras. However, when she pointed out that Sean Connery lived off the *autovía*, their heads whiplashed back and forth like wipers in a hail storm.

Nicola shuffled beside him as she dug into her bag for her

lighter. Mike reached between his feet for the carton of duty-free cigarettes and, snapping open the cellophane, handed her a fresh pack. She lit one, revolved the cassette in her Walkman and settled back with her eyes shut and her chin raised. He smiled at this habit of hers. It wasn't that she was scared of getting a double chin: quite the reverse, her chin was tiny and it barely cupped her face. She was sensitive about it and constantly pulled at the skin or stretched out her neck in an attempt to firm up her jaw. This often had the effect of causing people to think she'd spotted someone more interesting across the room.

Mike gazed out at the dark hills and rewound their relationship. They had met when she came to *Sorted!* magazine as a temp. Although her arrival had led to a marked improvement in grooming amongst the staffers, Mike's only concession had been to rake a comb through his tangled brush of hair. He hadn't thought he stood a chance with this effervescent blonde. After all, who'd want a sub-editor twelve years past his sexual peak? He'd immersed himself in his copy-editing and had studiously ignored her.

Opportunity came by default. One slack day in February, the staff drew up a list of her more visible attributes and held a sweepstake on who'd be first past the bedpost. Mike, having arrived late due to a dose of flu, found her weeping at the word processor. Apparently, she'd found the list and had called them all animals. Someone had then corrected her by saying 'Mammals'. Her response was to start lobbing potted plants as they retreated to the pub to re-evaluate their attitudes. Mike discovered she was on the rebound. Her ex, Gavin, was a car salesman whose hobbies were his Maserati, other women and his Maserati. He slipped into the role of transitional man with a mixture of gratitude and ill-concealed glee.

The following month was a sexual marathon which culminated in pet-names and thrush. Come April, they had stopped writing weekly love-notes to each other. Soon after that, their differences emerged. She was twenty-two; he was thirty-one. She was a compulsive clubber who wanted to be out six nights a week; he wanted to sit at home, watch the telly and gripe. It was around this time that she had suggested the holiday.

Mike thought she was being ironic. Two weeks in the Costa

del Sol? 'I learn it from a *boook*,' he'd joked in a passable imitation of Manuel from *Fawlty Towers*. Nicola explained that her family alternated holidays between southern Spain and Ibiza. However, this year they had chosen Disneyland, which she didn't much fancy because it sounded childish. He'd considered it. On the plus side, it was an affordable and stress-free way of spending a fortnight. On the negative, he preferred the kind of holidays where you avoid other English people, the sort where you find struggling with foreign languages and customs exhilarating; not that he'd been on one, of course, but he had been to Norfolk. In the end, he agreed to go.

Now he wondered if he would regret it. Still fresh in their minds was a row along the lines of the classic 'move in or break up' argument. They had parted for a week and really only got back together because of the unrefundable deposit.

'We are now arriving in Fuengirola so those of you who are staying at the Hotel del Playa please remain in your seats.'

Mike gazed at Sarah. She looked like she wanted to be elsewhere. She made no eye contact with her charges and wasn't bothering to maintain even a superficial smile. In fact, she didn't seem like your typical tour rep at all.

'If you're at the Hotel Bella Vista, we'll be dropping you first, so—'

The coach became a jungle of grabbing, stretching limbs.

'—please wait until the coach has stopped,' she added with an exasperated sigh.

He chuckled.

'What's up?' asked Nicola, plucking out her earphones.

'We're nearly there.'

'What were you staring at?' She craned round a shuffling blouson jacket to get a better view. 'Oh, I see. Pretty, isn't she?'

'Is she?'

'Course she is,' she said, shooting him a mean look.

Concealment wasn't Mike's thing. His sole game of office poker had resulted in the loss of a week's wages and the suggestion that should he wish to take it up professionally, he should consider playing in a mask.

* * *

The hotel complex was a toffee-coloured clump of high rises. Money had been spent on the palm-filled atrium, the dining room and the sea-facing suites. It had not been spent on their room. Even the lifts had more carpeting. They threw their bags on the bed and searched in vain for the view promised in the brochure.

'Bella Vista? More like Bela Lugosi,' snorted Mike.

'You should go down and ask for an upgrade. The brochure said that all the rooms have a sea view.'

'Didn't say which sea. Technically we're facing the Atlantic.'

'Can't see that through the lift shaft, can we?'

The mechanism acknowledged them by squealing like an abattoir.

'Too late to do anything about it now,' he said, wiggling a toe through a hole in his trainer.

Too weary to argue, Nicola went to the bathroom and thrust the duty-free vodka under the cold tap. Once it had cooled, she poured two hefty measures and laced them with warm Coke. They slugged them down as they unpacked. Mike finished first and picked up a book. Tired and tipsy, he found the words had come adrift and were moving about the page in a holding pattern.

'You won't do anything, will you?'

She had drained another measure. Neat, this time.

'You never take a risk. That's why you're not a proper reporter.'

He dropped the book on to his lap. 'I was a reporter. On *City Life*. Until it folded.'

She lit her thirty-seventh cigarette of the day. 'Are we going to have a good time here or what?'

'This is just Blackpool with Sangria.'

'You didn't have to come'.

Too exhausted for another bout, he searched for the quick way out, preferably one that didn't involve faking illness or facing the problem.

'I'm going for a swim,' he announced, putting both feet through one leg of his trunks.

'At midnight? Where?'

'There's a pool, isn't there?'

'It'll be locked up. You'll get us into trouble.'

'Aah!' He waved a superior finger, tried to tap her nose, missed and poked her in the eye.

Nicola blinked rapidly, crinkling up one side of her face. 'Do what you like. I'm going to bed.'

Mike shot to the surface, spouting water and fresh mucus. He thrashed to the side of the pool, levered himself up on to the tiles and dashed to the nearest wall. As he leaned back for support, his head hit a switch and the scene was flooded in light. The body was dressed in a black suit. The jacket had filled with air and bobbed, swollen, like a boil on the water.

Instinctively, Mike looked up. A man with a tanned face and a white moustache gazed down at him from a balcony on the third floor. As their eyes met, the man quickly disappeared inside. With a shiver, Mike scrabbled against the switches and doused the lights. Feeling safer in the dark, he crouched down and peered at the corpse through the slats of a sun-lounger. It twirled gently, face down. Mike listened for the sound of any approaching footsteps. There was only a whisper of Eurobeat and the hissing of the cicadas. He took a few paces forward to retrieve his clothes and was just about to slink away when the lights came on again.

Mike froze.

A hotel receptionist was standing by a door on the other side of the pool. He glanced at the foreign object in the water, then up at Mike. With a helpless grin, Mike pointed up at the sky. As the man came towards him, it suddenly occurred to him how complicated this was going to be to explain in Spanish. Somehow he didn't think there'd be much in the phrase book to cover this eventuality. The receptionist strode round the edge of the pool and came to a halt a few metres from him. He felt he ought to say something.

'Er, you have to get the manager. Umm. *Pronto?*'

The receptionist bent down on one knee and eyed the corpse like a snooker pro lining up a difficult pot.

Mike's voice rose up a notch. '*Comprende?* Get the manager. *El managero?*'

The man looked up. 'No need, *Señor*. This *is* the manager.'

The ten-mile stretch of water between Gibraltar and Africa is one of the most popular routes for drug trafficking. The Tangiers – Algeciras ferry carries some of it, taped into the walls of cars and container lorries or carried by human 'mules'. The bulk is sent by powerboat. These seventy-five horsepower 'Black Boats' constantly outpace the coastguards, speeding around the Rock of Gibraltar and aiming for the coastal strip between Estepona and San Roque. There, the cargo is dumped to await collection by the local hash gangs. A few days later, that contraband which has not been transported away to France, Germany or Holland becomes widely available in the resorts of Estepona, Fuengirola and Torremolinos. The penalty for the supply and handling of narcotics is high, but in setting this off against potential earnings, nine years in a Spanish jail is considered a mere occupational hazard.

Under a moonless sky, the craft left a slick of fizzling foam in its wake. As the coastline emerged, the outboard motor cut out and the boat slid forward, silently running. It slowed to a halt some metres off the shallows, its dark hull still invisible from the shore. Ramón Esteban had successfully navigated his way to safety. Behind him, in the stern, his brother Angel lay spread-eagled on the tightly wrapped bales.

'¿Hemos Ilegadó ya, Ramón?'

'Desde luego.'

Ramón held out a palm for a congratulatory high-five. Angel stood, swung an arm, missed and twirled backwards into the stern.

'*¿Hermano?* Why you go so fast?'

The elder brother didn't reply. Ramón had recently become a man of few words when a girlfriend had mistaken his sulking for deep character. Instead, he sucked on his teeth, hoping to irritate his sibling. Sure enough, Angel's pug-like face creased into a scowl. Ramón chuckled and raked a hand through his hair, leaving a smear of gel in his palm. Tall and lean, he preened constantly and took every opportunity to show off his muscled frame in a succession of low-cut T-shirts. By contrast, Angel, two years his junior, was a stubbly bear who probed and snuffled around behind him. Both native Andalucians, their career options were limited to joining the tourist industry or sliding into crime. They had chosen the latter, reasoning that the chances for self-advancement held more promise.

Angel picked at the polyurethane wrapping. Ramón slapped his hand away.

'*¡Idiota!* You'll break the seal.'

'How long we have to wait before they collect?'

'We wait for the light on the beach. Maybe one hour.'

'And until then?'

Ramón sighed. 'Think of the money. We have a good smoke later.'

'I want a smoke now,' pouted Angel.

'It's not our stuff.'

Angel's single eyebrow creased at the centre. 'But if we take a little is OK. There is always—' he recalled the words he had read on a cereal packet, 'settlement in transit.'

Ramón raised his hand to slap him but instead revolved his wrist to glance at his imitation Rolex. 'Maybe a little,' he shrugged. 'We have earned it.'

Angel lost no time in taking his penknife to the plastic.

Kevin wandered around Gatwick's north terminal in amazement. His mouth hung open as he trawled the duty-free shop, the boutiques and the mock-Italian coffee bars. He gawped at the range of commodities, thinking how simple it would be to stuff the more easily pocketable items into his rucksack. He stared gimlet-eyed at the painted assistants who shied away and fiddled under their counters.

Even here, in one of the busiest thoroughfares in the world, Kevin was an exception. His mole-like scalp was shorn to a sparse number-one, his eighteen-hole, cherry-red DMs were battered and bruised and his pudgy features were set in a permanent scowl. The tattoo on his right shoulder read 'MILLW', the result of a fight he'd initiated in a tattooist's. These attributes still terrified most people, despite the fact he was only five foot three in his white towelling socks.

He moved from outlet to outlet, dragging his rucksack behind him like dead prey. At the end of the concourse he loped round a giant steel sculpture and found himself in front of The Red Lion. It didn't look like a pub. It looked like a Eurostyle version of a pub with fancy booths and matching upholstery. Kevin sneered. He wouldn't normally patronise anywhere that offered both coffee *and* alcohol; not unless he was intent on creating serious damage. Today, however, he was officially on holiday.

In the duty-free shop, Detective Sergeant Anthony Russell was choosing a bottle of Scotch. Realising his charge was missing, his mouth settled into a long slit. Back at the station in Plumstead, his burgeoning jowls had earned him the nickname of 'Frog'. The wide nostrils confirmed it, braced, as they were, under a lumpy bridge and a smooth high forehead. His remaining hair was a dwindling mat which scrabbled northwards with each passing year. Tony now peered over the displays with a growing sense of panic.

Kevin had been a bad idea from the start. He had crashed his trolley into an escalator. He had barged to the front of the check-in. He had clambered into the luggage X-ray machine. When a burly customs official pulled him away, he told him that he 'wanted to know what his skellington looked like'. Had Tony been on duty, he would have thrown the little bastard to the floor and cuffed him right there and then.

He paid for four hundred B&H and a bottle of Johnnie Walker and scurried back to the main concourse. As he scanned the atrium for the troublesome troll, the last call for their flight to Malaga was announced. Tony moved quickly amongst the sun-worshippers, tripping over their bags and outstretched feet. Kevin was nowhere to be seen. He broke into a trot and covered the entire length of the departure lounge. The familiar explosion of a shattering pint glass brought him to a halt.

Angel took a massive pull on the spliff, releasing both a high-pitched giggle and staccato bursts of smoke. He rolled on to his stomach and passed the joint to his brother. '*Hermano*. I think my head is opening up'.

Ramón suppressed a smile as he twisted the joint between thumb and index finger. 'Moroccan. *Mi favorito.*'

'What star is that?' asked Angel, staring out to sea.

'Which star?'

'The one there. Low down, near the sea.'

Ramón shrugged. 'You are the one with the telescope at home. The one you never point to the sky.' He curled a bare foot over the black gear stick and began to massage his sole.

'It's getting bigger,' murmured Angel.

'You smoke too much of the *costo.*'

Angel wasn't listening. He was focusing on a widening circle of light. '*Si*, is bigger ... or maybe we are getting smaller.'

'*¡Mierda!*' Ramón screeched, springing to his feet and fumbling for the ignition.

'*Mierda. Guardacostas.* Coastguards!'

The light was swaying steadily towards them.

'What are we going to do?' cried Angel, stumbling over the nearest package.

'*Rapido*, throw them in the sea. *¡Todas!*'

Angel heaved the bales overboard, but they refused to drift away, clinging to the hull like guilty turds. '*Vamos. ¡Vamos!*' he shouted, shooing at them with his hands.

Ramón tried to turn over the cold engine without flooding it. He twisted the key, paused, swore and then smacked the casing. In the stern, Angel felt his bowels vibrate in fear as he gripped the last bale. It toppled into the water and sent him tumbling backwards.

A cone of lemon light washed across his panic-stricken face.

Looking up, he saw two uniformed officers silhouetted against the prow, their automatic machine guns trained directly at him. Suddenly, Ramón resuscitated the craft. The engine burst into life, choking and spluttering on the warm brine as they sped off towards open sea. Angel fell over again but didn't get up. This, he decided, would be a good time for a rest.

The coastguards didn't give chase. Instead, they cut their engines and drew closer to the bulbous packages. The pilot shut off the light and motioned to his partners, who lowered their weapons. He barked an order and they took up boat hooks and began to drag the sodden bales towards the hull. As the first package was hoisted aboard, the pilot grinned and began to unbutton his uncomfortable tunic. It was a size too small for him.

The evening flight was uneventful. Despite Tony's fears, the boy had quickly tired of baiting the stewardesses and, after a few lame jokes with the air-sickness bag, had slumped into a snorting doze. Due to the lateness of their arrival at Malaga, the butterscotch halls were deserted and the customs officials were eager to wave them through. Their coach, engaged by a tour company who'd slaughtered prices at every turn, didn't run to a guide. It slunk, low-bellied like a feral cat, down the N340 to Torremolinos. Reaching the resort, it negotiated the slender streets with surprising agility, pausing only to cough out passengers like fur-balls.

Their hotel, the MiraFlores, was an apparent misnomer since there were no flowers to see; only brick walls and white stucco arches smeared in grubby fingerprints. They stumbled through reception and rose in a clanking lift to their fourteenth-floor standard room. Tony threw down his suitcase and went to the bathroom to get a glass.

'You little sod,' he said, throttling a stiff measure out of the Johnnie Walker. 'You've been a right pain today.'

'Cheers,' said Kevin.

'I don't like this any more than you, son.'

The boy stuck a stubby digit into his right nostril. 'I hate coppers,' he said.

'Tough titty. Your uncle wants us here together. I didn't exactly want to share a room with a Neanderthal midget.'

Kevin extracted a wisp of mucus and examined it. 'Don't have to. I'm going out.'

'No you're not. We've got to wait here 'til he gets a message to us.'

The boy ignored him and tipped the contents of his rucksack on to his bed. Riffling through them, he selected a burgundy Fred Perry shirt.

'Kevin. We're only here for tonight. Let's get some kip, eh?'

No response from the boy.

Tony sighed. 'I'm going to take a shower. You want it after?'

'I wanna pint.'

'We'll go down to the bar. Give me ten minutes, all right?'

He reached for his sponge bag and stepped into the bathroom. The shower control required some fine adjustment before the water was bearable to human flesh. He undressed and clambered into the tub. After chasing a tiny bar of hotel soap around his feet, he gripped it long enough to lather his armpits, chest and flabby midriff. He moved directly under the jet and sighed with pleasure as the water washed away a little of his thirty-eight years of disappointment.

He thought of how he'd finally broken free of that desk job. Never again would he have to endure the laughter in the police gym. This was a chance, at last, to make his mark. Wait until Debbie heard the full details of his unexpected leave. He decided to call her when he'd dried off. For now, though, he celebrated his arrival in Spain by urinating copiously into the plug hole.

Tony emerged, pink and refreshed from the steamy cubicle. One tiny towel was knotted round his midriff and a second draped over his stooped shoulders. A third was in his hand, ready to rub at his thinning hair. As he scanned the room, his back muscles rapidly twisted into an impressive knot.

Kevin had gone.

3 ♪

'You sure that's what you saw?' asked Nicola, chewing on her muesli. 'You were pretty pissed.'

'No, I made it up,' said Mike.

They were eating breakfast in the icing-stucco dining room.

'We ought to tell someone. The police?'

Mike loaded butter on to a hard roll. 'We don't speak Spanish.'

'They'll have someone there who speaks English. Or we could try the embassy.'

He let out a sigh. 'I thought you wanted to be out in the sun, not stuck in some grotty office filling out forms.'

She slid a hand under her T-shirt and adjusted her bikini strap. 'Tell me again what happened? After you got out of the pool?'

'The porter asked for my room number and said I should go back to bed. Then he brought us a bottle of champagne. It's chilling in the bidet.'

'See anything after that?'

'From *our* room?'

She shot him a sarcastic smile. 'Sounds like he was trying to shut us up.'

'There is that.'

'Well then?'

'Well, what?'

She pushed her cereal aside. 'So we've got the advantage. I reckon we should go and see that tour rep.'

'Oh, we don't want to bother her,' he lied.

'We might be able to get something out of this. Like a decent room. There's that GuestTogether at eleven. We could have a word then.'

'If you want. Look, if you want to get down to the beach, then I could go . . .'

Nicola crumpled up a paper tissue, dropped it in her bowl and stood up to leave. 'You'll only cock it up and we'll be stuck in our Beirut death cell. I'll see you back there.'

Mike watched her retreating rear, wondered if he'd be the one to caress those legs once they had turned caramel.

'. . . And if you have any problems, I'll be at my desk between ten and twelve and then again at five until eight o'clock.'

Sarah slid off the table and gathered up her dockets. The guests filed out, anxious to avoid any eye contact which might plunge them into premature holiday friendships. A couple from Oldham had already made it their business to be Mr and Mrs Friendly and they stood like rocks in a stream as the room emptied. Nicola nudged Mike in the ribs. 'Go on then,' she whispered.

He took a few steps across the gaudy, patterned carpet. 'Excuse me, er – Sarah?'

'Yes?'

'I don't want to bother you, but—'

Nicola chimed in. 'Mike was in the pool last night when someone fell on him.'

'Well he shouldn't have been in the pool at night,' snapped Sarah.

'From the third floor,' added Nicola, darkly.

Sarah frowned. 'I see.'

'I wouldn't normally complain—' began Mike.

'He nearly drowned. He was bloody terrified,' interrupted Nicola.

'Well, not terrified,' countered Mike, trying to gain ground. 'But I didn't realise that the service included plummeting managers. It's not in the brochure,' he added, with a hopeful smile.

Sarah didn't return it. She explained that yes, there had been a report of an injury, but as you can appreciate, in a hotel of this size, accidents will happen and she was sorry for any inconvenience caused. She shifted her weight, ready to move off.

'Well that's not good enough,' said Nicola with the resolve of those well-versed in consumer programmes. 'We want a room with a sea view and a patio.'

Sarah held her gaze for a moment. 'I'll see what I can do. Will you be around later? Say, at lunchtime?'

Nicola crinkled up her nose. She was already missing valuable frying time.

Mike filled the gap. 'I'll be here,' he said.

A kilometre away in a shabby apartment, Angel was pulling at his bushy eyebrow in frustration. They had spent the entire night on the beach at Punta Mala and after motoring up and down in the shallows, had come ashore and scoured the inlet for the missing bales of hash. Returning empty-handed at daybreak, they found a venomous message on their answerphone. If the contraband was not forthcoming, it said, then they would soon find themselves deep-sea diving without oxygen.

Ramón staggered bleary-eyed through to the kitchen and lit the gas under a blackened coffee pot. Angel rose from the battered sofa and followed him through. '*Hermano*. What we going to do?'

Ramón winced and farted loudly. 'I don't know. You were the one who said we should get stoned.'

'But you agreed.'

'*Jodete*. Never again.'

Ramón stuffed a hand into his shorts and began idly rearranging his genitals. Angel gazed up at him in awe. In the last year, his brother had made enough from his illicit dealings to buy an open-top Isuzu Trooper Jeep with roll-bars and quadrophonic CD. Surely his innate resourcefulness would soon emerge? Instead, the elder brother dug a hand into the sink and plucked out a grime-encrusted cup.

'We tell him it was an accident,' Angel said. 'We did the right thing by getting rid of the *porro*.'

Ramón pinned him to the wall, pressing an elbow into his thorax. 'It does not matter how we lost the stuff,' he hissed. 'All that matter is it is gone. You know how much that costo would fetch on the streets?'

Angel declined to hazard a guess, what with his windpipe imploding.

Ramón answered his own question. 'Four hundred million pesetas, *¡maricón!*'

Angel planted a hairy knee in his brother's groin. Slipping from the grasp, he hopped around, wringing his hands in sorrow. '*Lo siento. Lo siento.* I would never hurt you, Ramón.'

'You in big shit. Deep *mierda*,' he wheezed.

'But, you took me there. It's your fault.'

Ramón kicked his legs from under him. Angel clattered against a stack of unused pans.

'I will put the blame on you,' sneered Ramón. 'I will tell them you are *estúpido*. I will say you gave the stuff away.'

He turned to the stove. The hot black liquid had spluttered on to the ring, snuffing out the gas. As he bent to the hob, Angel suddenly flew at him with arms windmilling. Ramón stepped neatly aside as his hirsute sibling crashed into the wall.

Tony Russell awoke drenched in sweat. Leaving the window open all night had only encouraged the mosquitoes to hold a running buffet on his pallid skin. He scratched his ankle, drawing blood as he surveyed the empty bed next to him. The previous night, he'd spent a good hour trawling the bars of Torremolinos without success. On his return, he'd attempted to contact his wife, but had been unable to unravel the hotel's complex dialling system. Frustrated, he went to bed with Johnnie Walker.

He needed grease to dilute his hangover. Pulling on slacks and a short-sleeved shirt, he unlocked the door. Outside, a gaggle of elderly maids were hoovering the corridor at a decibel level on a par with that of a jet engine. Gripping his forehead, he struggled downstairs. He had missed breakfast and the room was a desolate desert of limp cornflakes and dry bran. Deciding to brave a street-side café, he shuffled across the reception area. As he passed the desk, it occurred to him to check if any messages had come through. He veered left and hung on to the formica counter. The receptionist looked him up and down, then busied himself at the pigeon holes. Plucking out a scrawled note, he handed it over.

'Licky Shamrock pub. 12.00. Sitting outside table,' it said, in scrawled, halting biro. The porter explained in far more detail than was necessary that the Shamrock was actually on the main through-route, but way out on the town borders. Tony said he'd walk but the man cast him a knowing smile and offered to book a taxi. Muddled by dehydration, he succumbed and staggered to the heavy chrome doors. Outside, the heat threw a sharp flame under the gruel in his cranium. He moaned, clutched at the railings and prayed that the cab would be air-conditioned.

Lap lap lap lap.

Something pinky-grey and decidedly off was blurring Kevin's vision. It felt like a sandpaper loofah dragging back and forth across his face. He raised a chubby hand and grabbed it. This produced a muted yelp and a rapid panting. He peered at his catch and found he was holding the slippery tongue of a giant black wolfhound. As he released his grasp, the dog stood back and cocked its head to one side, eyeing him with suspicion. Kevin stared right back.

The dog stood at least a metre high. Its raven pelt was greasy and tufts stuck out at random angles. Each paw was the size of a small frisbee. The ears were battered but alert and gobs of spittle dripped from its muzzle. Kevin locked on to the gun-metal eyes. Slowly, its thick tail began to fan the air, causing a stray burger-wrapper to take flight. The dog let out a crisp bark, leaped into his arms and bathed him in a stringy lather.

Kevin stroked the matted fur and took his bearings. He was lying on a pile of black refuse sacks between two bins in an alleyway. Had he been thrown out of a disco? Or had he collapsed there after consuming his own body-weight in San Miguel? Either way, he decided, it must have been a good night.

'What we gonna call you then, boy?'

He recalled a horror film he had seen on the telly. 'Hound of Dracula.' What was the dog called? Sultan? Dog from hell? Sultana? Raisins? Soltan. That's it. He said the name aloud. A ragged paw flopped on to his chest.

'Soltan it is then,' said Kevin. He sprang to his feet to go off in search of breakfast. The mutt lolloped joyously behind him.

Known as a rich man's paddling pool, Puerto Banús is a few kilometres down the coast from Marbella. It attracts the moneyed of all nations, most of whom are reluctant to talk about how they came by their wealth. The resort has a casino, a string of apartments and a plethora of shops, bars and restaurants perched around the harbour. Owning a yacht there is a mark of status. These twin-engined, triple-decked, 10-berth luxury craft rarely cruise the Mediterranean, being more often employed as floating casinos or as venues for summer-long parties.

Felipe Luis Eduardo Ozorio stood at the prow of one such craft, the *El Rey de los Perros*. A Castillian by birth, Ozorio was the acknowledged leader of a vicious hash gang known as Los Perros de la muerte. The name was intended to mean the 'Dogs of death' but had been misheard so often as the 'Dead dogs' that the name had stuck. He had only recently settled in the Costa del Sol. In six months, the rangy twenty-six-year-old had carved out a niche-market in drug dealing, racketeering and theft. He was quite the rising star.

'Felipe?' José, his second-in-command, had appeared on deck. He carried a chilled glass of lemonade on a silver tray and wore a puzzled expression on his acne-pitted face.

Ozorio eased his RayBans down from his forehead and lit a fresh Fortuna.

'*¿Sí?*'

'You are not worried about last night?'

That morning, after consuming churros con chocolate and some of the finest Columbian product, Ozorio had been informed of the death in Fuengirola. The hotel manager had been one of their middle-men; one whose access to clean currency was deemed beneficial to the gang. In consequence, the hotel safe often housed more than passports and car keys.

Ozorio took the drink and sipped it. '*Venga*, José.'

He ushered the tall lieutenant inside and down through the polished beechwood cabins into the hold. There, Ozorio opened a hatch in the floor to reveal several plastic-wrapped packages.

'*Colega*. I have my vengeance. All you need is a boat, some uniforms, a couple of scared smugglers.'

José smiled at his brilliant friend. Felipe had always shone, both growing up in the slums of Madrid and at school when he had applied himself diligently to mathematics. This had paid off in many ways, not least in his ability to calculate the best possible cut on any given drug deal.

'So when do we move it on to the streets?' José asked.

Felipe Ozorio slid an arm around his shoulders. '*Mañana. Sera otro día*,' he purred, raising his eyes to his cabin and tapping a nostril with his finger.

*   *   *

Kevin was enjoying himself. Torremolinos was sunny and cheap. Also, Soltan had an amusing trick of nipping at passing waiters. In the last two hours he'd also discovered the casual Spanish attitude towards paying for a beverage. Consequently, he and the dog had taken to consuming several beers in a number of bars and running off without paying. As they strolled along the front in a beer-haze, they noticed a shiny-faced young man coming their way. He wore a garish jacket with the sleeves turned back, *Miami Vice*-style.

'Hello, here on holiday then?'

Kevin grunted and clicked his fingers. Soltan dropped to the ground.

''Cos I was wondering if you were aware of the enormous opportunities out here for people such as yourself to enter into no-risk investments?'

The youth left a pause, expecting his potential client to respond. Kevin didn't, so he continued.

'You probably think this is one of those awful time-share deals. Well, you needn't worry. Nobody's forcing anyone into anything these days. It's all been tightly regulated. Tell you what, though.' He smiled conspiratorially. 'We do have a very, very special offer at the moment. We can give you, yup, that's right, *give* you a free drink and six thousand pesetas – that's about thirty pounds in real money – ha ha! To come and look at one of our show ho—'

The youth never completed his sales patter; not because there seemed little likelihood of a sale, but because Kevin had head-butted him to the ground.

Tony Russell sat outside the Lucky Shamrock, which was a mirage of green amidst the native colour scheme of terracotta and blinding whitewash. He nursed a coffee which, under the exhortations of the patron, had been laced with a good measure of Drambuie. Staring at the thundering traffic, he felt his arms prickling in the heat. Debbie had made him promise to take plenty of factor twelve and apply it at all times. 'You can't take the sun,' she'd said. 'Your skin's far too sensitive.'

Tony hated having sensitive skin. You didn't go smashing into crack dens in Thamesmead with sensitive skin. He wondered whether this was one of the reasons why his chief superintendent had lashed him to a desk for the last three years. As he mulled it over, he failed to notice the white Rolls-Royce Silver Shadow with the jet-black tinted windows which had slowed to a halt near the kerb. It paused only briefly, before sliding away into the shimmering heat.

Mike had changed three times. Discarding shorts on the grounds that they made his legs look like hairy spaghetti, he settled on jeans and a clean white T-shirt.

Sarah wasn't at her desk. On asking at reception, he was told she would probably be in the Bar España, a local haunt in a side street some blocks away. With his legs already beginning to sweat, Mike followed the directions and came to a tiny, shaded entrance on a corner. He paused before going in. On the one hand he was disappointed that she'd forgotten their rendezvous; on the other he was delighted she wasn't the type of person who ate in the gaudy English pubs.

He stepped inside. A group of yabbering Spanish men were clustered at the shining, chrome bar. Spinning fans cooled the room and fluttered the strips of lottery tickets tacked to the walls. A television squatted high in a corner spewing out a daytime soap. There were several wooden tables, two of which were occupied by toothless old men playing draughts. Behind them, Sarah sat alone picking at a plate of *tapas*.

He approached her. 'Hello.'

She showed no sign of recognition as she looked up.

'Mike Trent. I came to see you earlier today. You said to come back at lunchtime.'

'Did I?'

'I'm staying at the Bella Vista. My girlfriend asked if you could see about getting us another room.' Still nothing. Mike lowered his voice. 'I was the one with the magnetic attraction to dead managers.'

'Oh, right. You'd better sit down, then.'

He smiled. 'I'll just get a beer.' He moved to the counter and waited for the barman to tear himself away from his friends. Shit, he thought. What is beer in Spanish?

'*¿Cerveza?*' queried the barman.

He nodded.

'Trouble is,' said Sarah as he re-joined her, 'it's high season and all the rooms are fully booked. I could try one of the other hotels.'

'Not if it's too much trouble.'

She bent to take another mouthful and a ringlet of hair fell across one eye. 'Well, yes it is actually.' She tucked the loose strand behind an ear. 'I'd have to cross-reference the bookings with all the other travel companies.'

'But that's your job, isn't it?'

She rested her fork on the plate. 'I suppose it is.'

'Don't get me wrong,' he ventured, 'but you don't seem much like a tour rep. Where's that happy, smiley everything's-just-lovely-super stuff? Or have you been out here too long to care?'

'Three weeks. That long enough?'

He sipped his beer. 'And before that?'

'I ran a travel agency back in Hammersmith.' A flicker of suspicion crossed her face. 'Why all the questions? You a journalist or something?'

'Used to be. I'm a sub-editor on a magazine.'

'Shouldn't you be trekking off to Tuscany or somewhere recommended in the boring parts of *The Sunday Times*?'

'Less said about that the better,' he replied, liking her all the more.

'Why?'

'My girlfriend booked it a while ago. I thought it was a joke.'

She hooded her eyes.

'You had to be there.'

She drained her glass and ordered another for herself in fluent Spanish. Mike took out his cigarettes.

'May I?' she asked, fanning two slender fingers at the packet.

He pushed them towards her. Sarah lit up and blew a luxuriant plume of smoke into a sunbeam.

'About what you saw. It was probably an accident. These things happen a lot out here. We do all we can for safety, but you can't watch over people like babies.'

'I saw someone on the balcony.'

'And?'

He backed down. 'It was only a glimpse. I mean, I wouldn't recognise him again.'

Sarah rested her chin on her hand and tapped ash into the tin tray. 'OK. Look, it was the manager. The police took the body away late last night. If you want to follow it up, then I can put you in touch with them. How's that?'

The question hung in the air.

'Well, it's not really my problem. I'm on holiday, for God's sake.'

She seemed satisfied. '*Mañana por otra dios,*' she said.

'Sorry?'

'*Mañana* culture. They do things in their own time out here. When they get round to following it up, you'll probably be on your way home.'

'I've only just got here.'

'Well, there's plenty to do. You should go see Ronda or Mijas.'

He thought of how Nicola would react to that suggestion. A pursed mouth shaping the question 'Why?' came to mind.

'No, I reckon I'm stuck here for a fortnight,' he sighed, hoping for sympathy. When none came, he changed tack. 'So tell me about Fuengirola? I heard it's chock-full of criminals.'

'No more so than London.'

'That's the party line, right?'

She narrowed her eyes, assessing him. They were hazel.

'There's a lot happens here that the tourists never see. Drug problems, organised crime. Some bars you don't go into unless you can prove you've got a criminal record.'

'Really?' he said, pleased to have got something out of her at last.

'Yes, really.' She stubbed out her cigarette, crushing every ember.

Mike felt a little braver now. She'd allowed him to stay long enough in her company to share a morsel of information. It was time to probe a little deeper.

'So how come you left London? You obviously had a better job there.'

'Good question.'

'It is, isn't it?' he said, pleased.

'I'm here because of my sister, Lana.'

'Oh. Is she a tour rep as well?'

'She was teaching English in Malaga.'

'What's she doing now?'

'Not much,' said Sarah, getting up to leave. 'She's dead.'

4

Jackie Drake perched on a bar stool and smoothed her Versace dress over her toffee thighs. Slim to the point where a charity might be initiated on her behalf, her taut muscles demonstrated the gruelling hours she had spent competing with her reflection in the gym. Only the stippled crow's feet around her eyes betrayed her age. Passing for mid-thirties, nothing bolstered her confidence more than the catcalls of local men. That, and the cocaine she shovelled into her pert nose. She sipped a fresh gin and smiled up at the barman. 'Have one yourself, Sam.'

Irish Sam reached for his tankard. 'Why not?' His voice was a Glasgow burr. He drew a pint, downed it in one and wiped the froth from his snowy moustache. He then reached out a muscular arm and began to shuffle a beer towel along the counter. Jackie stopped him by grabbing his wrist. She traced a fingernail over one of his tattoos, a faint blue nude which was bound in a python.

'What's the news then, Sam?'

He scanned his empty pub for potential eavesdroppers. 'Job done,' he said.

Her finger moved towards a clotted heart on his bicep. Underneath it were two curlicued scrolls with the names in each removed. Sam took his cigarette from its notch in the glass ashtray.

'There was some bleedin' tourist in the pool. Probably one of those Nazis trying tae get his towel down first.'

She stopped at a blotched dagger. 'John need to know about this?'

'Och, no.'

'All right then.' She focused on the furry line of the blade.

'You tell him it's kosher,' added Sam. I'll deal wi' the loose ends. I like to be professional.'

She leaned forward so he could see the deep crinkle where her breasts jostled together. 'I'm at a loose end Sam.'

He grinned, revealing a row of perfect, pearly white teeth. 'Away wi' yer. I was talking business.'

'Yeah, I know.' She sat back on her stool. 'Got to relax sometime, though.'

'Aye,' he said, looking her up and down. 'How's about a game, then?'

Her tongue poked out and moistened her upper lip. 'Yeah, why not?'

Irish Sam went off to fetch the scrabble.

Nicola sat on a damp towel on the edge of the bed as Mike smoothed globs of moisturiser into her burning shoulders. She winced and shrugged him away. 'If you can't do it properly, then don't do it at all.'

He rubbed the remaining cream on his shorts. 'It's not my fault you got burned. You look like you fell out of a burning building.'

'Is that meant to be funny?'

'Course not,' he said, glaring at her back.

She reached for a cigarette. 'Anyway, you sat in the shade all afternoon. What's the point of being here if you don't get out in the sun?'

He held up the bottle of duty-free vodka.

'Go on, then,' she sighed.

He poured them each a stiff measure and took his glass to the window. A long lilac shadow had crept across the wall opposite, dividing the view into two neat triangles. The room was still stifling. He reached for the catch but faltered, having remembered that ventilation was impossible without filling the room with the growl of lift machinery.

'Mike,' said Nicola, her voice weaker now. 'Can you close the curtains?'

He did so, bathing the room in a golden half-light. While she rested, he thought of his conversation with Sarah. She'd only shown him scant interest but he'd detected an empathy in those hazel eyes. Or was he imagining it? And anyway, what the hell was going on? What was all this about Lana, her dead sister? Nicola moaned softly. He flicked on the bedside light and saw perspiration on her raw face.

'You all right?'

Her eyes blinked open, but she wasn't focusing.

'I think you've got a touch of sunstroke.'

'I'm fine,' she murmured.

He went to the sink and soaked a flannel in cold water.

'You better take it easy for a bit.'

He patted it slowly across her forehead and down under her jutting jaw. He enjoyed being in doctor-mode, it being the one way he could be sure of being useful. He brought her cups of water. He straightened out the bed. He called reception when she puked up a bolus of scampi. It took three reminders before an irate porter arrived and cleared up the mess with the grace of a butler who had recently discovered Socialism.

Afterwards, Mike retired to the bathroom to wrestle with his holiday constipation. Skimming through a pamphlet, he discovered that 'Fuengirola comes alive at night when thousands of British, German, Dutch, Italian (and even Spanish!) visitors are catered for by many restaurants, bars and discoteca.' He flipped to another page which featured a photograph of the beach cradled by white Toblerone hotels. The caption read: 'The front has a view of the finest bitches in all Spain.'

Outside, as the last rays of sun sank behind the Sierra de Mijas, a promenade had begun. Extended families of well-turned-out Spaniards spread out across the wide pavements; children played under the benign but watchful eyes of rotund matrons; old men smoked, lost in memories; African immigrants hawked their wares; tourists failed to find the perfect restaurant. Mike saw none of this from his room. He learned instead that Spain has five television channels, all of them incomprehensible to him.

By eleven, Nicola had recovered enough to complain of hunger and had asked him to get her some chips. He tore himself away from the Spanish equivalent to *Countdown* – which seemed to involve only vowels – and found a burger bar near the hotel entrance. Back in the room, she devoured them and began to hunt through her closet for a dress.

'You sure you're all right to go out?'

'I'm fine.'

'Where are we going?'

She threw a tiny top on to the bed. 'Opera? Poetry reading? Clubbing it, of course.'

He stifled a yawn.

'Come on, Mike. We're on holiday!'

He reached wearily for his wallet, noting that she used his name more in irritation than infatuation these days.

She applied her make-up, then sat on the bed to lace up her new Nikes. 'Ready, then?'

Nicola stood up, wavered, sat down again and vomited soggy chips on her feet.

He helped her to undress and put her back to bed.

'Turn the light out, my head's spinning,' she said in a pained voice.

'I was going to read.'

'Read in the toilet.'

He went to the bathroom and stared at his reflection in the mirror. The gaunt expression of his father glowered back at him. He shook it away and pulled at the skin under his eyelids, before washing his hands and face.

'I thought you were tired?' she murmured as he came back into the room and put on his jacket.

'Not any more. I'm going for a walk.'

'Do what you like.'

He doused the light and slipped out into the corridor.

Tony lay uncomfortably in the square tub with his legs draped over the rim. After the failed rendezvous at the Lucky Shamrock, he'd taken a cab back into the centre of town and had spent the afternoon scouring the bars for Kevin. There had been sightings. On learning that Tony knew the midget menace, an irate bar-owner from Sheffield demanded he pay for two jugs of Sangria and a cheeseburger. A beach attendant described a 'crazy English with fierce creature' who cut a swathe down the beach, scattering the sun-loungers and uprooting the parasols.

Lastly, the manager of a German restaurant told him that a burgundy-booted elf had marched past throwing Nazi salutes. After that, the leads had dried up. Kevin had gone to ground.

Tony scratched at his itching scalp, wishing he'd listened to his wife's advice about wearing a hat. He wondered if Debbie would be home yet. What was it tonight? Pottery? He pulled a flannel from the water and squeezed it over his smarting face. Evening classes? In July? Insecurity surged through him. Tony was about to struggle from the tub and tackle the phone when he heard a faint click.

Suddenly, a pair of strong hands were digging into his shoulders and holding him underwater. He fought for breath as he was wedged further into the bottom of the tub. Bucking his legs, he tried to aim a kick at his assailant. Something hard whacked against his shins, sending a jolt of pain through him. He choked and thrashed his arms ineffectually. Another blow, this time driven deep into his stomach. The air fluttered from his lungs and he breathed in soapy water. He tried a futile upward thrust, but his limbs were already growing leaden. Slowly, unconsciousness began to gather him up in its embrace. Darkness. Then light. Light and sound. The pressure lifted and the roar of life returned. He was hoisted up and over the rim of the tub, alternately spewing liquid and gasping for air. As a glimmer of strength returned, he flailed at his attacker. He was rewarded with a sharp crack to the neck.

'Where is boy?' said a voice. It had the texture of roasted coffee.

He raised his head and saw a bulky young Spaniard in a waiter's uniform.

'Call this sodding room service?' he spat.

The man repeated his question as he produced a wooden table tennis bat. Before Tony could reply, the man had smashed it flat on to his face. An incisor cracked and he tasted blood.

'I don't know where he is, you dago git.'

The waiter threw a towel at him. Tony struggled to his feet and tried to wrap it around his waist.

'You not go to bar with boy. *Porqué?*'

'This towel's too small. Get me another one.'

The waiter snorted and took a step forwards. Tony tried to fend him off with one hand, his other cupped protectively around his genitals. The Spaniard was too quick. In an instant, his arm was forced halfway up his back. The waiter frog-marched him into the bedroom and threw him to the floor. From the ground, Tony heard a drawer opening and an exclamation of pleasure. In one smooth movement, the man cuffed Tony's right wrist with his own handcuffs, flipped him over and secured him to the metal frame of the bed. He then removed the key and slid it into the pocket of his tight trousers.

'Where is boy?'

'I don't sodding know. He went out last night and he hasn't come back.'

Tony had always suspected he'd fold under questioning.

The waiter stared at him with eyes as hard and black as stereo equipment.

'He's out there somewhere,' added Tony, hoping to placate the man.

A silence fell, broken only by the muffled sound of a family arguing in the room below. Tony probed his chipped incisor with his tongue. It felt large and metallic. The Spaniard ran a hand through his ebony hair and picked up the bat once more. Tony flinched. A smile flickered across the man's face as he holstered the weapon in his back pocket.

'*Vale*. Enjoy your stay, *maricón!*'

With that he tore the phone from its socket, placed it under his arm and left the room, locking the door firmly behind him.

Having wandered the entire length of the front in both directions, Mike was about to turn back. Earlier, when stopping for a beer, he'd been surrounded by drunken revellers and had decided then that Fuengirola wasn't for him. He'd now reached the end of the chains of hotels. Ambling off into a deserted side street, he found himself in a thin alley with whitewashed walls. A thudding beat shuddered towards him. A blue neon sign on a nearby wall read, Discoteca Solly Sombra. He decided on a nightcap.

The club was empty save for a lone barman totting up at the till. Bullfight posters hung on bare brick walls above red banquette seating. The bar was a forest of bamboo and dried palm fronds, a theme which was carried throughout the club.

A couple of steps led down to the small dancing area, above which a mirrorball revolved unevenly. Beneath it, the polished floor looked better suited to a game of Twister. A gangling black youth in a multicoloured shirt was massaging twin turntables in the rear.

Mike hopped on to a bar stool and ordered a *cerveza*. The barman served him without interest and went back to his accounting. He sipped his beer and let his gaze slide back to the dance floor.

'Fonky Sombrero gonna slip you into some good lovin' now with the ever-juicy Denice Williams,' growled the DJ in a syrupy baritone. As he bent to find another record, Mike noted that the man wore a battered *sombrero* which had slipped down on to his back, where it hung like a lazy halo.

A lone couple hove into view and began to twirl slowly. The girl's arms were limp around the man's waist and his head lolled sleepily on her neck. She looked English; he looked tanned. Mike felt a slight breeze behind him and turned to see an attractive foursome who had taken a few paces into the club. They paused to acclimatise themselves and to decide whether or not they were going to stay. Mike slumped against the bar hoping to appear cool and damaged and therefore interesting.

They turned and left.

The couple had now been joined by a plump girl in an unwise lycra dress. She looked pale from too much alcohol and was urging her friend to leave. The dancing girl broke loose from her potential lover and seemed to see him afresh. As they disappeared from view, Mike made a bet with himself. He smiled when, moments later, the women reappeared with their arms linked in solidarity. The man followed forlornly, a child forbidden his sweets. All three went outside and Mike found himself alone. He wondered whether the DJ would continue to spin tracks for his benefit. Perhaps he should request something?

The music stopped.

He watched self-consciously as the DJ packed up his records with quiet efficiency. He pulled out the plugs behind the console, came up to the bar and stood next to him. Mike stared straight ahead but, to his embarrassment, saw the man studying his reflection in a mirror behind the bar. He caught the face before looking away. Smooth umber skin which took on a cobalt hue in the blue light. The mouth was broad and straight, the lips full. The eyes gave away nothing. There was a faint crescent on his left cheekbone from an old scar. He was well over 6 feet tall.

'Howyadoin, mon?' said the DJ, slipping on to the seat beside him. 'MC Fonky Fonk. I and I say, the one an' only master soun' machine.'

Jamaican, thought Mike. The man gave him a brothers' hand-shake, bending his thumb back in the process.

'How's it going?' asked Mike.

'Not bad,' said the Fonk, reverting to pure London.

He relaxed a little. 'So what do I call you? MC Fonk? The Fonkmeister? Mr Fonk, Esquire?'

'Clive,' said Clive.

'Mike,' said Mike with a private smile.

Clive sprang two bottles of San Miguel from behind the counter and handed one to him.

'D'you live out here, then?'

'Been here about six months,' said Clive.

'Make a living?'

He sucked on his beer. 'There's plenty of work if you look for it.'

Mike scanned the empty room with heavy-lidded eyes. 'If this is work, then I'm in the wrong job.'

'Place is packed weekends,' replied Clive flatly.

'But it's Saturday.'

'Competition, man. You been to Maxy's?'

Mike shook his head.

'What about Poser's? Fat Ronnie's?'

'I only got here yesterday.'

'Ah.' Clive raised a finger. 'Fuengirola virgin.' He chugged more beer and his hair, a clump of beaded rat-tails, swung from side to side like a curtain.

'Not exactly a roaring success, this place?' Mike said.

'I get paid.'

'Much?'

Clive sucked his teeth. 'You're London, ain't you?'

'Tooting.'

'Posh.'

'Nah, it's a shithole,' he said, trying for street points.

'Not compared to Dalston,' Clive said. 'You the Clapham end?'

'Brixton end,' replied Mike, shunting his address down a social notch.

'Sarf London?' said Clive, adopting a gruff, barrow-boy growl. 'No bleedin' tubes. No cabs. Shithole.'

Mike retaliated. 'The north's better? Pissed tramps in Camden. The Northern Line. Arty-farty dinner parties in Hampstead?'

Clive smiled, reached into the pocket of his baggy cotton trousers and fished out a tin of Golden Virginia. 'Smoke?'

'Sure,' said Mike, expecting to be offered a vermicelli of dried-up baccy.

Clive prized it open to reveal four neatly rolled joints and slid off his bar stool. 'I like to chill out on the beach after the gig. Coming?'

Mike nodded.

'We'll take some more beers. Make you forget Tooting.'

'And Dalston.'

'And Dalston,' agreed Clive. 'Shithole,' he added.

'. . . So Nicola's in the hotel room now doing an impression of a dead beetroot.'

Mike shut up then. It was only after he'd given his new friend a comprehensive account of his relationship to date that he remembered why he had stopped smoking dope. He always talked too much.

They were sitting barefoot on the beach, their toes digging ridges in the cool sand. Clive said nothing for a few moments, then blew a perfect smoke ring. 'Seems to me it ain't got much future.'

Mike nodded, glad to find the justification for his next statement. 'Know anything about the tour reps?'

'Like what?'

'I dunno. There's one at our hotel. Sarah. She's a bit different. Sulky but gorgeous. Lovely smile.'

'Sulky?'

'Yeah, but with a figure that makes you want to scream into a pillow.'

'She'm gatta big battam?' giggled Clive, reverting to patois.

'No, tiny. Like . . . like two peaches in a silk bag.'

'Trouble.'

Mike took the joint, inhaled a little too quickly and coughed hard. As he leaned back, the stars seemed to undulate against the canopy of the sky. He sat up quickly and concentrated on the lapping waves. 'So why's this better than England?'

Clive drew a lazy circle in the sand. 'London's gone to shit.'

'That's a given.'

'No jobs. Get your GCSEs and you still end up working in some post-room or KFC. I tell you, that Colonel Sanders never freed *his* slaves.'

'But lots of black people work in London.'

'Not from Holly Street Estate.'

Mike's eyes seemed to be bulging in their sockets. He worried at them with his knuckles.

'Nothing there for me,' added Clive.

'Family?'

Clive sucked on his teeth, then threw his empty bottle into the sea. It bobbed once or twice, then filled up and sank. 'So tell me mo' bout this sulky bitch,' he said in a tone that would have given Isaac Hayes a run for his money.

'Nothing to tell.' Mike glanced at him. 'Bet *you're* fighting them off.'

'Nope.'

A tremor shot through his bowels. Shit, he's gay, thought Mike.

'I meet a few. No one regular.'

Mike relaxed.

'Some babes round here just like the idea of me y'know?'

'How d'you mean?'

'Holiday rules. If they don't get a Spanish guy, then this colour's next.' He pinched his arm. 'Come all the way to Spain when they could've shagged me in Hackney . . . Didn't, of course,' he added with disdain.

'What about the native women?' said Mike, affecting an all-purpose black accent he'd borrowed off Robin Williams.

'Spanish girls keep it real quiet.'

'So, have you . . . ?'

'Mm-hmm.'

'And?'

Clive guffawed. 'If the Pope knew what Catholic repression did to those women, he'd have disbanded the church long ago.'

Mike laughed as Clive wiggled the roach deep into the sand.

'I lived with an English girl for a while,' added Clive.

'Yeah?'

'Bad shit. Came home one morning to find the police trashing my place. They hauled me down the station for five hours. Turns out her body was found behind one of the discos. O.D'd on smack.'

'Jesus.'

'If I'd known she was into that, I'd have thrown her straight out, man.'

'There a heroin problem out here, then?'

'Yeah. Used to be up in the north. Madrid. Valladolid. Barcelona. It's everywhere now.' He stared at the sand. 'Fuckin' shock man. Never thought Lana was into that shit.'

Mike's head cleared rapidly. 'Lana? Did you say Lana?'

'Yeah, nice kid.'

'But this girl I was telling you about. Her sister's called Lana.'

Clive stared out at the sea. 'So?'

'So Sarah must be her sister. D'you know her?'

'Nope.'

'Look, I reckon you two better meet up. How about tomorrow?'

'I sleep in the day.'

'How about tomorrow night, then?'

Clive gave a slight nod. Mike stood up and began to pat the sand off his jeans. 'D'you want to meet us here or what?'

Clive arched forwards and stretched to his full height. 'No, you better bring her to the club. We need the punters.'

5 ∫

Tony Russell's second night in Torremolinos was worse than his first. Once his assailant had left, he dragged the bed across to the window and closed it, pulled the orange bedspread around him and fell into an uneven doze. He awoke aching all over and with his manacled hand mauve from the pressure of the handcuffs. Desperately needing to piss, he jerked the bed to the bathroom door, only realising then that there was no chance of getting it past the frame. He moaned and thumped the tiles with his free arm. He'd just managed to get his feet round the waste bin when he heard a gentle knock at the door. For a second, he imagined Debbie entering with a steaming cup of tea and a perfunctory kiss. He was dismayed to find it was the same brutish waiter. Carrying a full breakfast tray, the Spaniard strolled across the room and placed it on a chest of drawers.

'Come on, you've had your fun,' barked Tony in his best beat policeman's tone. 'Undo the cuffs.'

The waiter smoothed a hand over his freshly shaven chin. '*No creo*. Boy still not here.'

'At least bring the bloody breakfast over. How am I going to eat it from here?

A shrug.

'And I need a sodding piss and all!'

The Spaniard raised a hirsute eyebrow and sighed. 'The guests, they are more trouble every year.'

With that, he produced a roll of packaging tape, tore off a long strip and bound and gagged Tony where he lay. Satisfied, he went to the door and waved the 'Do not Disturb' sign before leaving. Tony tried a few muffled shouts but they were soon dampened by the army of hoovers in the corridor.

Basted in coconut oil, hundreds of holiday-makers were frying themselves under an angry sun on the beach at Fuengirola.

'Mike. Do my back.'

Nicola was lying face down on her lounger. Mike put down his paperback and took the oily carton from her outstretched hand.

'So where did you get to last night?' She asked. 'You didn't get in till past three.'

'I met a DJ. Black bloke from Hackney.'

'Thought you wanted to meet the locals.'

'He is local. He lives here.'

Nicola had awoken fully recovered and delighted to get back to her holiday. Unable to rouse Mike, she had breakfasted alone and then secured their places on the beach. He, on the other hand, had risen disorientated at eleven. His first coherent thought being to find Sarah, he dressed and went down to the desk. A frizzy-haired girl stood there, smiling vacantly.

'It's her day off, actually. But if you'd care to leave a message?'

He didn't. Joining Nicola on the beach, he lathered himself in high-protection lard and lay back on a slatted couch. The sun was oven-hot and the screeching of children made it impossible for him to focus on his book. He rolled over to display his under-arms, but found it too uncomfortable. He tried lying on his side but it made him sweaty. Mike settled in the end for sitting astride the lounger and squinting at the horizon.

'What d'you want to do tonight?' asked Nicola, now sitting up with a cigarette.

'I have to find that tour rep. What was her name . . . ?'

'Sarah. And you know it. Why?'

'The guy I met last night knew her sister. The one who died. I ought to tell her. It might be important.'

She took a drag and her smoke ribboned into nothing. 'Why d'you want to bother with that sulky bitch?'

'Just trying to help.'

'Like she helped us? You fancy her, don't you?'

'No.'

Nicola left a pause just long enough for him to feel uncomfortable.

'It doesn't matter, you know. She's obviously your type.'

Mike said nothing, suspecting a trap. When he didn't respond, she looked down and stared at her towel. 'Look. We're not married or anything. I fancy other people too, sometimes.'

'Like who?' he asked, hurt.

'Doesn't matter.'

'No, who?'

'Well – Tom's all right.'

'Tom? He'd shag anything that moved. And a few things that don't.'

'I only said he's all right. Didn't say I was going to jump all over him.'

He felt a knot of anger in his gut. Tom worked in their office. He was a lithe, six-foot Australian intent on sleeping his way through the female population of London. He had already graduated in osteopathy back in Sydney and bore a strong resemblance to a younger Mel Gibson.

'Don't know what you see in him,' he grunted.

She smiled knowingly. 'It's all right, Mike. There's nothing going on.'

'Good.'

'Why don't you just admit to it? You fancy this moody cow, don't you?'

He fussed with a cigarette, playing for time. Nicola had opened up the negotiations and now it was up to him to state his position. His thoughts raced. Has she got some prepared ultimatum? Or worse, a pre-emptive strike? If Sarah had feelings for me then, then I'd at least have some ammunition.

Nicola rearranged her bikini bottoms and sat up.

He took a deep breath. 'Look, Nicky. We both know it's not going to work between us. We're only hurting each other and we should end this quickly, like tearing off a plaster. We'll both feel better and maybe we can find some other people that can do us some good.'

He watched her splashing about in the waves.

Good thing I didn't say that out loud, he said to himself.

*   *   *

Sarah sat sipping *café con leche* and scanning the passers-by through her sunglasses. She'd changed out of her itchy uniform and into a white vest, long patterned skirt and high wedged *espadrilles*. She glanced often at her watch, noting that it was past midday and that the man had not yet arrived. She felt no rush of excitement, only a leaden atrophy which slowed her every movement. She'd chosen a café away from the hotel so as to avoid unwanted recognition. Nevertheless, she felt exposed. She was tempted to leave now, run to her apartment, pack and catch the next plane back to London. She could be home by nightfall, safe in her tiny flat with its bright walls and its sluggish plumbing. She could climb into bed and sleep it all off like the last symptoms of a virus.

Her cigarette was a limp grey tube in the ashtray. As she stared at it, a shadow fell across the circular steel table. Looking up, she saw a stocky, middle-aged man with a kind face and greying temples. The pale blue trousers, white shirt and soft leather briefcase indicated a nondescript professional. He could easily be a lawyer or a bank clerk. In fact, there was nothing about him to mark out his dealings with death.

'*Señorita* Rutherford?' he enquired politely.

She rose, nodded and shook his finely boned hand. He waited for her to resume her place before drawing up a chair. Now that the encounter was unavoidable, she tensed up and felt her armpits grow slippery with moisture. '*¿Quiere un café o una cerveza, Señor* Lucena?' she asked.

'English is fine, Miss Rutherford.'

He motioned to a passing waiter. '*Pogame un carajillo.*' A coffee laced with cognac quickly appeared.

'Thank you for agreeing to see me.'

He held up a hand. '*Es muy importante*, excuse me ... important to wait until things were less ... busy. You must first understand that what I have for you is in the highest confidence. Your sister's death is an embarrassment for many people here. *¿Entiendes?*'

She rushed in with her prepared explanation. 'Yes, look, Lana may have done drugs, but she'd never do—' she whispered the word, 'heroin.'

'I must tell you that the signs were there. The suffocation. The needle-marks.'

He placed his briefcase on the table. 'Will you be OK about seeing this?'

She closed her eyes an instant, hoping to shut out the truth, then nodded.

'First, let me explain. My department, pathology, as you know, performs autopsies on all suspicious cases. When the body was found with a young native in a similar condition, we at first thought it might be a suicide pact. The manner of death ruled this out.'

She concentrated hard on each word.

'When I was appointed to the case, I was told to report my findings to *El Comisario*, the chief in Fuengirola. First, it is undeniable that both she and the boy had taken *heroina*.'

He removed two black-and-white eight-by-tens and slid them across to her. Sarah studied them, finding it hard to place the two cold cylinders of dead flesh. It felt like they were playing a game, as if the pictures were of blown-up household objects she was supposed to recognise. Irritation nagged at her. Why the hell couldn't she recognise a part of her own sister?

'These are the arms of the two victims.'

'Victims?'

He ignored the query. 'Your sister – here.' He fingered one of the prints. 'Do you see the abrasions? The puncture marks?'

'Yes.'

'Do you notice anything unusual?'

She peered closely as he pointed to a dark smudge at the crook.

'Each victim received only one injection of *heroina*. The bruising on the vein indicates a clumsy attempt. Hardly,' he concluded, 'the daily dose of an addict.'

She wanted to shout in vindication. This was the proof. Proof that she was right and that all the explaining and justifying she'd done for Lana over the years wasn't in vain. 'I told the police she wasn't a junkie,' she hissed.

Lucena's eyes darted around the café tables and settled on hers. 'Please. This is dangerous for me.'

She gripped the rim of the table. 'I understand. And I appreciate your doing this. Please go on.'

Lucena rested his right hand on his left. Rather primly, she thought.

'The most common form of death in the addict is asphyxiation. The user often passes out and regurgitates in his sleep. The tongue becomes lodged in the windpipe and the result is suffocation. We are seeing more of this on the coast.'

'But that isn't what happened to Lana, is it?'

'No. Neither she nor the boy had vomited or swallowed their tongues. That was in my report.'

She felt anger now. 'Then why did they lie?'

'Please.' He downed the last of his brandy. 'Do not press me.'

She chewed on her lower lip, hoping he would divulge more. Lucena's cultured intonation reminded her of her father and the way he used words to coddle her. Then she remembered him in anger, shouting at Lana, his voice losing the softness and reverting to pure Edinburgh. A powerful, yet lyrical bellow that she did not possess. The family had moved to the home counties when she and Lana were little and she'd grown up with the flat, even tones of the English. She'd always longed to find that rage in herself, to release her anger and bark back at the pettiness of the Charlottes and Melissas at school. Somehow, it had never surfaced.

A smile crossed the pathologist's face. 'I have a daughter your age. She is studying nursing in Sevilla.'

Had he seen the connection?

'Is that why you're helping me?' she asked.

He placed a paternal hand on her shoulder. 'I am here because you have been an irritant these last weeks. The phone calls. The messages. People had begun to think I had taken a lover.'

Sarah's eyes fell to his hand. He took it away.

'I can tell you this,' he continued. 'I gave in the findings of my report as I have told you. What is then done with the case is immaterial to me. I am an observer, nothing more.'

'Then tell me. How did my sister die?'

Lucena removed two more photographs and held the first in

front of her. 'If you look at her wrists, you will see contusions here and here. I was able to lift fibres from under the fingernails. Household rope, very common.'

'So she was tied up?'

He revealed the other photograph. Lana's face looked, in death, like a child's attempt at a mask. Sarah thought that seeing it again would make her cry out. Instead she only felt numb.

'There are lesions around the mouth and cheeks. Pressure has been applied on the back of her neck. It does not indicate a blow. More possibly a knot. The cause of death was indeed suffocation. But I do not think she did this to herself in the street.'

It occurred to Sarah then how young Lana looked. Events flashed through her mind. Christmases, family holidays. Dressing up together. The dressings down when they went through their rebellious phases. Lana coming home with a nose-ring. Their mother calling it self-mutilation. Her reply. 'It's not bloody mutilation, it's a feminist statement! Says I control my body. I wouldn't want to look like a curtain-pole if this was just for a man!' Lana had then flounced out and had driven back to London, leaving her sister to mop up the damage.

As Lucena placed the photographs back in his satchel, she found herself swallowing hard.

'I'm sorry. I know this is distressing for you,' he said.

'How did the boy die?'

'His skull was broken in three places. A brain haemorrhage.'

She felt energy seeping out of her. 'So neither of them died of an overdose?'

Lucena fished out several hundred-peseta coins and placed them on the table. 'My autopsy report indicated that the heroin had entered the bloodstream but had not reached the heart. That is to say it was introduced after death.'

'Thank you,' she mumbled.

He leaned in closer. 'I am sorry to add that there is also evidence of sexual activity with the boy. His semen was present in both her vagina and anus.'

She wilted visibly. Lucena held her arm. 'Please say nothing to anyone about our meeting. If you do, I shall deny it. These copies,' he added, patting the case, 'will be returned to the file immediately. *Adios, Señorita* Rutherford.'

As he walked away down the leaf-shadowed street, Sarah felt her emotions bubbling to the surface. Lana wasn't just a disobedient menace, a convenient repository for her parents' tantrums. She was the victim of some terrible event. What the hell had happened to her here in Fuengirola?

Angel opened the door to the apartment and received a fist in the face. He reeled back, his lip spouting blood. The man stepped inside and landed a second blow to his jaw. Angel flew backwards on to the grubby linoleum.

John Drake slammed the door behind him and trod straight over Angel's supine body.

Hearing his brother's cry, Ramón ran from the kitchen, brandishing his switchblade. Drake slapped it out of his hand and gripped the boy by the face. 'You little fucker! Where's my fucking puff?'

Ramón garbled as the man dug his fingers further into his cheeks. Getting no coherent response, Drake flung the boy across the room. He landed on an orange crate, which splintered under his weight. Angel had crawled to his feet and was now cautiously approaching the steaming behemoth.

'*Señor* Drake, *lo siento*, many, many apologies, I—' He was cut short by another blow, which sent him reeling against the wall.

Drake stomped around the apartment, using his vast bulk to throw the furniture aside and smash the few ornaments their mother had left to liven up *Casa Ramón*.

'I'm going to lose my rag in a minute, you fucking dago ponces. That's a month's shipment down the bleedin' drain. Don't know why I bother with you, you fucking tossers.'

He wrenched Angel's Fender Stratocaster copy from its stand and hurled it at the fireplace. Its neck broke and the strings sagged into a useless tangle.

'I'm too good to you, that's what it is.' His bark was distinctly Peckham on a bad day.

Ramón and Angel cowered in the corridor.

Drake's anger subsided a little. 'Come here, you stupid cunts,' he said, slumping on the sofa. Wiping the sweat from his bald pate, he began to massage each finger in turn. The brothers inched back into the room.

'Come on,' he added, a forgiving parent now. He produced a gold lighter, sparked up a Royal Crown and spoke through the cloud. 'I must be your Father-fucking Christmas.'

John Drake had two things in common with the mythical provider. Firstly, he sported a white beard and moustache (although the beard was a goatee and the moustache was worn long and tapered) Secondly, he liked to remain an ethereal figure, one that never appeared on government records or paid taxes.

As he pulled out a wad of folded notes, Angel stared at it with undisguised greed.

'There you go,' said Drake, peeling off a handful and fluttering them across a pile of pornographic magazines. 'Fix up the place with that.'

Ramón took a chair and wrung his hands together. 'We had no way to know there was coastguard in the area. It come out of nowhere. I never saw one there before.'

'Yeah – funny that.' There was a twinkle of suspicion in Drake's eyes.

Ramón tried to purse his lips into a question, but it hurt too much.

Drake pinched his cocaine-singed nostrils and wiggled the tip of his nose. 'What I want you, and your sad sack of shit brother, to do, is keep your eyes open.' He glanced at the hairier youth. Angel's face was already showing signs of swelling. 'Any of that puff starts turning up here or down Estepona, you let me know. All right?'

The boys nodded like toy dogs in a car.

'And you,' he continued, jabbing a stubby finger at Ramón. 'I got a bit of work for you if you can handle it.'

Drake put an arm around Ramón's shoulders and led him away. Angel heard murmurings followed by the sound of the door closing. His brother returned to find him nursing his broken guitar.

'Not as bad as I thought, *hermano*,' Ramón said, trying to massage feeling back into his jaw.

'Bad?' squealed his brother. 'He broke every-cunting-thing.'

Angel had learned a new word.

'*Es bueno* he was not angry,' said Ramón blithely.

Stumped for a reply, Angel threw the remains of the instrument at his brother.

'But it'll be fun,' whined Nicola.

Mike shrugged, wincing as his shoulders crackled. His body had turned the same colour as his tongue. Nicola, after staying out for the whole afternoon, was burned all over except for two white patches: one under her watch strap and the other across her eyes. Whilst on the beach, she'd met Rod and Brian from Edgbaston, who teased and flirted with her and told her that they knew all the best clubs in Fuengirola.

'Not my thing,' said Mike.

She jutted out her chin. 'You're never up for anything. Name one thing we've done together in the last couple of months? Go on.'

'We went to that restaurant in Fulham.'

'With the office.'

She tore the shrink-wrap from a fresh packet of Silk Cut. 'Why is it always me who's got to suggest things?'

He stared at his feet, thinking, My toe-nails grow quicker abroad.

'Are you listening?'

'Yeah.'

'You really act like a child sometimes.'

He waved a hand for a cigarette. 'It's not just me. It's a thing we've got into.'

She threw the packet at him. 'No, Mike, I don't think it's a thing *we've* got into.' Her arms were crossed now, ready for confrontation.

'I don't want to argue.'

'You never do.'

He fell silent, thinking of his father's credo of letting things sort themselves out on their own.

'Well?'

Mike pulled off his T-shirt. 'I'm going for a shower.'

The water bounced off his body and sprayed the flimsy curtain in a fine mist. This relationship isn't working, thought Mike. It's dead. We're trying to resuscitate it through the electricity of argument. He closed his eyes and let the liquid pound his face. We're really just two single people pretending to be a couple. He reached for the shampoo, squirted a puddle in his hand and lathered his hair. But what if I were to end it? One, I'll be thirty-one and alone. Two, we're stuck here for another twelve days. Three, I'll be alone. He splashed soap into his armpits and tipped his head back under the nozzle. Have I got the guts to end it? He bowed his head and watched as suds poured down his stomach and dripped off his penis. Sod it. I'm going to do it.

He spun the dial and the flow ceased. Nicola. I think it's time we had a talk. He stepped out of the tub. Darling. I want to say something . . . about us. Water pooled across the floor. Baby – this isn't working, is it? He wrapped himself in his towel and wriggled into the new pair of *espadrilles* he'd bought that day. Nicky. I need my space. No, not that old one. He padded into the bedroom. She was curled up on the bed facing away from him.

'Nicola?'

She turned and looked up at him with tear-stained eyes.

'Mike. We need to talk.'

The sky had turned indigo and the lift was clunking as other guests ventured out for the evening. Mike felt as if he'd swallowed a bowling ball.

'It isn't working, Mike. We both know it,' she said flatly.

He released a fractured lupine howl. Nicola took a step forwards and hugged him. Mike held on tight for as long as he could, realising that this was probably going to be their last moment of intimacy. She finally extricated herself and stood back. 'It's for the best, Mike.'

'Wh-what are we going to do about the holiday?'

'We'll work it out.'

A wave of affection flooded through him. 'But it's been good. Hasn't it?'

'Yeah.' She kissed him firmly with swollen lips.

He wiped his eyes with the backs of his hands and let out a shuddering breath. 'You know what's so stupid, Nicky? I was thinking the same thing in the shower. About us splitting up. You beat me to it.'

'Competitive as ever,' she said, without rancour.

'I would have said it, you know.'

'It's OK. I believe you.'

'I'm just trying to find my self-respect.' He pretended to look under the bed. 'I'm sure it's here somewhere.'

She picked up her lighter, but changed her mind and threw it on to the dresser. 'Why couldn't you have been more like this before?'

'Like what?'

'Vulnerable. Funny.'

'So you like me now, do you?'

'Always did.'

A grin crept across his face. 'Any chance of a last shag then?'

Smiling, she reached for his hand and pulled him towards her. They kissed hungrily and shuffled to the bed as they disrobed. He toppled on to her, feeling himself rise as her pelvis snuggled against him. She wrapped her legs around his thighs and dug her heels into his buttocks. Freeing his right hand, Mike reached down to manoeuvre himself into position.

'Oww,' she grimaced.

'What is it?'

'Sunburn. Don't worry. Carry on.'

She cried out again as his chest met hers. They tried it with her sitting astride him, but her inner thighs were too raw. They tried spoons, but he couldn't get a grip. He detumesced, which made it worse. Frustrated, she turned over and thrust her bottom in the air. He managed to enter her, but she yelped as his flanks chafed against the back of her thighs. Eventually, they conceded it wasn't going to happen.

'What shall we do now, then?' asked Mike, smoking.

'Want to come to that disco?'

'Suppose so. What about us? I mean, what are the rules now?'

She started to dress. 'We'll make it up as we go along.'

'So we go as a couple, but . . . ?'

'We're free to do what we like – if that's OK by you?'

He nodded, thinking he ought to seal the bargain in some way. The bond of sex had failed and they had already agreed on a post-relationship contract. With exaggerated politeness, Mike leaned over and shook Nicola's hand.

Ramón, wearing a hooded sweatshirt, lycra shorts and giant Nikes, stood at the bar in Maxy's nightclub. Angel, in a string vest and MC Hammer trousers which puddled around his ankles, fingered the plasters on his face. '¡Vay! Ramón. ¿Qué te parece esta? What you think of that one?' he shouted.

Ramón rolled his eyes. 'Italian. Ni intentes. No chance.'

They wandered to the shore of the dance floor and surveyed a sea of bodies. A fresh wave broke as Culture Beat's 'Mr Vain' boomed out of speakers. Angel moved to pounce, but Ramón stuck an arm across his chest, holding him back.

'Wait, idiota. Pick your target first.'

'But the good ones will be gone. What about the bald girl with the earrings?'

'That's a man, maricón!'

When the song came to a close, Ramón poked his brother in the back. 'We should go now to check the streets for the porro.'

'I want to find a woman.'

'You could not find one if she was sitting on your face. Venga.'

Angel didn't hear him. He was watching an adolescent in big trainers and a tiny skirt. Ramón shot out a hand and pinched his cheek. 'I have to go to work now. You look out for the hash in here. ¿Vale?'

'Sí, sí. Adios.'

Leaving Angel to contemplate the potential loss of his virginity, Ramón shouldered a path through the crowd.

* * *

Mike went downstairs to check out the rep's desk and found the dark cubby hole unattended. There was noise coming from the bar. Inside, a Flamenco floor show was in progress, cheered on by a crowd of peeling families. On the low stage, a woman in red chiffon was stamping her feet as if they were on fire; her partner, an ageing Casanova, strummed a guitar and yelled encouragement. A small child crawled under the man's chair, only to be nudged away by a gleaming cowboy boot. Mike swung the door shut behind him and went to join Nicola and her new friends.

The streets were packed and the air was scented with a cocktail of frying onions and the starchy odour of chips. They strolled along the pedestrianised area and were quickly swallowed up in the throng. Gypsies hawked shawls, stallholders held out T-shirts, girls on rollerblades buzzed around them like angry wasps. Rod and Brian ignored it all and made straight for the Lancashire Rose pub. As luck would have it, another foursome had just left and there was a space outside. Mike drew up a metal chair and gawped at the heaving, multinational bar. Brick-faced brawling Liverpudlians aside, it could have been an ad for the EEC. They ordered jugs of San Miguel and Brian handed round some Doves. Mike passed on the Ecstasy, explaining that he preferred stimulants which you could smoke or drink. Nicola shot him a hard stare and launched into a discussion about Handbag vs Jungle music. He soon became edged to the fringes of their space and, as they fell into a giggling huddle, he turned away entirely and watched the passing parade.

An empty stomach and too much lager dulled his senses. Before he knew it, Mike had joined them in a sweaty nightclub. The others disappeared on to the dance floor and he found himself on his own once more. He sipped the watered-down beer and winced as the relentless beat puckered his eardrums. After ten minutes, he decided to leave. Clambering up on to a metal gantry, he spotted Nicola down in the maelstrom. She was pumping her limbs ecstatically in front of Rod and Brian, who had both stripped off their shirts. All three were grinning inanely, arrogant with chemical energy. He dropped down and forged a path through to her.

'I'm going,' he yelled.

No reaction. He did a little mime, which, in her space-cadet trance, could as easily have meant 'the bill please'. Mike snaked his way out, almost losing a shoe on the glutinous floor. Cool air chilled the sweat on his sopping shirt. He took it off and flapped it in the air as he walked back along the front. Arriving at the Bella Vista, he found the reception area deserted. Probably all in the pool, he thought.

On a whim, he went over to the rep's desk. Sarah was sitting staring blankly at her files.

'Been trying to find you,' he said, trying to appear nonchalant.

'It's my day off.'

'So you really love this job after all.'

'No.'

'You look tired.'

'Thanks.'

'Let's talk in monosyllables, shall we? Me. Have. Some. Thing. Tell. You.'

'What?'

He raised his eyebrows.

'What do you want to tell me, Mister Trent?'

Sarah sighed. She had spent the rest of her day worrying and had only come back to the hotel because she couldn't think of anywhere else to go. The job, at least, made her feel real.

'I met a bloke last night called Clive.' said Mike, brightly.

'Hope you'll be very happy together.'

'He knew your sister – if that's any help?'

Her eyes flashed with impatience. 'Of course it is. Tell me.'

'She stayed with him here in Fuengirola. Lana died of an overdose, right?'

She nodded imperceptibly. 'Where can we find this Clive person?'

'That would be why I've been looking for you.'

'Well?'

'He's working at this place down at the end of the—'

She was already halfway towards the exit.

'You're good at this walking out thing, aren't you?' said Mike, as he hurried after her.

Sarah stepped down on to the pavement and began fishing in her bag for her car keys. 'Didn't you have someone with you?' she asked. 'A girlfriend?'

'Ex-girlfriend. We just split up.'

'Oh shit. Sorry.'

He wondered whether to tell her about it. It might gain him a sympathetic shoulder, one that he could nuzzle up to and cuddle.

'Shall I get my car?' Sarah asked.

Scratch that, thought Mike. 'We can walk it. He's a DJ in a place called the Solly Sombra.'

'Never heard of that one.'

'Shall we go, then?'

'What about your ex? Will she be OK?'

'She makes friends quickly.'

Nicola buzzed around inside the heaving nest, feeling good about dancing, good about her body, good about her new friends and good about the funny little Spaniard in the vest and pantaloons dancing in front of her. He seemed either to be developing a new style of ballet or directing traffic.

Torremolinos, twenty-one kilometres up the coast from Fuengirola, has a lot in common with that resort. It has the same white high-rises, the same stretch of beach, the same motorway skirting its boundary and the same kinds of clubs, pubs and bars. The main difference is that Fuengirola doesn't have Kevin in it.

With a joyous shout and a stiff bark, Kevin and Soltan burst into their hotel room. Tony Russell lay naked, manacled to the bed and feathered in strips of brown tape.

'Oy, oy. What's going on here, then?'

'Where the pigging hell have you been?' spat Tony. He shrank back as the dog leaped on to the dresser and sunk his muzzle into the cold breakfast.

'I been out,' said Kevin.

'What's that bloody wolf doing in here?'

'Soltan's my mate.' He wrestled a sausage from the dog's jowls and threw it in the air. 'Soltan. Catch!'

Soltan achieved vertical take-off and caught the lump of gristle in midair. He landed with his paws astride the television.

'Why'd you name him after a bottle of suntan lotion?'

'I didn't. Soltan's the name of Dracula's dog.'

'That's *Zoltan*.' said Tony, unfazed by the extent of the boy's stupidity.

'No it ain't.'

'Yes it is.'

Kevin's beady gaze persuaded him not to take the argument any further.

'I bloody hate dogs,' scowled Tony.

'He hates pigs,' countered Kevin.

His cheeriness infuriated the policeman. Someone with so few prospects in life had no right to be carefree – especially since he himself was at such a low ebb. Soltan, paws scrabbling, righted himself and upended the set with a crash. He then dragged the rest of the meal on to the floor and devoured it.

'You been having fun, then?' asked Kevin.

'No, you little turd. Because of your disappearing act, the meet with your uncle never happened. Some maniac dago waiter turned up and acted like he'd seen *Reservoir Dogs* too many times.'

'Not a bad film, that.'

He ignored Kevin's pocket critique. 'Make yourself useful and go find him. He's got the bloody keys.' Tony rattled the bracelet, wincing as it cut into the raw skin.

'What's this dago look like then?'

'He's a waiter. Stocky bloke with a tan.'

'Could be any of them.'

'Exactly. Why don't you phone reception?'

Kevin went to where the phone wasn't. 'Phone's gone.'

Tony spelled it out. 'Yes. He took it. Otherwise I'd be calling the tourist board to complain about the service, wouldn't I?' Condescension was having no effect. 'So go down to the ground floor. Tell them that young master Drake has returned and is now entertaining in room 436. That should get the message through.'

The boy went to the door.

'And for Christ's sake don't disappear again.'

'Nah. I wanna bath.'

'What about this werewolf?'

'Play with him, will you?'

Soltan growled as the door closed. Tony let out a whimper as he once more cupped his genitals with his free hand.

They were zigzagging across the thin white streets.

'I flew out here to identify the body a month ago,' Sarah began. 'The Spanish authorities said it was a heroin overdose and my parents believed them. They wouldn't even come out here.'

'Parents,' sneered Mike.

'Thing is, Lana never took hard drugs.'

'Did you tell that to the police?'

'Didn't do any good. I asked the British consul about an investigation. He wouldn't have it. Said it was all under Spanish jurisdiction. Basically, he didn't want the bother.'

'How very un-British,' said Mike, struggling to match her pace.

'Just politics. There are fewer Brits coming out here now. The tourist industry is fighting a losing battle since everyone started going to Florida.'

'So you got fobbed off by everyone.'

They turned a corner into a street packed with cars. Sarah weaved around a Peugeot. 'Yes, but I couldn't live with it, so I came back.'

'That's brave of you.'

'Or foolish.'

'Or foolish,' conceded Mike, still impressed.

She stopped to disentangle the hem of her skirt from the bumper of an aged Seat. 'I took the job here as a sort of cover. I've been showing her photograph around all the bars and discos.'

'Didn't Lana write to you? Leave an address or something?'

'The letters stopped coming over two months ago.'

'But if she was living with Clive, then wouldn't the police have given you his address?'

'Like I said, they didn't want to know. Her stuff got sent home and all I got was the run-around. Filling in forms. Being sent to the wrong bloody offices.'

Reaching the end of the street, they found themselves back on the front.

'Oh,' said Mike.

'I thought you knew where this place was?'

'Let's cross over. I can get my bearings from there.'

They sat on the low sea wall to catch their breath. Behind them, the dark Mediterranean hissed against the sand.

'So anyway,' said Sarah, 'I've been pestering the pathologist who did the autopsy.'

'Autopsy? Don't they only do that in suspicious circumstances?'

'Exactly.' Her tone seemed to have lightened a little.

'Well, we are in tune.'

'Except I'm a quicker walker.' She wiggled her shoes at him. 'Even in heels.'

'Oh yeah?' said Mike. 'I'll race you to that corner over there. The club's only a bit further on.'

'You're on,' said Sarah, jumping up and striding off. Mike, going as fast as he could, soon reached the cusp between walking and running. Unable to keep it up, he began to skip, bounding past her and chuckling as he scuffed against the ground.

'Cheat!' she shouted, giggling. She broke into the same lolloping movement and sailed past him, thrusting an arm on to his chest to slow him down. He swerved off to her left and ran the rest of the way, arriving breathless at a poster-covered wall.

'You're the cheat,' he wheezed.

She smiled, a broad-toothed smile with a slight gap between her front incisors. Mike took it in like sunlight, savouring the tight little crescents of the dimples on her cheeks. Then, as quickly as it had appeared, her face clouded over and the smile went away. 'Let's go,' she said.

* * *

Blue flashing neon dabbed at the walls of the thin alley as Mike led her to the door of the Solly Sombra. As he pushed it open, they were met by a wall of searing, orange flame. Mike and Sarah were flung to the ground as the air was sucked back inside to stoke the inferno. Scrambling half to his feet, Mike looked around. Sarah lay awkwardly in the doorway, her eyebrows and hair singed. He put his hands under her shoulders and pulled her away from the entrance. Propping her head up against a wall, he felt a sticky patch of blood in her hair.

A scream came from inside the building and thick black smoke pulsed out towards them. Inside the dark rectangle, streams of liquid fire came down in ropes from the bamboo rafters. Mike searched for something to act as protection. The only objects in the street were a cardboard box filled with rubble and a moped. Useless. Sarah coughed and clutched at her head. Mike took off running and returned a minute later, dripping wet from having plunged into the sea. He bent to touch her shoulder. 'You OK?'

She managed a grunt. He took a deep breath and plunged straight into the flames. The wooden cane crackled and spat around him as the dense smoke seeped into his lungs. He retched and fell to the floor. Suddenly, he realised why his mother had always made him carry a handkerchief. He pulled a fresh cotton square from his pocket, tied it round his face and crawled forwards on hands and knees.

There was no shouting now. As the front of the bar collapsed, he made out the prone figure of the barman lying folded up against the soft drinks cabinet. He was about to go to him when a raft of bamboo collapsed between them, spitting fire. He rolled back and away under one of the banquette seats. The vinyl had split open and the yellow foam gave off an acrid, green smoke. From the dance area, the multicoloured lights on the DJ's console were blinking irregularly. Using them as a beacon, he crawled down the steps and through to the back of the room.

Clive was unconscious. His right leg was twisted under him and his clothes were blackened with soot. His giant *sombrero* had slipped on to his face, protecting him from the worst of the falling fire. Mike lifted it away and saw he was breathing. He took hold of Clive's wrists and dragged him across the room. Suddenly, there was a loud thump from the kitchen. The walls shuddered and the glass on the posters around him shattered.

'Fuck,' he shouted, as adrenalin surged through him. He tugged and heaved at Clive's body, jerking it up the steps and into the bar. A fresh cloud of smoke shrouded them, stinging his eyes. He lost his grip, then dropped down and grabbed Clive's ankles. Hoisting the DJ's legs under his armpits, he wheelbarrowed him to the exit.

Sarah was holding her head in her hands. As he dropped Clive beside her, an explosion came from inside. Broken roof tiles flew into the air and rained down into the street.

Mike tore off his mask and gulped in fresh air. The smoke was like sandpaper in his lungs. He dry-retched, lost his balance and collapsed. Heaving and choking, he finally looked up with streaming eyes.

A blue light was strobing up the alley towards them, the plaintive wailing of sirens piercing the night as a police car squealed to a halt a few metres away.

'Sarah,' he gasped. 'Meet Clive.'

7

The ambulance took them to the hospital above the *autovía* near Marbella. Clive was rushed into surgery and Mike and Sarah were treated for smoke inhalation and shock. An hour later they were both released. Awaiting news of Clive's progress, they sat on hard plastic seats and nursed coffees in a long, fluorescent corridor.

'I feel stupid with this,' said Sarah, adjusting the bandage around her head.

Mike rubbed at a patch of gauze on his arm. 'Would you believe they gave me a tetanus jab? I was only in the water a minute.'

Before she could reply, a nurse approached and said a few words in Spanish. Sarah thanked her and stood up. 'We can go in now.'

The small ward contained a dozen or so sleeping patients. The nurse ushered them to a bed which had been sectioned off by a plastic curtain. She whispered to Sarah, drew the curtain aside and left. Clive was asleep and breathing softly with the aid of a respirator. His right leg had been plastered and was raised up on a contraption of pulleys and ropes.

'Is he going to be all right?' asked Mike.

'I guess so. She said his burns aren't too serious.'

'So what do we do now?'

Her voice was firm but drained. 'I'm staying here until he wakes up.'

'This must be really important to you.'

She gave a tiny nod.

Mike felt the exhaustion creep through him. The adrenalin

high of the rescue had dissipated and now he needed sleep. More than that, he wanted time to fathom out how he'd had the courage to leap into the flames.

Sarah drew up a chair and sat down beside the patient.

'Do you want me to stay?' Mike asked. She didn't reply, so he perched on the end of the bed. 'You, um. You were going to tell me about your meeting with the pathologist?'

'Well.' Her voice was a monotone now. 'He said it wasn't an overdose. She'd been gagged and she was given an injection of heroin after she died.'

'Shit.'

'They found a Spanish boy with her. That wasn't an overdose either. He had a brain haemorrhage.' She began picking at a snag in the bedspread, then, stopping herself, folded her hands in her lap.

'What are you going to do?'

'I don't know.'

'And you never bumped into Clive?'

'Nope.'

He felt he had to keep asking her questions. To slope off now wouldn't seem right – like leaving a funeral before the end of the service.

'What was Lana like?'

Her eyelids fluttered closed. She breathed in through her nostrils, then looked up at him as she exhaled. 'Rebellious. She left home at fifteen and bummed around a lot. I got landed with being the sensible sister while she was out having a good time.' A flash of annoyance crossed her face. 'Why are you so interested anyway?'

'I . . . I just am.'

Her face fell. 'Shit, I'm sorry. You must think I'm a real hard-nosed bitch.'

'Not at all,' he said, not sure if he meant it.

'I didn't even thank you for tonight.'

She stood and hugged him. He held her close, breathing her in and feeling her curls tickling his cheek.

'By the way,' he murmured. 'That was my full quota of heroics.'

He sensed he'd forced a smile from her. Even so, she stiffened and broke away. 'I've got to see this through, Mike. I have to know the truth.'

'Can't I do anything?'

'No, no.' She was brisker now, zipping up her composure. 'You've done enough already. You should get back to your holiday. Let me pay for a cab to take you back to Fuengirola.'

He refused, explaining that he had plenty of holiday money. He wanted to tell her he'd do anything for her. Anything that is, that didn't involve any more physical danger. Instead, he murmured wishes of good luck and crept to the double doors at the end of the ward. Looking back, he saw that she had already drawn the curtains and that her shadow was shrunken against the pale ochre plastic.

John Drake stormed into the Hotel MiraFlores in Torremolinos, his mood as harsh as the morning light scorching the shrunken palms in the atrium. He elbowed aside a German tourist from Dortmund and banged his fist on the bell. The night-porter ambled out of the office.

'Where's Pablo?'

The man eyed him sleepily and held open the office door. Inside, the stocky waiter looked up from his copy of ¡Hola! and shook himself alert.

'Come on then,' said Drake, turning towards the lifts.

They rose in silence to the fourteenth floor. Drake lit a cigarette and smoke trailed behind him as he marched towards room 436. Pablo loped alongside, fumbling for his set of keys.

'I release la policía last night. Boy is here.'

Drake dug into his trouser pocket and fished out a wad of notes. Peeling off a thick layer, he stuffed them into the waiter's hand. Pablo muttered his thanks, handed him the key and slunk off down the corridor.

Drake straightened his jacket, slipped open the lock and flung the door back on its hinges. There was a loud bark from Soltan. Tony Russell was asleep under a pile of crumpled sheets. Kevin was towelling himself dry after a shower. He wore nothing except a pair of yellowing underpants.

'Uncle John,' he yelped gleefully.

Soltan trotted over to examine the new creature. Drake held out a hand and the dog licked it.

'The fuck you been, Kevin? You was supposed to be here yesterday.'

Kevin looked only slight perturbed. 'I went out. I thought it'd be all right 'cos I'm on holiday.'

'Don't think, Kev. It's not in your nature,' said his uncle, wearily.

Tony Russell sat up, bleary-eyed. 'About bloody time,' he said, trying to muster up his animosity. Although he knew the face from mugshots and old borstal photographs, the man in front of him was no malevolent teddy boy. The greased-back DA haircut had become a bald dome with two white crescents of hair above the ears. He still had prison eyes, but the years under a hot sun had softened the features. His goatee and moustache gave him the look of an ageing Spanish grandee – albeit one with a belly that cried out for a transducer and ultrasound jelly. Judging by the Armani suit, the handmade loafers and the clumpy gold Rolex, exile had been kind to John Drake.

'You'll be Russell, then.'

Tony glared at him. 'I suppose it was your sodding gorilla that cuffed me to the bed.'

'Yeah. And?'

Russell shot a look at Kevin, who was now pulling on his jeans.

'So what was the point? It was that little sod that buggered off.'

Drake waved a hand to silence him. 'Well, he's here now ain't he? Kevin, get dressed and go wait in the motor – It's the white Roller out the front,' he added purely to annoy the policeman.

Kevin looked at Soltan. 'What about my dog, Uncle John?'

Soltan, having lost interest in the conversation, was slurping noisily at his testicles.

'This mutt yours, then?'

'Yeah, he's called Soltan. I found him.'

'Soltan? Ain't that a suntan lotion?'

'Told you,' Tony butted in.

Kevin folded his eyebrows in preparation for a scowl. 'Nah. Soltan. Hound of Dracula. Like in the film.'

'Zoltan!' said Drake. 'With a Zed. Anyways, lose him. We got three Dobermans up the villa.'

'Aww.'

'Off you go, there's a good lad,' said his uncle, wiping lather from his hand.

Kevin grabbed his rucksack and left the room with the newly christened hound lolloping behind him.

Drake closed the door. 'Right, down to business.'

'So what's the deal? How do we go about this?'

Drake was about to spark up a Royal Crown when he spotted Tony's duty-free B & H on the bedside table.

'Bennie Hedgehogs!' He strolled over and scrabbled inside the open packet.

'Be my guest,' deadpanned Tony.

Drake lit one and inhaled luxuriantly. Tony noted with satisfaction that he still smoked as if he was in an exercise yard – cigarette cupped in the hand and sucked between thumb and forefinger.

'I said only one copper and you kept to that. Pukka. Kevin may be thicker than a BLT sandwich, but he's got a nose for filth. Now, let's see them papers.'

Tony went to the wardrobe and pulled out his suitcase. He placed it on the bed, unzipped it and removed a sheaf of documents in a beige file. Drake showed no sign of eagerness as he took them. There was silence for some ten minutes, broken only by the slow curling of pages and the flick of Drake's lighter as he chained the policeman's cigarettes. As the last page turned, a grin surfaced on his face. He removed a fat little Mont Blanc pen, signed it twice and passed it across. Not wanting to admit he only had a biro, Tony took the pen and made his mark.

'Tiny writing. Sign of insecurity,' said Drake, watching.

Tony held it up. Drake took, capped and holstered the pen without taking his eyes off him. He parted his jacket and thumbed round his belt to tuck in his shirt tails. 'Right. You're going down to Estepona. Know where that is?'

'I'm sure it's on the map.'

Drake ignored the response and tucked the file under his arm. 'It's all squared up. You're booked into a place down there. Here's the address.' He handed him a card which was emblazoned with a hotel logo. 'Just wait for my call, all right?'

Drake left the room without pausing for a reply.

Tony took in the orange and beige furnishings with fresh eyes. The Hound of Hell and/or suntan oil was gone. Even Kevin's odour, reminiscent of beef-flavour crisps, was beginning to disperse. He crossed over to the curtains and released a blast of sun into the room. Peering out, he saw a patch of cerulean sea between the jagged blocks. It's all happening, he thought. I'm going somewhere at last. He permitted himself a smile for the first time since he had left England. Better take a shower and get moving. Tony turned and promptly trod in Soltan's leaving present.

Mike crawled under the sheets and spread a hand across to Nicola's side of the bed. He felt around, expecting to find a pair of buttocks to snuggle up to.

Nothing. He turned on the bedside light.

No Nicola.

He suddenly felt utterly alone. Getting up, he paced the room and ended up staring at his reflection once more in the tiny bathroom. As he cleaned his teeth for the third time, he thought about his over-reliance on women. The string of compromise girlfriends; leaping from relationship to relationship like stepping stones across some vast chasm. And now? Now he'd fallen through. He thrust a hand against his mirror-face. No. Don't see it like that. It's not commitment. I've been committed to lots of girls. They laughed at that down the pub, Steve and Mark. And then? And then they went home to their wives.

Mike slumped down on the toilet. He knew what the trouble was. Something in him rebelled against the smooth gear changes of a well-oiled relationship. He inevitably rode each fling into the ground with a continual application of the brakes.

He went back into the bedroom and sat on the bed in his pants. So it was all over with Nicola, just as it had been with Katie and Donna and Alison. And she'd been the one to break it off. She was out there now, doubtless in the first rush of lust with another. He parted the scrawny curtains and watched the dawn dilute the sky. He smoked another cigarette and poured himself a vodka and flat Coke.

What about Sarah? I left her up there in that hospital. I could have stayed and helped her out but I walked away like I always do. If there was an Olympic event for avoidance I'd take gold . . . and then feel so bad I'd hand it back.

Mike swirled the brown liquid around in his mouth, his teeth and his resolve turning as soft as rubber.

Nicola pulled on her mini-dress and sat back on the dried-out leather sofa. The apartment was a mess. A couple of tatty rattan chairs, a guitar with its neck broken, an orange crate, empty liqueur bottles piled high in the brick fireplace, dog-eared posters of Claude Van Damme frozen in combat poses. She reached for her shoes.

She had danced until three with Rod and Brian. The Spanish guy had tagged along, gazing at her adoringly with puppy-dog eyes. She had loved everyone at that moment and so, when he kissed her, she had responded by grabbing his bottom and forcing her nails in until he squealed with pleasure. She didn't understood a word he said, but it didn't seem to matter; the grammar of attraction was universal.

When they left the club, he led her away from the others. Veering off the wide boulevard, he hustled her along white-washed streets and up into the musky gloom of his flat. He'd lost no time in removing her clothes and she was soon vulnerable in her panties. Then the drugs had worn off and she had felt herself go cold. Suddenly, his eagerness became desperation; his jabbering, an irritating static. She'd pushed him away, crossing her legs and holding a cushion to her breasts. He had then plied her with tequila. Looking for a way out, she happened to glance at a pile of pornographic magazines. He mistook her disgust for interest. He brought them over and gave a jolting commentary, flipping through a glossy travelogue of mountainous breasts, nipple-tumuli and forests of pubic hair. She hoped he'd sense her evident boredom and give up so she could sneak away. However, his energy seemed limitless. He went to the bedroom and returned with a large lump of hash, which he slammed on to the sideboard. Grinning in encouragement, he performed a smoking motion with two fingers. She nodded and he rolled a spliff. Once it was lit, she made sure she took only tiny puffs.

That had been an hour ago and now she was thoroughly pissed off. The Spaniard had stumbled off to the rancid toilet, creating an opportunity for escape. She picked up her platforms and crept to the hall. The boy stopped her at the door and steered her back to the settee. She stood up again. He pushed her down and shouted at her in fractured English. The gist of his argument seemed to be that he was an impressive guy with his porn and his drugs and she should therefore be only too glad to surrender her body to him. This was a statement he reinforced by producing a gun.

It was large and silver. She shrank back as he waved it about in the air and posed with it. He aimed at her, then dropped to one knee and spun round to fire at an imaginary assailant.

Ramón entered, slamming the door shut behind him. '¿Angel, que pasa?'

As he entered the room, Angel turned the gun on him and made a soft shooting sound with his mouth. Ramón tore the weapon from his hand and slapped him hard across the face.

'¡Bastardo!' yelped Angel. 'What you do that for? It was not loaded.'

The other one was leaner and had a more angular face, but it was clear that they were brothers. He smelt faintly of petrol.

'Macarra. I told you not to bring girls here,' he sneered, waving the pistol at Nicola.

Angel felt his smarting cheek. 'Where else I gonna bring her?'

Ramón put the gun on the sideboard and saw the slab of dope. 'You show her this – and this?' he said, indicating both objects.

Angel lowered his eyes to the floor. Ramón said something in Spanish which, she suspected, concerned his brother's amateurish seduction technique. They studied her as if she were a piece of fruit on a market stall. She squirmed and looked away as they conversed in hurried Andalucian, all vowels and shrugs. The taller one took a step forward. Angel winced, clearly expecting another blow. Instead, Ramón lit a Fortuna and blew the smoke at her.

'You English, yes?'

She nodded.

'You know how to get to your hotel from here?'

'We're a couple of streets off the main road, aren't we?' she ventured.

'Wrong answer.'

Ramón dropped to one knee, his face inches from hers. The oily smell was pungent now.

'Because of my *estupido* brother, you have seen too much. We have to keep you here.'

Her heart sank. His pragmatism masked something far more dangerous. She considered jumping up, shouting, heading full pelt for the door.

'Look. I won't tell anyone. Just let me go, OK?'

'Ramón smiled but his lips were taut around his teeth. 'No.'

She opened her mouth to scream out, but his hand was already there.

8

Drake's villa, high up in the hills behind Fuengirola, looked down on the resort like a proud parent. Access was difficult. The road leading up to it was a series of chicanes which first curled around the new developments and the unmade golf courses. It then rose up high into scree and scarp before petering out to a dirt track. The entrance was protected by iron gates which were set in a high wall and topped with prowling security cameras. A palm-bordered gravel drive led to the plastic-columned front portico.

On the rear terrace, the sun had already begun its daily task of bleaching the parasols, the matting on the sun-loungers and the paint on the wooden chairs. The raised patio looked out over a vista of marram grass bordered by roses, shrubs and a row of neat lime trees. Beyond that, a crenellated white wall hid the property from prying eyes. The centrepiece of the garden was a turquoise pool, which rippled with snakes of light.

A table had been laid for breakfast. There was a jug of fresh orange juice, a pot of tea, a basket of croissants, jams and pats of butter. Eschewing these, Kevin was tucking into an English breakfast. John watched as he shovelled beans, sausage, fried egg, mushrooms and a slice into his face.

'Didn't they feed you at that hotel?'

'I wabm't mere for breakfaff,' Kevin said, spraying a mist of bean juice.

Drake sniffed, then swallowed, tasting a reassuring metallic twinge.

'Kevin?'

'Yeah?'

The boy slurped at a mug of tea as his uncle lit up a pur-loined B&H.

'That copper, Russell. He give you any grief?'

Kevin shook his head. Not a wise move, since he hadn't closed his mouth. Tea spattered the table top.

'Good,' said John. 'The filth never know when to leave well alone.'

'He was a wanker. Could've had him anytime, Uncle John.'

A smile flickered under Drake's moustache. 'Toe-rag was after me for a job back in the seventies.'

Kevin grabbed a fistful of buttered bread.

'So anyway. How's your dad?'

'All right.'

'Bob's asked me to look after you.' He paused. 'Might be a bit of work going, if you want it.'

Damp dough squeezed between Kevin's canines as he grinned.

A gentle tapping came from behind them as Jackie teetered out on her mules. She wore a silk robe tied at the waist. It fanned out as she walked, revealing plenty of tanned leg.

'All right Jacks? I was just telling the boy we might find him a bit of work.'

She poured herself a bowl of muesli. 'That's nice.'

'This is great, Auntie Jackie,' said the boy, nodding at his plate.

'Haven't lost my touch, then.' She waved her spoon at her husband. 'Grumpy here's always telling me I don't do his bacon right.'

'She does it all limp when I want it salty.'

'Burned more like,' countered his wife.

Kevin smiled at them both. It was just like a proper family.

John licked a finger, dabbed it on the tip of Jackie's nose and held it up for her inspection. She took the digit in both hands and sucked off a trace of powder.

Drake's mobile phone crowed into life. He punched its buttons and waddled off, his flip-flops smacking on the tiles. Jackie gave Kevin a critical glance. He was wearing only his cherry-red DMs and jeans. His chest was white and hairless and a baby roll of fat spilled out over his belt.

'We could go shopping later,' she said, smiling. 'Down Marbella.'

She pronounced the second syllable of the word louder and more brightly. 'Get you some shorts.'

'I'm all right in me jeans.'

She continued her friendly stare as John trotted down the steps and on to the grass. He suddenly tore the phone away from his ear. Counting hurriedly to three, he held it up again.

'Get rid of her, you stupid dago ponces!' he bellowed. '*Si. Pronto!*'

'Anything the matter?' called Jackie.

'No hassle,' he replied cheerily, then lobbed the phone into the pool.

The dining room at the hotel in Fuengirola was teeming with pink, peeling bodies. The Germans had annexed the buffet, liberating the liverwurst; the French lapped at their coffees, silently cursing the non-smoking signs and the English huddled in a corner, complaining quietly to one another about the service.

Mike sat on his own sipping coffee. He hadn't slept. At six-thirty, he'd taken a long shower and then dressed. He was one of the first to arrive at breakfast. Having nothing better to do, he took his time over the meal as he considered his position. Nicola's probably having a brilliant time right now, he thought. She's on some roof terrace with the Marbella jet-set. And Sarah? She's out of my league. Back in London she'd be one of those people with friends in Chelsea. Dines in Notting Hill and knows what a terrine is. He curled his lip. Yeah, Notting Hill legs. She wouldn't be seen dead with me in Tooting, the rotting tooth of South London. He drained his cup.

'Sod it!' he said aloud. An expectant hush spread across the diners.

'Bollocks,' he added, causing a middle-aged hausfrau to redden. He strode out amidst turning heads and the rustling of shellsuits.

Tony Russell went down to reception to make his calls. First, he had to contact the Home Office. He was halfway through dialling when he realised that this was too public a space to report his progress. Deciding to phone them later, he rang his wife instead. Debbie answered on the second ring.

'Where have you been? I thought you were going to call me?'

'I tried but I couldn't get through.'

'What's the weather like?'

'Bloody hot.'

'Are you using the lotion and the moisturiser?'

'I haven't been out much,' he replied, darkly.

Twin hoovers suddenly roared into life as the maids attacked the expanse of carpet around him. He pressed the phone closer to his ear.

'Where are you?' asked Debbie.

'Torremolinos. It's like Eltham dipped in whitewash.'

'How long are you going to be there?'

He raised his voice. 'I'm just leaving for Estepona. I'll try and call you this evening. Six o'clock be alright?'

'Hang on.'

He visualised her on the kitchen extension, stretching the cord over to the melamine board; the one with all her courses and appointments written on it.

'Six is no good. I've got my evening class.'

'I meant to ask you about that.'

The vacuums came alongside the booth and bumped against the skirting.

'Tony? I can hardly hear you. You under a flight path or something?'

'Cleaners. I'll call you later, all right?'

'Not till ten. I've got car mechanics.'

'OK Debs.' He sighed wearily. 'Love you.'

'Love you too.'

He hung up. Car mechanics? That's a new one. He picked up his case, went to the reception desk and leafed through the guide-rack for a bus timetable. Finding one, he learned that there was a regular service from Torremolinos to Estepona. If he hurried, he could catch the 11:15.

He took a cab to the depot, bought a ticket and walked out on to the shaded forecourt. When he couldn't see his bus, he put down his suitcase and stopped a passing driver. 'Estepona?' he asked.

The man growled a stream of indecipherable Spanish. When Tony didn't react, he pointed to a farting juggernaut in an oily bay off to his right. Tony rushed over and managed to squeeze through the doors just before they hissed shut. The bus belched acrid fumes on to the cracked concrete and then inched out into the blazing sun.

On the spot where Tony had briefly rested his case, a dog was snuffling vigorously. He pricked up his ears, padded forwards and barked at the disappearing bus. Coming to a halt at the rim of the shaded area, he then lay down and lowered his head on to his sable paws. Passing by, a bus driver bent to stroke the forlorn animal.

'*Hola. Que bonito eres.* You miss your bus? I go next bus, yes?'

Soltan barked, ran around in a quick circle and then went off to pee on an Australian backpacker.

Clive 'The Fonk' Watson opened an eye and took in the opaque plastic, the IV bag and the white tube that was his right leg.

'This may hinder your athletic career,' grinned Mike who was sitting next to him.

Clive mumbled into his respirator, then raised an arm and pulled the plastic hemisphere from his mouth. 'Wha' happen?' he croaked.

'You're in hospital.'

'I hate hospitals.' He tried to moisten his lips with his tongue. 'Someone could die of thirst in here.'

Mike reached to the bedside table and poured him a beaker of water. 'Would you believe there's a bloody bar downstairs?'

Clive took the drink and swallowed painfully. 'I'm all mashed up.'

'You've been in a coma for ten years. We've lost the pound and they hanged the monarchy in Trafalgar Square.'

Clive narrowed his eyes and moved his free leg under the sheets.

Mike tried again.

'OK, how about this? I pulled you out of the Solly Sombra last night. Remember much?'

'Not a lot. Smoke, fire, falling stuff.'

'Whole place burned down. I'd say it was the work of a music-lover.'

Clive held up his beaker. 'Respect is due. Thanks, man.'

Mike reddened. He wasn't good at taking compliments. He usually denied them until the donor gave up and agreed he wasn't all that noble or kind.

'I found Sarah, by the way. She was with me last night. She said she was going to wait by your bed until you woke up.'

'That's cool.'

'Oh, and my girlfriend's missing,' he added. 'Well, my ex-girlfriend.'

'You lost two women?'

'It's a gift I have,' he deadpanned.

'So, when do I get to meet this Sarah?'

'She should be around.' Mike leaned forward. 'Can't miss her. Fantastic body, great tits, long tumbling hair—' He paused as Clive's gaze slide over to his right. 'She's standing right behind me isn't she?'

Clive nodded with his eyes.

'Do go on,' said Sarah. 'I'm sure you could be more shallow.'

Mike smiled wanly.

She yawned. 'One of the nurses let me use a room to get some sleep.'

Mike stood up and offered her the chair.

'Why did you come back?' she asked. 'Male-bonding ritual is it?'

'I thought you could use a little help.'

A little harshness crept into her tone. 'What about asking me first?'

'Do you need any help?'

'Yes,' she said flatly.

Mike decided he had made the right decision.

'How are you feeling?' asked Sarah, as she took the chair and faced Clive.

'Like one of the steaks in Big Ronnie's. Burned.'

'I really need to talk to you about Lana.'

Clive pursed his lips. 'Fire away,' he said.

'She lived with you, yeah?'

'Only for a couple of weeks.' He paused and took a sip of water. 'Listen, Sarah, I was really freaked by what happened. You tell me what you know first, OK? I don't want to upset you.'

She glanced up at Mike. 'Did you tell him about the pathologist?'

'Nope.'

She looked back at Clive. 'So you didn't know she was murdered?'

'Shit, no!' Clive jerked himself upright and dissolved into a spasm of coughing. Sarah quickly grabbed the respirator and held it to his mouth. He gulped in oxygen, then put it aside. 'Tell me.'

He listened in silence as Sarah explained the details of the autopsy. When Clive finally spoke, there was sorrow in his voice. 'I hadn't known her long. We met in Sparklers Nite-Spot when I was a barman there. She was looking for work. Had no bread. I said she could crash at my place until she got sorted.'

Sarah said nothing, wondering about the nature of their relationship.

'Never saw much of her round the flat. Sparklers was a rip-off, so I started DJ'ing. One-nighters in Estepona and Torrie-town. Sometimes she came along and I'd fix her up with drinks and a meal.'

'The last I heard of her she was teaching in Malaga,' Sarah interrupted. 'Didn't she mention that?'

He thought for a moment. 'Might have. I know she thought there was money down here with the season coming up. Trouble was, she didn't want to be a propper or a waitress, so it was tough getting work.'

Sarah crossed her arms tightly against her chest. 'What about the night she died?'

'I hadn't seen her for a day or so. That was normal. First thing I knew, the police busted in on me, trashed my place and hauled me off.'

'How did they know she lived with you?' asked Mike, wanting to be included.

'Keys had my address. They kept her set.'

'They never showed them to me,' said Sarah.

'After they questioned me, the cops said I should think about moving on,' continued Clive. 'And that's about it.'

'Why didn't you go?' asked Mike

'Solly Sombra was easy money. Owner said a black face pulls the crowds. Didn't think he meant the Klan.'

'Must have been just about the only place I never checked,' said Sarah. 'And I went through the book.'

'Should have looked under firewood,' offered Mike.

They fell silent. Nurses clattered in the background. A blind was opened and fresh sunlight illuminated the curtains. Clive turned to look up at a grey locker which stood by the side of the bed. 'Is my jacket in there?'

Mike opened it. 'Yeah.'

'Should be some keys in the pocket.'

He fumbled around and produced a set with a metal, skull-shaped fob.

'Take them. Police took Lana's stuff, but you never know. Might be something of hers lying around.'

'What's your address?' asked Sarah, reaching into her bag for a notepad and pen.

'Calle Padre Espinosa. Number 43. Flat B.'

She wrote it down. 'Thanks Clive.'

'You guys saved my life.'

'All in a day's work,' said Mike, grinning.

'You're going to milk this, aren't you?' said Sarah.

'You bet.'

They drove back to Fuengirola in Sarah's car and parked in the old town. The shops had closed for lunch and the street was deserted as the midday sun threw the beaten-up trucks and dusty cars into sharp relief. Clive's building was a four-storey block with an arched door set into a wall. Mike rotated the keys until he found one which worked on the outer door. It opened into a cool, tiled vestibule. In front of them was a plant-studded stairwell which led up to the first floor. Mike went in, but Sarah stood hovering in the doorway.

'You coming?' he asked.

This is the last place where Lana was seen alive, she thought.

'Sure,' she said, nervously and followed him inside.

A sign on the wall indicated that Apartments A, B and C, were off to their right. Mike quickly located Flat B and sprung open the black oak door. The inner hallway was dim and cool, illuminated by a few slivers of sun which bled through a metal shutter. Sarah shivered and rubbed her arms. Mike closed the door behind them and went to roll up the blinds.

'Don't,' she said.

'Why not?'

'Just don't.'

They crept into the main room. This, too, was in darkness. Beanbags lay around a wooden table which sat on a frayed hessian carpet. There was an aged cabinet full of mismatched glasses. Landscapes and religious icons hung on the bare plaster walls. Sarah slumped on to one of the cushions.

'You sure you're OK?' asked Mike.

'I'm a little tired, that's all.'

'Can I get you anything? If there is anything.'

'Soft drink?'

The refrigerator in the kitchen contained only a bottle of flat lemonade. He found some tumblers, filled two of them and brought them through. Sarah cupped her hands around her drink.

'It's weird. I get no sense of her having been here.'

'Would you normally?'

She smiled to herself. 'She was one for marking her territory. Lana got a flat in Shepherd's Bush once with three other girls. She was the last one there but she was so messy that *they* moved out. You can imagine what she was like at home.'

With a pang of guilt, Mike realised he had mixed feelings about the dead girl.

Sarah continued. ''Course, by the time I left home and came down to London, she'd gone.'

'Where to?'

'Birmingham. She was in a play.'

'She was an actress?'

'Fringe production.'

'Oh, right. She wasn't, then.'

She frowned. 'That's not very kind.'

He mumbled an apology.

'You're right, though. She wasn't. She never really knew what she was.'

A smell of frying tortilla wafted in from somewhere outside. Mike's stomach gurgled loudly. He downed his drink. 'So where shall we start?'

'I'll look in the bedroom. You root around in here.'

Clive didn't have much in the way of possessions. Mike searched the drawers and cupboards and pulled out piles of vinyl records and a heap of magazines. He flicked through them, having a hard time resisting the urge to stop and read.

In the bedroom, Sarah pulled shoes and an empty box from under the bed and went to the wardrobe. It contained several pairs of jeans and a row of multicoloured shirts. She came to a faded denim jacket which was clearly too small for Clive. Smelling it, she recognised her sister's scent. She pulled it out and put it on, checking all the pockets as she did so. Finding nothing, she hugged it tightly around her and went into the bathroom. There was a bottle of patchouli oil on the side of the bath. She wondered whether it belonged to Lana or to Clive.

Mike was in the hall now, standing in front of a large and ornate tallboy. He rifled through the drawers, pulling out mini-cab cards, pamphlets and crumpled leaflets. Amongst them there was a ringbound notebook. It was full of handwritten notes. 'Sarah?' he called.

As she emerged from the bathroom, Mike held out the book for inspection.

With a gasp, she recognised Lana's loose scrawl and began to examine every page. There were scribbled names of clubs and bars, designs for clothes and doodles. In several places there was her trademark cartoon of a wide-eyed rabbit. She came to blank pages.

'I'll go through this in more detail back at my place.'

'You weren't wearing that jacket before. Is it Lana's?'

She smiled.

'Can I have another quick look at that?' Mike motioned to the book. She passed it over as if it were a first edition. Flicking through to the cardboard backing, he saw that a rough map had been scrawled on it in weak biro.

'Look at this.'

Sarah took it and studied the drawing. 'Well, that's the coast road. Marbella that way, San Pedro the other. The directions seem to lead to somewhere up in the Sierras.'

'What's up there?'

'It's pretty barren.' She pointed to a heavy blue line. 'That's the mountain route to Ronda, but these markings go off the road. There's nothing up there but hills and dirt.'

'Ah. The real Spain at last,' grinned Mike.

Nicola awoke face down on the sofa and bound in a green plastic washing line. Following the phone call, the brothers had secured her and had gone off to catch up on some sleep. Unable to move, she had fallen into a doze until the discomfort and the rising heat of the day awoke her.

'So, what we going to do?' asked Angel, now washed and dressed.

Ramón was gazing at a cracked mirror, combing and recombing his hair. 'Best thing is we take her up into the hills. Maybe near Alhaurin, then *pchh*!' He made a gun with his hand.

Angel looked shocked. His image of the outlaw life had not included shooting tourists – especially nubile ones. 'When are we going to do this?'

Ramón slapped his forehead. 'Oh yes. I forgot. You're very busy today. Right now, *maricón*,' he added.

The phone let out a long shrill tone. Angel grabbed it. His face fell as he recognised the voice. '*Sí, Mama. Sí, sí.*' He slumped a little with each exclamation. '*¿Hoy? ¿Toda la familla, en Istan? Vale. ¿Con Ramón?*'

His brother shook his head furiously.

Angel grinned. '*Sí, Mama. En una hora. A la dos. De nada. Adios.*'

Ramón fumed beside him. 'We cannot go for a meal with the family now!'

Angel shrugged. 'We have not seen Mama for days.'

The elder brother fetched his gun and, dragging Nicola to her feet, put the weapon to her chin.

'You forgetting something?'

'We could take her with us,' said Angel, meekly.

'She is your girlfriend now?'

The boy couldn't disguise his excitement. 'Mama has never

seen me with a girl. It might shut her up for one minute . . .
Mama don't speak English and . . . and this girl, she—' Angel
smiled at her, '*Hablas Espãnol?*'

'Fuck off,' said Nicola.

'See? She don't speak Spanish. No one in Istan speak English.
We take her to the meal, and then after—'

Ramón gave up. It was like reasoning with something under
a stone. He cocked the gun and grabbed his brother around the
neck. '*Vale.* But if anything goes wrong, you answer to Señor
Drake. *Comprendes?*'

9

'*Es Pablo en Torremolinos.*'

John Drake leaned back in his chair and pressed the stop button. The concerto cut out and silence returned to the study. 'What's up?' he said, cradling the phone to his ear.

'The *policia ingles* has gone, but there is something else you must know.'

Drake closed his eyes and breathed out slowly through his nostrils.

'There is much merchandise arriving here in town,' continued the Spaniard.

'Combat Alley?'

'Like the first day of a sale. Moroccan *costo*. Good quality.'

'Distributors. Local?'

'*Si.* It says Ozorio to me.'

'OK Pablo. Good work. You around tonight?'

'*Si, Señor.*'

Drake replaced the phone, stretched his fat arms and snapped off his Rolex. Rising, he moved around the desk to the centre of the room. In front of him was a large-scale model on a raised dais. The hand-painted sea was bordered at one end by a harbour and a length of shoreline. Two fleets of bench galleons were arranged in an arc, whilst the smaller pinnaces, angosys and biscayans were clustered in the harbour. Drake pulled at his goatee and surveyed the scene. Picking up a galleon, he admired the fine detail he had painted on the rows of cannon and on the square-rigged mainmast. He then replaced the ship and set about bringing the fleet closer to the harbour. Satisfied, he stood back and fished out a cigarette. He flung open the double doors, paced through the lounge and came out on to the patio.

Kevin lay prone in the pool in a transparent inflatable chair. In a concession to Jackie, he'd cut his jeans down to ragged shorts. There was a discolouration in the water around him.

'Kevin,' admonished Drake, 'you pissed in my pool?'

The boy pointed at a tumbler which lay on the bottom of the pool. 'Nah. Spilt me drink,' he slurred.

'Wonder why my brother wanted to get rid of you?'

Kevin kicked his legs and the chair surged backwards.

'If you're bored, you can come with me tonight. Someone up Torrie-town needs a slap.'

'Oh yeah!' Kevin raised both thumbs to his uncle, lost his balance and tipped over into the water.

The pebbles spat against the bodywork of the Peugeot 205 as it bounced over the pot-holes. The car slewed from side to side, trying to conquer a landscape which had known only centuries of neglect.

'Hold it. Hold it a minute,' said Mike, studying the hand-drawn map. 'She's marked something here. Looks like a tree. Or a spider.'

Sarah forced a groan out of the handbrake.

Mike looked around. Stalks of hard straw on the verge shone gold in the still heat. The valley below was a dustpan of russet earth smudged with the purple shadows of eucalyptus trees and olive groves. The sky was a solid slab of blue. Sarah lifted herself up from her seat and peeled her moist dress from her buttocks.

'I think it's that one,' said Mike, trying to catch a glimpse of her thighs. 'Over there where the track turns.'

He pointed to a gnarled tree on a rise. Its bark had been cut away, leaving it exposed like a freshly peeled orange.

'The cork tree?'

'Is that what it is?'

'Yes, and don't ask me how they whittle it down to get it in the bottles.'

She put the car in gear and crawled forwards.

It was early afternoon now, the hottest part of the day. They had left the serpentine switchbacks of the main road and had dipped down, crossing a dried-up riverbed before rising up into the Sierras. Drowsiness nagged at them and smoking cigarettes only dehydrated them all the more. They had brought bottled water, but it was now warm and unpleasant to drink.

'That must be it,' Mike cried out.

'You sure?'

A villa had been cut into the hillside. Its cracked terracotta roof was studded with lichen and the peeling white walls were submerged in dead vines. The only sign of an entrance was a single pillar of bricks. Sarah drove past and stopped a hundred metres further down the track.

'I said that was it,' said Mike, sharply.

'I'm not driving straight in there. God knows what we might find.'

They parked and walked back to the house. Behind the pillar, the ground fell away to reveal a dusty courtyard. The front door was blistered black iron and the windows either side were engulfed in bougainvillea.

They found a thin passageway to one side of the house. It led through to a small patio bordered by curved railings. Mike peered over and gave a low whistle. They were perched above a drop of several hundred metres. The ground, far below them, was a patchwork of furrowed ochre slabs. There were no signs of human habitation. Mike decided it was truly unspoilt and therefore highly desirable. Sarah had slipped between two yellowing sun-loungers and was peering through a pair of sliding glass doors. A beaded curtain obscured her view. She put a hand to the door and shook it away, scalded.

'I suppose this is where you reveal your gift for lock-picking?' asked Mike.

She spat on her hand to squeeze away the pain. 'No.' She wrapped the hem of her dress around her hand and tried the hot metal once more. 'It isn't locked.'

She slid it open and paused, waiting for signs of movement. Hearing nothing, she parted the curtains and stepped inside. The beads rattled, waving themselves to a halt. With a shrug, Mike followed her in and adjusted his eyes to the gloom.

Bare walls, wicker furniture, a brick fireplace. The adjoining kitchen had only a simple sink and a hob with an empty bottle of gas underneath it. The only indication of the twentieth century was a battered fridge-freezer which buzzed intermittently. Mike prized it open and found it contained several cans of beer and a bottle of vodka.

'Maybe this place belongs to an alcoholic goatherd. That, or someone didn't finish his twelve-step programme.'

Sarah went off to investigate further as he fished out a Dos Equis. He dug out a bottle-opener, prized it open and sucked greedily. Strolling through to the smallest of the bedrooms, he found her on hands and knees, straining to grab at something under the bed.

'What is it?'

'I can't reach.' She stood up. 'Let's move the bed.'

As they jerked the bed away from the wall, its metal legs left jagged lines in the dust. Sarah reached into the gap and retrieved a tiny silver chain. She sat on the mattress and fed it through her fingers. She grasped it tightly, tears brimming in her eyes. 'This is Lana's ankle bracelet,' she choked. 'I gave it to her two Christmases ago.'

'Are you sure?'

''Course I'm sure.'

Mike stepped forwards to hold her, but froze as he touched her shoulder.

'What is it?'

'There's a car coming.'

In seconds they had pushed the bed back and were at the patio doors.

'Wait,' whispered Mike loudly.

They stayed motionless as the car drew up outside. There was the clunk of a door, then footsteps coming directly towards them. Sarah quickly closed the doors.

'Back to the front of the house,' he urged.

They scampered through to the hall, then Mike pulled her into the bathroom. The sink was grimy and the iron bath rusted. The window was a sheet of bright green. Mike undid the catch and found it wouldn't give.

'Are there bars on the other side?' asked Sarah.

'I don't think so . . . Ah!'

It sprang open a bit, revealing a tangled sea of bougainvillea.

He pushed harder at the springy growth and there was soon room enough for a person to slip through.

'Go on. You first.'

She hoisted herself up on to the window-ledge and jumped out to the ground. In a moment they were back in the courtyard, blinking in the glare of the sun.

A shining blue Mercedes stood there, incongruous against the ruined villa. Sarah immediately ran off and dropped down behind the outer wall. Mike joined her, gasping for breath and sweating profusely in the sudden heat.

A man emerged from the front door. He was old, a homunculus in pale jeans and a silk shirt that would have suited someone twenty years his junior. He walked with a stoop, the angle of his back indicating a curvature of the spine rather than poor posture. A pot belly hung underneath him like a sloth gripping a tree trunk. Sarah etched his face in her memory. A weaselly mouth and sallow cheeks. Deep lines scored across the forehead. Small, beady eyes. His head appeared hairless but, as he bent to the car boot, a silver ponytail fell on to his rounded shoulders. Removing a bulky tripod, he carried it inside, then returned for a long silver fan which Mike identified as a lighting umbrella. He made three further trips: two for some battered suitcases and one for provisions. The last box clinked, indicating it contained more drink. Finally, he closed the front door, clambered back into his car and started the engine.

'What now?' asked Mike.

'We'll follow him.'

'Follow him?'

Mike was about to object when he realised she had left his side. He caught up with her at the car. 'Let's give him a minute,' he panted, bending to the driver's window. 'Another car out here's going to look odd.'

'OK. Can you remember the number?'

He nodded.

'Write it down.'

He found a pen in the glove compartment and was looking for paper when Sarah's impatience got the better of her. She gunned the engine and spun the car round in a semicircle.

They followed in silent excitement. Back on the main mountain route they relaxed enough to hold back and let a few cars get between them and the Mercedes. They passed a new urbanisation and the road began to straighten out. Soon the coast was visible in the heat haze and the blue and white markings of the Marbella town boundary appeared on the kerbside. They came to the motorway junction as the Merc turned off towards Puerto Banús.

'We can't park in the harbour,' said Sarah. 'We'll stick out like a sore thumb.'

'Why?' asked Mike, enjoying a tingle of excitement he hadn't known since childhood.

'You'll see.'

She drove them to the giant Hypercor supermarket and parked in its subterranean car park. As they emerged on to the street, Mike realised why her Peugeot would look out of place. Every car was a Rolls, a Ferrari or a BMW. It was as if all the top of the range cars had come out here for a holiday.

They hurried through to the quayside.

The harbour was full of luxury yachts which were sprinkled in a profusion of masts, satellite dishes and radar. Around them, the quay was skirted by exclusive restaurants and shops. Brand names shouted at them from all sides. Versace, Dolce and Gabanna. DKNY. Bond Street-sur-Mer. Mike's head reeled with the cultural bends, having surfaced from the third world to the first in under half an hour. Feeling under-dressed in his T-shirt and Top Man shorts, he found it impossible not to gawp at the display of naked money.

'Over there,' said Sarah, pointing to a jetty.

The withered man trotted up the gangplank of a triple-decked yacht and disappeared inside.

'What now, genius?' asked Mike, yawning as weariness crept up on him once more.

Sarah peered through her sunglasses. 'Can you make out the name?'

'It says the *Maiden Voyage*.'

'Well, I'm going to stake him out.'

'Aren't we taking this detective thing a bit too far?'

'I'm only going to sit in a bar and watch what goes on.'

He rubbed his eyes. 'Look, I'm really tired. I ought to go back and see if Nicola's all right.'

'OK. I need time to think anyway.' There was a trace of hurt in her voice.

'Shall I come back later?'

'It's up to you.'

'Right. That means yes, doesn't it?'

'No, that means it's up to you.'

'I just need some sleep,' he said crabbily. 'Then I'll come back.'

If she was relieved, she wasn't showing it. 'How about eight o'clock? Relieve me of my shift?'

He nodded, wondering if he should give her a goodbye hug. Sarah solved it by hugging him. Mike walked away delighted, then realised he had no idea of how to get back to Fuengirola.

Nicola was sitting in the street on a long trestle table amidst twenty Spanish people who were all talking at once. The tiny village of Istan, up in the Sierra Bermeja, was at least fifteen kilometres from the coast. Ramón sat to her right, drinking copiously and arguing with anyone in range. To her left, Angel snuggled close and continually planted wet kisses on her neck. Opposite them was Mother, a leathery matriarch clearly in a state of extreme excitement. She gesticulated. She made imploring eyes at Nicola. She pushed plate after plate of tapas in her direction.

The entire town seemed to be celebrating in the geranium-bedecked streets. It was not the Spain Nicola was used to. Waiters scurried in and out of the bars bringing plates of spiced meats, tortillas, *jamon y queso* and calamares. Wizened farmers in battered suits gummed their food and jovial patrons poured wine from earthenware jugs. Women chattered as their children shrieked and ran around unfettered. Two old men duelled Flamenco rhythms on their guitars, egged on by the syncopated clapping of the bystanders. Nicola was bewildered and scared. For a last meal, it certainly had all the trimmings.

Mother touched her hand again and uttered one of her long, seemingly consonant-free sentences. '*Esta demasindo delgada. Necesita engordar un poco.*'

Nicola shot her an earnest frown. 'Your sons are going to kill me.'

'*Come menos que un pajarito.*'

'They're taking me to the hills to shoot me. Don't you understand, you toothless old bitch?'

'*Como mi hijo puede salir con ella, no lo entiendo. Mi hijo, el puro virgen.*'

'Doesn't anyone speak English? They're going to kill me!' She put a finger to her temple, miming a gun. 'Bang bang.'

Everyone laughed as if it was the funniest thing they had ever heard.

Ramón was growing progressively more drunk, Angel, more frisky. She kept batting his hand away as if it were a stubborn mosquito. What if I try and get away? She thought. If they force me back, I'll start screaming and the rest of them will know something's up. There must be a policeman here. She scanned the joyous throng. It seemed unlikely. Ramón lined up some shot glasses and poured a dark liquid across them. The elder brother's worse. Maybe if I can get him drunk enough then he'd be less of a problem. She fixed on a false smile and chinked her glass against his.

More villagers arrived, some with soil-blackened fingernails from working the terraced hills. Looking askance at Ramón, she noticed the drink was finally taking hold. Angel was happily wolfing down bread and olives.

'I need to go to the ladies,' she whispered to him. 'You know . . . *Señorita's.*'

He waved at a nearby bar. She rose and shuffled behind the trestle tables, smiling at the catcalls and the upturned faces of the younger men. The street wound in a sharp bend up to the central Plaza. She remembered that this was where Ramón had left the jeep. A hand suddenly appeared on her shoulder. It was Angel, who was grinning and waving a finger at her.

'I think you are trying to get away, no?'

'I was looking for the toilet, scumbag.'

As he steered her back towards her place, a sudden cheer rose from behind them. They turned to see four men carrying an enormous monkfish on a silver platter. It was the ugliest thing she had ever seen. Nearly two metres long, it had club-like fins and greeny-grey plates instead of scales. Long dorsal spines emerged from its backbone and, surrounding the jaw, were a row of tassel-like outgrowths. The grotesque mouth was a maw of curved teeth, its gullet grey and ribbed like the inside of a tyre. It gaped open in surprise as if it couldn't believe anyone would bother catching it.

The villagers clapped and cheered. Even Angel released his grip to join in. Nicola saw her chance. She took two steps forwards and reached for the plate. The flesh had been pre-cut into sections so when she pulled, the whole head came away in one. She winced and thrust the open mouth over Angel's face. It covered his head like a slimy balaclava. The villagers fell off their chairs, spluttered into their drinks, cried out in shock. Even the children fell silent.

Then, almost in slow motion, someone pointed at the fish-headed boy and emitted a high-pitched shriek of laughter. Angel spun blindly, his curses muffled by the fleshy carcass. The teeth had locked on to his collar and he couldn't get a grip on the slimy scales. Slowly, the faces in the crowd softened, their eyes sparkled and the engine of hilarity spluttered into life.

She didn't hesitate. She scrambled under the table, tore the car keys from Ramón's waist and ran off up the street. As she reached the corner, she risked a glimpse over her shoulder. Angel was pirouetting and stumbling around as the crowd applauded. The person who had started the fun was bent double, weeping with laughter.

'Mothers!' spat Nicola as she leaped into the Jeep.

10

Mike climbed out of the cab at his hotel in Fuengirola, consulted the phrase book and handed a fistful of notes to the driver. The heat had driven the tourists to the beach or to their rooms, so reception was empty. He collected his key, took the lift to the sixth floor and rattled the large plastic fob against his door. It was dark inside and it didn't look as though the maid had been. Reaching for the light switch, he was suddenly thrown to the floor. At first he thought it was a shock from the socket. As a foot impacted on his back, he gathered otherwise.

'Stay down, you wee bastard,' said a bellicose Scots accent.

He stayed down, what with being unable to move. The foot pressed harder.

'What did you see?' demanded the voice.

'Nothing,' he grunted. Mike's left arm was promptly wrenched upwards and almost pulled out of its socket. He cried out in pain.

'None of that, sonny.'

His aching arm was released and the foot placed on his head.

'Perhaps your memory needs a kick-start? Friday night. You were taking a dip. What d'you see?'

He realised this had nothing to do with Sarah. This was happening because he was in the wrong place at the wrong time. Or the right place at the wrong time. Either way, he wished he hadn't gone for that midnight swim.

'I didn't see anything. Not even the body.' As he winced at his own stupidity, the pressure increased.

'One stamp on your scrawny little spine and you'll be eligible for the Paralympics.'

The foot lifted and Mike shrank into a foetal position. He decided that if he was going to die, he wanted to die like a man – bawling and pleading.

'One thing I know for sure is you haven't been to see the bobbys,' said the voice to itself. It came closer. 'Why not?'

'I didn't want to cause a fuss.'

There was a boom of laughter. Seeing this as a promising sign, Mike tried to turn over. He was rewarded with a swift kick to the ribs.

'Let's keep it like that, eh? Keep our noses out of other people's businesses. Savvy?'

Mike lay still and as silent as possible, given that he couldn't control his moaning. He hoped that the man would eventually tire of hurting him. The feet stood astride him now and burly hands lifted him up by the armpits. As he was thrown on to the bed, his face hit something sharp. He refocused and saw the corner of his own suitcase.

'Might be an idea for you to cut short your vacation.' The voice seemed almost jovial now. 'After all, it's not turning out too well, is it?'

He considered this. 'Yes. You're absolutely right.' Mike gasped.

A hand grabbed him by the hair and lifted his head up. Tears sprang into Mike's eyes.

'I packed your stuff. Never let it be said I'm not considerate.'

Both his and Nicola's clothes had been thrown into their cases. Their passports lay between them on the bed.

'Hope you enjoyed your stay,' concluded the Scotsman.

Before Mike was able to compose a reply, he was forced back down on to the bedspread. He didn't move again until he heard the door close.

The sun's last rays turned the white hotels to amber gold as the lights winked on across the town of Torremolinos. Waiters placed paper squares over the café tables and fastened them with metal clips. Locals wandered home with their shopping. Youths on mopeds buzzed around, looking for girls. A white Rolls-Royce purred along the main strip. Inside, Kevin pushed buttons on the radio as his uncle halted outside the Hotel MiraFlores.

John Drake flicked a butt on to the pavement and turned to his nephew. Kevin was a painful shade of pink from his day by the pool.

'Least you ain't gonna stick out, being that colour.'

The boy shrugged. Sunburn didn't bother him. John tooted the horn.

'Uncle John?'

'Yeah.'

'Can I go find S . . . Zoltan?'

'That oily mutt? You played with the Dobermans all afternoon.'

'It's not the same.'

Ignoring him, Drake twirled the tips of his moustache into a fine point. Pablo appeared from the front entrance and hurried over.

'*Buenos tardes, Señor.*'

'All right Pablo? Take the boy here and pop up to Combat Alley. Get me one of their dealers. I'll bring the motor round. Be by the Palladium.'

'No problems.'

Pablo stepped a respectful distance away as Drake spoke to his nephew.

'Kev. You go with this bloke.'

'But he's a dago.'

Drake gave Kevin a stern look. 'Kev, you're just watching for tonight, all right? Look and learn.'

Kevin clambered out. Once he and Pablo had disappeared, Drake lit a fresh cigarette and pulled away.

Combat Alley is a small park bordered by wide pavements and a plethora of bars. It rarely comes alive until well after midnight, when it begins to resemble a refugee camp with fresh supplies. Proppers, buskers, dealers, addicts, tourists and hundreds of teenagers flood into the tiny square, looking for drugs. Even though it was still early, the more entrepreneurial dealers were already out making a killing from the less price-conscious.

Kevin and Pablo stumbled back to the car with a scared youth between them. He had dyed blond hair and his stubbly face was ashen. Drake unlocked the rear doors and the three of them clambered in. He reversed the Rolls out of the throng, then manoeuvred it back on to the main street. They drove in silence, heading north towards the smaller coastal resort of Benyamina. Neon washed their faces.

Pablo kept a firm grip on his captive. Kevin had his eyes on the street, hoping for a glimpse of his lost pet. Drake asked if anyone would like some music. Without pausing for a reply, he pressed a button and the 'Blue Danube' flowed out of the speakers. He hummed along as they crept past the shopping area into the steep scarps of the housing estates. As they pulled off the main road into a warren of nondescript streets, the dealer whispered to Pablo in Spanish.

'What's he on about?' asked Drake.

Pablo leaned forward. 'He say he know nothing.'

'Well, he must know something. Height of the Eiffel Tower? Mozart's last concerto? Winner of Euro ninety-fucking-six?'

Kevin chuckled in the back.

They cruised through disintegrating suburbs. Crab-grass had overtaken the pavements. Street lights flickered. Scrawls of graffiti advertised poverty and dissent. There was an odour of rotting food from the torn rubbish sacks which were piled along the kerb sides. Drake pulled over near a block of flats and doused the headlights. The buildings above them cast a shadow which fell in the shape of a tombstone. Drake turned round and leaned an elbow on the back of his seat.

'Let's make this quick, then. Where'd you get the stuff?'

The dealer appeared not to understand. Pablo spoke to him and the youth spilled out a few hesitant sentences. Drake raised a chalky eyebrow.

'¡Maricón! It could be anyone, from what he say,' shrugged Pablo.

Drake sucked in air. 'Not good enough.'

Pablo translated this by smashing the back of his fist on to the boy's nose. Blood spattered the dealer's dusty sweatshirt.

'Now,' said Drake, certain that the language of violence had crossed the linguistic barrier. 'You ain't working Combat Alley without speaking a bit of English, so let's cut all this native bollocks. ¿Entiendes?'

The boy nodded, crimson dripping from his shattered nose.

Drake spoke with a patronising air. 'Did you get the *porro* from Ozorio?'

'Yes.'

'How much hash you got?'

'I have almost one kilo. You want?'

John flicked a dismissive hand. 'What is it? Moroccan?'

'*Sí.*'

'What?' Drake said, peeved.

'Yes.'

Drake twisted round to face front. He held Pablo's eyes in the mirror.

'Kevin?'

'Yes, Uncle John? Oh shit. Shouldn't have said your name. Sorry John.'

'Don't matter. Go with Pablo now. You'll learn something.'

'OK.' Kevin bounded from the car like a dog let off its leash.

Ten minutes passed before the boy returned and slid into the front seat.

'Fuckin' 'ell,' he said, in a mixture of amazement and surprise. 'Fark-in El-luh,' he said again, for emphasis.

Drake nosed the Rolls back on to the main road and they were soon speeding towards Fuengirola along the busy N340. The evening was blood-warm and cicadas drummed out in the dark brush. Jasmine scented the air, interspersed with whiffs of brine as they skirted the sea. A crescent moon caught waves off the Mediterranean, reflecting shimmers of waxy light.

Kevin was bursting to talk about it.

'Know what he did Uncle John? He only cut his cock off. Stuffed it in his mouth and then bleedin' stabbed him.'

Drake kept his eyes on the road. 'Pablo walking back then?'

'Yeah. Said he needed a drink. I need a pint after that.'

'Method's a bit crude, but it gets the message across to Ozorio.'

'Who's he?'

'Spark us up, will you Kev?'

Kevin searched out a fresh pack amidst the detritus on the dashboard. He coughed as he lit one for his uncle.

'Shouldn't smoke, Uncle John. It's bad for you.'

'Yeah, yeah,' said Drake having heard it all before. 'Anyway. It's a religion out here. When in Rome—'

'But we're in Spain.'

Drake resisted the temptation to belt him one. Instead, he took a deep drag, crushing the filter between his nicotine-stained fingers.

'Ozorio's an oily little toe-rag from Madrid. He come down here a few months ago and tries to muscle in. I had a shipment due the other night, only he goes and has it away with the whole bundle. Has his blokes dress up as coastguards.' He paused for effect. 'Listen to this, Kev. Half the dealers up the coast are selling my fucking puff.'

'So that was the warning then?'

'Yup.'

'Fucking hell,' said Kevin.

They sat in silence for a moment.

'Kevin?'

'Yeah?'

'No swearing in front of your auntie, all right?'

Mike was curled up with the sheets pulled over him. Following the Scotsman's visit, he'd put a chair against the door, thrown everything off the bed and fallen into a deep sleep full of robust dreams. Through his haze, he became aware of a distant rattling. He rolled over and spread his cheek on the pillow. 'Ten muw minnis,' he mumbled.

He fought to stay submerged but the noise continued, increasing in volume. He pulled the pillow over his head until it became unbearable. Opening one eye, he saw a fluffy lava of orange. The bedspread swam into focus and he realised he was still in Spain.

'Mike,' cried an hysterical voice.

Nicola. He leaped up, fell over one of the cases and crashed to the door. As he pulled the chair away, she burst in. Nicola was a quivering mass of nerves. Her bare feet were cut and bruised, her dress torn, her body covered in a patina of dirt.

'Christ. Th-they nearly killed me Mike. What am I going to do? Oh, Jesus.' She fumbled to light a cigarette and paced up and down, wired on panic.

'Nicola. Nicky, what's happened?'

She faced him, her features twitching and the smoke from her cigarette shaking into jagged lines.

'I was kidnapped,' she howled.

He hugged her close, ignoring his own aches, which had returned like an unwelcome guest. Heaving sobs racked her thin frame as he edged her to the bed, sat her down and began to rock her. The cigarette dropped from her hand and smouldered on the tiles. He stared at it but did nothing as her tears subsided. She swallowed, let out a small burp and took halting breaths. Mike fetched a glass of water. She grabbed it with both hands and began to explain.

'I-I went off w-with this Spanish guy. Last night. Back to his place. He was a real – a total creep.'

'Did he? Did he hurt you?'

She shook her head.

'He showed me all these drugs and guns and porn and stuff. Like, like that was going to make me shag him.'

Mike made a mental note not to bother trying that one.

'But then his brother came home. He said that they were going to keep me there because I'd seen all their stuff.'

'Can you describe them?'

Her breathing became a little more regular. 'They were Spanish. I don't know. They called themselves Ramón and Angel.'

'Angel?'

'It's pronounced Ang-hell. Sodding hell is what he was!' she spat.

'And the other one, Ramón?'

'He was older.' She wrinkled up her nose. 'What's that smell?' Seeing the burning stub, she threw her glass of water at it. 'He was a right bastard. Then they got this phone call from some bloke. Then . . . then they said they had to kill me!' A tear trickled towards her chin. 'They took me up to some village in the middle of nowhere for a meal.'

'They were going to kill you with Spanish food?'

'No, arsehole. They were going to shoot me afterwards! Up in the mountains.'

He hugged her again. 'How did you get away?'

She told him.

He couldn't stop a smirk. It became a chuckle and then a high-pitched hysterical giggle. Soon they were both laughing until it hurt, which didn't take long. Mike bent double over the bed, moaning in pain. He told her about his adventures and concluded with a blow-by-blow account of his recent beating. Nicola stared at their passports, which were lying on the carpet.

'Well, that's a bloody good idea,' she sniffed.

'What?'

'Leaving. That's exactly what I'm going to do. I'm going to have a shower and then I'm going straight back home to England.'

She disappeared into the bathroom. Mike sat with his face in his hands and thought about it. Why stay? He'd been beaten up and almost cremated in a fire. He didn't even want to *be* on this holiday. And what about telling the police? A kidnapping? A beating? They should report *this*. Then he remembered what Sarah had told him in the café about them taking their time. About the slim probability of bringing about a resolution. He snorted angrily. When had he or *his* family seen any justice? Look at Mum, living her half-life in Eastbourne. Dad gone to his grave a beaten man. A victim of terrible circumstance.

Nicola emerged from the shower draped in a towel. She was calmer now. 'D'you want to call for a cab? Maybe we can get a stand-by ticket?'

He picked up the receiver and held it to his ear until the high-pitched tone broke into his thoughts. He pressed 9 and ordered the taxi.

They were soon dressing and packing. Nicola's mood had lightened and she even sang a current hit as she folded, tucked and pushed things into her case. Mike moved as if through water. Nothing made sense.

'Nicola?'

'Yeah?'

'You say someone *told* them to kill you?'

She started as if a wasp had landed on her face. 'They told me about it in the Jeep on the way up to the village. They were just pretending they couldn't speak English. Bloody dagos.'

'We're not exactly bilingual are we?'

'Yeah, well. Look, this guy Angel was apologising. He said his boss said I had to go. I said, "Well if you feel so bad about it then let me go." He said he couldn't. His boss would have his *cojones.'*

'That's bollocks.'

'No it isn't.'

'No – I know that word. It means "bollocks".'

'Mike. Stop pissing around and let's go.'

He sat down. 'It's all a bit extreme isn't it? They could have just dumped you back in town. Even if you'd been able to identify them, they'd have had plenty of time to hide their guns and drugs and what-not before the police arrived.'

She spun on her heel and faced him. 'Forget about it Mike. This isn't one of your poxy lefty investigations. This is real. This bloke, Drake or whoever he was, was giving them orders. They were so nutso they were going to go along with it.'

He stared at her in shock. 'Drake? Did you say Drake?'

'Yes. Drake. They spoke to him in English. Now let's go.'

She checked and rechecked the wardrobe and bedside tables to make sure they hadn't forgotten anything. Mike sat frozen to his seat as his world imploded. The air around him seemed tangible, a hot soup of fear. Had she really said it? He thought of his family. Of how the mention of the name was tantamount to invoking an evil spirit. A demon who had torn away the foundations of their trust and had brought death into their semi-detached lives.

'Nicola.' His voice was hoarse. 'Tell me again who it was they spoke to.'

She called through from the bathroom. 'Drake. Like ducks and drakes.'

'You're certain?'

'Yeah. They were shit-scared of him.'

Mike began to sweat profusely. It suddenly seemed that it had all been predestined. Drake, who had never been apprehended. Spain. It was obvious. Where else did the villains end up? With a slow, syrupy certainty, Mike realised he had fallen into the maelstrom.

Nicola had her make-up on now. She was standing by the door with her case and their room key.

'Mike. Are you coming, or what?'

'I'm not sure.'

'You haven't even packed.'

'I . . . think I might stay for a while.'

'What?'

'I can't really explain.'

'It's that Sarah girl, isn't it?' she said, rolling her eyes.

'No. Something else.'

'Like what?'

'Drake.'

'You're bloody mad.'

'It's something from a long time ago.'

She opened the door. 'Well, I'm going right now. You coming or not?'

Their eyes met. Hers shone with anger and impatience. His were filled with fear and shock. He gazed at her silhouette in the door frame as she fidgeted, shuffling her fingers around the handle of her case.

'Mike?'

He continued to stare until there was only the frame and the dull light in the empty corridor.

PART TWO

In her silver sandals, copper dress and metal bangles, Jackie Drake was dressed to kill; that, or disrupt radio signals. Perching on the toilet in her bathroom, she held a mirror in one manicured hand and a rolled-up five-thousand peseta note in the other. The door opened and her husband barged in. John was wearing a shirt, a tie and a boxy jacket. His legs and feet were bare.

'You had enough of that, Jacks?'

She bent to the cocaine.

'I don't want you out of your head while I'm talking to the mayor.'

She shot him a defiant look and hoovered a line of powder into her right nostril. John smudged a finger across the mirror, then jerked it around his gums. 'You seen my gold cuff links?'

'Which ones?'

'The initialled ones. With J. D. on them.'

'Don't ask me.'

He padded away. Jackie smoothed out her dress and came through into the bedroom. Crossing an acre of ivory carpeting, she closed the blinds and shut out the twinkling lights on the distant coast. John was absorbed in perusing a row of shoes at one end of a long built-in wardrobe.

'What was you up to earlier?' she probed. 'Kevin come back full of beans.'

'We was up the coast.'

Clearly, he wasn't about to offer more, so she sat on the queen-sized bed and rifled through her bag for her cigarettes. 'This going to be a long session tonight?' she asked.

'Dunno. Why?'

'I was thinking about later.'

He winced and straightened his belt. 'It still hurts, love.'

'I told you to see someone about it.'

'It'll sort itself out.'

She blew smoke and palmed the lighter. 'It's been months now, John. There anything you ain't telling me?'

'Like what?'

'Like there's a million young tarts out there.'

He came over and held her face in both hands. 'Twenty-two years, lover. I ever done the dirty on you?'

She tilted her head upwards to look him in the eyes. 'You ain't done it with me in nearly six months.'

He released her, then moved off towards her bathroom.

'Where you going?'

'See how much of that gramme you—' His voice tailed off. Jackie stubbed out her cigarette and marched straight in behind him. John had plucked her stash from a marble sill and was unwrapping the paper parcel.

'I don't want you gabbing nineteen to the dozen,' he said, by way of explanation. He tipped the cocaine into the sink. She shot out a hand to stop him but he shouldered her away and turned on the tap.

The drugs turned to mush.

'You ain't coming tonight.'

'Good,' she pouted. 'I'll go see some of my friends.'

He thought for a moment. 'Nah. You better stay here and babysit the boy.'

She glared at him. 'Kevin don't need looking after.'

Before he could reply, there was a crash from downstairs. Kevin had been riding Emily the Doberman through the hall and had just sent a precious sextant flying from its stand. Drake raised his eyebrows. The point had been made.

The cab crawled to a halt amidst the throng in Puerto Banús. Mike emerged with his case and counted out the exact amount on the meter. For this he received a sneer, a finger and a faceful of fumes as the car moved off. Gazing around, he suddenly felt like a washer in a pile of rare coins. The men had over-groomed hair and heavy watches. Their pastel-coloured shirts were embroidered with designer names and their trousers had creases as sharp as surgical tools. The women were divided into two camps: the younger in jeans which had been artfully torn at the knees by Orientals in sweatshops; the elder in trouser-suits and ostentatious jewellery. They were all, he noted, as brown as white people can go before attracting police attention.

He found the bar where they had agreed to meet. It was now seething with people, in-bred types whose idea of conversation appeared to be calling out each other's names in surprise. He tunnelled through and found Sarah dozing at a table near the rear. She didn't see him so he placed a gentle hand on her shoulder. As his fingers massaged her neck it sent a delicious shiver to his loins.

'Hi,' she yawned. 'What time is it?'

'About nine.'

They ordered *café con leche*. Omitting Drake's name, he explained about Nicola's departure and then told her of his beating. Sarah gave no indication that she knew of the Scotsman.

'So I thought it might be better if I checked out,' he added. 'Either that or I add "unprompted violence" to my complaints about the service.'

'Where are you going to stay?'

'Thought you might have some suggestions – seeing as you're my tour rep.'

'Not really, no.'

'I suppose staying at your place is out of the question?'

'I haven't got a spare bed.'

'No problem. I can sleep on the floor,' he lied.

Without replying, she turned her gaze to the harbour. 'I've been watching his cabin cruiser all day. He's got a team of flunkies delivering all sorts of stuff.'

They paid and went outside. Most of the yachts were sleeping in their berths, their masts tinkling gently in the breeze. Only the *Maiden Voyage* was ablaze with light. On deck and inside the long cabins, waiters scurried about carrying magnums of champagne, trays of glasses and platters of food.

'Either he's throwing a party, or Pavarotti's coming to visit,' said Mike.

Sarah gave his clothes a critical glance. 'That's not your best gear, is it?'

'No, my Batman pyjamas are in the case. You suggesting we gatecrash?'

'Mm-hm.'

He clapped his hands together. 'Right. I'll go buy some cans of cheap lager.'

She smiled sardonically. 'We'll have to do better than that. Let's go back to mine and change.'

Sarah's flat was tucked away in a small block behind some offices in the centre of Fuengirola. Inside, a row of doors opened off a long burgundy corridor. She announced she was going to get some sleep and wandered off to the bedroom at the far end. Left alone, Mike examined the spartan living room. It had a short couch, a desk strewn with her files and a bookcase half-filled with yellowing paperbacks. There was a small portable television. He went to turn it on but realised its noise would probably wake her. Instead, he made himself a cup of tea in the kitchen, noting gladly that she had English teabags instead of the local ones, which never percolated properly. He came back into the living room and tried to settle. The couch had wooden rungs at either end and, no matter which way he turned, he couldn't get comfortable. Finally, he spread the cushions on the floor and used his jacket as a pillow.

He awoke to the sound of footsteps padding past in the hall. The bathroom door creaked open and a shower nozzle spurted into life. His watch read midnight. Rolling his dry tongue around his mouth, he realised he was desperate for a piss. Five agonising minutes later, he was relieving himself in the kitchen sink when she walked in.

'Shit. Sorry,' he said, zipping up. Sarah's hair was an aura of tight glistening curls. She looked small in her white towelling robe. 'I was bursting, but I didn't want to disturb you.'

'Should have come in anyway,' she said flatly.

She placed a pan of water on the gas and lit it. Mike struggled to put aside the image of her behind a flimsy shower curtain. Naked.

'Course not,' he said finally. 'I'd have to put up with your wet naked body behind a flimsy shower curtain.'

'How awful,' she said in mock surprise. 'Tea?'

He nodded and smiled at her back as she reached into the fridge.

'Milk?'

'Please.'

They sat and drank at a metal table which looked as if it had been borrowed from a street café. Sarah seemed more refreshed now and he told her so.

'I have to get eight hours, otherwise I turn into an animal,' she replied.

'Me too. Eight, ten or thereabouts.'

'I can break it up with naps but I have to get the full eight somehow.'

'Me too,' he repeated, overjoyed at this personality dovetailing. This was the first step towards unity. He always tried to agree with everything a woman liked so that it would appear they had a lot in common.

'Got anything to eat?' he asked.

'Cheese. Bit of old bread.'

'Any mango chutney to go with that?'

She made a face. 'Sweet and savoury? Together?'

'Just joking,' he said hurriedly.

She lifted her feet on to a chair and studied them. They were perfect: straight toes; no corns or callouses; slender ankles, her cuticles pink against the light tan. Mike wanted to kiss them.

'So, tell me more about yourself,' he asked.

'Like what?'

'I dunno. Usual stuff. Where you're from.'

'Scotland. At least, my family are.'

'You don't sound it.'

'My parents moved to Gloucestershire when I was young. Dad's got his practice there.'

'Practice?'

'GP.'

'Fiery temper, the Scots,' Mike said, fishing.

'Och aye,' she deadpanned.

'That explains the tousled, temptress hair.' He reached out and curled a lock of it around his fingers. Straightening it out, he let a long corkscrew spring back and flop down on to her forehead.

'Finished playing?'

'No.' Mike reached out both hands like a movie monster and loosened another batch of tendrils.

She pushed his hands away and shook her wet hair at him like a dog. Mike screwed up his eyes as the droplets sprinkled his face. Sarah laughed, and when he opened them up again, flung her hair at him once more.

'Best way to shower,' he said, grinning.

She raked her hands through her thatch and sat back, serious now.

'OK, let's get on to our plan of action.'

'What plan of action?'

'We need to get aboard his boat. Find out something more concrete.'

'Yeah, well. I expect he's dying to spill the beans.'

'Well, it won't do us any good sitting around here, will it? I'm going to get dressed.'

Sarah rose and went to her room. She reappeared ten minutes later in a long black cotton dress which was cut low at the back.

'What d'you think?' she asked, twirling around.

'Very nice – for a woman.'

She gave a friendly growl. 'That T-shirt won't do.'

'Wrong colour?'

'No, the slogan.'

It read: 'Same shit, different day.'

'But I haven't brought any smart clothes.'

She thought for a moment. 'Tell you what. We'll drop by the Bella Vista on the way. One of the waiters might have something in your size.'

'Great,' he muttered.

In the exclusive restaurant of the Marbella Club Hotel, John

Drake lifted a forkful of chicken to his mouth and eyed his dining companion. Señor Juan Alberto Ruiz Márquez was not only the Mayor of Fuengirola but also the owner of many of the prestigious coastal properties. A slender man with a high, intelligent forehead, he sported a sable wedge of moustache which drew attention away from his long, chisel-like chin. He exuded an air of priestly gravitas which often caused those around him to pause before speaking. At present he was inspecting a morsel of sole marinière which he had separated from the bone with surgical precision. Drake took a gulp of Chardonnay and wiped chicken fat from his goatee.

'Let's call it an occupational hazard.'

Márquez hooded his eyes. 'It was a regrettable incident. We expect this of the tourists, but I do not like to hear of people – my people – being thrown from high buildings.'

Due to his standing in the community, Márquez was happy to ignore protocol and discuss business at the table.

Drake reached for a toothpick. 'Can't argue with that. Only he was passing a lot of merchandise through that hotel.' He slipped the sliver of wood between his incisors. 'Your boys find anything in the hotel safe?'

Márquez steered a napkin around the rim of his glass of mineral water. '*El Comisario* was pleased to inform me of the recovery of a quantity of cannabis and amphetamines.' He paused for effect. 'That and a large sum of money that bore little relation to the hotel accounts. *Sí, lo hicimos*. Yes, we did.'

'Good. It's my patch and I won't have all this.'

Márquez sighed. 'Los Perros de la muerte are a problem to us all but there is little I can do to stop them being here. They are, after all, *Españoles*.'

Drake shuffled his Rolex around his wrist like a worry bead. 'I done you a favour on this one. You ought to be protecting my interests.' Nothing came back from Márquez so he changed tack. 'You hear about the other night?'

'The fire?'

'Who d'you think *that* was down to? The Russians?'

'They are making their presence felt here, but—'

'Bollocks. Ozorio knew I owned the gaff.'

'I see. I did not think things were escalating in this manner.'

Drake slapped his palms on the table. A bolt of pain suddenly shot through his stomach. He tried to swallow it away. 'These slags ain't even locals. This is your northerners. You can't trust 'em.'

Márquez stroked his chin and let his hand slide to his neck. He began to tug at the skin. 'Perhaps we are getting a little excited. One incident in a pool. One unsafe building catches fire. This does not amount to warfare.'

Drake knew better than to argue. Márquez was a man on whom he'd built a castle of trust in the last decade. He straightened the cutlery and reached out a chubby hand for his cigarettes. 'You'll keep an eye on all this, then?'

Márquez blinked once.

'Pudding?' queried Drake.

The mayor pulled a face and placed his hands on his flat stomach.

'You eat like a fly,' spat Drake, peeved to have been denied his indulgence.

'Let us talk of other things. I believe we were discussing a Mercedes convertible. I find the cream leather interior most acceptable.'

Drake blew out a plume of smoke and refilled his glass. 'It's outside, old son.'

Márquez raised an eyebrow. 'Walnut dashboard?'

A nod from Drake. The mayor put his napkin to his lips. 'Then I shall do all I can, *Señor* John, to maintain equilibrium.'

John held up his glass, then downed the wine in one.

Jackie and Kevin were relaxing in the lounge. They were surrounded by portraits of seafarers, paintings of battle scenes and cabinets which contained maritime memorabilia. The boy lay on the rug with his boots up on the black leather couch. Jackie sat with a fluted glass of blue curaçoa and vodka. She was barefoot and her dress had ridden up around her knees. They had started their evening at the bar, working their way through a spectrum of cocktails and a clutch of joints until lightheadedness drove them to a horizontal position.

'What d'you want to do now?' she slurred. 'Monopoly?'

'Nah. Used to carry one of them get-out-of-jail-free cards. Don't work in real life.'

As they giggled, Kevin came close to dropping a foot through the heavy glass table. Jackie twisted round and sat up.

'I'm going to powder me nose.'

As she leaned forwards to hunt for her sandals, Kevin noticed that her ripe breasts formed a nice straight line when pressed together.

'Can I have some Chas, Auntie Jackie?'

'I don't think your dad would approve.'

Her voice was stern but he could tell her heart wasn't in it.

'He ain't here. Anyways, I done coke before. And speed.'

She rose, swaying beside the arm of the couch. 'What about your uncle?'

'He won't mind,' he said, giving her his crocodile grin.

Moments later, they were kneeling on the rug as Jackie chopped up the cocaine. 'Mustn't tell John,' she said, concentrating. 'This is my personal stash. He don't know about it.'

'Nod's as good as a wank.'

She formed four curved lines and the boy bent to them, snuffling like a pig in a trough. He lay back and inhaled violently as she vacuumed up the remains. They blinked, sniffed and swallowed.

'What now, then?' asked Jackie, her eyes sparkling.

Kevin jumped to his feet. 'Kiss-chase.'

'I'm a bit old for that.'

'No you're not,' he replied, kneading her shoulder with a pudgy hand.

She wriggled out of his way and poked him in the stomach with a scarlet talon. 'All right, Fat Boy. You're on.'

They scampered from room to room, shrieking like children. Jackie's workouts in the Marbella gym allowed her to outpace him with ease as she ran gazelle-like across the cool marble floors. She went in and out of the rooms and then upstairs. Kevin, who'd borrowed a pair of his uncle's voluminous shorts, was slowed by the flapping trunks. He stopped running and instead began to prowl silently.

Jackie came to the top of the balustrade and froze, listening for movement. She heard only the beating of her own heart. Tiptoeing carefully down the staircase, she went across to the kitchen and pushed the door back on its hinges. Kevin wasn't behind it. She turned back to the lounge. Empty, only the hollow eyes of the portraits. Glancing over at the patio doors, she saw they were open. She crept outside.

The purring of cicadas filled the warm air. A group of ants had scaled the low terrace wall and were demolishing a nub of discarded bread. She scanned the dark waters of the pool. Suddenly, Kevin let out a cry and jumped at her from behind the door. Pinning her arms to her sides, he smothered her face in dry, pecking kisses. Laughing, she pulled her hands free and pushed him away. Kevin grinned, her lipstick smeared across his mouth like jam.

'You little bugger,' she chuckled.' I thought you was upstairs.'

'We can go upstairs if you like.'

She swallowed her laughter. 'I don't think so.'

'How about a swim then?'

She often bathed nude at night. It was a simple pleasure she loved to do alone, lying there floating, gazing up at the stars and thinking of nothing. It wouldn't be the same with Kevin splashing around her like a terrier. She watched as a ripple hurried across the water.

'Maybe another time, Kev.'

She turned to face him, only to find that Kevin had pulled down his trunks to expose the largest penis she'd ever seen. Her mouth fell open in surprise. She shut it quickly, lest he got the wrong idea. The cock was rising towards her now, its girth increasing as blood pumped into the thick muscle. Slowly, the glistening pink head emerged from the foreskin. She found it oddly reminiscent of her husband pulling on a roll-neck sweater. The boy's face had a serene yet quizzical expression, as if he were the proud owner of a prize marrow and awaiting the award of his rosette. She looked him straight in the eyes.

'No, Kevin. Definitely not. No.'
'Aww.'
She stepped neatly around his engorged cock and strode back into the house.

12

They parked in a lot opposite the Hypercor supermarket. Mike clambered out of the car and felt his armpits moistening in the humid air. 'I still say I look like a bloody waiter,' he said.

Sarah had borrowed a pair of trousers and a jacket from one of the hotel staff.

'Stop fussing. We've got enough to worry about. Stick with me and don't say anything.'

'I'm an embarrassment, am I?'

'No, Mr Paranoid. I might have to pretend to be Spanish. *¿Hablas español?*'

'No, *Señorita*,' he replied, wondering why he only understood the language when she spoke it. They wandered through to the quay and discovered that the on-board party was in full swing. Coloured lights had been strung along the decks and scores of partygoers were drinking and dancing inside. The sound system soared around the harbour, booming out Ibiza dance hits and perennial club favourites. They moved across to the jetty.

'Shit,' said Sarah.

A monolithic slab in a dinner jacket was standing at the top of the gangplank.

'With knobs on,' agreed Mike. 'What now?'

'Let me think.'

They watched as the great, the good and the not-so-good ambled past. Two leggy girls in tiny dresses stumbled in their direction. One was bottle-blonde, the other sported bad-hair-day highlights which made her look like an irate tabby cat. Sarah squeezed Mike's arm. 'Wait here.'

She strode across to them. 'Lucy. Hi!' she brayed in a voice which suggested years of gymkhanas and in-breeding.

The pair jerked back like alert squirrels.

'Sarah,' she added. 'Jeremy's sister.'

'Oh *Jeremy*,' said the blonde, then air-kissed Sarah and turned to her friend. 'This is Olivia.' Olivia had bushy eyebrows and the air of a newscaster reporting a royal death.

'Where are you staying?' asked Sarah.

'Marbella Club,' she replied tersely. 'It's a bloody *hole*, actually.'

Mike watched as they went into a girlish huddle. After a moment, Sarah broke free and came over to fetch him.

'This is Neil,' she said, brightly. 'Neil. Lucy and Olivia.'

'Hullo.'

Lucy giggled. 'Is it fancy dress?'

He gave her a watery smile. 'No, I simply hadn't a *thing* to wear.'

They found this awfully amusing. The tabby one folded her beetle-brows and peered at him as if he were some kind of exhibit.

'Neil . . . ?'

He realised he was expected to give a curriculum vitae and possibly whip out a copy of *Burke's Peerage*.

'Neil Downe,' he said, getting into the swing. 'Of the Berkshire Downes.'

Sarah fired off a grimace which could have frozen lava. 'OK, everyone,' she chirruped. 'Where are we off to?'

The blonde waved a slender arm at the cabin cruiser. 'Over there. Frightful people but there should be plenty of charlie.'

'Super,' said Mike and Sarah.

The girls led the way, and they followed them up on to the deck, relaxing visibly as the hulk remained oblivious to their presence. Clearly eager to lose them, Lucy and Olivia went straight to the dancing area and disappeared into the throng. Sarah lifted two glasses of champagne from a passing waiter and came outside.

'How did you know them?' asked Mike, aghast.

Her grin was big and smug. 'Never seen them before in my life.'

'Then how did you know one was called Lucy?'

'Inspired guesswork.'

'What if you'd been wrong?'

'Then I would've tried Melissa, Charlotte, anything horsey.'
She punched his arm. 'Kneel down, indeed!'

'We got on board. Now what?'

'Mingle.'

She drained her glass and went back in. Mike drank his
champagne. Warmed by the alcohol, he began to eavesdrop
on the various conversations. He detected English, German
and Dutch accents and there was even the odd Arab in white
robes. The women were in another league from those he met
at cramped parties in Tooting. These were the kind he'd usually
see with a staple across their stomachs. Some were Scandinavian,
others Mediterranean. Nearly all of them had bare midriffs and
were showing off their stomachs like hot children. One such
dusky maiden had just broken away from two Spaniards, leaving
them deep in a heated argument. Mike threw back his drink and
decided to make the most of the situation. He straightened his
tuxedo, adopted a suave pose and went inside – only to spend
the next ten minutes fending off demands for fresh nibbles.

'*¡Maricón!* She was going to be my girlfriend!' said the younger
of the two Spaniards.

'Eat my dirt, Fish Boy.'

'You always get the girls,' pouted Angel.

'Maybe that's because I don't smell of fish!' crowed Ramón.

Angel barged into him, sending his drink flying into the water.
His elder brother responded by gripping his sibling in a head-lock
and cuffing him several times with his elbow.

'*¡Jodete!* I hate you,' cried Angel. 'I tell Señor Smale that you have
VD and herpes and that none of the girls must go near you.'

Ramón pursed his lips and flapped his hands against his throat
like gills.

Angel stamped his foot on the deck.

'When you going to stop this?'

Ramón considered the question. His eyes brightened. 'In one
year – your next mating season!'

*   *   *

Sarah trawled the party, gleaning what information she could. There appeared to be two strata of guests: the first were yacht owners and expats; the second, businessmen with deep tans and the arrogance of too much money and too many drugs. Going below, she discovered that the eye of the party hurricane was centred around the farthest cabin. Its door was kept closed but occasionally opened to disgorge grinning executives.

She waited in line outside the toilet while she assessed the situation. Two girls emerged from the far cabin. Both were in their late teens, skimpily clad and, judging by their accents, Andalucians. They took their places behind her, enabling her to overhear their conversation. One was complaining of stomach-cramps and telling her friend that she wanted to leave. Her protestations fell on deaf ears but a name kept cropping up which sounded like 'Snail'. Sarah presumed that this was their host. Reaching the front of the queue, she was obliged to slip into the cubicle. She put her ear to the door but heard nothing more.

Mike was sitting alone on the upper deck.

'I thought you were going to mingle,' she said testily.

'I have mingled. I'm mingled out.'

'What did you find out?'

'Most people prefer the chicken.'

She ignored the comment, having news of her own. 'I think our man's in the back. I'm going to try and get in there.'

'Better hurry, then. People are leaving.' He pointed to a group who were wandering off along the jetty.

'Give me ten minutes.'

'And then what? Do I burst in armed with some vol-au-vents?'

Sarah crinkled up her nose. 'What are you on about? Just stay here and wait for me, OK? I'll be back soon.'

Barry Smale wore cowboy boots, leather trousers and a black silk shirt stretched taught as a balloon over his paunch. In his low canvas chair, he looked like a rock 'n' roll version of Buddha. Behind him, screens were set into the walls, each one showing a different pornographic film. The two Spanish girls had returned and were gyrating in front of him. Showing no interest in either the movies or the girls, Smale instead concentrated on his latest guest, a bearded Dutchman in an Armani suit. Carmen, the skinnier of the two dancers, was now urging her friend to slip her arms around her in a lesbian clinch. She refused, pulling away and clutching at her stomach. Carmen pushed her aside and, ensuring her pudenda was at Smale's eye level, strode up to her withered host.

'*Lo siento, Señor Smale*, she—'

Her friend broke in. '*Señor*. I no feel so good.'

Smale eyed her like a sick animal. One that ought to be put out of its misery. The girl wilted visibly and rushed to the nearest window. With trembling fingers, she worried open the catch and thrust her head out into the cool air. Carmen groaned at the sound of vomit raining on the water below.

Smale's rasp was a shovel digging into gravel. 'Get her out of here.'

Carmen pulled the girl inside and frog-marched her across the room.

'And for fuck's sake find someone else. I wanna start the shoot in an hour.' He shot a long-suffering glance at his associate and continued his business.

Angel wasn't enjoying the party one little bit. Ramón had successfully persuaded a nubile Swede to give him oral relief in a dinghy – an achievement he had crowed about way beyond Angel's limited attention span. He'd then left with the girl, issuing his brother with strict instructions not to return to the flat that night. What Ramón didn't know was that, earlier, whilst still smarting over the fish incident, Angel had sneaked into his room and borrowed a Glock 9mm pistol. His original intent was to drive up into the hills on his moped and maim some cacti with it. Now, drunk, and with the gun nestling in his belt making him feel all virile and powerful, he reconsidered his options.

Sarah was dawdling in the corridor when Carmen led her sagging friend out of the cabin. Seizing the opportunity, she took the girl's limp arm and helped manoeuvre her off the cruiser and on to the jetty. Carmen, showing a remarkable lack of interest in her *colega's* well-being, dumped her unceremoniously on an oil drum.

'*Gracias por su ayuda,*' she said to Sarah.

'*De nada.*'

'*¿Eres española?*'

'*No, soy inglesa.*'

'*Me llamo Carmen.*' She looked Sarah up and down. 'You know Smale?'

'*Un poco.*'

'What are you doing in Banús?'

'Looking for work,' said Sarah, shrugging.

Carmen's eyes lit up. '*Ven conmigo.*'

She steered her back on board and fixed her with a limpid gaze. 'You need money?'

'Desperately.'

'I have to find a girl right now. For film.'

'I'm an actress,' lied Sarah, remembering the camera up at the villa. 'What sort of film?'

Carmen fanned a braceleted hand. 'Erotic. Very simple. Only you and me. It is big money for tonight. Ten thousand pesetas. You interested?'

'Sure,' said someone.

Sarah realised that it was her.

Carmen adjusted Sarah's cleavage and, before she knew it, she had been hustled into the front cabin. Keeping her fears in check, she scoped the room, taking in the leather seats and the expensive Italian furniture. Finally, she saw the pumping and spurting on the screens. It suddenly became clear that this branch of acting wouldn't be one that required an Equity card.

Smale was alone now, immersed in one of the screens. A brace of women were clustered in a slippery tank and were writhing and sliding over one another. His face registered no excitement or interest.

'*¿Señor?*' Carmen enquired, flashing her biggest smile. 'This girl, yes?'

He looked her up and down. Sarah felt her legs and upper lip trembling.

'Turn round,' he croaked.

She did so.

'It's girl-on-girl. Piece of piss. You done it before?'

She took a sharp breath and spoke in her best Mockney. 'Yeah, course.'

'You're English.'

''S'right.'

'Got a name?'

'Sarah,' she replied, having had no time to think up a plausible alias.

He tilted his shiny skull at Carmen. 'She told you the deal?'

She nodded as Smale raped her with his eyes. 'You ain't the filth. I can smell filth,' he said, tapping his aquiline nose.

She tried not to make her relief too evident.

'Not bad. Not bad at all. You're dirty, you are.' Smale forced a creak from the seat as he stood up. He lifted a nicotine-stained finger. 'All right, English. You're on.'

'How much, then?' Sarah squeaked.

'Eight thousand potatoes for the night.'

The price had plummeted somewhat. Smale placed his hands on her hips and turned her round with dry fingers. They scrabbled crab-like over her abdomen and up to her breasts, feeling their weight.

'Anythin' wrong with you?' he asked, a bronchial wheeze underpinning each word. 'No inverted nips or nothin'?'

'No.'

'Good. Got any specialities?'

She wondered whether to mention her degree in business studies.

'Golden showers? Deep throat. Fisting. Animals?'

This is the oddest job interview I've ever attended, thought Sarah. She was tempted to ask about the work conditions and a pension plan and hoped he wouldn't notice she'd broken into a cold sweat.

'We're doing oral, anal and dildos. Bit of bondage and all.'

'OK.'

'Ejaculate?'

He said it as if he were offering her a sweet.

'Sorry?'

'D'you ejaculate when you come? Some birds do. Mind you,

we'll fake it with a hose under your arse.' He smirked. 'Usually do.'

She was saved from further panic as the door burst open and a short Spanish boy stumbled into the cabin. He was plainly the worse for drink. 'Señor Barrysmale!' he exclaimed, spreading his arms wide.

Smale looked as if a swarm of mosquitoes had flown into the room. 'Angel,' he said frostily.

The boy took a step forward, his eyes on the women. 'You are doing film tonight? You let me watch, yes? You always telling me it's OK, ¿Sí?'

'Look, son. It's business. I don't want you whacking off in front of the birds.'

Angel clearly hadn't understood. 'I come, yes?'

Unfortunate choice of words, thought Sarah.

'I help. Hold lights. Make drink. No money.'

Smale took hold of Angel's arm and pushed him towards the door. 'Another time, all right?'

Angel looked over his shoulder at Sarah and Carmen. 'But is pretty girls. Beautiful girls.'

Smale had his hand on the door now. 'You talk to the guv'nor. He'll set it up for another time.'

Angel wasn't going to be put off so easily. Pulling out his gun, he waved it in the air and strutted around, shouting curses. The two women instantly dropped to the ground and crawled under the banquette seats. Smale waited until the boy was in range and shot out a withered arm, gripping Angel's gun-hand and bending it backwards. He was stronger than he looked.

'All right,' he barked. 'Don't lose your rag. I can use someone to help me do the lights. But that's all.'

Angel hugged him.

'What a fucking tea party,' Smale muttered, prizing himself free.

Angel, beaming, came towards Carmen and Sarah. '*Hola*,' he said, puffing out his chest.

'Put the shooter away,' barked Smale, busying himself in the search for a light meter.

Angel put the gun on to the cushioned seat. His fancy taken by Carmen, he quickly cornered her and turned on his limited charm. Sarah, ignored for a moment, saw her chance. She called over to Smale who was rummaging through a drawer.

'Can I have a pee before we go?'

'You got five minutes.'

She dropped her handbag to the seat and covered the weapon. Angel was eye to eye with Carmen. She reached down, slipped the gun inside her bag and left.

'The man's called Barry Smale,' she said, buzzing with adrenalin. 'I persuaded a Spanish girl to get me in there. We're going up to the villa now to make a dirty movie.'

Mike stared open-mouthed. 'Good. Nothing squalid then.'

Sarah frowned. 'I had to go along with it to find out more.'

'And appearing in *Big'n'Busty Two* is going to help?'

'I'm not going to *do* it. I'm going to get some answers with this.'

She showed him the gun.

'Jesus. Where'd you get that?'

'A Spanish kid came in with it. I nicked it off him while he wasn't looking.'

'Bloody hell. How many times did you see *Thelma & Louise*?'

She shrugged.

'Do you know how to use it?'

'Yes,' she said quickly. 'No,' she said, a little slower.

Mike took the gun and removed the clip. It made a satisfying snap as he slid it back in. He checked the safety and felt the weight of it in his hand. 'It's loaded.'

'How do you know?'

'Oh, you know—' he said blithely.

'Mike. Come on.'

'Oh, all right. The staff at the magazine went on a trip to a firing range. We tried out all the guns. It was all very puerile and childish really . . . And a bloody good day out.'

'Well, it's come in handy.'

'Sarah, this is crazy.'

She rummaged in her bag for her car keys and held them out. 'There'll only be him, the other actress and the Spanish boy up there. What I reckon we'll do is this. You follow us in my car, get close to the villa and keep watch until I get inside. Then you sneak in through that bathroom window and burst in on us. I'll pull the gun and we'll figure it out from there.'

He thought for an instant. 'There's just one teeny-tiny problem.'

'Which is?'

'I can't drive.'

'Oh for God's sake,' she hissed. 'Then follow us in a cab.'

She went below. Mike crept off the cruiser and watched from a safe vantage point on the harbour wall. Moments later, Smale emerged. Mike decided that he looked badly in need of another six dwarfs. Angel came next. Make that five dwarfs, he thought. After that a willowy, ebony-haired girl trotted out followed by Sarah. Smale spoke to the hulk in the jacket and gestured at his craft. The man nodded and began to round up the last of the stragglers. The foursome went up the jetty and clambered into Smale's Mercedes. Hearing the roar of the engine, Mike ran quickly through the shopping area to the main street.

He had no trouble in finding a cab. As he climbed in, he saw the Merc turn the corner and prowl towards them. It came to a halt at a set of lights.

'Follow that car!' barked Mike, thinking, I've always wanted to say that.

'*No entiendo.*'

'The car. Follow,' he wailed.

The driver remained immobile. Mike scrabbled for his phrase book and, flipping through the pages, cursed their inability to serve up even a simple cliché.

'*El coche,*' he shouted. Follow wasn't in the book. 'Mercedes.' He gesticulated wildly at the street.

'*No hay ningún Mercedes aquí,*' said the driver.

He looked round. The car had disappeared.

13

Smale drove hunched up against the wheel with Angel jabbering at his side. In the rear, Carmen lay dozing next to Sarah, who turned to peer out of the rear windscreen. Seeing only blackness, she realised she had made a big mistake. What if Mike didn't show up? She knew she couldn't go through with it alone. Pull a gun? On all three of them? Any one of them could easily disarm her. And then what?

Oral. Anal. Dildo.

The words flowed like a perverse tongue twister. The first, she mused, wasn't something she made a hobby out of. The second? One of her ex-lovers had once tried it and she'd quickly guided him back to the proper orifice. The third, well, she'd rather use her fingers.

OralAnalDildo.

The dark mountains swelled in and out with each curve of the road. She looked back again. Still nothing. The hum of the engine dropped a few notes as the car slipped down a gear and picked up the grittier score of the dirt track.

Oralanal.Dildo.

She shivered. Exploring the darker side of sexuality was a trail which Lana had blazed: her stories, often told in long, giggling phone calls, had filled Sarah with a mixture of fascination and terror. Maybe, she wondered, maybe this is what this is all about. Not about how Lana died, but how she lived.

Oral. Analdildo.

It sounds like a Czechoslovakian puppet troupe, she thought. The Great AnalDildo and his three cock-ring circus. The half-smile died on her face as they rose up towards the villa.

*   *   *

Mike stood on the quayside and tried to remember a time when he'd felt worse. He pictured himself at age nine, convincing a school friend to jump off their garage roof while clutching a handful of balloons. The theory was simple enough. 'They're lighter than air so you won't fall,' he'd told the boy. After the ambulance had left, his parents had sent him to his room to bone up on science and guilt. Supper was withheld.

He paced up and down now, torn between going to the police or beating his head repeatedly against a lamppost. Glancing at his watch, he saw it was nearly three a.m. He went to the nearest bar, rattled the doors and found they were padlocked. Shit, thought Mike. Even if I went to the police and managed to direct them to the villa, then they're going to find her in the middle of a porn film. She'll be arrested and charged and God knows what else. That's going to put a serious kink in our relationship. He lit a cigarette. Christ. I've got to do something. He took a couple of drags then tossed it aside and wandered up to the slumbering *Maiden Voyage*. The lights on the rigging had been turned off and only a small lamp glowed in one of the cabins. He moved closer, thinking, I'm going to regret this. He crept up the gangplank and tested the handles on the doors to the rear cabin. Locked. He pulled his hand away sharply. There must be an alarm system. He froze and listened. No bells or sirens, just the masts clanking in the soft breeze. He peered through the nearest porthole. There were no wires visible on the inner frame nor any blinking lights in the cabin. Feeling more confident, he crossed the deck and clambered up over the railing. There was a slightly open porthole down by the main cabin. At feet and eye level, metal rims projected out from the hull ringing the craft. He swung out and, using them as foot- and handholds, inched his way towards the prow. Once he had reached the window, he bent down and grasped the top of the frame. He recoiled, recognising the acrid odour of fresh vomit. Holding his breath against the smell, he levered open the porthole and slipped inside.

Silver ropes of reflected water danced on the ceiling. Mike adjusted himself to the soft swaying of the boat. The cabin was a half-oval with banquette seats and rows of drawers set into the walls. He made out the dead screens as his night vision kicked in. Each one was squatting on a video recorder. A remote control handset lay discarded on a chair, so he took it and ignited the nearest one. It flared on and heavy metal ground out of the speakers. He scrabbled for the volume control, frantically fingering the calibrations to mute. On screen, a woman lay sandwiched between two hairy men, one entering her from behind as the other forced his penis deep into her throat. He ejected the tape, and took in the printed title on the spine. *Banging Miss Daisy*.

'Cultured man,' muttered Mike. Another guilt pang gripped him. Sarah's up there with him, doing God knows what. He balled his fists impotently as he thought of what to do next. The answer, when it came, seemed entirely rational. Steal the tapes. At the very least, they might provide clues or evidence Better yet, they might provide a link to Lana's death. He removed the ones in the machines and burrowed into the drawers beneath the screens.

Twenty minutes later, his collection included *Anal Sluts, Die Bitch Die* and *Fuck me Suck me, Kum on me*. Some had Dutch or impenetrable Arabic titles but the covers were similar; women with pendulous breasts and expressions which were a cross between lust and mock hurt. Wondering if he'd missed anything, he crouched down on all fours. There were slender drawers at floor level. He removed the drawers above them and reached inside to pluck out still more tapes. The labels on these were hand-written and appeared to be jottings of timings combined with meaningless initials. These were clearly not meant for public consumption. He made up two piles, ten from the private stash and ten from the others. Looking to find a suitable container, he opened the door and tiptoed along the passage. There was a galley off to his right. He rifled the cupboards and found a roll of plastic bin-liners. Scurrying back, he tore two off the roll and double-bagged the tapes. Gripping the neck of the sack, he clambered outside. The water lapped lazily against the hull. Clamping his booty between his teeth, he moved hand-over-hand until he reached the deck. He jumped down, shouldered his catch and darted off into the night.

* * *

In the bathroom, Carmen was pouring herself into a rubber sheath dress as Sarah fastened on a leather corset. She struggled with the buckles and laces, moving as slowly as a child preparing for school. Thoughts came fast. How stupid can I get? This could be just how Lana died. Perhaps she even wore these clothes. She sniffed at the stiff hide. There was no trace of perfume, only a musty animal smell. She remembered a time when she was fourteen. Lana had bought a tight black leather skirt and had urged her to try it on. When she complied, her sister helped her to complete the outfit with a jacket and a pair of her high heels. She then backcombed Sarah's hair, made her up and stood her in front of the full-length mirror. She saw not herself, but a paradigm of sexuality, a cipher of attraction. Lana, of course, said she looked great and insisted that they go to the pub to laugh at the reactions of the men. She refused and changed back into her jeans and army greatcoat. They went for the drink, but ended up sipping shandies in frosty silence.

Carmen had now pulled on a pair of elbow-length black gloves and was hunting through the dressing-up box for a whip.

On their arrival, Smale had produced three large cardboard boxes and had announced that they would start with a little 'domination'. Angel had, of course, offered to help the girls dress but was told to shut up and set up the lights in the bedroom.

'Shoes,' said Carmen, glancing over at her.

Sarah slipped back into her pumps.

'No, no. *Allí*. Over there.'

The nearest box contained several pairs of thigh-length, patent leather boots. They had been left unzipped and flattened down, deflated fetish objects from some other scenario. She found a pair that were her size and slid her legs gingerly into their long shiny skins. Carmen tipped herself into a pair of stilettos and bent to the mirror to check her make-up. Sarah zipped up the boots and tried a few halting steps. She fell backwards into the shower.

'What is wrong?' asked Carmen.

'Not used to heels this high,' said Sarah, lamely.

'*¡Dios Mío!* You done this before, yes?'

She must have paused a little too long because Carmen stopped applying her mascara and turned to her with a frown.

'You never done this, no?'

Her reply was a smile that begged for sympathy.

The girl sighed. 'Just do what Smale tells you. Think of making love to your husband.'

'I'm not married.'

'Then think of me as . . . your best girlfriend.'

Sarah had an image of them strolling through Habitat in their bondage gear.

'Pretty babies?' called Angel, popping his head round the door. 'You come now?'

Sarah grabbed her bag, feeling the weight of the weapon inside it.

It was hot under the lights and both girls were soon perspiring freely. Smale outlined the story. Sarah would enter first, then Carmen was to force her over a chair and beat her on the arse. Sarah would writhe in pleasure as Carmen then grappled her and pushed her on to the bed. Carmen would then strip for Sarah, French-kiss her, unlace her corset and start sucking on her breasts. She'd then move on to cunnilingus – which Smale referred to as 'giving her a good licking'. Sarah's role would essentially be passive. Once Smale and Angel had reset for the close-ups, the girls would perform soixante-neuf and then masturbate one another. After that, Angel would be dispatched to fetch the garden hose for the cum-shot.

Was this really Lana's world? Sarah wondered. Did she come here willingly or was she drugged and forced into it? Panic was close. She gripped her bag and fingered the clasp.

Now?

Smale took a light reading and rasped at them to take their positions. 'Action,' he wheezed. 'And make it good.'

She strode into the frame with as much gusto as possible and spread herself over the chair as if doing a warm-up exercise.

Now?

Carmen played her role with the relish of an actress who thinks it might lead to better work. However as the first blows rained on her behind, Sarah yelped and froze. Smale swore at her and began again. She held still as Carmen threw her on to the rancid mattress and sat astride her. Carmen peeled off the rubber dress as if removing a condom.

Now, oh God, now.

She thrust out a hand but couldn't reach her bag. Carmen moved in for the French kiss. Her breath was unexpectedly sweet. Sarah couldn't go through with it. She turned her head from side to side like a child avoiding an over-zealous grandmother. Smale kept filming. Finally, Carmen held her face in her gloves and gave her a movie kiss, all movement and no penetration.

Angel had been strangely silent during the proceedings. As Carmen sat up to loosen the rest of Sarah's corset, she happened to glance in his direction. The boy was pummelling away inside his trousers.

'*¡Eres un sucio bastardo!*' she shrieked.

Smale shut off the camera and barked at Angel. Carmen joined in, insulting the boy's manhood with a stream of invective. In response, Angel leaped on to the bed and grabbed hold of Carmen's breasts. The lights toppled over and exploded. Pitch blackness and the smell of frying dust, then silence. A dull thud as Carmen punched Angel in the stomach. Smale hit the main light. Sarah was standing on the bed with the gun trembling in both hands.

'Don't move!' she screamed.

Carmen and Angel shrank away as Smale, in the line of fire, raised his hands to head height.

'What's all this?' he croaked. 'Feminists?'

Angel moved at the edge of her vision. She swung the gun in his face. 'Don't move, you little bastard.'

Her gave her a broad grin. 'How you know my gun is loaded?'

'It's loaded.'

He moved a little closer.

'Don't,' she spluttered.

He reached up for her wrists. Sarah raised a booted foot and dragged the long blade of the heel down his leg. Angel fell away, screaming out as a red stripe appeared on his matted calf. Smale moved towards her. She pointed the barrel at him but he continued his approach. It's make or break, she realised. She had to show she meant it. Holding the gun low, she squeezed off a shot.

The recoil slammed her back against the wall. The noise was

much louder than she'd expected. It left a high-pitched ringing which sang around the room like a trapped bird. As it subsided, the smell of cordite stung her nostrils. She blinked back into focus. The silence was replaced by a howl and a shuddering burst of tears. Angel lay awkwardly on the floor, clutching at his right foot. Blood welled up through his fingers.

'*¡Madre Mía!* My foot! You blow hole in it. *¡Puta!*' His lower lip trembled as he faced her. 'All I want do is make love. Only once.'

Carmen crossed herself and spewed out a litany of saints' names.

Sarah stepped down, forcing Smale to back away. 'I want to talk to you about my sister.'

'Who's she? The fucking Terminator?'

She marched him back into the lounge. The patio doors were open and the sky had turned to pale milk behind the beaded curtains. She waved the gun at a chair. Smale sat heavily, his paunch expanding to fill his damp shirt.

'Lana. Remember her?'

'Lot of birds come up here,' he wheezed.

'What about dead ones?'

His tone was that of a specialist who knew his field and ached to bore with its intricacies. 'Snuff movies? No one gets killed in them. That's all hype and bollocks.'

'I think something happened to her here.'

'Oh yeah?'

'Were you involved?'

'Not me, love. Not my style.'

'Who, then?'

Smale let out a long breath. 'What's all this about? Why don't you put the shooter away if you wanna rabbit?' He smirked. 'Tell you another thing, darlin'. It would help my concentration if you packed them tits away.'

She realised that her breasts were still exposed through the laces of the corset. 'Carmen?' she called. 'Get my clothes, will you?'

Still petrified, the actress went to the bathroom and returned with her dress. Sarah told her to get some gaffer tape from the bedroom and tie Smale to the chair with it. Sobbing, she did as instructed, then asked to be excused so that she could tend to Angel's foot. Sarah nodded and the girl left the room.

She went behind Smale and slipped on her dress, immediately feeling better in her own clothes.

'My sister had a map leading to this villa,' she began, as she sat on the sofa opposite the withered gnome. 'I found her ankle bracelet in the bedroom. Tell me what happened here.'

'I dunno nothing about it.'

Sarah winced inwardly as she realised that the threat of the gun wasn't enough. There was only one other option. Torture.

Smale spoke again, his eyes puckering in the pallid light. 'Let me ask you something. You think I'm the only one what uses this place? Know who owns it? Any idea of who runs things round here? Names? Anything?'

The gun wilted in her lap.

'So you got a dead smack-head, and what else?'

'Her bracelet.'

'Anyone can plant a bit of Tom. I don't think so, love.'

Her eyes lit up. 'Wait a minute. I never mentioned heroin was involved.'

He remained expressionless.

She leaped up and pushed the barrel of the gun into his guts. 'You killed her. Tell me what happened.'

Smale cried out. 'It weren't me.'

Suddenly the pistol flew out of her hand. As she fell to the floor, she realised what had happened. Angel had crawled unseen into the room and had thrown himself at her. She scratched and clawed at the boy until he landed a punch to her chin. She howled and thrust out an arm for the gun. Angel got there first, kicking it aside with his good leg. It skittered off and bounced out on to the patio. He began to slap at her face and chest, his arms raining down on her like paddles. She brought up an arm up in defence but he pinned it to her side. She spat in his face. He wiped it away. She brought her knee sharply up to his groin. Angel moaned and keeled over.

Sarah scrambled outside on all fours and fell on the gun. She had it by the barrel when Angel leaped at her once more. The pistol sailed out of her hand, over the parapet and away, down into the valley. Fortunately, Angel's trajectory was misjudged.

He continued past her and smashed his head into the iron railing, knocking himself senseless. She sat, panting in relief and exhaustion. The sharp morning air brought her to her senses. She needed time and distance to sift the fresh facts and consider a new strategy. With the urge to flee taking over, she went back inside and crossed to the bedroom. Smale's jacket lay folded on a chair. She fished the car keys from his pocket. Carmen was now huddled in a corner, looking up at her with panda eyes.

'I still get paid?' she whined plaintively.

She took out Smale's wallet. It contained only twenty thousand pesetas in notes – about a hundred pounds. He had clearly no intention of paying them the full fee. She threw the money at Carmen.

'You take it. And if you're going to carry on with this, you should get yourself a union.'

Sarah let herself out of the front door, unlocked the Mercedes and gunned its engine under an anaemic sky. She'd driven only a few hundred metres down the track before she stopped the car. Resting her head on the soft leather steering wheel, she began to weep.

Mike managed to find a cab and ordered the driver to take him back to Fuengirola. As they sped past the white outcrops of the resort villages, his worries came flooding back. I've failed her, he thought. When it comes down to it, I'm an observer not a participant. And that's why I ended up in journalism. Thrills without commitment. Bloody excuses, excuses, excuses. Billboards sprung up around them as they neared the town. *Rebajas. Muebles*, soft drinks, show homes for the latest developments.

What if she's actually done it? he wondered. Maybe she's got all her answers and she's escaped? Perhaps she's back at her flat right now, waiting for me. With a jolt, he realised he didn't know her address. He fumbled in his jacket pocket for his cigarettes. His fingers found an irregular shape. Clive's keys. Breathing a sigh of relief, he scanned the fob and read out the address to the driver.

Safe in Clive's apartment, he decided to hide his plunder. He went to the lounge, opened a wooden armoire and thrust the sack inside. Too obvious. He pulled it out and stuffed it behind

Clive's records and magazines. Still no good. He washed his face in the bathroom. Looking up from the sink he saw, reflected in the mirror, a cylindrical water heater fastened high up on the wall. Perfect. Standing on the bathtub, he wedged the package securely between the tank and the wall, then went to catch up on some sleep.

Mike awoke refreshed, but starving. There was nothing in the kitchen except crackers, flour and a tube of tomato paste. He dressed, locked up and came outside into the street. The day was bright, but the air was not yet warm. His stomach growled. He hadn't eaten properly in two days. What I really need, he thought, is a proper English breakfast. He wandered among the side streets until he found one in which bars and cafés featured predominantly. The one on the corner looked friendly enough. It had olde worlde English lettering on the sign and the blackboard menu promised a good selection of coronary-inducing meals. The door was open, so he walked in and took the nearest table.

It was decked out like a London pub, all nicotine-yellow with dim lighting and a faintly clandestine air. The tables were tarnished by over-use and the walls hung with framed photographs of people he didn't recognise. Sportsmen, he guessed. Mike was the only customer. A delicious aroma of frying bacon wafted from the kitchen and sent his salivary glands into overdrive. Grabbing the menu, he raked his eyes down it, thinking, bacon, eggs, sausage, mushrooms, beans, fried bread and a steaming mug of tea. Engrossed, he didn't even look up as the waiter approached.

'Everything. Bring me everything on this menu.'

A single blow clubbed him into unconsciousness. Had he known the name of the man who had suggested he leave the Costa del Sol forthwith, Mike would never have walked into Irish Sam's bar.

14

That morning, the *policía municipal* in Fuengirola received an unusual number of calls; some were from local bakers who reported looting, others concerned a disturbance at the beach. A crowd had gathered there since dawn and their numbers had grown alarmingly. Under the command of Sergeant Carlos Jésus Sánchez, a police van was duly despatched to the scene.

Screeching to a halt, they found the sea barely visible through a dense cloud of smoke. Sánchez, a teetotal Christian who had been a keen supporter of Franco, surveyed the mob with a sneer. He stepped down from the van and collared a passer-by. When asked why the fire department had not been summoned, the man merely shrugged and gave a blank smile. Pushing him aside, Sánchez told an officer to make the call and issued orders to disperse the throng. The squad moved forwards in a phalanx formation and the crowd pushed them back with enthusiastic catcalls. They surged in once more, this time breaking through to the epicentre. The people here were more docile and many were lying unconscious on the sand. A cart selling *churros con chocolate* had been tipped over on to its side and every last smear of chocolate had been wiped from the steel bowl. Sánchez, having lost sight of his men, forged his own path and immediately saw the cause of the disturbance. Several bales of cannabis had been piled on top of one another and were blazing merrily. Those members of the mob without access to tobacco and Rizla papers were simply inhaling the smoke. Sánchez cupped his hands to his mouth and ordered them to disperse. No one moved. He barked another caution.

'¡Tados! Leave now, or you will all be under arrest.'

A high-pitched giggle scampered across the crowd. They moved towards the sergeant and, seizing him, forced him deep into the smoke. Due to the onset of apathy, his fellow officers were unable to reach him for some time.

Sarah's morning passed in a blur. She took the Mercedes back to Puerto Banús, left it on the quay, then went back to her car. Needing desperately to recount the night's events, she drove to the hospital in Marbella in the hope of talking to Clive. On her arrival, she was informed that he had checked himself out. Throwing up her hands, she stomped back out into the crisp sun. Deciding to shower and sleep, she then made for her flat. As she pulled into her street, she wondered if Mike would be encamped on the doorstep.

He wasn't.

She was now crouching, fully clothed, in the shower, drenched by the pounding water. Where the hell is he? she thought. Why didn't he follow me last night? She closed her eyes and felt the water drumming against her face. More immediate worries bubbled to the surface. Angel's injured and Smale's tied up – but for how long? She cursed herself for not having had the presence of mind to disable the telephones at the villa. Peeling off her sopping dress, she wrung it out and threw it into the sink. She stood under the water again. Her body felt alien to her. It was as if, in going ahead with the charade, she'd crossed a personal ravine. Now she was on the other side, a new country, a perplexing place whose customs and morals she could not comprehend. Had there been an element of complicity in entering Smale's perverted world? The uncertainty of it all caused her to twist into tears once more.

She turned off the shower, clambered out of the tub and trod a wet trail into her room. She curled up on the bed, hoping fervently that sleep would erase at least part of the pain. She decided it wasn't worth risking going to the police at this stage. But what to do next? She closed her eyes. Her thoughts began to fragment slowly and the orange inside her eyelids shaded to black.

*   *   *

Bang bang bang.

Pause.

Thud thud thud.

Bang bang bang!

John Drake came outside to discover the cause of the noise. Kevin was smashing a basketball against the garage door and had already created a few sizeable dents in the white metal.

'Knock it off, Kev.'

As Kevin dropped the ball and sloped off towards the pool, John wondered if he'd been wise to take the boy up to Torremolinos. Perhaps he was more sensitive than he thought? He picked up the ball, threw it at the hoop and was blinded by the midday sun. Looking away, he blinked furiously, strobing black ovals in his vision. The ball ricocheted off the backboard, bounced away and came to rest in a row of shrivelled rose bushes. The earth beneath them was bone dry. Drake sighed. He'd had the gardeners working full time to keep the lawn and plants from dying off. It was a losing battle. Water rationing had already been introduced in the cheaper resort villages. If the heat kept up then he'd soon lose the whole garden. He'd taken a few steps towards the ball when his mobile bleated.

'John-john? Barry here.' Smale's voice sounded even more phlegmatic than usual. 'Got a little problem.'

Drake listened with increasing rage as the events of the previous night were described to him. 'Where the fuck are you now?' he spat.

'Still here. She took the Merc.'

'What's she know?'

'She knows about the girl. Knows it weren't smack. Not a lot else.'

There was a pause. At the other end, Smale held the phone away at arm's length. He would have preferred to conduct this call from a greater distance, such as another time zone.

Drake was calm now. 'So she can't point the finger at you.'

'She pointed a shooter at me. And her tits.'

'You cunt!' he bellowed. 'You fucking with me, you little toe-rag. You fuck up my shit you slag and I'll fuckin have you.' There was an audible intake of breath. 'Cunt,' he added.

Smale trembled, wondering whether it was feasible for a phone to melt. Drake continued to rant for some time. There was a noise in the background which sounded a bit like a basketball bursting.

'John-john, what am I gonna do about this?'

The line went quiet. Drake's voice came back with a new sense of deliberation. 'First, you clear out that villa. Strip the place top to bottom. She's bound to send the filth up to have a butcher's. Second, I want you out of the way for a bit.'

'What, on the cruiser?'

'No, on a fucking tricycle. Take her up to Benalmadena and bung her in harbour till I square this up. Wait for my call.'

'What about my motor?'

Drake let out a long sigh. 'I'll send one of the locals.'

Barry sighed with relief. Drake always came through. There was always the torrent of rage and the malicious insults, but afterwards, a magnanimous gesture.

'What about Angel?' he asked. 'His foot needs looking at.'

'Fuck him.'

Drake cut him off, then called Ramón. Afterwards, he went inside and consumed one gramme of cocaine, three-quarters of a bottle of tequila, sundry pills and, to level things off, a sizeable quantity of hash.

Clive was receiving visitors. He had taken a cab home and had gone to his landlady for a spare key. When Sarah turned up, she first insisted on fetching some basic provisions from a local shop. She now sat in his living room with a bowl of coffee cupped in both hands. He hobbled in on his new crutches.

'You been busy, ain't you girl?'

He fell heavily on to a beanbag.

'How are you going to get up from there?' Sarah asked.

'Don't care. Anything's better than that hospital.' He opened his tobacco tin and began to roll a spliff. 'For medicinal purposes,' he explained.

She toyed with his Zippo until Clive clicked his fingers for it. When he reached out, he took her hand and squeezed it in empathy. He lit the joint and the smoke made a shelf in the light. 'So,' he began. 'Let's go over this. We got Lana's ankle bracelet and the map you found. You reckon Smale knows more than he said, right?'

She nodded. 'I never mentioned heroin. But *he* did – so he must know.'

'He could've read about that in the papers.'

She shook her head. 'He knew all right.'

Clive took a drag. 'Trouble is, this is what they always call circumstantial evidence. Seen it on telly.'

'That's more or less what Smale said.'

They fell silent. A wisp of blue smoke curled in the hot air.

'I'm really upset,' said Sarah.

'I know.'

'And I think I'm going to cry.'

'Go ahead.'

He held on to her as silent tears spilled from her eyes and rolled unheeded down her cheeks. After a while, she sat back and wiped her face on the sleeve of her T-shirt. 'Sorry about that,' she said. 'It's a girl thing.'

'*No importa.*' He grinned.

'OK. What now?'

Clive traced a finger across a plaster on his temple. 'What was this Spanish guy's name?'

'Angel.'

'Can you describe him?'

'God, I don't know. About eighteen, short and hairy. Big baby clothes.'

'Not much to go on.'

'There is the bullet in his foot.'

'True.' Clive worked a finger under his cast and began to scratch. 'Did Smale say anything else? Something we might be able to use?'

'He said lots of girls went up there. He implied it was owned, or at least used, by other people.'

'A regular haunt for the porno club.'

He raked his hands through his beaded hair. Sarah shuddered as she flashed on an image of the curtains up at the villa.

'Sarah?'

'Yes?' She noticed his irises were chocolate brown.

'That was pretty cool what you did up there.'

'Stupid, I thought.'

'Lana would have been impressed.'

She paused a moment, then ventured, 'Clive. Did you sleep with her?'

He shook his head without hesitation. 'I had a bad thing before I came out here. Not ready to jump in again.'

'What about other men? Boyfriends? It might be important.'

'Don't think so. She usually slept in here and I would've sussed it.'

Sarah took and lit a cigarette. 'You know, no one thought much of her back at home. She was always letting people down and causing trouble. She was one of those people who carve a wake.' She blew smoke and closed her eyes. 'Sometimes I don't know why I came.'

'Blood, I guess.'

He placed the joint in the ashtray and rolled the end off it. 'OK. Let's get real.' He smiled at her. 'Can't sit around here all day taking drugs.'

'But you said we had no evidence.'

'Smale's making hard-core movies. We'll tell the police about that.'

'That a good idea?'

'You know how things work here. We'll say you were at the party and the guy tried to get you involved. Give them enough to get them on our side.'

'But I'm in that film, aren't I?'

'Chances are he's got rid of it already. I say we go ahead with the police but hold back on Lana for now. If they get anywhere with this Smale guy and want to know more, well, we might stand a chance of getting her case reopened.'

Sarah's face lit up. 'That's brilliant. You should be a lawyer.'

Clive scowled. 'We going to the pigs, or are you going to sit here and insult me all day?'

Light bled through three tiny squares of bottle-glass at the end of the cellar. One bare brick wall was piled high with crates of bottled beers; the other was lined with barrels. Mike came to and looked around foggily. Tethered to a pillar in the centre of the vaulted room, he soon discovered that struggling only tightened his bonds. He called out for help but it brought no response. He shivered as his fears began to infect him like a virus.

What the fuck have I got myself into? I should have gone home and forgotten all about this. Drake was a ghost. My father's ghost, not mine. He sneezed loudly and tried to reroute his thoughts. Picturing Tooting, he saw the shoddy shops, the traffic, the dog shit-laden park. Suddenly, he ached for home.

There was a tramping above him as customers clomped back and forth. A jukebox flared into life with a selection of sixties' hits. He tried calling out again. Nothing. He didn't feel like singing along with the Kinks, so he lowered his head on to his right shoulder and passed into an uneven doze.

A sharp squeak shocked him back to consciousness. The squares of light had crept further across the floor and a dish-washer throbbed steadily above him. Suddenly, Irish Sam was staring at him with piercing blue eyes. Too tall for the low cellar, his head was cocked to one side. It was the first time Mike had seen him clearly. A sandy mop of hair rested on a face which was panel-beaten by experience. Deep lines criss-crossed the tanned forehead and two others slashed down from his nostrils almost to his chin. The white bushy moustache hid thin lips.

'Y'all right there? Anything I can get you?'

'Yes, breakfast. And I'd like to leave now, please,' said Mike politely.

The tall man chuckled.

Mike wondered whether to try reason and quickly discounted it. He formed a rudimentary plan which involved crying and begging.

'You are fucken' stupid. I tell you to leave and you walk into my pub,' said the man, laughing in disbelief.

Mike laughed too, but it was the humouring kind.

'The fuck did you do that for?'

'I told you, breakfast. I didn't know it was your place. I don't know the area. I'm a tourist, remember?'

Sam's lower lip slid out momentarily. 'Irish Sam's. Finest beer in Fuengirola. A family pub with all you'd expect at home and more. I wrote that. It's on the sign outside.'

Mike make a mental note to add, Today's special, torture – if he ever made it out alive.

The Scotsman took hold of his forehead in the span of one

giant hand. 'Whassa game then? I tell you to fuck off and you're still here?'

'I'm on holiday.' whined Mike.

'Dinnae give me that shite. You saw me from the pool.'

He banged Mike's head up against the pillar. Mike grimaced as the pain ricocheted around in his cranium. 'I won't be recommending this place to my friends.'

Sam took Mike's cheeks with the thumb and forefingers of both hands and waggled them. It made an unpleasant squelching noise. 'Funny guy.'

'Fucking psychopath,' spat Mike.

Sam's voice dropped a notch. 'As it goes, when I was doing ten in Barlinnie, the doctors did say I was a were bit touched. Mind you, what do the quacks know, eh?'

'Let me go. I won't bother you again. Honest.'

The Scotsman's expression stamped this option into a lifeless wreck. 'D'yae ever hear that joke about the two pieces of string? One goes to this party and—'

Mike prepared himself to laugh as if hearing it for the first time.

'—I'm a frayed knot,' came the expected punchline.

They laughed loudly.

'So,' said Sam, with conviction, 'I'm afraid not. You don't get out. You come under the category of "loose ends".'

Had he been in a better mood, Mike might have appreciated the juxtaposition of the dual string comments.

'And all loose ends have tae be tied up.' He gave Mike a meaningful look and then left, closing the cellar door firmly behind him.

15

Kevin was chasing the Dobermans, Emily, Charlotte and Anne, round and round the lawn. On the patio, Jackie was lolling in a deckchair and marinading in her liquid lunch. John, at the wrong end of a severe drink and narcotics binge, was asleep on a sun-lounger. His mobile chirruped beside him.

'Yeah, what?'

Unable to summon up the energy for another tantrum, he listened and grunted and slid further down until his flip-flops fell off the end of the lounger. Once the caller had finished, he used his forehead to push in the aerial and wriggled his toes back into the shoes. Lurching upwards, his gut almost threw him off balance. Taking a step forward, he trod in something sticky. With a sigh, he remembered what it was. Kevin had heard Jackie use the expression 'hot enough to fry an egg' and had tried it.

He shuffled down the steps, across the marram grass and belly-flopped into the pool. The water scissored upwards, splashing and hissing on the tiles. He emerged, blowing water and mucus from his nose. He went under again and again until the repeated dousings pulled him back to full consciousness. Wringing moisture from his beard and moustache, he levered himself out of the pool and stamped wet footprints into his study.

Cool air and a couple of lines of Columbia's finest soon had him gritting his teeth and stoking up a fire of righteous indignation. 'Kevin!' he bellowed out of the window.

The boy and the dogs turned as one. Jackie murmured something in her sleep and rolled over on to her side.

'Kevin. Study!'

This was a treat. On his arrival, his uncle had made it clear to him that the room was out of bounds. Kevin ran into the villa and skidded to a halt at the double doors. John motioned him inside, closed the doors and pointed at a long brown sofa. The boy sank into it as Drake began to pace the room, smoking.

'Kevin, I brung you out here as a favour to your dad. You got two choices. Either you has a decent holiday and buggers off home come September. Or,' he paused for effect, 'you can work for me out here.'

Kevin sat up and the leather squealed against his thighs. 'Brilliant, Uncle John,' he said.

'What time you got, Kev?'

He looked at his wrist and saw only bare skin. Earlier, he had discovered that his watch wasn't waterproof and had left it at the bottom of the pool. John picked up the remote, aimed it at the television and surfed channels until he found a news report. A young and glamorous female reporter was standing on the beach at Fuengirola. In the background, the smouldering heap of cannabis had been cordoned off by fluttering tape; a cluster of policemen were keeping the crowd at bay as a JCB prepared to move in. As the pretty anchor woman gave her piece to camera, she failed to notice a commotion behind her. Sergeant Carlos Sánchez staggered wild-eyed into shot. His tie was knotted bandana-style around his forehead and his tunic was unbuttoned to reveal a pristine vest. On reflex, the reporter held the microphone to his face. Sánchez grinned lopsidedly and slipped a horny hand deep into her cleavage.

'¡Qué bonita!' he hooted, scooping out a tanned breast.

The report cut away to a library shot and Drake jabbed the screen dead. 'That was my fucking smoke, Kev. Ozorio done this to take the piss.' He tossed his cigarette aside. 'That slag's saying my puff don't matter to him, so he's gone and torched the whole bundle.' His nephew looked blank. 'It's a statement, Kevin,' he added.

The only statement Kevin knew of was one you made in a police station.

'Power,' said John, sensing it still hadn't sunk in.

'Oh, right,' said Kevin sheepishly.

'I'm gonna arrange a meet. We're gonna discuss his terms.'

'His terms? I thought you said . . . ?'

Drake gave a sly grin. 'Yeah. You're going instead.' He lit another cigarette from an onyx lighter on the desk. 'It's like this. I ask him for a meet, face to face. I come over all desperate, like I'm losing it.' He smiled like a shark. 'Then I sends you. That'll piss him right off. No offence, son.'

Kevin hadn't taken any.

'Right. You go out and play while I give him a bell.'

Kevin left the room, pleased to have attained a position as negotiator with such ease. To celebrate, he ran across the lawn and wrestled with the dogs until they yelped. Drake made the call and strolled outside to find his nephew.

'It's all sorted. Ever been to a bullfight?'

'No, Uncle John.'

'Ramón's coming over. He'll drive you up the bullring in Torremolinos. Do as he says, right?'

Kevin raised two chubby thumbs.

Stepping out of the police station in Fuengirola, Clive and Sarah donned their shades against the glare of the afternoon sun. His arms aching with the pressure of the crutches, Clive suggested they rest up. They found a nearby bar and ordered tapas and beers.

'They weren't very helpful,' said Sarah, running her hands through her hair and catching a knot.

'Least they're going to check out the villa. That should buy us a little time.'

'So what do we do now?'

Clive raised his mummified leg on to a chair. 'Can't do anything much. Besides, we don't know what they know.'

'Who? Smale or the police?'

'Police. They might know about Smale already.'

'You've got a suspicious mind, Clive.'

'Yeah, well. We've got to think ahead.'

She sipped her drink and gazed up at him. With a guilty flush, it occurred to her then that, back in England, she would probably cross the street to avoid him.

'Clive?'

'Yo.'

'Did you get a lot of hassle back home? You know, being . . . ?'

'Tall? No.'

'You know what I mean.' Her dimples made a brief appearance.

He leaned forwards. 'Tell you something. I bought a car when I was eighteen. Right old banger. It was taxed and MOT'd, the lot. Thing is, every time I went out in it, I kept getting pulled over.' He lowered his eyes and toyed with his plate. 'Shit. If I was going to nick a motor, it wouldn't have been an X-reg Polo. I got so pissed off I started taking the bus. Car sat in the street for six months until the local kids stripped it down.'

'I'm sorry.'

'Not your problem.' He gulped at his San Miguel and swilled the dregs around the glass.

'What d'you think's happened to Mike?'

'You like him, don't you?'

'He's all right.'

'You mean you haven't decided yet.'

Her turn to concentrate on her beer.

'I guess,' said Clive, stretching his arms behind his head, 'that when he shows up, it's either going to be at my place or yours. Ain't got nowhere else to go.'

They allowed the *when* to hang in the air. Sarah had already begun to wonder about the *if*. If he was all right. If he hadn't chickened out and taken the next plane home.

'Wait,' she said, remembering. 'He's got that set of keys you gave us.'

'My place then.'

She drew a zigzag in the watermark left by her drink.

'I don't want to go back to mine anyway.'

'Good,' said Clive, rapping his knuckles on his cast. 'I need a slave.'

Ramón's jeep, stereo pumping at top volume, screeched to a halt outside the Plaza de Toros in Torremolinos. He and Kevin clambered out and scrunched to the entrance. Judging by the roars from inside, the *corrida* was already under way. They pushed through the turnstile and came into a chilly, vaulted atrium. Climbing up several flights of stone steps, they emerged into the stands. Down below in the bright sandy circle, two toreadors sat astride their horses and taunted a perspiring bull. Failing to shake off two coloured *banderilleros* in its flanks, the bull slowed to a lethargic trot. The *picador* approached with his *muleta*.

Ramón led Kevin down the raked cement steps of the amphitheatre. Their seats were in the sun and, despite wearing sunglasses, they still had to cup their hands over their eyes to see. The *matador*, carrying a third stake, paced forwards. The expectation in the crowd grew heavier. The bull pawed the ground, but the *matador* kept steady eye contact. He swished the *capa* across the animal's head as if pulling a shroud across a dead relative. A whip of applause cracked the air. Suddenly, in one swift movement, he thrust the knife deep into the animal's neck. It hauled itself around in a semicircle, shaking its head in a rain of sweat. The bull lost momentum, sank to its knees, keeled over and finally lay still. Ramón yelled at the bullfighter to remove the bull's ear. As if in response, the *matador* produced an *espada* from his belt and went about the task with the practised ease of a butcher.

Kevin looked around. A tall, pock-faced young man was making his way towards them from the shade. He wore a linen suit with a plain T-shirt and tasselled loafers without socks. Ramón immediately stood up and shook the man's hand. He introduced him to Kevin as José.

'All right,' said Kevin.

José gave Ramón a questioning glance and beckoned them to follow him. All three climbed back up the aisle and skirted the perimeter before resettling in the *sombra* seats. He and Ramón then began to converse in Spanish so Kevin turned to the ring. The carcass was being dragged away and the next animal had not yet been released. He prodded Ramón on the shoulder. 'What's going on then?'

'He has been sent by Ozorio. He is very angered that *Señor* Drake is not here.'

'Tell him tough shit. His boss ain't here neither.'

Ramón shot him on insouciant look and turned back to José. Kevin busied himself with kicking away at the concrete steps with his heels. Moments later, an announcement came over the loudspeakers and a cheer went up. Another bullfighter had entered the ring. As he paraded up and down, José rose and applauded loudly, exhorting the others around him to join in. Ramón followed suit.

'What's up?' asked Kevin, tugging at his sleeve.

'The *novillero* is Ozorio's brother from Toledo. It is his first time in the ring. This is a proud day for their family.'

'Why ain't Ozorio here to see it, then?'

Ramón shrugged. 'Maybe he is. In one of the boxes.'

Kevin felt his temper slither out of his control. It was *he* who was meant to be the negotiator. He began to clench and unclench his little fists. 'He should be down here talking to us.'

Ramón put a hand on his shoulder. 'Is not how things are done.'

He shrugged him away. 'When we going to talk business, then? Uncle John says I got to report back and that.'

Ramón turned away and carried on talking.

Two *toreadors* entered the ring as a fresh bull was released. The black beast was a ball of energy in comparison to the last animal. The *novillero* took up his position in the centre. He stood proud and composed, his embroidered waistcoat glittering in the sunlight. He unfurled his *capa*. The bull didn't hesitate. It charged headlong, missing him by inches. A rumble of displeasure staggered through the crowd. Kevin was momentarily impressed. This bloodthirsty quality in the Spanish reminded him of damp Saturdays at the Den. The *novillero* was clearly not having a good time of it and the bull was beginning to tire him out by forcing him to leave his position. The crowd leaked hisses. Kevin glanced up. José was commentating on the match to anyone within radius. He poked Ramón on the calf.

'When's this going to finish, then?'

'We must wait. It is a matter of honour,' replied the Spaniard sharply.

'Bollocks it is.'

Kevin had had enough. He stood up, trotted down to the edge of the stands and leaped over the barrier. He fell three metres and landed squarely on the sand. Even the bull looked over in surprise.

Ignoring the shouts and the frantic waving of the *toreadors*, Kevin strode purposely forwards. Ozorio's brother was too engrossed to notice him until it was too late. He came up behind him, deftly removed his sword and lobbed it aside. The crowd went berserk. The bullfighter looked on in shock as Kevin grabbed his cape, threw it down and trod it into the dirt. He tried to snatch it up but the boy put a boot to his chest and pushed him down. The bull shuffled from hoof to hoof, its bovine consciousness unable to comprehend the meaning of the scuffle. The diminutive skinhead locked eyes with the animal, daring it to defy him. The bull snorted in response. Dripping saliva and mucus, he backed up a few paces and charged.

Kevin grinned.

Andalucian culture thrives on stories handed down from mouth to mouth and from generation to generation: tales of strife which concern the vagaries of the weather or the Moorish oppressors who ruled the land for so many centuries; fireside tales of bravery or unrequited love; tales of families rent asunder in the Civil War. Their parables usually exclude outsiders but, in this case, the story of the Englishman who fought the bull bare-handed stands a good chance of becoming legend.

Kevin did indeed grab the bull by the horns, forcing the animal to a dead halt. It reared its head and lifted him off the ground. Kevin soared upwards and sailed in a somersault before bearing down on that muscular neck. Using tactics learned in the dead streets of New Cross, he started kicking. He kicked at its flanks; he trod on its hooves; he booted it in the neck. The speed and ferocity of the attack so surprised the bull that it froze for an instant. This gave Kevin his chance. In a move that would have caused even Hemingway to drop his drink in surprise, the skinhead drew back his fist and felled the bull in one punch.

Mike listened as the outboard motor cut a swathe through the sea. It was dark now; dark and damp. Irish Sam had returned to the cellar after nightfall. Mike had been unshackled and forced down on to a rank square of old pub carpet. He was rolled up in it, secured fast and hoisted over Sam's shoulders. Unable to see, he relied on his other senses as he was carted outside into the street. At first there was traffic, then a thump and blackness. He was inside a container which smelled of petrol and fish. When the engine started he realised it was the boot of a car. The journey lasted a short while before the boot opened and he was lifted out. The smell of brine. Another jolt and he was rocking gently. A chugging from an outboard motor as they moved out to sea. He worried enough space between him and the carpet to crane his neck upwards. The lights of Fuengirola were receding into the distance.

'You're not really going to do this, are you?' he yelled.

'Back with us, are ye? Not for long, though, eh?'

'I'm just a tourist, for fuck's sake.'

Sam chuckled to himself. 'I should charge you, then.'

'People will be looking for me. My girlfriend. The police.'

Sam remained silent, concentrating on his course.

Considering his imminent death, Mike tried to will the slides of his memories on to his mental screen. All he could imagine was a dark slab of pure fear. The engine cut out and the boat idled to a halt.

'This should do it,' said Sam, more to himself.

Mike began to thrash inside the tube. Given time, he reckoned he could free one of his hands. Strong arms now lifted him up.

'Wait!' he barked. 'Just tell me one thing.'

'Last request, is it?'

'Yeah.' He wriggled his arm furiously. 'Why d'you call yourself Irish Sam when you're obviously Scottish?'

Sam threw him back on to the deck and bent down so his face was visible to Mike. He put a hand to his forehead and lifted up his sandy fringe. There was a thin mesh where the skin met the hair.

'Irish jig, see?'

'Thanks,' replied Mike, sardonically. 'That's put my mind at rest.'

Sam hauled him up once more, grunting with the exertion. 'See, it's a wee bit like tossing the caber. Except there's no prize.'

Mike freed an arm.

'Stop your pissing about, will ye?' said Sam, feeling the movement.

'Sod you,' shouted Mike, thrusting out his hand. He tore the wig from the Scotsman's head and spun it into the sea. Sam roared, dropped him and dived in after it. Landing with a thump on the boards, Mike rolled back and forth until he had worked both arms free. He slithered out and stood up. Sam, thrashing about in the water, located his sodden mop, stuck it on his head, then attempted to clamber aboard. Mike kicked his hands away. The Scotsman went underwater and came up bald. He gripped the sides. There was a short boat hook in the stern. Mike grabbed it and swung at Sam as he hoisted himself up again. It dug deep into the Scotsman's left armpit. Mike put his weight behind it and pushed hard. Sam fell overboard, leaking blood.

The chunky outboard motor had two black gear sticks on the casing. Mike chose one at random and pulled it down. The engine spluttered into life and the boat surged forwards. He looked round. Sam had got hold of the casting-off rope and was ploughing through the water behind him. Mike pulled the gear further. The speed increased to thirty knots and the boat veered sharply to starboard. Locating the rudder, Mike twisted it to the left and right. Sam let out watery curses as he was buffeted in the wash.

Ramming the gear up to full speed, the craft spun in a wide arc towards the shore. Stealing frantic glances behind him, he realised that Sam was pulling himself closer to the boat. In panic, he pulled the other lever. The engine went into neutral, catapulting them round and smashing Sam's body into the hull. Mike went back into gear and made for shore. Sam held fast, unable to get closer for fear of being chewed up in the propeller. They approached the beach at top speed. Two hundred metres. One hundred. Fifty. Mike leaped free and plunged into the warm shallows.

He surfaced, wiping his hair from his face. The boat had flung itself at the sand like a weary swimmer. It nosed down, carving a deep scar before it flipped high into the air. It catapulted on to an outcrop of black rocks and exploded in a ball of copper flame.

16

'Morning, Kev,' said Jackie, entering his room with his breakfast on a tray. She placed it beside the bed and leaned over to ruffle his hair. Kevin cracked open a sleep-encrusted eye, which he focused on her legs under a pale silk robe.

'Once you've had that, John wants a word in his study.'

Kevin grunted acknowledgement and waited until she'd gone before sitting up and rubbing his face. His uncle and auntie had been out when Ramón brought him home. He'd let himself in, fought off the Dobermans and had found a cold meal waiting for him in the kitchen. He ate it in front of the telly and then went straight to bed.

The Study.

As he dragged a toothbrush across his uneven teeth, it occurred to Kevin that John might be upset about yesterday's events. He dressed slowly, stuffing a bacon sandwich in his mouth before trotting downstairs.

John Drake was poring over his maritime model. He wore a fresh cotton shirt and pale slacks and his goatee was combed to a fine point. He smelled of strong cologne.

'Come on in, son.'

The boy sloped in, head down. John repositioned a high-masted Biscayan and bent to the tableaux to squint at the battle.

'Saw your little escapade, yesterday.'

'How?' asked Kevin, perplexed.

'On the telly.'

As his uncle straightened up, Kevin prepared himself for a barrage of ear-bending and physical violence. He decided to take it like a man, or at least, a short man. As John approached, Kevin saw powder gleaming in his moustache.

'Brilliant, boy!' said Drake, clapping him hard on the shoulders.

Kevin's face lit up.

'Couldn't have thought of anything better meself. How d'you get out of there? All I saw was one big ruck.'

'Went out the back,' grinned Kevin. 'Where them bullfighters come out of. Ramón was in the Jeep. Looked a bit pale for a dago.'

Drake steered him towards the desk. 'They went apeshit when you floored that bull.' He let out a full-throated laugh. 'Top man!'

'I thought you'd be angry.'

'Nah. Tit for tat. They piss me off. I give 'em aggro. Sod Ozorio and his piss-ant operation.' He slid open a drawer. 'Shut yer eyes and hold out your hand.'

Kevin did so and Drake slapped a slab of hash on his outstretched paw.

'There you go. Enjoy yourself.'

'Thanks, Uncle John.'

''Cos you might want to lie low for a bit.'

'Oh, right,' replied Kevin, not realising the reverence in which the Spanish hold their cultural events. Were he to return to the *corrida* in Torremolinos, he would, no doubt, be set upon by incensed locals. The previous night, in fact, several British pubs had been attacked by youths on mopeds and the tourist office had been lightly grilled.

Sarah spent the night at Clive's flat. After phoning the tour company and concocting a lie about contracting food poisoning, she cooked him a roast chicken which they washed down with a bottle of vino tinto. Later, Clive offered her his bed, explaining that it didn't matter where he slept, what with his leg in its current state. She accepted gratefully and fell into a deep sleep. Clive returned to the living room and sat up long into the night.

The phone punched a hole in his dreams. Using a crutch, Clive knocked the machine from its stand and dragged himself to the receiver. Afterwards, he washed, dressed as best he could and made coffee. Sarah padded into the kitchen in a long T-shirt.

'Who was it?' she yawned.

'Police. They said there's nothing up at the villa and no sign of Smale's cruiser in the harbour. Said he was registered there but he sailed without giving details of his course.'

'So it's a dead end.'

He poured the coffee into two glass cups. 'Worse.' He held up a crutch and bounced the rubber stop against the fridge door, closing it. 'Getting good with these, aren't I?'

'What's worse?' asked Sarah.

'They asked if we'd like to come in and answer some questions.'

'It's optional, then?'

'What do you think?'

She sipped her coffee and gathered up her hair. 'How long have we got?'

'Day or so. *Mañana*.'

She scrunched it up under a butterfly clasp. 'But all we have to do is tell the truth.'

Clive looked at her as if she'd farted. 'You better drink some more coffee. It was you who said the police were connected with Lana's cover-up, remember?'

'Shit. With knobs on.'

'Reckon you better get back to your place. They don't have your address yet.'

'What about you?'

'I was coming to that.' Clive lit a stub from the ashtray. 'I had a long think last night. I really want to help you, Sarah, but well, this is all too heavy. Soon as Mike turns up, I'm going down to Estepona for a while. I've got a room there I can use.'

She felt herself falling inside.

'I'll get some work down there. I'll leave you the address in case you need to get hold of me.'

Clive turned away from her and looked out of the window. In the alleyway outside, an elderly woman was placing a small bag of refuse in a bin. Pressing it down with a leathery hand, she began to fan at the flies.

'I'm really sorry, Sarah,' he added. 'I can't hack this.'

'What about this place?'

The woman went inside, Clive looked back at her. 'You can use it.'

'And Mike?'

'He'll turn up soon.'

She flared up. 'You know he won't come back. We both know he's buggered off back to England.' Her lips were pursed and her neck grew taught with tension. 'And anyway, I thought you were going to help me.'

He was defensive now. 'Hang on. I never promised anything.'

'Fine. Go to Estepona.'

Clive took a step towards her. 'Look, Sarah. I know you're pissed off, but what can I do with this?' He rapped his knuckles on his cast.

Saying nothing, Sarah went to the bedroom and slammed the door behind her. Clive hobbled to the door and knocked, but she refused to answer.

Angel's foot resembled a large, mummified turnip.

Having eschewed the services of the hospital, he instead took a cab back to *casa Ramón*. There, he bathed his foot in vodka. The bullet had mashed his little toe but otherwise he was still able to walk. Using a bread knife, he cauterised the wound and waited for the pain to subside to a throbbing agony. He bound the foot in a bandage and was soon able to stop sweating and shaking for minutes at a time. Secretly, Angel was rather proud of himself. There had never been anyone remotely connected to medicine in the Esteban family and he felt like quite the pioneer. After sleeping for sixteen hours straight, he awoke to find his foot had swelled to double its normal size. It occurred to him then that perhaps he should have sterilised the bread knife. Or even washed it first.

Ramón arrived at ten in the morning with a message from Drake. Their orders were to find the girl and to report back. To that end, Ramón had already been busy in Puerto Banús and Marbella and was about to start in Fuengirola. 'My very own younger brother,' he had told many of the bar-owners, 'was shot by an insane *puta*.' He couldn't bring himself to add 'in the foot', so he exaggerated his brother's condition, putting him critically ill in hospital.

Privately, Ramón had another shame to conceal. He had only escaped from the Plaza de Los Toros by feigning an epileptic fit in front of Ozorio's lieutenant. Then, once José had gone to locate a doctor, he had scooted off in the other direction. Leaping into the Jeep, he accidentally slammed the gear into reverse, an action which the emerging skinhead interpreted as a brave gesture of help. They had driven away at speed and had barrelled down the *autovía* to Fuengirola. There, he had suffered the further humiliation of witnessing the skinhead in a celebratory mood. His evening was spent apologising to various patrons and trying to quieten the boy down – which was like trying to soothe a rabid dog.

Ramón pushed those events to the back of his mind. He selected a loose jacket, a low-slung T-shirt and a pair of faded denims and began to preen in the mirror. Angel, full of righteous indignation and tequila, followed him outside to the Jeep. He sat in the passenger seat and began to invent a series of improbable tortures for the Englishwoman.

The calls came in on Ramón's mobile as they scoured the town. Sarah had been sighted in a bar at Puerto Banús, but the barman was certain she wasn't a regular. Contacts in Marbella drew a blank, which now left several possibilities. There was Estepona and Torremolinos or worse: she could be staying in any one of the many development villages.

Angel's hobbling slowed him up considerably and Ramón soon ordered him to stay in the Jeep. Finally, a nightclub owner recalled Sarah as the girl who had shown him a photograph some weeks previously. *Bueno!* thought Ramón. She must be here in Fuengirola. He decided to try the hotels. A receptionist suggested that his best option would be to talk to the tour representatives. They would have a list of all the English guests and a woman on her own would be unusual. The brothers Esteban spent a further hour alternating spells in the blistering heat with shivering in air-conditioned lounges.

As Ramón strode into the Bella Vista, he stopped a florid couple from Oldham who were on their way out. 'Please? Where can I find tour company person?'

The wife smiled up at him. 'D'you mean Sarah, love?'

Ramón flashed his teeth. '*Sí*. Sarah.'

She looked at her husband for acknowledgement. 'We've not seen her for a while, have we, love?' The man stared straight ahead. 'Food poisoning or summat,' she continued. 'That's what the other girl said.'

'Other girl?'

'At desk.' She pointed to a pale girl in a cubby hole.

The woman was about to speak again but Ramón had already crossed the floor. She turned to her husband and found him struggling in the swing doors. A hairy teenager with a bandaged foot was tugging furiously on the other side. The rep's name-tag read 'Kimberley' and she was making an idle doodle look like brain surgery.

'*¡Hola! ¿Donde está Sarah? ¿No está aquí hoy?*'

She had a flat Midlands accent. 'Sorry, I don't speak much Spanish actually. Only phrase-book.'

'Then I speak in English. Can you tell me, where is Sarah?'

'She's ill. They sent me to fill in.'

He flashed his most charming smile. 'You have her address?'

'Can't give it out, actually. It's company policy.'

He leaned over and chucked her under the chin. 'For me? . . . Kimberley.'

Angel had won his battle and now reached the counter. Ramón waved an arm at him. 'You see, my brother is a good friend with Sarah.'

Angel flashed an inane grin.

'You know it is her birthday tomorrow?' Ramón added.

'No, I didn't, actually.'

'He was going to send flowers. We do not have the address.'

Kimberley considered this request under Ramón's limpid gaze. She'd only been in Spain for a few days and was still sizing up the talent. Having taken the job in the hope of meeting Antonio Banderas or similar, she wanted to discover what the indigenous population were like in bed.

'What's it worth?' she asked with a sly grin.

He shrugged. 'Maybe I take you out sometime?'

'I come too,' added Angel.

Ramón trod on his damaged foot. 'I take you to the finest restaurant in Marbella in my *fantástico* Jeep. Hip-hop trip music.'

'When?' asked Kimberley, playing hard to get for all of a minute.

'*Esta noche*. Tonight.'

She frowned. 'I've got to organise the entertainment in the bar. It's Flamenco.'

He tried to conceal his sneer. 'What time you finish?'

'Eleven.'

'Is early. I come here after.'

She pulled out a file, flipped through the plastic sheets and found Sarah's address at the back. She wrote it down.

'*Voy*,' said Ramón, taking the paper. 'I see you tonight. Yes?'

She nodded, already wondering what to wear.

The brothers Esteban were half-way to the door when Kimberley called out, freezing them to the spot. 'Hang on. You didn't tell me your name.'

'Javier,' said Ramón.

'See you tonight then . . . Javier,' she said, giving them a little wave.

Sarah, more upset than angry with Clive, had returned to her apartment for a change of clothes. They'd agreed to wait for Mike until seven. If he didn't show by then, she'd go back to the *policía municipal* and give them the full story. If this brought no result, she told Clive, she would go to the airport and take the next flight home.

As she packed, she became aware of a scratching at the door. At first she thought to call out. She swallowed her voice. There were often break-ins in the apartments and a woman upstairs had recently been beaten. Wishing she had thought to double lock, she crept into the kitchen and scrabbled in the cutlery drawer for a knife. The front door suddenly splintered and crashed back on its hinges. A second later Ramón strode into the room. She let out a scream and retreated. Her hand found a cold cup of tea. She threw it in his face, then followed this up by flinging the cup at him. It bounced off Ramón's forehead and he went down. Angel hobbled in behind him.

'English *puta. Hijo de puta.*'

'Shit. Not you again.'

He went for her and she landed a kick to his knee. Angel let out a howl. She jumped back against the freezer compartment of the fridge. He limped forwards again. She swung it open, fumbled around amidst the ice and belted him with the first thing that came to hand. It was a packet of frozen fish fingers. It caught him full in the face, sending a rain of orange crumbs to the floor. Angel collapsed. She spun round. The other one wasn't there. Then the table loomed up at her.

When she awoke she was sprawled on the floor and surrounded by the crushed contents of her fridge and freezer. Fish fingers had been ground into the tiles and torn teabags were sprinkled everywhere. Sarah felt sick and dizzy. There was an argument going on in her living room. One of the Spaniards was pleading for the right to kill her there and then; the other one advising him against it. She wondered if her hearing had been affected as the first one seemed to be saying something about a magnetic attraction to fish. There was a flurry of activity. A punch, a groan. Books fluttering through the air. Glass breaking. Finally, a low moan. She hoped they had beaten one another unconscious. However, a sharp rap on the door brought them scurrying past in the corridor. English voices.

A bald, middle-aged man waddled into the kitchen. His white goatee and moustache lent him a cultured appearance, but was nullified by the paunch and baggy tracksuit bottoms. His face was tanned to a pale leather and his eyes were dark and piercing, the pupils shrunken to dots. He was followed by a circus midget in burgundy boots, tight yellow T-shirt and ragged cut-off jeans. The man poked a lighter at a cigarette and blew smoke. Behind him, the Spaniards hovered like eager footmen. He waved them away and they scuttled off. As the outer door closed, the skinhead picked her up and propped her on a chair. He leered at her, his jaw jutting out like a promontory on the burning beach of his face. The older man pushed him aside and crouched to her eye level.

'Who the fuck are you?' she spat.

John Drake pocketed his lighter and snorted a grey cloud in her face. 'An interested party.'

17

'So I swam ashore and hid on the beach.'

Mike was engaged in gutting Clive's fridge. 'I was in this cove surrounded by cliffs. There was a road sign up on top. Torreblanca del Sol?'

'That's not far,' said Clive.

'I was too knackered to walk, so I found this old rowing boat and slept underneath it. Woke up this morning and the place was full of neo-Nazis.'

'Huh?'

'Windsurfers. Hitched a lift back with two Nordic gods.' He guzzled a Coke. 'Where's Sarah?'

Clive told him the story to date.

'What a woman,' said Mike, amazed.

'Yeah, think of the damage you could do if you worked together.'

'I'll take that as a compliment.'

'And that Scots guy? He sounds like a right psychopath.'

'That's what I told him.'

'Not a good move.' Clive took a wooden spoon, rammed it into his cast and wiggled it from side to side. 'Dropped ash down there last night. Itches like buggery.' He pulled it out and sniffed the handle. 'Where'd you stash these tapes, then?'

Mike went to the bathroom and pulled the bin-liner from its hiding place.

'Think we should check them out now, or wait for Sarah?'

Clive shrugged. 'No time like the present.'

Clive went through to the living room and collapsed on to a

beanbag. Mike sat on his knees in front of the video with the remote in one hand. 'Ready then?'

'I guess so, Doc.'

He slipped in the first tape and pressed play. Clive began to tremble. Soon he was howling with laughter and emitting helpless, high-pitched shrieks.

'This is hardly *Carry On up the Khyber*,' frowned Mike, perturbed.

'I never saw porn before,' said Clive, wiping tears from his face.

'What, never?'

'Never got round to it.' He chuckled again. 'That woman with the enormous jugs? Jesus, that ain't horny. That's a medical problem. There's enough milk in one of those to feed Rwanda.'

Mike reached for the other pile. The unlabelled ones. 'Let's try one of these. And try to be serious.'

'OK, Doc.'

Couplings. Trios. Bondage. Golden Showers. Coprophilia: a parade of perversions. The settings were mostly nondescript hotel rooms; empty, anonymous places which held no clues. They rejected them more quickly.

'This is getting us nowhere,' Mike said.

'Better check 'em all.'

He pushed in another. Static filled the screen. 'Nothing on it,' he grunted.

The image wobbled, flickered and came into focus, revealing the villa in the mountains. There was no sound. A topless girl was sunning herself on the patio. Behind her, a motorbike came into shot. The rider dismounted and removed his helmet to reveal a youthful Spanish face. The girl took off her sunglasses. The youth approached, picked up her bottle of tanning oil and dribbled it down her chest. He began to massage her breasts, tweaking each nipple to hardness.

'Turn it off,' barked Clive. 'That's Lana.'

Mike reversed to her face and held it there. 'Think we should skim through the whole thing. For clues?'

'Let's wait for Sarah,' said Clive, sharply.

'She should be here by now.'

'Phone's over there.'

Her answerphone voice filled Mike with a soft pleasure. He spoke after the short beep. 'Hi, it's Mike. I'm at Clive's. I managed to get hold of a tape of Lana. You'd better get over here and see it, soon as poss. See you soon. Bye.'

At the other end, John Drake stood over the machine like a wolf eyeing his prey. Sarah, slumped in the chair, moaned in frustration as the message ended. Drake grabbed a fistful of her hair.

'Who's this Mike geezer, then?'

She grimaced as he tightened his grip. 'A friend.'

'Clive?'

'Another fucking friend.'

'Popular, ain'tcha? Where they staying, then?'

She pursed her lips. Drake gave another sharp tug.

'Don't bother trying it on, love. I'm fucking fairy fingers next to the lad here.' He motioned to Kevin, who was picking at his teeth with a fork.

'They're just people I met out here. I don't know where they are.'

Drake sighed like a parent who knows that his child is lying. 'Kevin, have a look-see. See if she's got an address book. Diary or something.'

The skinhead fumbled around the kitchen, then grinned gormlessly. 'Nuffink here.'

'Try the bedroom.'

The boy emerged with her handbag, carrying it as if it were an unexploded bomb. Drake tipped the contents on to the table and her make-up clattered in all directions. Sifting through her possessions, he fished out her notepad. The top sheet was blank save for the tour company logo. He stroked the surface with a finger, sensing tiny indentations. Placing it flat on the table, he lit a cigarette and took several deep drags. He made a cylinder of ash, which he tapped on to the page. Smearing it from side to side, he noted that a faint image was beginning to emerge. It was Clive's address. Sarah had written it down in the hospital and had then torn off the top sheet. Drake held it aloft. She couldn't hide her dismay. He smiled, took out his pen and rewrote the address over her hasty scribble.

'Kev. There's some videos at this gaff.' He handed it to his nephew. 'Run over and get them for us, there's a good lad. There's a street map in the motor.' He tossed his car keys to Kevin and the boy sauntered off.

Drake unclipped his mobile and punched buttons.

Barry Smale was downing his fourth Pina Colada of the day in the front cabin of the *Maiden Voyage*.

'Baz? John. How's it going?'

Smale put down his drink. 'All right John-john. Lot quieter up here as it goes.'

'Do us a favour, mate. Go take a look at your collection.'

Drake heard the sound of drawers opening. It was accompanied by Smale's breathing, which became heavier by the minute. When he came back on line, his voice was pinched. 'There's a few missing.'

'Don't I fucking know it you shithouse! Can't you keep your house in order just once, you cunt?' His tone dropped to a patronising lilt. 'You check them tapes and tell us what's missing, then Uncle John will sort it out.'

'OK, John-john,' he said, his voice small.

Drake shot out a foot and kicked Sarah off her chair. She fell heavily and cried out in pain.

'Barry?' asked Drake, calmly.

'Yes, John?'

'Piss off.'

Smale scrabbled around, pulling out tape after tape and chaining cigarettes with trembling fingers. He paced, shooting out intense stares as if the missing items might magically reappear. Realising his hopes were futile, he poured a fat line of cocaine on to a glass-topped table. Producing a silver tube, he inserted it into a cavernous nostril and traced a jagged line across the powder.

Mike had decided he couldn't wait any longer and had asked Clive for directions to Sarah's flat. He staggered along now, blinded. The street was a sheet of white sunlight and the heat scorched his lungs. Reaching the shade of an alleyway, he saw, coming the other way, a short, brutish-looking boy with a florid face and shorn, velcro hair. He was reminded of an Action Man he'd once cremated in his back garden. They turned sideways to pass one another.

'Awright?' said Kevin.

'All right,' murmured Mike, and carried on.

He arrived at her apartment to find the door broken and signs of a struggle. Sarah's bag lay spread-eagled on the kitchen table, violated. The answerphone eye was winking. With increasing trepidation, he played back his own message. He rang Clive's. There was no answer.

Clive lay on his back with his right eye swollen and his nose bleeding. 'Enneff, baftarbs,' he mumbled.

'NFT?' asked Mike, incredulously.

'NF. National Front.'

A cold spear of shock ran through him. 'It wasn't a little skinhead, was it?'

'Yeah.'

'Shit. I saw him in the street.'

He helped Clive to a sitting position and, because he couldn't think of anything else, made him a cup of tea.

'He took the tapes, then?'

Clive slurped the hot liquid, wincing as it ran over his split lip. 'Yeah.'

'Then we're buggered.' Mike stared around impotently. His gaze fell on a dying pot plant. The leaves had been fried to a crisp khaki. 'D'you think Smale's got Sarah?'

'Maybe it's that Spanish guy she shot in the foot. Angel.'

'He started. That's the same name as the bloke who kidnapped Nicola.'

'Lot of Angels round here.'

'Don't think so,' Mike snorted.

'According to Sarah, this one had a gun.'

'So did . . . the one who kidnapped Nicola.'

Their eyes met.

'Wait, wait, wait,' said Mike. He lit a cigarette and began to pace. 'If it's the same guy, then Angel works for Smale – right?'

'Connected to him, yeah.'

'And to Drake, because Nicola said that Drake gave the orders to kill her.'

'So?'

'So Smale, Angel and Drake are all part of the same mob.' Mike's heart began to race as his suspicions multiplied. A spectre was growing real. Silver specks danced in his vision and his mouth filled with saliva. He swallowed hard to suppress a wave of nausea.

'You all right?' asked Clive.

Mike leaned on the wall to steady himself. When he finally spoke, his voice was parched, hollow. 'I know Drake.'

He slid down the wall and shut his eyes tight. 'Well, my old man did. He was a bank manager. Got injured in a raid. When they found the safe empty, they took out their frustration by shooting him in the leg. Stubborn old git, my dad. Out of hospital in ten days. Got a mention in the company newsletter.'

'When was this?'

'Jesus, years ago. I was only eleven. Remember going to the hospital with Mum. Miles of bloody corridors and that horrible disinfectant smell.'

Clive studied his face. 'Looks like you need a beer.'

Mike nodded and Clive fetched four bottles from the fridge. They opened them in silence.

'My dad was offered compensation but he turned it down. Went to another branch in Wandsworth. Thing is, he was developing some sort of agoraphobia. Had to force himself to go out. Weekends, he never left the house.' Mike slammed down his drink and the froth trickled over his fingers. His knuckles were white. 'Course, you can get all the fucking counselling you want *now*.'

Clive looked at the floor.

'There was a mistake, some lost transaction. Mister bloody Honesty says it's his responsibility. They let him go. No disability pension. Nothing, except for constant pain because his thigh hadn't healed properly. Then it was the dole for four years. Dole and drink.'

'Didn't he take up the compensation thing with anyone else?'

'No. He'd turned it down once, so that was it.'

'Is he all right now?'

'Nope. By the time I got to college, he turned into a right alky. The police were his private minicab service.'

Clive prized the empty bottle from Mike's hand. 'What is this? I mean? Drake? What are you . . . ?'

'Oh yeah. Cut to the chase, right?' snarled Mike.

'I, I didn't mean it like that.'

Mike suckled his fresh beer. 'Didn't see him for years. Not until I came back down from Leicester. It was about eighty-nine. Dad had wasted away.' He raised a finger. 'But he was sober. He'd been through all that AA shit, but he still couldn't get a job. Wanted to get the Star Trek money instead. Some scheme to sell seeds, or something. I helped him do the forms.' Mike took a shuddering breath. 'Interview was on a Tuesday at four. I waited home with Mum. Six o'clock comes and he's not back. By eight she's cracking up. She's crying and hugging me and telling me all these things about him, saying it's been hell since the accident. Saying she'd nearly walked out on him a hundred times.' Mike's voice took on the proud air of the martyr. 'And then the police turned up.'

'Oh, shit,' Clive murmured.

'He'd got the money. Been standing at Borough tube with a bunch of flowers for Mum. Thing is, he still hated crowds. He was probably waiting for the rush hour to die down. I dunno. Anyway, the transport police reckoned he tried to get off a packed tube and got his jacket trapped in the doors. Wasn't much left of him. Just plenty of blood and some fucked-up roses.'

There was a long silence.

'That bank robber fucked up his life,' said Mike, cold now. 'Our lives,' he added, correcting himself.

'Was it Drake?'

'The same gang did another raid in Whitechapel. They got half a million and fled the country. Dad recognised Drake when the police got him to look through the mugshots. How do I know this?'

'What?' Clive asked.

'Say, "How do I know this?"'

'How do you know this?'

The words came out in a torrent. 'Drake, fucking Drake. It

was all he ever fucking talked about. The bastard who crippled him.'

'You sure it's the same man?'

'I don't know,' Mike wailed.

He pressed his hands to his face and held them there as tears spilled out of him. Motes of dust poured through the sunbeams. After a while he took his hands away and began to massage his stubble. He gazed around with bloodshot eyes, scanning the bulky furniture, the deflated beanbags, the dusty television and the dead slab of metal that was the video. With a sudden cry, he scrambled to the machine. He pressed eject and the vital tape spewed out of its dark innards. He held it aloft in triumph.

Clive smiled weakly.

'Come on,' exhorted Mike. 'This is the tape. What's wrong?'

Clive took a long, deep breath. 'It's something I told Sarah. I'm really sorry, Doc. It's all this. It's way worse than at home. Serious, man. I'm going to Estepona. Gonna look for work down there.'

'What?'

'Can't do this shit. You want to be a vigilante, then fine. I can't do it.'

Mike raised his fist to smash it down but held it in the air. He lowered it slowly. 'All right.' he said, calmer now. 'Just one thing. Can you help me look for the little Spanish runt tonight?'

Clive held his gaze. 'OK.'

'This is my wife, Jackie.'

Jackie, in leggings and a spangled top, held out her hand.

'Pleased to meet you,' she said. 'You look hungry.' Without waiting for a reply, she took Sarah's arm, led her straight to the kitchen and began to prepare a salad. After a few moments, Drake came in and beckoned to his wife. They stepped out into the marble hall.

'What's going on?' she asked, wiping her hands.

'She's been asking questions about Smale. Do us a favour. See what she's got to say.'

She gave him a puzzled look.

'I gotta go out. Kevin's in charge of security.' With that, he kissed her on the forehead and went off to change.

*　　*　　*

Jackie and Sarah ate their evening meal at one end of a long wooden dining table; Kevin demolished his food at the other. Sarah was still too stunned to think coherently. It didn't make sense. After being threatened, attacked and dragged into Drake's car, she had been brought to a palatial villa and was now being treated like an honoured guest.

'You look good in that,' said Jackie between mouthfuls.

She was wearing one of Jackie's full-length dresses. Jackie had removed her clothes while she showered, replacing them with a few choices of her own which she had neatly laid out on the bed.

'Thanks,' said Sarah, who'd have been happier in a skirt and T-shirt.

Jackie's chatter was a constant stream which she dipped into only occasionally. Skimming, she learned that they had come out here in the late seventies. Jackie had been a young bride and there'd been some difficulties in starting their new life here. She'd eventually adapted to the lifestyle and now had many friends in the Costa del Sol, their names passing by in a forgotten blur. Her husband had built a business on his savings and had become a person of good standing in the local community. Reading the subtext, she decided John Drake was, in reality, a villain who'd come to southern Spain to escape extradition. The rapid expansion of the resort areas and lax planning laws allowed many such people to prosper unheeded.

Jackie went on to extol the virtues of this earthly paradise. The weather; the shopping, the sports facilities and, of course, the celebrities. Tarby, Cilla, and Brucie were often seen in Marbella and she spoke of Sean Connery as if he were a local god.

'Him out of *The Untouchables*?' Kevin broke in. 'I seen that.'

'No, Kevin,' said Jackie, admonishing. 'He was the proper James Bond.' She smiled knowingly at Sarah.

'What? Before that ponce Dalton?'

She turned to Sarah. 'So, what do you do out here?'

'I'm a rep for a tour company.'

'Really.' Jackie poured her another glass of wine.

Sarah noted that it was vintage St Emilion. Furthermore, the food had been excellent. Ordinarily, she would have praised her hostess, but considering this might be her last meal, she decided against it. Despite herself, she was also impressed by the villa. Jackie had earlier given her the tour, with Kevin loping behind them like a malevolent butler.

The living room was spacious and stylish, a cross between hacienda and Habitat. There were Persian carpets and old sea-chests lining the walls; above them, genuine oil paintings. Some depicted sea-battles, others naval portraits. She placed them as sixteenth century and, if not masterpieces, then still of some value. The nautical theme was taken up by the framed maps and the brass sextants and compasses which were displayed in cases about the room. The kitchen was of the latest design, with granite work surfaces and shining stainless steel appliances. She had begun to reassess her notions about class and taste.

'That must be interesting?' asked Jackie, referring to her job.

'Why am I being kept here?'

Jackie spread her arms wide and her bangles rattled on thin wrists. 'Not that bad, is it?'

'That wasn't the question.'

'You're a guest.'

'Then I'm free to leave.'

'I wouldn't put it like that.'

Kevin perked up and grinned.

'Since you ask,' said Jackie. 'You tell *me* why John wants you here.'

Sarah noted with irritation that she smiled at the end of every sentence.

'Because my sister was murdered and your husband knows something about it.'

'Does he now?'

'Yes. Lana was involved in one of Mr Smale's pornographic films. She was later found dead in the street.'

'What's that got to do with John?'

'You tell me. Is he involved in porn as well?'

She laughed, a sweet tinkling sound. 'John? I don't think so.' She glanced over at the boy. 'Kev. Why don't you go off and play while us girls have a chat?'

He didn't move.

'Kevin,' she said, a little more harshly.

He slunk off. Shortly, from somewhere out in the garden, they heard the sound of yelping dogs being thrown into deep water.

'Now,' said Jackie. 'John's asked me to look after you.' She leaned over and brushed the curls from Sarah's face. 'So, let's be friends, eh?'

It was night in the fairy-lit streets of Fuengirola and Mike and Clive's search for the wounded boy had been fruitless. They had spent a great deal of time and money scouring the main nightclubs and now the bars were beginning to close. Stumbling out of another Dionysian pleasure palace, Mike helped Clive into the cab which they had hired for the evening. The driver didn't even look up from his paper.

'Let's call it a night,' said Mike.

'Well, if you're sure?' answered Clive, who was getting the hang of sarcasm.

Mike looked out at the gaudy neon along the main strip. Sarah was in danger and there wasn't a thing he could do about it. He sparked up a cigarette and glanced at the astronomical sum on the meter.

'Shit. I reckon we're going to have to do a runner.'

Without rustling a page, the driver pressed the automatic locks. As they closed with a clunk, Mike hooded his eyes.

'Oh, so *now* I get a driver that understands English,' he said.

18

Ozorio's yacht was moored at the marina in Marbella. The previous evening, after instructing his associates to search out and maim the British skinhead, Felipe and José had stoked their anger with amphetamines and strong liquor. This led to several large holes being kicked in the cabin walls and the inevitable breaking out of weapons. Gunfire echoed long into the night, causing little actual damage except to a flock of martins, which were forced to change their migratory route.

It was nearly midday when Ozorio surfaced. He staggered on deck, praying for fog to match his mood. No chance. The sun had feathered the clouds to nothing and the temperature was topping thirty-five degrees. Felipe moaned when his mobile bleated. His cranium was a bubbling chemical frenzy that no amount of vitamin C or saline solution had been able to soothe.

'*¡Bastardo inglés! ¡Jodete!*'

It was John Drake.

'Appreciate your position, son. I'm offering a truce.'

'I accept nothing from you. *¡Maricón!*'

'Give it a rest. The boy was over-excited that's all. Don't worry about it.'

'*¡Jodete!* You insult my family.'

'Which is why I want to make amends.' Drake's tone had the cheeriness of a football fan whose team has just hammered the opposition six-nil. 'I want to make a deal,' he added.

'No deals.'

There was a pause.

'Very favourable on your side.'

'*¡Hijo de puta!*'

'How's about this? My connection in Tangiers. Free reign in Torremolinos and a meet with some contacts.' Drake sniffed. 'I know you're having trouble down here, not being a local and that.'

The implication he was a born and bred Andalucian momentarily escaped Felipe.

'*Está loco*,' spat Ozorio. 'Why would you do that?'

'Let's talk about it tonight. You and me.'

The man was either a fool or this was a trap.

'Where are you setting this trap?'

Drake chuckled. 'How's about a spot of dinner in Banús. On me.'

'*¡Jodete!*'

Drake continued undeterred. 'You bring your yacht so's you got protection. One man each, and no one's tooled up.'

'"Tooled up?"'

'No weapons.'

'We will be armed,' warned Ozorio.

'Suits me. Thing is. Puerto Banús? Bit public, innit?'

Ozorio realised that even he couldn't get away with an assassination under such conditions. But then, nor could Drake.

'What about your mad boy?'

'He's been dealt with. Won't see him again.'

There was a pause. '*¿A que hora?*'

'Ten. You ever had curry? There's a t'riffic Indian down there.'

Drake scratched his belly and looked up at Sarah's bedroom. The curtains were still drawn. He called Ramón and then his old friend, Irish Sam Calhoun.

'What's up, Jock? You sound a bit down.'

Sam's voice was thick with mucus. 'Had a wee problem the other night.'

'Sorted?'

'I lost my syrup. And my boat.'

'Ain't like you, Sam.'

The Scotsman sighed. 'Jesus fuck, John. Some fucken tourist saw us when I done that bit of bizzo the other night.'

Drake raised his eyebrows.

'I had a word with him, only the cunt didnae leave. He walks into my place, happy as Larry.'

'Careless.'

Sam sneezed. 'I has him away on the boat only he pulls a stroke. Had to swim about five fucken miles. Been in my cot the last couple of days 'cos of all the shite they put in the water.'

'I'll have a word with the local filth. Stop 'em sniffing around.'

Sam grunted. Loose ends.

'Anyways,' continued Drake, brightly, 'remember that aggro up the Rock?'

'Aye.'

'You got any of that old Semtex lying about?'

'Be glad to get rid of it.'

'Pukka. I'll be sending Ramón out your way. And my neph-ew.'

'Kev's here, then?'

'Yeah.' Drake's tone became excited. 'He was on telly the other day.'

John rang off and smiled to himself. It was all falling into place. He went inside and called up from the hall. 'Kevin!'

The boy came to the balustrade.

'What you doing up there?'

'Nuffin'.'

Kevin had been peering at Sarah's sleeping form through the keyhole in the hope that she'd roll over and be all naked.

'Gonna have some fun later,' said his uncle. 'You like fire-works?'

The boy nodded like an excited puppy.

Sunlight hammered the tarmac between the sturdy coaches at the bus station at Fuengirola. Clive had a full rucksack and was about to board. On Mike's insistence, he was to take the tape and keep hold of it until either one of them were able to reach him. In the meantime, Mike was going to continue the search for the injured boy on his own.

'This is it, then,' said Mike.

Clive wedged his crutch under one arm and gave him a hearty handshake. 'Nice knowing you, guy.'

'That's encouraging.'

Clive's gaze fell on a concrete stanchion over to his left. Amidst a gathering of backpackers, a Spaniard with a bandaged foot was whispering to a pair of lanky Antipodeans who were fishing out crumpled notes.

'Don't look now,' said Clive.

Mike wheeled round.

'But that's him.'

Angel didn't see them. He was too busy explaining that five thousand pesetas was only worth a minute number of Australian dollars.

Mike broke into a broad grin. 'Right.'

Clive placed his crutch on to the footplate and swung on to the step. 'Guess I'll see you around then, Doc.'

Mike didn't answer. He was already striding across the forecourt.

Sarah entered Drake's study and peered at the scene on the table top.

'The Armada, right?'

'Yeah,' said Drake, pleasantly surprised. 'Good to meet another historian.'

'I thought I was history,' she deadpanned.

Drake laughed. 'Very good. Yeah. Big hobby of mine, as it goes. That's my ancestor up there.' He waved a hand at a portrait of Admiral Sir Francis Drake which took pride of place on the wall.

Sarah gazed at the painting, doubting the veracity of his statement.

'The explorer and great naval commander,' added Drake.

'Or mass-murderer. Depending on how you look at it.'

'History's written by the winners, love.'

'Unfortunately.'

He steered her to the low sofa and poured out fresh coffees for them both. 'Jacks tells me this is about your sister,' he said, as if asking a question of a potential employee.

'That's right.'

'What you got?'

'You're the one that brought me here. I'm not saying anyth—'

Drake slapped her hard across the face, and the force of

the blow knocked her horizontal. He lit a cigarette while she recovered.

'I told you not to fuck me about. It ain't worth it.'

She glared at him. 'You bastard.'

He raised his hand again. Sarah tried to grab his arm but he seized her by the throat and threw her down once more. Giving no pause, he dragged her up by one arm and punched her in the stomach. Sarah doubled over, gasping for breath.

'If I have to, I'll do damage. Tell us again what you told Jacks last night.'

Sarah coughed and retched and shrank away. Her thoughts raced as she recovered from the blow. Telling him what he already knows won't be giving anything away. And it might buy me a little time. She sat up on the sofa.

'My sister Lana was killed in Fuengirola. It had something to do with a porn film. They said it was heroin, but that was a lie.'

Drake remained impassive. 'What about them tapes, then?'

'What tapes?'

His right hand balled itself into a fist.

Seeing it, she cringed. 'Look, I really don't know anything. I was lucky to get out of Smale's villa alive.'

'So was he, from what I heard.'

'My sister's bracelet was in the bedroom up there.'

'And?'

'And I think she was murdered. No, scratch that, I know she was killed.'

Drake's face became a mask of stone. He had sunk away from her, back into a place of torment. An arena where morality and reality pummeled one another, enmeshed in a struggle from which there was no victor. The fight had ceased many years ago but still there were the memories. Many memories. When it came, his voice was icy. 'What would you do if you found out who killed her?'

'I'd have them arrested.'

'Failing that?'

She thought hard. 'I don't know.'

Smoothing his moustache between thumb and index finger, he went to his desk and pulled out a snub-nosed revolver. Sarah recoiled as he thrust it at her. Drake turned it around by the barrel and held it towards her. 'Take it.'

Hesitantly, she took the gun and rested it beside her.

'I'll tell you this for nothing,' he said, his voice a low purr. 'Not much escapes me round here. The girl?' He paused for effect. 'Let's say I done it. Say I killed her. So go on. You got the shooter. Use it.'

Sarah gazed at the hard metal; that familiar object from countless films and television shows, the cultural icon. Bang, bang you're dead. She'd been too wired to think properly when she took Angel's weapon. At the villa, she had acted purely out of terror. Firing at the boy had been an act of desperation, not a calculated attempt to kill. But this? Here and now in the smooth light of Drake's study? Who is this man? Does he actually want me to end his life?

'Come on love. I ain't got all day.' Drake's implication was that the task was of no more importance to him than taking out the rubbish.

She curled her right hand around the butt of the gun and slipped her index finger to the trigger.

'OK. I'm leaving. Back off.'

She stood up, but Drake moved in front of her.

'You'll have to do better than that.'

Anger and pain coursed through her. She lifted the weapon and pointed it at his stomach. 'Did you murder Lana?' she asked.

He smiled facetiously. She raised the gun with shaking hands and the world suddenly stopped. There was no sound or movement, only focus. Focus on the twist of his smile. On the long white moustache, the darkness of his irises, his tanned flesh, his eyes, his lips. His hand.

Before she could react, he snatched the gun from her. He pulled the trigger without hesitation. Sarah shut her eyes, expecting to be blown into infinity. There was a tiny click and then silence. Drake locked the gun away and strode off as Sarah curled into a quivering foetal ball on the couch.

It wasn't hard to follow Angel as he hobbled around selling his wares. The armed *guardia civil* by the ticket booth either hadn't, or didn't want to notice his transactions. The boy then sloped off to a bar where he ordered a large gin-lemon. Mike found a bar across the street and watched as Angel downed two drinks. Afterwards, he rose and limped off into the warren of streets behind the bus station. He followed at a discreet distance until they came to a series of shabby apartment buildings near a row of shops. Angel entered via an iron-gated door and disappeared into the gloom. Mike waited a moment, then stepped inside.

Throbbing heavy metal music led him to a panelled door at the end of a gloomy corridor on the first floor. Deciding that he needed the element of surprise, he crept outside again. The block was balconied along the first floor with Angel's apartment directly above him. Its windows were open.

A sweet smell of frying onions wafted out from another flat. Other than that, all was quiet for the *siesta*. A dusty Citroën van was parked by the shop next door with a ladder lashed to its roof. Mike realised that if he climbed on top of the van, he could reach the balcony.

He scrambled up and over the balustrade and crept along, taking care to avoid the bright vases of geraniums. He came to Angel's window, where the music was loudest. A television flickered inside. On the screen, three oiled, naked women were writhing and spearing one another with dildos. Somehow Angel's viewing choices didn't surprise him. He counted silently to three and dived into the room.

The boy let out a strangled cry and stopped masturbating. Having landed on Angel's penis, Mike righted himself and instinctively gripped his own groin in sympathy. Angel curled up, his injured member rapidly detumescing. Mike grabbed the sheet, bundled Angel up in it and threw him to the floor. He kicked him hard in the ribs, then stopped and strained to listen for other sounds in the flat.

Nothing. Good, no brother. What now? Tie him up? Find some rope. He went to a chest of drawers and scrabbled around inside. Pants! Angel moaned, so Mike trod on his injured foot. Wait. Think. Nicola said there were guns here. They weren't hard to find. Ramón had them mounted on his bedroom wall like trophies. He took an automatic pistol and lifted the mattress. The cartridges were underneath in boxes on the floor. He stepped back into the hallway at the exact moment Angel's hand touched the phone.

'No, we don't want pizza,' said Mike, levelling the gun at his chest.

The boy raised his hands and the sheet puddled around his ankles.

'You do speak English, don't you?'

'No,' said Angel, understanding perfectly.

'Your name's Angel, right?'

'*Sí.*'

'Got a message from Nicola.' He cracked him across the face with the butt of the pistol. Angel's body made a satisfying slap as bare flesh hit the floor. He looked up. A long drool of blood and spittle spooled from his mouth.

'Sorry,' said Mike. 'You all right?'

Angel spat on the floor.

He held the pistol closer. 'Drake's your boss, isn't he?'

'*Sí.*'

'And he's got Sarah, right? The beautiful sulky girl with the frizzy hair?'

'*¡Puta!*'

'No – Sarah.'

The boy nodded.

'I want you to take me to Drake. Do you drive?'

Angel held up his mummified foot.

'We'll work round that. You got a car?'

Angel shook his head 'Ramón has the Jeep.'

'What about a bike?'

'I have Vespa.'

'Good,' said Mike, relieved. 'For a moment there I thought we were going to have to do something illegal, like stealing a car.'

19

The El Rey de los Perros nestled into Puerto Banús under an ultra-marine sky. Suspecting treachery, Ozorio had ordered several of his men to position themselves around the harbour. Already in place, they milled around, examining the garish paintings in the galleries and tutting at the prices in the restaurants. A light breeze ushered away the last of the day's heat as Felipe and José stepped on to the quay. Privately disgusted by Drake's choice of meal, Ozorio explained to his friend that a bloated stomach and swamp-like wind was a small price to pay for this capitulation.

Hidden behind a boathouse, Drake, Ramón and Kevin watched as Ozorio's yacht hove into view. John gave out instructions and received a gleeful double thumbs-up from Kevin. He then strolled across to Valli's bar, where Irish Sam was waiting for him.

'The fuck is that?' he blurted out. Sam was wearing what appeared to be a dead squirrel on his head.

'Fucken ponces,' said Sam. 'I asked for the sandy brown.'

They ordered lagers.

'Right,' began Drake. 'Here's the deal. I've been getting grief off these bastards. I need you with me for the meet with Ozorio. Some of his team's here already.'

'Want me to deal with it?'

Drake fanned a hand. 'Nah. I've had a word with Mister Mayor and he's upped the police presence.' He motioned at two men who were stood at the bar. They wore chain-store suits, their jackets bulging with cumbersome walkie-talkies. 'Spot the filth,' he added. 'Ten points.'

Sam's frown made deep tramlines on his forehead. 'Police protection? You goin' soft in the heed?'

'I'm a respected citizen,' replied John through hooded eyes. 'Anyways, I got a little something planned. You sort it out with the boys?'

Sam nodded. 'He's a card, that Kevin. So what's afoot?'

'You like surprises, don'tcha?'

'Aye.'

'Well, you'll love this.'

The boys made for the end of the harbour with Kevin shouldering a heavy rucksack. Ramón walked faster, urging him on. 'Hey come on. Maricón,' he chided.

'Got to be careful with this stuff.'

'Vale, vale. Let's go. *Vamos.*'

They sloped past the last of the yachts, arriving at a stone turret at the far end. They slipped over the harbour wall and landed on wet sand. Ramón had earlier scouted out the area and had decided that their best approach would be by water. To that end, he had hired a small dinghy. He unveiled it and tore aside the tarpaulin, then pushed the craft into the sea and jumped in. Kevin strode into the water, eased down his pack and clambered aboard. Ramón took up the paddles and manoeuvred around the rocks which marked the neck of the harbour. They sculled alongside the first of the luxury yachts and bumped into its hull.

'Go easy, you prat,' whispered Kevin, loudly.

'*Sin problema.* I very good with explosives.'

'What? Matches?'

'No. I bomb a *discoteca* last week.'

'Not with Semtex,' snorted Kevin, gripping the precious cargo.

'With much *gasolina.* I get plenty vouchers. Free CD. Def Leppard.'

Kevin sneered. 'Which boat is it, then?'

'Third one from here. I count from other side.'

'What if it's guarded?'

Ramón put aside the paddles and removed a shining revolver from the inside pocket of his jacket. Kevin's eyes lit up. 'Let's have a look?'

'No.'

'Go on. Gi's it,' he said, thrusting out an arm which caused the dinghy to lurch wildly.

'*Mira. Mira.* British *idiota*.'

'Gi's a sodding look, then.'

'*Mañana*.'

'You want a smack?'

They windmilled their arms at one another, only coming to their senses when a paddle slid into the water. They came alongside the third boat and threw a rope over the outside rail. Ramón tied it fast and quickly shimmied up on deck. Passing the rope to Kevin, the boy tied it to the rucksack. Once the explosives were aboard, Kevin scrambled topside, denting the hull with his steel toecaps.

At the behest of Drake and Sam, both competitive eaters, Felipe and José had been forced to sweat through a particularly toxic Chicken Vindaloo. Each spoonful caused a lava flow in Felipe's gullet as he cursed the protocol which dictated that they eat before doing business.

Sam flashed a savage grin at the squirming Spaniards, then snapped a popadum into shards and ladled it with chutney. John, at his side, smirked as he gulped back his lager. This was to be his night of glory. Recent events had contrived to test him to his limits and yet he had come through unscathed. He always came through. He felt a shiver of immense power coursing through him, a mixture of confidence and the result of a vast line of cocaine he'd just snorted in the toilets.

Ozorio slid a hunk of Nan bread over his plate and disengaged his fork.

'You enjoy that, then?' Drake asked.

'I would have preferred something stronger,' replied Ozorio, tempting fate.

José took his master's signal and dropped his serviette to mask his unfinished meal.

'It is time to deal, yes?' said Ozorio.

Drake and Sam exchanged glances.

'What about pudding?' asked Sam, disingenuously.

Drake snapped his fingers and a waiter appeared. 'Dessert menu,' he barked.

The Brits made great show of examining the choices. Drake then snapped the menu shut and waved the waiter away.

'*Bueno*,' said Ozorio. 'Now we begin. First, you say you make compromise. I say no. I will tell you what we demand. We take all your business in Fuengirola and in Torremolinos. *Y también*, all along the coast. If you want to sell *chocolate*, then you give us half of all your profits. You will inform your suppliers that *Los Perros de la muerte* are now the main customers.'

Drake turned to Sam. 'Well, that's his hand. What d'you reckon?'

Ozorio's shining forehead reddened. He wanted to dab at it but to lift the napkin would be to admit defeat. Instead, he placed an elbow on the table and jabbed a finger at Drake. 'You have no choice. Your organisation is small. Your power diminishes by the day.'

'Listen, boy. I been here a lot longer than you. I set things up so they run nice and smooth. Anyone who butts in gets a smack. That means you, the Russkies or any other firm.'

'The old must surrender to the new.'

'Yeah, and you'll have this place a smack-head's paradise before we know it. Crack. Guns, aids, the lot.' A solitary vein began to throb on Drake's temple. 'You toe-rags come down here and think you can fucking waltz it. I done years of graft before your lot showed up.'

'Is called progress,' said Ozorio releasing his best snarl.

Drake steepled his fingers against his nostrils, trying simultaneously to assume a professorial air and sniff back a searing chemical trickle. 'Let's look at this in the historical context. Know much about the sixteenth century?'

Ozorio shrugged.

'We was maritime nations, Spain and England, right? Only your lot decided to invade us. Our Queen sends Francis Drake to put the kibosh on it. Now, he's got a bunch of galleons and pinnaces and he sets sail out of Plymouth.'

Ozorio and José assumed the posture of schoolboys faced with dull facts and superior knowledge.

'. . . Frankie adds two men of war to the fleet. Turns out he was preparing for a scrape long before he got the call.'

Sam smiled encouragingly.

'They captures a Spanish boat at Finisterre and susses out Cádiz harbour's full of shipping. Know Cádiz do you, Ozorio?'

'Of course, but . . . ?'

Drake held up a hand. 'Three days later, they sails up to the harbour.'

Ozorio shot a bored glance at José. Drake turned to the lieutenant. 'Oy. You listening, son? You heard of Sir Francis Drake?'

'*Sí*,' muttered José.

Drake's litany was well polished. 'Circumnavigated the world, went round the Cape of Good Horn. Brilliant tactician, sailor and naval commander.'

'He killed many people in our colonies,' retorted José, remembering that his version of history differed from the one he was hearing.

John lit a fresh cigarette. 'Least you got an opinion.'

José was secretly pleased at the compliment.

'Even if it's the wrong one,' added Drake, deflating him. 'Sir Francis always released his prisoners. Now, your Spanish, they used to chop off a swordsman's hand and cut his heart out. No bleedin' manners.'

José racked through dusty classroom facts for contradictory information.

'So,' continued Drake, 'he arrives in Cádiz and the place is chocker. 'Bout sixty ships.' He numbered them on his fingers. 'A Genoese angosy; a carrack belonging to the Marqués de Santa Cruz; twenty confiscated Dutch ships—'

Ozorio tapped a solitary finger on the table. It was ignored.

'Drake sees his chance, tells the other poxy British captains to fuck off and goes in like a bleedin' wolf in a henhouse. Bosh!' Drake smashed his fist on the table and rattled the cutlery. 'He sinks the big galleon. Bosh! The Spanish leg it. By nightfall the whole British fleet's pillaged your ships.' He gave a shark-grin. 'Destroyed ten thousand tons of shipping.'

'What is your point?' asked Ozorio, plainly fed up.

'Next day, the Duke of Medina Sidonia sends reinforcements. Too bloody late. Drake's out of range. He pulls out the harbour, only the wind's dropped. Stays another night. What do your bunch do?'

'You tell me.'

'You set light to your ships.' He turned to Sam. 'It's called a fireship. You ram your enemy with one of your own burning boats. Know what Drake said? He goes, "They're doing the job for me."'

The Brits burst into explosive laughter.

'I had enough,' said Ozorio.

Drake eyed him like a captive pupil. 'Early the next morning, he brung our fleet out with no damage to *any* of the British ships.' He leaned forward. 'He took your lot out, mate. They called it "Singeing the king of Spain's beard."'

Ozorio stood up. '*¡Imbécil!* You waste my time with these stories. José, *venga*. We go now.'

Drake pulled him back to his seat. 'It's a lesson in tactics. Call it a warning, if you like.'

'What warning?'

Drake glanced at his Rolex. 'Take a butchers out the window.'

Steven Aldridge was enjoying his lottery winnings of £11,406,107. As he'd imagined, the vast increase in his personal portfolio hadn't changed him at all. It had, however, changed his friends and family into mercenary leeches – so he promptly cut them out of his life without a penny and not one iota of regret. His wife Linda was upset. She reasoned that a share was due to her and the kids, if only because their nine-year-old son Darren had selected the winning numbers. This held little sway with Steve, who asserted that a wife and two brats were a hindrance to his finer pursuits. He walked out on them and his job in the electronics firm in Loughborough and moved to a London hotel. All attempts at contact were met with silence. Steve was far too busy, what with the spending sprees, the drinking bouts and the rental of expensive whores. After a month of this, he decided he needed a change. A holiday. He'd recently begun a relationship with Pam from Altringham whose oral talents were legendary around Euston. Negotiations with her pimp soon released her from her obligations and he set about her Higginsian re-education with lavish gifts.

They spent a month or two exploring the Caribbean and Florida before he announced his intention to buy a fifty-foot luxury yacht. They paid cash, took ownership in Miami, hired a crew and set sail. Two days off the Keys, Steve asserted that the international jet set were begging for his presence. They dropped in on Cannes and St Tropez before settling on Puerto Banús. By now, Pam had become an irritant. He found her childlike insistence on fresh jewellery rather wearing and she, in return, thought him a callous oaf; an oaf who might rescind her meal ticket at any opportunity. They had already been excluded from the better on-board parties and soon discovered they had little in common with the wealthy, except for money and a perma-tan. Unwilling to mix with the *hoi polloi* in Torremolinos, they spent their days on board their floating gaol. On this particular evening, they had rowed over a call which Pam had made to a 'friend'. They had then proceeded to drink themselves into oblivion in separate cabins. The explosion tore the life out of them in less time than it takes to sign a cheque.

As the ball of flame sent him flying into the water, Kevin realised that Ramón's knowledge of explosives was scratchy at best. While he doggy paddled to the nearest jetty, the Spaniard's organs spattered the harbour in delicate crimson strokes.

Inside the restaurant, windows shattered and a blast of heat seared across the room. Diners scattered; waiters leaped to the ground; Sam's new wig flew from his pate and landed in a trough of Massala. They were the only ones to remain seated as the carnage settled. Once his ears had stopped ringing, Drake clapped his hands together and rubbed them in satisfaction.

'Like I said.' He poked a chubby digit at Ozorio's chest. 'A warning. Looks like you wanna get another boat.'

Ozorio looked out at the orange cloud, the screaming hordes and the plume of thick black smoke. He took a sip of lager, rose from the table and threw down a few coins.

'*Señor* Drake. That was not my yacht.'

20

The aged Vespa ground into every pothole as they climbed the
dirt track to Drake's villa. Mike rode pillion, clinging on tightly
with the revolver pressed into the boy's back. Reaching the solid
iron gates, Angel killed the flatulent engine. The whispering of
cicadas filled the darkness. There was a small barred porthole
set in the wall through which they could see the hacienda. The
colonnaded porch was festooned with hanging baskets of geraniums and illuminated by lanterns. Around them, myriad insects
swam lazily in the soupy air. Noting the security cameras on the
gateposts, Mike crouched on his haunches and tried to figure out
a way of getting inside. Folding fast under questioning, Angel
had explained about the guard dogs. Subsequently, Mike had
forced the boy to purchase four hunks of brisket which were
now soaking through their wrappings in his jacket. There was
an intercom set into the wall at head height.

'Angel. Buzz them and tell them you're coming in.'

The boy limped to the gate as Mike pulled the bike off the path.
Angel buzzed once, then again. Turning to Mike, he spread his
arms in a gesture of despair. Mike pointed the gun at the console.
Angel pressed once more and it rustled into life. Above them, a
red light on the security camera blinked on.

'*Es Angel, Señora* Drake.'

There was a click and a smaller door set inside the main gate
sprang open. Without thinking, Mike ran forwards and pushed
Angel through the gap. They sprawled together on the gravel
driveway. Mike rolled aside and raked his gun in a wide arc,
taking in the lawn and the fat pineapple palms which lined the
drive. The porch was a short dash away. He rose on the balls

of his feet and prepared to run. Suddenly, he was aware of a low drumming coming from the side of the house. The surly Dobermans appeared and bounded towards them at full stretch. As he fumbled in his jacket, he wondered why they hadn't tied up the dogs. Perhaps they mistrusted Angel as much as he did? He wrenched the bloody packet free and tossed the steaks into the path of the approaching hounds. Charlotte, Emily and Anne stopped in their tracks. They sniffed at the air, then lowered their snouts and set to devouring the meat.

What now? thought Mike as the adrenalin pumped through him. Better deal with the boy first. Cut down the opposition. He rapped Angel on the back of the head with the butt of the gun. Angel moaned, swore and clutched his head. Annoyed, he hit him again. Angel gnashed his teeth but remained steadfastly awake. The boy flapped his arms at him and Mike's next blow glanced off the boy's shoulder. He gave in and trod hard on Angel's damaged foot. The boy swooned to the grass verge, unconscious. He pulled him off the path, dumped him under a bush and sprinted to the back of the house. Paws on gravel. One of the Dobermans had taken pursuit. He leaped on to the terrace, tore off his jacket and threw it at the snarling dog. Charlotte shredded it as efficiently as a government official in a fraud scandal. Bending double to catch his breath, he peered through the half-open patio doors. The room appeared to be empty. He stepped inside and positioned himself behind the muslin curtains. A cool blast of air-conditioning curdled the sweat on his back.

To his right, there was a hallway and a flight of marble stairs curving upwards; to his left, a pair of double doors. He parted the curtains and stepped inside. Naval memorabilia in cases, oil paintings on the walls, low leather sofas, two women staring at him in surprise. One was sassy, deeply tanned and just the right side of middle age. The other was Sarah.

'Hi,' said Mike.

'Hello,' said the women.

'And you are . . . ?' said Jackie, rising to meet him with a drink in her hand.

'That's Mike,' slurred Sarah.

She was wearing a dress that seemed a little on the tarty side.

Her hair, piled on her head, made an amber halo in the soft light. She seemed bemused. He wondered if she'd been drugged.

'I thought you were in trouble,' he said, feeling a little foolish now.

Jackie moved towards him.

'If you could just stop there?' He waved the gun.

She smiled at him. It was a nice smile, one which reminded him of travel agents and eager hotel staff.

'Well,' said Sarah. 'Shall we go then?'

'You OK?'

'Her husband nearly killed me, but apart from that – fine.' She bent to tie up her espadrilles.

'D'you want to stay for a drink?' Jackie asked.

'Another time perhaps. Nice place, by the way.'

'I designed it. The clutter's John's.' She waved a bangled arm at a case full of ornaments.

Sarah came and stood beside him.

'Mrs Drake, is it?' he enquired of Jackie.

'Call me Jackie.'

'D'you mind calling the dogs off? Don't want to get torn apart on our way out.'

She pressed a coquettish finger to her lips. 'Sorry. Forgot about them.'

Mike swung the pistol at the front door. 'Please.'

She tottered in front of them, pausing as she reached the hall. 'Sure you won't stay?'

'No thanks,' said Mike, privately cursing his middle-class upbringing which was undermining his lone gunman act.

'John'll be home in a minute.'

He was stumped for a reply. On the one hand, he wanted to whisk Sarah back into safety and into his arms; on the other, he almost relished the prospect of facing his adversary. The decision was made for him when John Drake burst through the front door with a bedraggled Kevin at his side.

'The fuck are you?' he spat.

'A man with a gun,' said Mike, sweeping the pistol towards them.

Under Mike's supervision, Kevin brought out some kitchen

chairs and bound his uncle with gardening twine. Drake took this in his stride and glared at Mike the whole time. Sarah restrained Kevin and Jackie. Once she was certain all three were secured, she slapped Drake hard across the face.

'That's for scaring the shit out of me, you bastard.'

Drake offered no reply. Mike poked the gun in Kevin's shoulder. 'You beat up my mate, didn't you?'

'Piss off.'

'Language, Kevin,' hissed John with an eye on his wife.

Mike used a curtain-tie to gag Kevin. He had never liked skinheads, not even scale model ones.

'He knows about Lana,' said Sarah, who had sobered up fast.

'Got a few questions to ask him myself, actually.'

Mike stared at his nemesis. The man was old and fat, quite unlike the rangy youth his father had described to him in his alcoholic rants. Despite this, Mike sensed that this was someone you didn't reckon with unless you knew what you were doing. Furthermore, it was only the gun which elevated him to Drake's division. He cocked the trigger. 'John Drake?'

'Who wants to know?'

'I do. Does the name Trent mean anything to you?'

'Should it?'

'Probably not. Why don't you think back to 1974?'

'Bollocks to you.'

He held the gun closer. 'Barclays bank in Beckenham.'

'What about it?'

'You robbed it with a shotgun.'

'Not me, son.'

He pressed the barrel into Drake's forehead.

'If this is a contract, then get on with it,' warned Drake. 'Who you from? The Petersons?'

'Mike,' interjected Sarah. 'What's this all about?'

'Old wounds,' he replied, pulling the gun back from Drake's head. It left a red, indented circle.

She was aghast now. 'What do you mean? Are you some kind of hit man?'

He was about to deny it when they heard a buzzing in the air. Growing, it was as if a swarm of angry hornets were about to invade the house and envelop them all. The glass doors exploded and the avenging Angel burst through on his Vespa. He was screaming at the top of his voice and his ballooning foot rested on the handlebars like a battering ram. A thousand shards of glass sprayed them all. The moped bounced over the sill, skidded across the shiny floor, spun a full circle and scattered them like skittles.

Jackie was first to break free. She scampered across the floor, grabbed the gun and centred it on Mike and Sarah. They slowly raised their hands. A dazed Angel recovered next. Using a penknife, he freed Kevin and his employer. Drake rubbed his wrists, took the gun off his wife and gave her a gentle peck on the cheek. 'Cheers, love,' he said.

Jackie went to the bar and poured herself a stiff shot of vodka. Following her lead, Kevin grabbed a beer and threw one to his uncle.

'Right then,' said Drake.

He opened the debate by punching Mike full in the face. His nose spurted blood and his eyes watered with the pain.

'I don't stand for this. You come into my gaff and hassle my family. What's your game?'

Mike probed his nose gingerly. It was already beginning to swell. 'I'm not a hit man,' he mumbled.

'Never!' replied Drake with sneering sarcasm. 'What's this about Beckenham?'

'You shot my dad in a bank raid,' moaned Mike, realising the hopelessness of his situation. Drake jabbed him hard under the ribs. Winded, Mike doubled over. Drake followed up with another punch to the gut, then used the back of his hand to swipe him across the face. One of his rings gouged a trench in Mike's cheek. Sarah took a step forwards. Drake swung the gun on her.

'You know I'll use this. You sit down like a good girl.'

She sat.

Mike was on all fours now, his face webbed with trickles of blood. Wheezing, he clambered to his feet.

Drake eased out a crumpled pack of Royal Crowns. 'Where was this again?'

'Beckenham branch of Barclays. There was nothing in the

safe, so you took it out on the manager. My dad. You shot him in the thigh.'

Drake flung a weary look at Jackie. 'You work in a bank, you take the risks.'

'You sick fucker,' shouted Mike, no longer caring about his fate. 'How can you destroy a man's life like that? For no reason?'

Drake punched him in the kidneys and Mike slumped to the floor once more. Drake staggered backwards, his face twisting into a grimace of pain. A vein began to drum excitedly on his temple. He shook uncontrollably and went pale.

'John? John love?' Jackie barked in concern.

Waving her away, he propped the gun on the back of the sofa and clutched at his groin. He bit his lower lip until it bled. Massaging his lower stomach with both hands, he took deep breaths as the pain subsided. 'You wanna sob story?' he snarled. There were flecks of blood and spittle in his goatee. 'I'll give you a fucking sob story.'

He plucked the gun from the seat and, holding the barrel down, paced around Mike.

'My younger brother, Barry. Sixteen he was. Always on at me to take him out on the job so I lets him come in on a B&E. Offices in Stepney.'

Jackie wasn't smiling now.

'Fuck-all there,' he continued. 'We're about to leg it when the filth shows up. Baz only panics, don't he? Bolts up the stairs and falls out a bleedin' window.' Drake's face went a violent crimson. 'Broke his effing neck. Dead on impact. That good enough for ya?'

'That was an accident,' barked Mike.

'So?'

'Shooting my father wasn't.'

Drake's voice was thunder. 'Who d'you think you are, cunt? Come up here with this load of old bollocks? Shit happens. Live with it.'

Mike's heart beat a fast tattoo inside his chest. This was a canvas of pure malice. There was no peace in those shrivelled eyes, no forgiveness in the twisted mouth. He did not doubt for one moment that Drake was capable of killing him there and then.

The man lumbered around, every muscle pinched tight in pain. He thrust out an arm to grip a chair, his forearm vibrating with tension. Jackie put her arms around his shoulders. 'You'd better lie down, love.'

He nodded imperceptibly. 'Kevin. Cellar key's on the door by the kitchen. You and Angel take 'em down there. I gotta rest.'

The boys took hold of their captives.

Jackie guided her husband towards the staircase. He paused by the marble balustrade. 'Angel? By the way. Well done, boy.'

The young Spaniard bowed slightly. '*Gracias, Señor* Drake.'

He took a step up. 'Angel?'

'*¿Señor?*'

'I got good and bad news for you.'

Angel assumed a quizzical expression.

'Good news is, you're promoted. You're working for me full-time. You're on sixty thousand potatoes a week, starting tomorrow.'

Angel beamed. This was a significant improvement in his lifestyle. Now he'd be able to afford clothes, a car, women. They would flock to him like seagulls to a fish. No, not a fish. Never a fish. Never again. He couldn't wait to tell Ramón and the family.

'Bad news is,' continued Drake, 'Your brother's snuffed it.'

Angel took it out on Mike and Sarah, prodding and poking them with the pistol as Kevin followed them down into the brick cellar.

'I shoot you, *bastardo inglés* in the head,' he spat.

Mike was less than impressed. 'If you're not too busy playing with yourself.'

'I take you to the mountains and leave you to be eaten by vultures.'

'Buzzards,' corrected Sarah.

'*Que?*'

'It's buzzards, not vultures, in Spain.' She couldn't comprehend why she was being so facetious. Perhaps it was the relief after the torrent of rage upstairs.

'You should see his porn collection,' added Mike. 'Makes Guccioni look like an amateur.'

As they reached the floor, Kevin decided he'd had enough. He head-butted Mike to the floor and began kicking him ferociously. Sarah howled, then leaped on the skinhead's back and tore at him with her nails. Crimson welts appeared on his skin but Kevin shook her aside as easily as throwing off a coat. She fell against a pillar then jumped up and ploughed in once more. Angel waved the gun this way and that, screaming obscenities. He couldn't get a bead on either of them. To shoot at random might jeopardise his new position by wiping out the boss's nephew. As quickly as he had started, Kevin stopped kicking.

'Gi's the shooter.'

Angel cradled it. '*¡Jodete!* No, I am security now. I keep.'

'It's my turn.'

'*Señor* Drake says me. I save his life.'

Kevin pouted, struggling with the notion of beating the crap out of Angel as well. Sarah took the opportunity to aim a kick at him. Kevin grabbed her foot and sent her flying. She folded on to the dirt floor. Satisfied, he gave them an uneven grin and stomped off with Angel hobbling behind.

They had a few seconds to scan the vaulted space before the lights went out. Arches. A pile of discarded furniture. Empty side-rooms intended for use as a wine cellar.

Then, pitch blackness.

Sarah crawled to him. 'Mike? Are you all right?'

''Course not. It bloody hurts. And this is the second time I've been locked in a cellar.'

'We're totally fucked, aren't we?'

He felt the touch of her hand.

'You know that saying about religion being the province of the weak and the damaged?'

'Mm.'

'I think it's time we pretended that the little baby Jesus is going to save us.'

He felt her warmth as she drew close. They cradled one another and tried not to weep. After a while, she reached out a hand and accidentally poked him in the eye. Mike slid down and rested his head in her lap.

'We're not giving up now,' she said defiantly, then softened. 'I never knew all that stuff about your dad.'

'Never got the chance to tell you. When Nicola mentioned Drake's name, I just knew I had to stay.'

'I thought you came to rescue me,' she said, a little hurt.

'That as well.'

He nuzzled against her stomach and she stroked his hair.

'Now who's brave and foolish?' she said.

'Both of us.' He sat up and searched out her mouth, the darkness bridging the chasm between kissing and not-kissing. There was no hesitation, no holding back for fear of rejection, only need and urgency. Her lips were salty and responded quickly. They moved around and over his own in a soft, undulating rhythm. He tasted her with the tip of his tongue, pressing deeper as they locked mouths. His hands went to her face and cradled it. She covered his hands with hers. Realising she had automatically closed her eyes, she opened them and still saw nothing. A calm overtook them as they meshed together and felt their bodies falling away, crumbling like dust. Soon, there was nothing of them left but the kiss.

It didn't last. The fear saw to that.

21

The explosion at Puerto Banús caused havoc in the harbour. The plain-clothed police attempted to round up Ozorio's men, who refused to give up without a fight. Skirmishes broke out, knives were drawn and blood was spilled amidst the panic-stricken hordes. When the emergency services arrived, they found their access blocked by the stream of cars leaving the scene. Their stubborn refusal to move caused the fire to spread unchecked and consequently, six more luxury yachts were gutted. Saudi Arabians were whisked away by their armed bodyguards and other yacht owners ran through the streets with priceless ornaments and paintings. The British contingent demonstrated their solidarity by heading for the airport en masse. Mr Connery was away filming in Los Angeles and was unaware of the events near his home.

The Spanish press and television channels started searching for a scapegoat. The first rumour came from an *El Pais* reporter who intimated that the Basque Separatist Movement had been involved. Shortly afterwards, the identity of the deceased lottery winner came to light. An acquaintance of Mr Aldridge's quickly verified that he had no political or terrorist connections. Or any connections to speak of. A second theory bloomed from this unlikely flower. It was posited that a disenchanted member of the lucky winner's family had ordered a contract killing. This was rubbished by the police as they had enough on their plate with all the regular contract killings in the area. The harbour was then cordoned off and forensic experts moved in. The news made all the front pages, except for the Spanish edition of the *Sun*, which had managed to persuade the TV anchor-woman from the incident at Fuengirola to appear top-less.

Ramón's remains were never identified.

The story continued to garner headlines until the police reports were completed. The presence of Semtex made it simpler to pin the whole thing on the IRA and this seemed to pacify all parties concerned.

A few days later, Steven Aldridge's widow was notified she was to become the recipient of a little under six million pounds. It transpired that her husband had neglected to change his will in his flurry of spending, boozing and whoring.

Smeared in Chicken Vindaloo, Felipe Ozorio rose with great dignity, shook broken glass from his clothing and told John Drake in no uncertain terms that they would meet again. He went to his yacht, helmed the craft to a safe berth in Marbella and drunk himself into a stupor. The next day, he breakfasted on orange juice, *tostadas con miel* and some class A drugs. He then summoned José, and any other cronies who had evaded police custody, to his cabin. There was much discussion over the method but accord was reached before noon. Drake was to be stopped, and stopped now. His operation was to be terminated with extreme force and with as much show as possible.

Tony Russell was not enjoying himself one little bit. On leaving Torremolinos, his skin had erupted in a rash of dermatitis so virulent that even Jesus would have shaken his head and passed swiftly on to the lame and blind. The unguents he used to calm it only seemed to encourage the mosquito population of Estepona to feast on his torso. Unable to spend more than an hour in direct sunlight, he endured his waking hours in the pubs and bars. The boredom was alleviated with alcohol, but his beer consumption gave him a constant hangover and an interesting yeast infection.

His hotel, which was called the Madrid and known as the Shit Hilton, was a monument to poor service and plumbing. Built in the late sixties, the water supply coincided with the outside temperature in that it was boiling during the day and tepid at night. The walls creaked, the electricity was intermittent at best and the meals provided basic nourishment if you happened to be a small, foraging creature. Tony ate his meals in a local burger bar and bathed only as and when his sores allowed.

He had spent his first sweltering afternoon trying to negotiate the bureaucratic maze of the Home Office on the phone. On finally reaching his brother-in-law, he found that the man was not best pleased. Chief Superintendent Frank Croucher did not suffer fools or relatives gladly and was most unimpressed when Tony explained that he had simply handed over the documents. Tony held his ear away from the torrent of abuse and forced a hollow laugh when Frank reminded him that his 'holiday' was at the taxpayer's expense. He demanded that Tony check in on a daily basis and, if no progress was made by the following Monday, he was to return to England. The thought of it filled him with dread. Coming back to Plumstead under a cloud had not been on his original agenda.

His flagging spirits were further lowered when he contacted his wife. Things had gone downhill in the marital department as Debbie had had 'time to think' and had taken matters to her solicitor. She refused to specify her reasons for wanting a divorce but he suspected that a certain evening class teacher was involved.

The rest of his week passed in a miasma of drink and self-recriminations. His day began with a full examination of his dressings and then a trot to the nearest bar. He would buy the *Sun* and read it from cover to cover before strolling to the El Alcazar for a liquid lunch. After *siesta*, he made his call to England. With nothing to report, his comments soon became glib and unflattering to the constabulary in general. His evenings were spent strolling through town or wandering along the beach. There, he found the warm Sierra wind quite pleasant, except when it whipped sand into his open sores. The local children had christened him '*La Rana*'. He didn't know what it meant, but judging by their elaborate mimes it had something to do with a small amphibious creature. A gang of prepubescent bullies would often tail him with jeers and chants. He bought them off with cigarettes and took refuge in the darker *bodegas*.

Friday arrived and, although it was still blisteringly hot, his sores had healed enough for him to spend the morning in the sun. Relaxing over a beer in an outside café, he suddenly thought he was hallucinating. The tables and chairs scraped backwards and a dark shadow was looming towards him. Tony blinked uncertainly. Was it real? Had he overdone it in the sun? When the growling black mass took a chunk out of his leg, he knew it had substance.

Genealogically, Zoltan was a mongrel soup; forty per cent labrador on his mother's side, and on his father's, pure wolf. It was this that gave the dog its acute sense of smell. It had taken him five days to travel down from Torremolinos, a jaunt which included sundry bitings and chasings and concluded with Tony's left leg.

The policeman limped inside and hopped on top of the soft drinks freezer, cowering there as three burly staff armed with brooms removed the snarling hound. Afterwards, Tony stoked up on cheap scotch, fled to his hotel room and hid for the next twenty-four hours. On Saturday, he felt a lot better. His skin had peeled and he decided to brave the sunshine once more. He bought a pair of garish trunks and sneaked two grubby towels out of the room. He went to the beach, rented a sun-lounger and began to baste. Midday came and went and he still hadn't shown any signs of burning. To celebrate, he went to the busy beach bar. It was a place he had avoided, not wishing to be a figure of derision for the bronzed clientele. He had passed by often enough, tantalised by the cooking smells, the cool jugs of beer and the long-limbed, firm breasted teenage beauties.

He took a seat under the straw awning and gave his order. The tuna salad was crisp and the beer refreshing. Chasing the last of his olives around his plate, he wondered if he might just stay in Spain. His dream fragmented at the sound of low growling. With infinite precision, he eased from his seat and moved towards the counter.

Zoltan let out a crisp bark and froze him to the spot. Tony reached for the rolled-up paper in his back pocket. Easing it out, he prepared to cram it into the dog's drooling snout. Zoltan pawed the tattered lino matting. Tony lifted a fluttering hand to cover his jugular. He was dimly aware of someone approaching him. The stranger whistled to the dog and a chunk of meat landed on the ground. Zoltan immediately bent to it, tore off a hunk and swallowed it down. He then sat up on his haunches, wagged his tail and drooled a puckered puddle in the sand.

'Jesus. Thanks. That monster's been following me everywhere,' said Tony, breathlessly.

'No sweat.'

His rescuer was a tall young black man with one leg in a grubby plaster cast.

'Can I get you a drink?' asked Tony.

'Sure. Why not?'

'Tony Russell,' said Tony, thrusting out a damp hand.

'Clive,' said Clive. 'And I'll get them. It's on the house.'

Buzzt buzzzt. Bzzzzztt.

'Yeah?'

'It's me. Sam.'

'Come on in.'

Irish Sam was sporting a beret emblazoned with the insignia of the paratroop regiment of the Scots Guards. He had never belonged to that troop, but he felt entitled to wear the cap since he'd won it in a fight in a bar in Cyprus. The beret also covered up a bright orange curry stain on his skull. He paced through the house and joined Drake in his study. John proffered a rolled-up note.

'Mornin' Sam. Charlie?'

'No. Ta.' Calhoun lit a cigarette. 'Kevin all right?'

'He's in the games room with the Spanish boy. Seem to be getting on.'

In response, there was a muffled thud as a snooker cue hit flesh.

Sam rolled his hand over an antique globe. 'Whassa position wi' Ozorio and his crew?'

Drake pressed a finger to his left nostril and sniffed. Once his hearing had returned, he settled in his chair and beckoned Sam to be seated. 'Reckon I'll have a word with Márquez. Tell him last night was down to the dagos.'

'Think he'll go for it?'

Drake mimed the placing of an invisible wad of money into

a pocket. 'Anyways, we got something rotten in the cellar. Like you to deal with it.'

Sam raised a bushy eyebrow.

'I was gonna give it to Kevin or Angel but I don't reckon they're up to it.'

'Always use a professional.'

'It's a bloke and a bird. She was sticking her nose in where it ain't wanted. Had to bring her up the villa, find out what she knew.' He sipped his third *cortado* of the day. 'Actually, it's a fair bit, as it goes. Smale's been a right nonce about all this. Got a bleedin' mouth on him, that one.'

'What about the other fella?'

Drake sighed. 'I come back last night and he's only standing there with a shooter. Give me all this bullshit about some job back home. Reckon he's contract. Petersons, probably.'

'Old business, eh?'

'They never fucking leave it alone, do they?'

'Want me to do it here, then?'

Drake nodded and the Scot rose from his seat.

'There'll be something in it for you,' said Drake.

'Cheers. Wanna come down the bar for a bite to eat later? And bring Jackie along. I ain't seen her in a while.'

'All right. You cookin'?'

'Aye. Got a cracking shepherd's pie in the oven.'

'Love a bit of the old cottage pie,' said Drake, moistening his lips.

Sam frowned. 'Shepherd's.'

'What's the difference?'

'You use lamb in cottage pie. Shepherd's is beef.'

'Whatever.' Drake moved across to a wooden chest in the corner and undid the chubby padlock.

'Lot of people make that mistake,' added Sam.

Drake opened the chest to reveal a cache of weapons. Two Hockler and Koch semiautomatics, three pump-action shotguns, assorted grenades, a Uzi and a wide selection of handguns which included a Glock 9mm, a Remington, a Beretta and a Colt .45.

'What's your pleasure?' Drake asked in the amiable manner of a barman.

'Sometime,' said Sam, 'I'll make youse both cottage and shepherd's pie. You'll see the difference.'

Hooding his eyes, Drake pointed to the weaponry.

'I'll take old faithful there.'

He handed Sam a smooth black Beretta.

'You cook that Haggis stuff, then?'

The Scotsman pulled a face. 'Sheep's intestines and blood and that? Turns ma fucken stomach, so it does.'

'Thought you Jocks loved it.'

'Not me,' he shuddered. 'Are the guests ready?'

'Yeah. Key to the cellar's in the kitchen. By the microwave.'

Irish Sam Calhoun flicked on the light and tramped downstairs. Mike and Sarah shielded their eyes against the sudden glare, staring rabbit-eyed as the tall Scot came into focus.

'Not you!' gasped Sam and Mike.

'Who is it?' asked Sarah.

'The bloody Scotsman who tried to kill me,' Mike said.

'You wee shite.' Sam waved the pistol. 'Stand up, the pair of youse.'

They did so.

'Can't we talk about this?' asked Mike, instantly regretting it. He had never known a psychopath to change his mind after a light chat.

Sarah felt the blood draining from her body.

Sam's mood was jovial. 'You're a lying bastard. Thought you was supposed to be a tourist.'

'You mean this isn't the tour?'

Sam took his time in checking the chamber of the pistol and Sarah wondered whether to risk running at him. She decided that he looked like a man who was used to being run at.

'Any last requests?' muttered the giant.

'Yes. Tell me who murdered my sister,' said Sarah, despite her fear.

'Who's that then?'

'Lana. She was killed up in Smale's villa.'

'Better ask Smale about that.'

'I did. He didn't tell us anything.'

Sam shook his head. 'I'll tell you one thing and one thing

only. It was an accident. Just like this.' He raised the pistol and fired.

The bullet careened off the ceiling and buried itself in the floor. The cause of Sam's poor aim was a yell from Kevin. All three froze and listened, their ears ringing from the noise. The air smelled metallic. There was a loud whump, a running of feet, a burst of muffled gunfire and Kevin's shaven head appeared at the top of the stairs.

'Uncle John says get up here now. It's a seige.'

Sam glared at his captives, uncertain of his priorities. Mike and Sarah prayed silently. Another burst of gunfire. Abruptly, the Scot turned on his heel and took the steps four at a time. It was several moments before they moved and clung to one another in relief.

In a dog pound in Estepona, Zoltan pricked up his ears and scrabbled against the wire netting. A doggy sense was alerting him that his master was in trouble.

The dark human with the long white paw had seemed friendly enough and Zoltan had not objected to being led away from the policeman. He was fed, watered and put in a large cage. White-paw brushed down his oily coat and told him this was a doggy hotel. Zoltan knew a prison when he saw one and swiftly sunk his fangs into the human. He received a mouthful of plaster and no reaction to his best bite. Perhaps white-paw was a superior being? After all, he was a deeper colour than the rest, which, in doggy society, indicated nobility. Other humans surrounded him and speared his flank with a needle. He came to in a communal area and set about terrorising or mating with the other dogs until they moved him to a single cage. Now, he barked furiously, flung himself against the netting and pawed at the concrete floor until his pads bled.

Chunks of the perimeter wall had been blown away by mortar shells and a deafening hail of bullets was reducing the front of the house to rubble. Ozorio and his men had arrived with an arsenal of weapons and intended to make full use of them. They crouched behind their Jeeps and used the walls for cover as they pumped round after round at the villa. The garden furniture was ribboned and tattered, the palms pruned to a jagged mush. Flowerpots and hanging baskets had exploded into fragments and there were gaping holes in place of the windows. The garden was peppered in chunks of plaster and garnished with trails of smoke. Only the sun beamed contentedly, catching winks off the rifles and the ricocheting bullet casings.

The Dobermans were playing in the garden when the attack began. Emily died first, flattened by a chunk of falling masonry; Anne, ridden with bullets, tumbled into the pool: Charlotte was despatched as she bounded through a fresh hole in the wall. Inside the house, bullets punctured every surface. They splintered furniture, perforated paintings and minced the maritime pieces. Mortar shells thumped on to the roof, causing rubble to pour into the bedrooms.

'Where's John?' called Sam as he reached the kitchen.

Kevin and Angel had dragged over the weapons chest and were loading up. 'In the games room,' shouted Kevin, before striding into the lounge and opening fire. His first spray went wild and took out a glass cabinet – one that he had been making strenuous efforts to avoid all holiday. His second volley was more accurate as he steadied his aim on the Jeeps, now visible through the outer wall.

'Caaannntttts!!' he shouted.

'Fuck's John doing in there?' bellowed Sam.

He received no reply as Angel, too, had joined the fray. The boy leaped behind the remains of the sofa, screaming a litany of fresh curses as he let off the odd round. Leaving them to it, Sam dashed to the games room. There was a pinging noise. John Drake was bent over the flashing lights of a pinball machine. He was engrossed in the game.

'All right, Sam?' he called out, as he bucked the table to increase his score.

'Fuck you doing? The house is confetti.'

He continued to focus on the lights. 'Yess! Twenty-four thousand!! Double up, double up.'

Noting the rim of white powder round Drake's nostrils, Sam wondered if his friend hadn't overdone it. Drake flipped catches and fought the machine. It uttered a succession of beeps and flashes. Then there was a tinkling scale of tones. 'Fifty thousand.' Drake punched the air 'Yess! Winner.'

'Fuck's sake, John!'

'Sam, do your history. It's only the bleedin' Armada.'

Calhoun pressed his lips together. 'Don't get it.'

'Drake! He finished his game of bowls at Plymouth first.'

Sam's face frowned in confusion. 'What about Jackie?'

'Upstairs. Under the bed prob'ly.' Drake released the levers on the machine, bent over and clutched an armour-piercing rifle. Being an Eastern European make, it was so heavy that he could barely lift it. He grunted, pulled it to his knees and swung it up to his chest. Drake staggered back a few paces, clasping it to his swollen stomach.

'Got enough firepower, there?' chided Sam.

Drake grunted again.

'Fuck's sake. Let me take it.'

'No chance.'

A shell thudded into the roof and the kitchen ceiling erupted in a rain of plaster.

'Make sure you use them grenades,' added John.

They stumbled over the wreckage and into the hall. Sam buried two automatic pistols in his belt and fished out the Uzi. 'This should do it,' he said, admiring the gleaming metal. Then he sighed.

'What's the problem, Sam?'

'My fucken pie's gonnae be ruined.'

Sweat poured down Drake's face. 'Right then.' He aimed the rifle and screamed in the direction of his attackers. 'Let's go have these cunts!'

With that, he waddled into the hail of bullets.

'There's a bloody war going on,' said Sarah.

'There goes my travel insurance.'

She forced a grim smile. 'If we stay here, they'll kill us.'

'Unless they get killed first.'

'And we'll be killed if we try to get away.'

Mike listened to the monsoon of fire. 'I reckon we should stay here. We're protected by the roof. They can't survive this.'

She chewed her lip. 'Nope. I don't think so.' And she started up the stairs.

* * *

Drake and his men were replying with confidence. One of Ozorio's Jeeps had exploded, killing one of his men and knocking two others senseless. They lay spread-eagled on the ground, ignored by the others who continued to pulverise the building. Casualties inside were limited to Angel, who had been hit in the shoulder. Sam fired indiscriminately, his orange dome spraying sweat in a glistening arc. Kevin was on the floor, trying to pick off the men like ducks in a shooting gallery. Drake was in his study, pumping shells out of the window. His face was twisted in rage as he fired and fired and fired again.

Mike followed as Sarah clambered over the rubble in the kitchen and through into the games room. Having had time to familiarise herself with the layout of the house, she went straight to a curtained door at the far end. Moving the material aside, she found the door was locked.

'We've got to get this open. The garage is through here.'

'OK.'

Mike ran back, took a handgun from the chest and fired at the lock. The recoil sent him flying on to the snooker table. Seconds later, there was a low rumble and a timber buttress speared the pinball machine. As its lights flickered out, Sarah tugged the door open.

There were three vehicles in the dark garage: Drake's Rolls, Jackie's Shogun and Sam's Sierra. Mike went to the Rolls, Sarah tried the Sierra. She found the keys amidst a pile of discarded papers and drink cartons on the passenger seat.

'Mike,' she called, as she jumped in and opened the passenger door. He clambered in beside her.

'Seat belt,' she warned.

'What the hell are you going to do?'

'A drive in the country? See the sights? How should I know?'

She thrust the gear into reverse and pressed her foot hard on the pedal. The car shot backwards, buckling the garage doors as if they were paper. The rear bumper snapped off as the car whirled in a semicircle. It came to a shuddering halt in the basketball court. Out of the line of fire, they took a moment to accustom themselves to the light.

The villa was a smoking husk. Half the roof had caved in and craters dotted the yard. The shrubbery and vegetation had been decimated and the garden was covered in a fine patina of dust. They were facing a pair of iron gates, behind which the ochre scarp of the hills rose sharply upwards.

'I reckon there's an access road behind there,' Sarah said. She shifted into first, then second and rammed the gates. The impact threw them back in their seats as they smashed through. Landing in a shallow ditch, she kicked into reverse once more and the car jerked out of the hole. The track followed the perimeter wall and curved round towards the front of the house.

She gritted her teeth. 'Hold tight.'

The tyres squealed as the car spun forwards and bounced between the wall and the hillside. Deep gashes appeared in the bodywork. On the curve, the hill fell away to nothing and the valley stretched out in front of them. The car sailed into thin air, plummeted down and smashed on to a switchback a few feet below. The windows shattered, a tyre exploded and the impact almost destroyed the suspension.

Mike and Sarah felt as if they'd fallen through their bodies.

The car, still in gear, reared up and slewed dangerously close to the next drop. Sarah pummelled the brake, lifted her foot clear and applied the pressure again. The Sierra came to a halt, inches from a deep ravine. She reversed back to the road. The car spluttered and groaned, but carried them onwards and away.

They headed for the coast with the burst tyre flapping like a sheet in the wind. Behind them, a priapic pillar of smoke rose into the flat cerulean sky.

22

A stillness hung over the villa. The left side of the building had collapsed and smoke curled languidly in the hot air as the rubble settled. Sam was tending to his wounds. One bullet had creased his left shoulder, another had clipped his right thigh. Angel moaned softly and clutched at his bloodstained arm.

Kevin was entirely unharmed and still full of beans. Overjoyed at having survived a real live shoot-out, he stomped upstairs and scrambled through the bedrooms calling out Jackie's name. His aunt lay trembling under the marital bed with an empty bottle of vodka. Hearing a whimper, Kevin fell to the floor and tried a calming smile. It was like coaxing out a reluctant cat. Eventually, she held out a hand and allowed herself to be helped up. Jackie stood, then swayed, and then vomited all down her front. She waved him out of the room, tore off her blouse, put on a fresh T-shirt and washed herself as best she could. Kevin then helped her to negotiate a path down the broken staircase.

'Where's John?' she croaked as she entered the lounge.

Sam and Angel looked round. The study doors were gone, revealing a waist-high heap of plasterboard in place of Drake's model.

'Where is he?' she screeched.

'Jackie, love.' Sam took a step towards her.

She started to cry. 'He's bloody gone and done it this time.'

There was movement in the rubble. Slowly, a gap appeared and a chubby finger wormed its way to the surface. The plaster shifted as an arm emerged. John Drake, rising like a phoenix, got to his feet. He was covered in a patina of chalky dust and trickles of blood ran across and down his torso. Other than that, he seemed intact.

'Anyone got a fag?'

Jackie broke into heaving sobs. Kevin took her in his arms and cuddled her, his hands sliding surreptitiously down to fondle her arse. She slapped him away.

'Christ Almighty,' breathed Sam. 'What a scrap.'

'Saw 'em off though, didn't we?' said Kevin.

Drake picked up a crippled galleon and placed it on top of the pile. 'Right.' he said, his tone regaining its authority. 'Who's hurt?'

Angel raised his undamaged arm.

'Jacks – you all right?' She nodded limply. He pointed at Angel. 'Get the boy down the hospital will ya? Go see Doctor Garcia. He's a mate.'

'Ain't we goin' after them, Uncle John?' Kevin asked.

Drake smoothed his beard. 'Not yet.'

'But they fucked up our house.'

'Don't swear, Kevin.'

'Shut up!' shouted Jackie, throwing her arms wide. 'Look at this place. Just look at it. This was my home!' Her face reddened. 'It's all gone. Whole bloody lot, and you're worried about Kevin swearing in front of me? Well, fuck you John!'

The men shuffled in embarrassment. Sam finally broke the silence.

'Lissen. I know a couple of navvies. We can get this place fixed up in no time.' He turned to Jackie. 'You and John can stay in my quarters, if you like.'

She smiled ruefully. 'Thanks Sam, but that ain't exactly the point.'

'What is the point, Auntie Jackie?' asked Kevin.

She snorted. 'Ask your uncle.'

Drake fished out a crumpled pack of Royal Crowns. 'There's a good side to this, as it goes.'

'What's that?' Kevin asked.

'They never checked the casualties. Must've reckoned we all snuffed it.'

'True,' agreed Sam.

'Hold up,' said Drake, starting. 'Did you deal with our guests?'

'Aww shite.' The Scotsman paced quickly out of the room and soon returned.

'Bastards had it away wi' my motor.'

Drake's face betrayed nothing as he dug out his mobile. 'Let's get things sorted. Sam, you check outside, see if any of 'em are still hanging about. Kevin, you better bury the dogs.'

Everyone remained where they were.

'Come on, chop chop. Not the end of the world.'

With that, Drake clapped his hands together, hoisted his mobile on to his shoulder and strode off to make some important calls.

They made it to the outskirts of Fuengirola before the suspension collapsed and the car fish-tailed to a halt.

'What now?' asked Mike, clambering out.

Sarah shrugged. 'We'll walk it to my flat. Pick up my car.'

'Then go and find Clive in Estepona?'

She nodded. They walked the last kilometres into town, arriving parched and weary at her apartment. Making straight for the kitchen, they took turns in slurping from the cold tap and splashing themselves with water. Both changed into fresh clothes and Sarah collected her bag from the bedroom. As she pulled the zipper, she paused. A wave of dizziness came over her as she suddenly felt like a stranger in her own life. Bracing her hands on the walls, she guided herself back to the kitchen and entered, shielding her eyes from the bright sunlight. 'I think the shock's getting to me.'

'We've got to keep going. We could still be in danger.'

She looked at the floor. A column of ants had invaded the room and were forming sinewy lines which radiated out from the squashed provisions.

'Do you think they're all dead in the villa?' she asked quietly.

Mike said nothing and, taking her arm, led her outside. The Peugeot was scalding hot and they had to spit on their fingers in order to open the doors. Sarah racked the cold air blower up to full and started the engine.

'Been thinking,' said Mike, as they pulled away. 'I reckon it's time I learned how to drive.'

'Why bring that up now? Jesus, we nearly died up there on

the road. Another foot further and we'd have slid down that
ravine.'

'Well, it seemed like fun.'

Sam sauntered into the study cradling two cans of beer. Drake
was about to speak but first excused himself and went to the
toilet. He emerged a couple of minutes later. His face was
ashen.

'Y'all right there John?'

'It's nothing.'

'You wanna get a check-up. You ain't up to it, pal.'

'Yeah, yeah,' he grunted.

Sam threw him a beer.

'It's just the Charlie,' he added, smoothing a palm over his
shining head.

'You wanna get some exercise. Come down the gym wi' me
and Jackie,' suggested Sam.

'I'm built for comfort,' Drake replied, wincing as the pain
started up again.

Sam upended his beer, wiped a forearm across his mouth and
threw the can aside.

'Oy. Don't bung your rubbish in my study.'

Sam rubbed his moustache. 'Call it a privilege. I took out two
of them bastards.'

'How d'you know it was down to you?'

'I just know,' said Sam, gruffly.

'Bollocks.'

'Bollux to you.'

'Fuck off.'

'You fuck off.'

They broke into smiles and Sam thrust out a horny paw. John
shook it firmly. 'Owe you one Sam. You're a diamond.'

'Cheers, pal.'

'Now. It's time we dealt with a major source of aggro.'

'Ozorio?'

'Not that toe-rag. We'll do him later. Someone who's been
pissing me right off for a long time. You around tonight?'

Sam sucked on his teeth. 'Have tae get someone to run
the bar.'

'Don't worry about it. I'll cover your overheads.'

Sam looked up at the blue square where the roof used to be. 'Got no overheads yoursel' at the moment.'

His friend ignored the quip. 'We'll get Jackie and Kev to do it. They can kip over your gaff.'

Sam nodded.

'Sorted,' said Drake. 'We'll meet down Marbella. Fill you in tonight.'

'Where we going?'

'Fishing.' Drake clapped a hand on his friend's shoulder. 'Gawd, we been through it, you and I.'

Waves of heat rose from the road, distorting the town. Estepona was deserted and they soon located Clive's address in a block near the sea front. It was guarded by a stubborn concierge who informed them that the occupant of the flat was out. They persuaded him to take a message and then had a late lunch in a nearby restaurant. Tired and preoccupied by their thoughts, they ate in silence.

Back at the apartment, Clive had returned and was overjoyed to see them. He kissed Sarah on both cheeks and shook Mike's hand until it hurt. His cast was now a battered shell and he had dispensed with his crutches. He fetched cool *cerveza*'s, moving in a series of jerking hops and arcing his damaged leg forwards like a minesweeper. The main room was furnished with a battered sofa and well-used wooden cane chairs.

'Belongs to a guy in Brighton,' explained Clive. 'When he's not renting it out, I come down here and keep it clean for him.'

Mike took in the pile of dirty plates and takeaway cartons.

'Better hope he doesn't come back soon.'

Clive sat in silent amazement as they told their story. He only interrupted when they got to the war at the villa.

'Only thing on the news was a bomb in Puerto Banús. IRA.'

They did not react. As Londoners, the activities of the IRA were as tedious to them as a cancelled train.

Mike summed up. 'So now we know they're all connected. Drake, Irish Sam, Smale, Angel – and that bloody skinhead who beat you up.'

Clive sneered.

'He's Drake's nephew,' added Sarah.

A broad smile grew on Clive's face.

'What?' asked Mike.

'You two,' he said, shaking his head. They all grinned at one another as the sun cast the first rays of evening light into the room.

'What now?' Clive asked.

Sarah sighed. 'I still don't know what really happened to Lana. The Scotsman told us it was an accident.'

'Like he'd say otherwise,' countered Mike.

'What about this tape?' she asked.

Clive fetched it and handed it to Mike. 'You guys going to carry on with this?'

They exchanged glances and Sarah gave a tacit nod.

'This is sick stuff,' warned Mike, turning the film in his hands. 'Let's get it over with, then.'

'Hang on,' said Clive. There was a small portable TV, but no video recorder. He left the flat and returned with a machine he'd borrowed from a neighbour. Mike connected it up and, as the film began, he kept his eyes on Sarah.

'That's her,' she said as Lana appeared.

He pressed pause. 'D'you want to go on?'

She nodded. The Spanish lover stripped off Lana's bikini and carried her to the bedroom. He mounted her and began to thrust energetically. Without the sound-track it was like watching an old silent movie and Mike half-wished there were something to distract them, like piano music. Sarah remained glued to the screen. The Spaniard took Lana from behind, his doughy buttocks moving rhythmically up and down against her. Before his orgasm, he pulled out, turned her over and shot his semen all over her chest. Sarah shielded her eyes but allowed the film to continue. There was a cut and Lana reappeared, now gagged and bound to the bed. The boy began to drool spittle on her rectum. As he revolved his finger around her anus, Sarah grabbed the remote and stopped the tape. Her hand fell loosely to her side and the handset clattered to the floor. Clive, sitting nearest, held on to her. 'It's OK,' he whispered.

'Sarah,' murmured Mike. 'We've got to find out who was behind the camera.'

Her eyes were bloodshot and her chin quivered. Clive slid away and Mike took Sarah in his arms, wrapping himself around her and burying her hair in his chest. Clive slunk out of the room, returning with a tray of teas. Mike and Sarah had separated and were now holding hands like children.

'So it's either Drake, Smale or Irish Sam.' Sarah said.

'Maybe all of them,' added Clive.

'And hopefully they're all dead.' snorted Mike.

Clive poured tea. 'Not Smale. He's gone. Least that's what the police told us.'

A seagull landed on the windowsill, jerked its beak from left to right, pecked the glass a couple of times and took off into the humid air.

'I met a policeman,' said Clive, changing the subject. 'British one, on his tod. He was having a rotten time being chased by a wild dog. He's staying at the Shit Hilton.'

Sarah blew on her cup. 'What's he doing here, then?'

'Dunno. Got a lot of coppers here. Some of them are out here on holiday with the villains they're supposed to catch.'

'At the taxpayer's expense,' sneered Mike.

'Yeah, well. According to him they passed a law. Supposed to make it easier to extradite them.'

'That makes me feel a lot better,' said Mike scornfully.

'Called the Alien Law,' continued Clive. 'They had thirty days to get out or they were stuck here for good. They stayed. Anyway, this copper – Tony – hey, CopperTone.' He grinned at his joke. They didn't laugh so he filed it away for future use. 'He said that the EEC are getting tough on drugs and porn.'

'Why did he tell you all this?' Sarah asked.

'Dunno. He wanted someone to talk to, I guess.'

Mike scratched his stubble. 'You seeing him again?'

'He said he was going down to Gibraltar.'

'He might be able to help us.'

'How?' asked Sarah.

'He might know more about these people,' urged Mike.

'You have great faith in bureaucracy.'

'Sorry. Lost my head for a minute there.'

Clive began to roll a joint.

'Hang on,' said Mike, growing enthused. 'You got nothing out of the Spanish police, but these criminals are English. Maybe they're exporting porn back home?'

Sarah shook her head. 'They'll stick to mainland Europe.'

'We could at least show this tape to the policeman.' Clive and Sarah did not look convinced. 'He's got to be interested. It's a murder, for God's sake. Sex and death, that's what promotions are made out of.'

'He won't want to get involved,' Sarah muttered.

'Oh well, let's forget it then.'

Clive licked a Rizla paper and stuck it down. 'Mike's right. Can't do any harm.'

Sarah closed her eyes. 'Look, I'm really, really tired.'

'You still want to find Lana's killer, don't you?' asked Mike.

'I suppose so.'

Clive chimed in. 'I'm not working 'til Wednesday. I'm cool to go down to Gib. I'll try and find him.'

Mike took Sarah's hand 'Well?'

'OK, but I really need a rest.'

'You treat my places like a hotel,' said Clive archly.

Her mouth turned up at the corners.

'Give me a couple of days.' he added.

'What shall we do in the meantime?' asked Mike.

She gave him a watery smile. 'I reckon it's time you got your holiday. Why don't I show you the real Spain?'

'And this isn't real enough?'

23

The evening sun flowered into a hot star in the tinted windows of the bar at the Marbella Club hotel. Irish Sam was lining up shots of Glenfiddich as John alternated vodka-Cokes and neat brandy in the same balloon glass. Both were wearing slacks, shades and long-sleeved shirts which hid their injuries. Sam, who had made an emergency trip into town, also had a new hairpiece: a silver helmet which gave him the air of a malevolent lounge singer.

Drake reached out for a bar snack but decided against it. Instead, he sparked up a Royal Crown. 'Goin' back to that trouble we had up at Smale's villa—'

'Aye,' said Sam, arcing a peanut into his mouth.

'He was after me to come in as a partner. That's why he asked me up there to watch him make that porn flick.'

'Hardly your department.'

'I was curious, I s'pose. Couldn't figure out why he wanted me in. I mean, he's got all his A-rabs and his flying Dutchmen, ain't he?' Drake's voice lowered to a rumble. 'Way I see it's this. One of his backers pulled out. That cowson ain't exactly big-time and since he don't deal with the locals he reckoned on getting muggins here interested. Anyways, I has a shufty and it turns out he's after doing a bleeding snuff movie. You know me, Sam. I ain't into all that shit.' He folded his arms on the bar. 'Smale throws a wobbly and you know the rest.'

The Scot bumped his glass on the table.

'And we cleared up for the wee toss-pot.'

'Only that ain't the end of it. He kept the bleedin' tape, didn't he? With that and what he knows, wanker's gonna blackmail us, I reckon.' He grabbed a palmful of nuts and crammed them into his mouth.

'Bastard,' said Sam, gripping his cigarette more tightly.

'Last time I do him any favours. I'm getting grief off everyone now. There was that bloke from the Petersons, that bird sniffing about . . . And,' he paused for effect, 'Ozorio suddenly knows where I make my drops. Someone's pulling my chain, Sam.'

'Aye, some wrinkled little fucker.'

'Let's not be hasty,' said Drake, rubbing the salt off his palms.

Sam took off his shades. His eyes were small and hard. 'No. Let's be fucking hasty and do him.'

'Not 'til we know what his game is. And I wanna get that tape. I reckon he's still got it.' Drake drained his glass and glanced at his watch. 'I told Smale to meet us on the marina at ten. He's coming in from Banalmedena.' He put a hand on the Scotsman's wrist. 'By the way. I ain't told him nothing about what happened today up the villa.'

Sam snorted. 'Reckon he doesnae know already?'

Drake stood up, squinting in the amber light. 'Should've sorted this sooner. Anyways, I'll have a slash then we'll be off.'

He waddled into the toilet and stared at his reflection in the mirror above the basins. His face seemed pallid, the skin puffed up around the eyes. His goatee and moustache were still matted with dust and they felt heavy and uncomfortable. Haggard, he thought, That's what I look. Then again, it could be the light in here. Everyone looks crap in the bogs. Fucking fluorescents.

He urinated and failed to squeeze out more than a few drops. Zipping up, he put his forehead against the cool tiles as he sensed a familiar pain spreading outwards from his groin. As it puckered into a bolus of agony he ground his teeth and clenched his fists, hoping to displace the tremors. It slowly subsided. He wiped the sweat from his face with a hand towel and fished out a small bejewelled tin. Placing it on the side of the sink, he carefully opened it and sniffed a pinch into each nostril. Refreshed, he returned to the bar and fought with Sam over the tab.

The *Maiden Voyage* moved across the horizon and laddered the seam where twilight met the sea. It slowed and navigated the entrance to the marina, then slid smoothly into dock by a concrete jetty. Smale came ashore and tied up, his silver ponytail bobbing on his shoulders as he worked the prow rope. He glanced up as the two men strolled towards him. 'Ahoy there,' he wheezed.

No response. Figuring that they hadn't heard, he waited until John and Sam were alongside him. 'All right boys? Where we going? Boozer?'

'Nah,' said Drake, nodding at Smale's cabin cruiser. 'Thought we'd take her for a spin.'

Before he could object, Calhoun and Drake had stepped up on deck. Smale freed the rope, coiled it and tossed it aboard.

'Mind if I take the helm?' Drake asked. 'Ain't had a go on one of these in ages.'

'Be my guest.'

Smale followed them to the pilot's cabin and demonstrated the controls. Drake reversed confidently and they were soon out of the harbour and heading for open sea.

'How's you then, Sam?' asked Smale. 'Ain't seen you for a while.'

'Fair tae middling.'

Drake brought her round and set an even course towards the horizon. Smale and Sam stood either side of him, admiring his handling of the craft as he increased their speed to twenty knots.

'Where we off to, then?' Smale asked.

John gazed at the lights of Marbella and the dark Sierra mountains behind. He noted with a little pleasure that a small flurry of cloud was drifting inland towards Ronda. 'Think I'll take her down to Puerto Banús. See where we go from there.' He looked across at Sam. The Scotsman acknowledged his tacit signal.

'Bazza?' Drake said, innocently.

'John-john?'

'How about you and Sam goes down below and sorts out some drinks and chemicals?'

Sam put a hand on Smale's shoulder and steered him away.

The centrepiece of the main cabin was a long, glass-topped dining table flanked by leather-and-chrome chairs. A well-stocked cocktail bar filled one wall. Smale went to it and searched out three tumblers, which he placed on the counter. Sam paused by a bowl of fruit on the table, selected an apple and bit into it.

'Ain't been on the *Maiden Voyage* before, have you Sam?'

Sam revolved the fruit in his palm and took another bite.

'What d'you reckon, then?' urged Smale.

'It's no a bad little tub.'

Smale shrugged. 'What's your poison?'

'Scotch. Neat. Vodka for the guv'nor.'

Smale poured the drinks, then produced a small bag of cocaine. Tipping a cone of powder on to the table top, he began to chop it with a silver razor blade. Sam swilled the liquid around in his glass while Smale formed three parallel lines.

'Wanna go first, Sam? It's primo Columbian.'

'I don't do Charlie.'

'How's about some of the old Billy whizz then? You Jocks love that.'

'In my younger days. Not now.'

'Fair enough.' Smale fished a short silver tube from a pocket. 'Don't mind, do you?'

'Gae ahead.'

Smale inserted the rod into his nostril and bent to the table. He had inhaled half a line when the impact of a chrome chair across his back smashed the tube clear through the side of his nose.

The cruiser slid through the sea as smoothly as a trowel through wet plaster. At the helm, Drake smiled to himself as he headed south-east. The stars above were a frosting of silver specks and the briny air was warm on his skin. He flicked his cigarette stub into the water and checked his Rolex. It had been a good half an hour since the other two went below. He slowed up and took his bearings. Satisfied, he put the engine into neutral and trotted down the stairs.

Smale's face was a war zone. His eyes had closed to purple slits and his nose was split from nostril to bridge, exposing the white bony cartilage. Blood poured from the wound, running over his lips like an obscene parody of lipstick. It flowed in rivulets down his turkey-neck and across his chest where it pooled in the folds of his bloated paunch. His shirt had been torn from his shoulders and pulled to waist level to restrain him. His liver-spotted upper torso was covered in short, deep gashes. Irish Sam held Smale's razor-blade in one bright red hand.

'You kids,' sighed Drake. 'Can't leave you alone for a minute, can I?'

Sam chuckled. 'He's no been very forthcoming. Says he knows fuck all about Ozorio and the tapes.'

Drake dropped to his haunches and faced the leathery gnome. 'Kept that fucking film on purpose, didn'tcha?'

Blood bubbled in his damaged maw as Smale tried to open his mouth. The voice, when it came, was a whisper. 'Only for meself, John.'

'Told you to get rid of that fucker.'

Sam eased the Beretta from his waistband.

'Hold up,' John said, leaning closer to his victim. 'I never liked you Smale. You're an oily little cunt.'

Rising, he wiped a finger along the table and rubbed his gums. He circled the broken man, taking in the frail torso, the ponytail matted with blood, the submissive posture. He eyed him with loathing as if Smale alone were responsible for his condition. Without warning, Drake punched him in the stomach with all his strength. Smale lurched forwards and fell, wheezing and spluttering, to the floor. Drake placed a foot under the body and rolled him on to his front. Smale let out a thin moan and fluttered a papery hand in surrender. Suddenly, there was a blinding flash and the room was bathed in white light. The beams sliced through the windows, bleaching the room as effectively as the hot Spanish sun. There was the sound of a powerful engine and the crackle of a tannoy.

'This is the Gibraltan coastguard. You are inside British waters. Come out on deck with your hands placed above your heads.'

Sam's face creased into a mask of hatred. He fired a volley of shots into the light. A return burst of fire took out the glass in the portholes as they dived for cover.

'Drop your weapons. Come out on deck.'

The light beamed in from both sides now.

'There's two of the fuckers,' blurted out Drake.

Sam smashed his fist on the floor. 'We can't be down as far as Gib.'

'We're fucked.'

Sam reloaded his pistol. 'Not me.'

There was a sorrow in Drake's voice. 'I ain't tooled up Sam. We've had it. We got one shooter against their automatics and I'll never get to the wheel.'

Feet landed on the deck above and thudded towards them.

Sam's voice was an incredulous screech. 'You're just gonnae give up?' Drake stretched out a hand. Only his index finger reached the Scot. 'No use in us getting killed. I'll sort it out with these cunts.'

The door burst open and the cabin swarmed with armed coastguards. Training their weapons on the ageing villains, they frisked all three, then handcuffed their hands behind their backs. Sam's gun and the cocaine were bagged for evidence and the cabin was searched for firearms and further narcotics. A stretcher appeared and Smale was rolled on to it. From Drake's supine position, he saw a pair of brown brogues. He raised his head to see a grinning, sunburnt face.

'Hello, John,' said Detective Sergeant Anthony Russell.

The coastguards shepherded the *Maiden Voyage* to the Algeciras side of the Rock of Gibraltar, where a British naval unit awaited them at the quayside. Smale was stretchered off first and rushed to the hospital block for medical attention. Drake and Sam were marched across a concrete apron which was bordered by low buildings and Nissen huts. They came to a stark, floodlit block rimmed by razor wire. Drake took it in. It was grim, efficient, institutional – a total contrast to the luxuriant villas and resorts he had known for the last twenty years. He and Sam were taken inside to be photographed, fingerprinted and relieved of their personal possessions. They were placed in separate cells.

Freed of his handcuffs, Drake massaged his wrists and scanned the cell. It was small and the only items of furniture were a thin bed and a rickety wooden chair. The walls were grey breeze block and the door a rusted army green with rivets around its perimeter. A wire-encased bulb bled light into every corner. There was, surprisingly, no graffiti. Reaching instinctively for his cigarettes, Drake remembered he no longer had them. He placed the chair under the tiny barred window, stood on it and peered out.

The Rock of Gibraltar dwarfed the harbour, its tall scarp rising to a sky tinged brown by the sodium lights of the camp. He felt a shiver go through him as the memories of prison came trickling back. The initial revulsion at the animal smell of other men, the endless months of regimented activity, slopping out, spot checks, the hatching of plans – to escape, to conquer the system, to build a new life. Then there were the complex bartering systems. The ever-present danger of sudden violence. The loss of libido, quickly replaced by a fetishistic fascination for one's own body. Finally, a descent into acceptance and torpor. He sat back down on the chair and listened to the sounds of feet in the corridor outside. Despite himself, he began to measure their frequency.

An hour later, the lock rattled and a guard opened the heavy door. He stood aside as D. S. Russell entered the room.

'You took your time,' said Drake.

'Paperwork. We had to search the boat. It's full of Smale's porn and plenty of class A drugs. Enough to add a few years to his sentence.'

'Fair dos.'

'Where's the money?' asked Tony.

'I ain't got it,' said Drake with a slender smile.

The policeman's tone wavered. 'What do you mean, you haven't got it?'

'Didn't say I *haven't* got it. I just didn't bring it with me.'

'But the deal was—'

'I give you Smale and Calhoun. What am I, fucking stupid? I call the shots on this, remember?'

'You're supposed to deliver all three of you *and* the money.'

Drake sighed. 'You have no idea. You ain't got a fucking clue of the graft involved in setting this up.'

'Not too difficult for a man of your abilities,' replied Tony in his best sarcastic tone.

'You'll get the money when and where I tell you. You think I was going to drop a suitcase full of dosh on you like it was Christmas? Your lot would fuck me over quicker than dogs round a bitch in heat.'

Russell fumed. 'What are you saying?'

'You got the sweetener, now you let me go. I'll be in touch.'

Tony almost screamed the words. 'Let you go?'

Drake rubbed his thumb and fingers together. 'Or no pota-toes.'

'I'd have to talk to my superiors,' said Tony, biting his lip.

'You do that. And bring us me fags. I'm gasping.'

Tony left the room. Shortly afterwards, the guard returned Drake's cigarettes and he chained three of them in quick succession.

Having roused Frank Croucher from his bed and suffered his full wrath, Tony arrived back at the cell looking both peevish and chastised.

'Well?' asked Drake, looking up.

'Since you've shown willing, Scotland Yard and the Inland Revenue are going to co-operate – but only up to a point.'

'Yeah – and the rest.'

Tony Russell let out a long sigh.

Drake stood up. 'What you worrying about, boy? You'll get your stripes for this.'

'This isn't just about promotion!' spat Tony. 'So what happens now?'

'You let me have a boat and I'll toddle off. You'll get the call soon enough.'

'When?'

'Take me a couple of days to sort it. You can go back up Estepona if you like.'

'To that shithole?'

Drake chuckled. 'Used to be quite a nice little hotel, that.'

'When? In the fifties?'

'Don't you get expenses?'

Tony's mouth formed itself into an amphibian pout. 'No,' he said.

Drake grinned. 'Good job the British taxpayer ain't being fleeced 'cause of me.'

Tony felt his back muscles tightening. He was about to explode when Drake clapped his hands smartly together. 'Right then,' he said. 'I'll be off. Better go pick up my Rolex before some thieving cunt has it away.'

Forty minutes later, John Drake was heading out of the harbour at the helm of an impounded speedboat. He took the time to wave graciously at Tony Russell, who stood seething on the quay as his quarry disappeared into the night.

24

Leaving Estepona that evening, Sarah drove Mike up the lazy switchbacks of the Serrania de Ronda. They rode in silence, passing acres of olive groves and silvery eucalyptus before arriving at the *pueblo blanco* of Jimena de la Frontera. It was perched on a hillside and veined by thin lavender streets. Geraniums peeped out from every balcony and the air smelled of jasmine and frying *tapas*. They circled the Plaza D'Espana at the foot of town, then lurched up into a warren of vertiginous alleys. Parking on a perilous slope, Sarah removed two wooden blocks from the boot of the car and wedged them firmly under the rear wheels. They found themselves outside a pair of rough oak doors. Sarah then obtained a set of keys from a widow next door. Opening up, she explained that the villa was a rental property and was presently between lets. In front of them was an inner courtyard, bordered by potted orange trees and vines. She showed him the house, then went off to shower. Mike ambled up to a bedroom on the top floor. It had white stucco walls and a terracotta tiled floor. He opened the wooden shutters to find that dusk had fallen and that the sky had become an awning of pure blue silk. He lay on the bed and closed his eyes.

He awoke fourteen hours later, blinking lizard eyes in the streaming sunlight. He was naked under the crisp white sheet. Sarah knocked and entered. She was wrapped in her towelling robe and was carrying a mug of coffee. She handed it to him.

'Hi. Sleep well?'

'Like the dead. Where are my clothes?'

She nodded at a rattan chair in a corner. 'I put them over there.'

He gathered the sheet around his neck and pulled a shocked face. Sarah smiled coyly.

'Right, here's the itinerary,' she said, all serious now. 'We'll spend the afternoon swimming at the local *piscina*. Then this evening I'm taking you for a meal. After that, there's a fiesta in town.'

He sipped his coffee. 'What, no shootings, kidnapping or explosions?'

'Not on this tour.'

'Fair enough,' he grinned. 'I'd had enough of 18–30 anyway.'

That same morning, Clive had taken a bus to La Linea de la Concepción and had crossed the border into Gibraltar to start searching for Tony Russell. He began with the local police station. Assuming him to be African, the desk sergeant promptly demanded that he turn out his pockets. It was only when he found Clive's British passport that he admitted grudgingly that, no, he wasn't aware of a policeman here on business. Had Mr Watson tried the naval base?

Clive walked down to the gates and was turned away by the armed guards. They refused to reply to his questions and remained stoic at their posts. He returned to Main Street and had a Coke. Feeling refreshed, he decided that Russell must be staying in one of the hotels. The town wasn't large and he could easily cover them all on foot.

He found the Gibraltarians friendly but unforthcoming. His description of a sunburned, middle-aged Brit covered most of the population and their wry comments about a black man searching out a policeman rapidly became tiresome. He worked methodically, checking every guesthouse in Line Wall Road, Engineers Lane and Governor's Street. Unused to the exercise, his legs began to swell with fresh muscle and his right calf turned raw where it chafed against the plaster cast. At the top of the town, he discovered the streets came to an end at the boundary to the nature reserve. Only one winding road led to the summit. He figured it was pointless to go any further. Scaring away an inquisitive Barbary ape, he hopped on to a wall, tore a branch from a eucalyptus tree and stripped it of its leaves. Using it as a makeshift crutch, he began his descent.

Working the bars now, he criss-crossed the myriad side streets without success. Hearing the same DJ on the radio in each one, it occurred to him to seek out the local radio station and put out a message. First, though, he would check the base again on the offchance that the guard had changed. A bleached white alley led down to the seafront. Halfway along, he came across a bar he'd missed the first time round. Parting the beaded curtains, he limped inside. It was empty. A spinning fan stirred the humid air, and numerous brands of gin adorned the wall behind the wooden counter. Adjusting his eyes to the gloom, he saw a man folded over a table in a corner. He was surrounded by empty San Miguel bottles and was plainly off-duty.

'CopperTone,' he growled, affecting a Bogart drawl. 'Of all the bars in all the world, I hadda search every goddam one for you.'

Tony twitched an arm and sent a bottle tumbling to the ground. As it rumbled away, the landlord appeared from a door behind the bar.

'Hey. No trouble,' he barked in a nasal Liverpudlian accent.

Clive held up his palms. 'It's all right. He's a friend of mine. Can I get four *café solos* please?'

'Dere's only two o'ya.'

Clive stuck a thumb in Tony's direction. 'One for me. Three for him.'

The Scouser cracked his knuckles and moved to the espresso machine.

It took a pint of caffeine and two borrowed aspirins before Tony was lucid enough to speak. 'What are you doing here?' he mumbled.

'Looking for you.'

Tony jerked his head up. 'That bloody dog hasn't turned up again, has it?'

'Nah, I'm here to ask a favour.'

Russell's face, already crumpled with sleep and drink, settled still further. 'From me? Don't think I'll be much help.'

'I like that. Positive thinking.'

Tony eyed him evenly. 'Spoke to my wife this morning. She's bloody shacked up with some sodding art teacher.'

'I'm sorry.'

'No you're not.'

'OK, I'm not,' he deadpanned.

Tony's mouth gave an involuntary twitch upwards. He'd spent his day trying to drown his sorrows, only to discover that they were persistent swimmers. His triumph over the capture of Calhoun and Smale had been short-lived. Drake was the real prize and his apologetic call to his brother-in-law had resulted in a highly personal dressing down. On the professional level, Frank had made one thing clear: the mission was of a highly sensitive nature and his failure to complete it would result in no less than his immediate dismissal. Tony had begged four days' grace. After that, replacement officers would be brought in to relieve him. In the meantime, Smale and Calhoun were due to be flown back to RAF Northolt on Wednesday night, where they would be met by Croucher.

'So, want to hear my story?' asked Clive.

Tony yawned. 'Why not?'

'I've got these two friends, Mike and Sarah. Sarah's out here to find out about her sister. She was murdered in a villa up in the mountains.'

'That's a matter for the locals.'

'They didn't help much.'

'How d'you mean?'

'They said she died of a heroin overdose, only Sarah got to see the coroner and he told her it was all lies. Someone was covering up big time.'

Tony frowned. 'Go on.'

'Thing is, she was doing this porn flick at the time. Mike got hold of the tape and we kind of wondered if you'd have a look at it?'

'Jesus. You pick your friends.'

Clive let out a staccato laugh. 'That ain't the half of it. I got roped in as well and got beaten up by a pygmy-brained skinhead.'

Goose-bumps galloped up Russell's arms. 'Not Kevin-sodding-Drake?'

'You know him?'

'Unfortunately,' sighed Tony.

'Now who's got the duff mates?'

'He's a bloody menace, that one.'

'His uncle kidnapped Mike and Sarah,' added Clive. 'He was going to kill them. A guy called Drake.'

Tony tried his best not to fall off his chair. 'Carry on,' he squeaked.

'He denied being involved with the flick. Then there's this other bloke, Smale.'

'Smale!'

'Yeah, real sleazeball. He makes the films, only we can't figure out where Drake fits in. I mean, why'd he try and kill Mike and Sarah?'

'Did he succeed?'

'They got away. There was a major shoot-out up at his villa. We reckon he's pegged it. Smale, we don't know about. He's gone missing.'

Feeling ahead of the game for the first time in a long while, Tony leisurely sparked up a Spanish Fortuna cigarette.

'Which d'you want first? The good or the bad news?'

'Whatever,' said Clive, arching his eyebrows.

Tony coughed on the harsh tobacco. 'Good news is I have Smale in custody right here in Gibraltar. I came out here to arrest him, another man and our friend John Drake. Bad news is that as of last night, Drake's still very much alive.'

Clive sat back in astonishment. 'Small world, guy.'

'It is, isn't it?' replied Tony smugly.

He went to the bar and ordered two beers. Clive drank deeply on his and begged one of Tony's cigarettes. Above them, the fan scissored the smoke in the muggy air.

'D'you reckon Smale could have killed her?'

Tony shook his head. 'He's a ponce and a pervert. Dealt in porn back home. Had a warehouse in Kent. It was raided and he skipped the country on a false passport.'

'Any chance we could talk to him about Lana?'

'Who?'

'Sarah's sister.'

'He's cut up pretty bad.' Tony gave a wry smile. 'Honour among thieves.'

'Is he conscious?'

'Just about.'

'You owe me one, CopperTone.'

'Sorry, no can do. And I'll have to interview your friends about Drake.'

Clive sucked on his teeth. 'Come on, Tone. You need information and so do we. You can give us ten minutes with the guy.'

Russell looked away. 'See what I can do.'

Clive's cheeks dimpled in relief. 'What's all this with you and Drake?'

'I'm meant to be taking him back to England. He's got a file thicker than a plumber's wallet.'

'I thought you said that the extradition thing wasn't working?'

'It isn't yet.' Tony lowered his voice to a whisper. 'He's turning himself in.'

'What?' Clive bellowed.

'He's bloody clever. He's done a deal with the Yard and the Inland Revenue. It's all very complicated but I was sent out here to see it through. It's all being done on the Q.T.'

'Is that why I got turned away at the base when I asked for you?'

'Didn't know you had, but yes. Probably.'

Clive folded his brows. 'I don't get it.'

'He offered to turn in Calhoun and Smale in exchange for a reduced sentence.'

'Is that enough?'

'Bollocks it is.' Tony rubbed a thumb against his fingers. 'Dosh. Moola. Mucho Dinero. He's buying his freedom. My brother-in-law's at the Yard. He gave me the job as go-between. All I had to do was follow Drake's instructions and I'd get all the glory. Right run-around he's given me. I even had to sign some contract, something to do with the tax people. I'll tell you this for nothing. That bastard's got every angle covered.'

'But he'll go to prison when he gets back, won't he?'

'Theoretically.'

Clive tried and failed to mouth a reply.

'Drake's little gift of Calhoun and Smale, along with a large amount of dosh payable to fuck-knows-who-really, means he'll get it down to a couple of years. Maybe not even that.'

'That's outrageous, guy,' spat Clive.

'It is, isn't it?'

'When's this all happening?'

Tony's jowls formed themselves into his familiar scowl. 'Drake won't say, but it had better be soon or I'm off the case.'

'Jesus. We'll have to get moving.'

'You and me both. And I want to see these friends of yours. Pronto.'

In the shower, Mike decided that since he hadn't been threatened, shot at or beaten up, it was turning out to be the best day of his holiday so far. He nearly went into shock when Sarah had emerged from the pool changing rooms in her lime-green bikini. To cover his burgeoning erection, he jumped into the water and surfaced with mucus sprouting from his nostrils. When she asked him to do her back, he energetically rubbed enough lotion across her shoulders, down her spine and deep into the small of her back to protect her from a small nuclear explosion. They swam and read and sunbathed and when the shadows lengthened, they padded back to the villa. Sarah had gone to reserve their table for dinner so he towelled himself off and admired his junior tan in the mirror. He heard a slam as the outer door hit the plaster walls.

'Mike,' she called, excitedly, 'The festival's started.'

There were children everywhere: The boys wore tiny *matador* outfits and the girls, *trajes de sevillania* – bright multilayered dresses to which they had added plastic bangles and make-up. The villagers lined the streets and threw confetti as the coronet and dulzaina players passed by. Then came a series of flower-strewn floats, each one celebrating the festival of the Virgen de la Macarena. They stood on the kerb, grinning with pleasure. Sarah raised her voice above the din. 'It's the *Feria*. The whole village saves up all year for this.'

'God, it's fantastic.'

'Sort of a harvest festival really.'

'No way. Where are the smelly old ladies with cakes?'

'It's essentially the same thing.'

He couldn't tell whether she was teasing him or not. 'But you've got to admit the coast is fake compared to this.'

'Oh yes. The terrible tourists. They've gone and kick-started the economy,' she said slyly.

'You're taking the piss, aren't you?'

She smiled mischievously and her tongue appeared between her teeth. 'Nothing wrong with tourism. I can't stand travel snobs.'

'I'm not a snob.'

'Never said you were.'

They followed the procession to the Plaza de España. The band played on and Sarah pointed to a cluster of marquees.

'There'll be flamenco dancing and fireworks there tonight. We couldn't have picked a better time.'

It was perfection.

'What are you grinning about, Trent?'

He wrapped his hands around her waist and kissed her on the lips. The noise and bustle fell away.

'Thank God,' she said. 'I've been waiting for that all *bloody* day.'

'Drake shooting him was the catalyst,' said Mike.

They were sitting outside on the first floor of a bamboo-canopied restaurant which overlooked the town. They sipped Rioja and nibbled on fresh olives as they waited for their meal.

'And that turned your dad into an alcoholic?' She frowned. 'That's a bit simplistic, isn't it?'

'Thanks, Doctor Freud.'

'I'm just saying that there could be other reasons. Maybe he always drank. You just never knew about it.'

He set his jaw and stared out over the terracotta roofs.

'People tell me I can be a little forthright,' said Sarah, blithely.

'Then they're right.'

'I'm sorry, OK?'

He took a mouthful of wine. 'After he died, Mum went to live in Eastbourne. Don't talk much about him now.'

'Maybe you should.'

As Mike put down his glass, she noticed a scar on his forearm.

'Where did you get that?'

He shrugged with his eyes.

'Oh come on. I love a good scar story.'

Her smile and half a bottle of Rioja was enough to make him talk.

'I used to be a bit of a crusader in the late eighties. Joined all the causes, went on the marches, bought the T-shirts. Middle-class war, basically.'

'Did you have a scraggly dog?'

'Lost it when the string broke. At that time I was a hack on a left-wing London rag. They sent me out to cover the Winston Silcott thing up in Tottenham. Saw myself as the friend of the people – Jimmy Stewart kind of thing. I got cornered by three black guys with knives on the Broadwater Farm Estate. I was shit scared. I threw my wallet at them and managed to get past. Legged it all the way to the nearest train. Bruce Grove, I think it was.'

'And the scar?'

'Crashed into a cycle courier outside the station. I'm not much of a fighter.'

She smiled. 'Well, you're doing all right out here.'

The sky had turned the colour of black ink and the sound of distant strumming guitars competed only with the chirrup of cicadas. Their meal had been excellent.

'I was always the conventional one,' Sarah sighed. 'Exams, university, decent job. All this is so not-me, it's incredible.'

Mike fought the urge to say 'Me too' again.

'I mean, it's like I'm turning into her.'

'Lana?'

She nodded. 'Least that would guarantee some attention from my parents.'

'You mean, she got it all because of being the black sheep?'

Sarah toasted him with her coffee.

'Sank you,' he said in a mittel-European accent.

She lowered her eyes. 'It was always me who helped her out.'

'How d'you mean?'

'Few months ago she got caught and arrested with some coke. She said it belonged to her boyfriend. The magistrate gave her a suspended sentence and a fine she couldn't pay. She tried to beg the money off Mum and Dad but they went ballistic. I stepped in and lent her the money. Her latest plan was to come out here and start again. Hence the teaching in Malaga.'

'And I bet you gave her the air fare as well?'

Sarah nodded.

Mike knew he was supposed to like Lana, but he felt only resentment.

'Do you ever think your altruism might have been misplaced?'

'Yes,' she said quietly.

A silence fell between them and a breeze lifted the tablecloth. Mike smoothed it down and put her hand in his. 'Tell me about your ex-boyfriends.'

'What's that got to do with anything?'

'I never knew Lana, but I know *you*. I want to know all about you.'

She told him about Neil and Steve and Greg and all the time Mike prayed that none of them had been particularly virile or sensitive. Luckily, her short catalogue was one of misjudged affairs and dismal one-night stands. Finally, she called the waiter over and asked for the bill.

'And there's no one else at the moment –' she added, rising. 'In case that's what you were worried about.'

They strolled to the fair and Mike found a game which involved shooting at a target on a barrel. The prize was a tiny cup of fortified Malaga wine and he easily won several. The palpable excitement of the crowd kept them enchanted as they walked round the stalls. In the main tent, two earnest young men were duelling on flamenco guitars as the townspeople clapped along in syncopated rhythm. Mike and Sarah joined in until their hands grew sore. Pushing aside the flap of the tent, Sarah stopped dead and turned to him. Mike shot her a quizzical expression. She abruptly kissed him on the lips, then pulled away and took him round to the back of the tent. They stumbled over a wall and into a dark, bone-dry field. Mike lay his jacket on the crumbling earth and Sarah stretched out to gaze up at the stars. He sat beside her, smoothing a hand along the length of her thigh and up over her stomach. She kissed him, then swung on top with her legs astride him.

'You're full of surprises,' he said, growing hard.

Sarah hitched up her skirt and Mike made an involuntary gurgling sound of pleasure.

'What about . . . you know?'

She produced a packet of condoms. He took a handful of her hair and kissed her, hard and hungry. She pulled off his T-shirt and cast it aside. He lifted hers up and over her breasts. As he began to suckle on them, she let out a low growl and pulled him tightly against her chest. 'Come on. I'm wet,' she whispered urgently.

He tore off his jeans in a frenzy, tugging them free of his trainers and kicking them away in a creased bundle. He rolled on to her and felt her soft baby stomach against his for the first time. He wriggled down and their loins met. A huge cheer went up and they were bathed in a million points of light. Multicoloured cones and spheres and phosphorescent flowers burst and blustered all around them. The firework display had begun.

Heaving with laughter, she rolled him aside. 'Oh no. Premature metaphor!'

They covered up and watched the display. Rockets pierced the sky with hissing howls and rods of light floated earthwards, accompanied by slowly descending whistles. They tried to embrace but the explosions triggered fresh chuckles. Finally, the spheres of vermilion and crimson faded to nothing and the valley sank back into slumber. He slipped inside her, releasing a sigh of ecstatic relief from them both. They moved slowly at first, holding the desire at bay. As their passion took over, Mike took care to perform well, pausing only for bouts of hysterical giggling.

PART THREE

25 ∫

Mike snuggled up to her warm body and woke her with fairy kisses.

'What shall we do today? Make love? Go back to the pool. Have sex?'

Sarah yawned and worried her knuckles in her eyes.

'We're going back to Estepona.'

Fear prickled him like the first day of term at a new school. He clambered on top of her and kissed her nose. 'When this is all over. Are we, you know, together?'

'You're squashing me.'

He rolled off her. Sarah leaned up on one elbow and her left breast made a perfect hemisphere in the morning light.

'You ought to know something. I don't take relationships lightly.'

Mike reached out for her, but she pushed him away.

'Can I trust you?'

'Of course.'

She smiled a little without showing her teeth.

'Are we going out then?' he asked.

Sarah lay back and pulled the sheet over her head. After a moment, he bundled her up in it, marvelling at her curves as he made a tight toga of her body. When she emerged, her face was set with determination.

'Come on. We'd better get going.'

In minutes, she was up, dressed and ready to leave. It wasn't until they were in the car that he realised she hadn't given him an answer.

They headed south to Castellar, then turned east on a small

road which took them to the coast at San Roque. As they reached the motorway, their calm evaporated. Mountains and flowers were replaced by scrub and diesel fumes as the lorries and coaches thundered past. Sarah wove in and out, tense behind her shades. Mike smoked, trailing his other hand out of the window in the hot air. They passed a hoarding perched high on the cliffs, a giant black bull advertising Veterano Conac. It was riddled with bullet holes. They fell silent as the television aerials and pylons pointed them towards the bustling high rises of Estepona.

Clive gave them a curt greeting and ushered them out of his apartment.

'We're going to Gibraltar.'

'Why, what have we done?' asked Mike.

'Tell you in the car.'

The twinkling Mediterranean grew large in the shimmering sun as they sped south once more. Clive, sprawled on the back seat, began to talk. They listened, aghast.

'When's Drake going back to England?' asked Sarah, finally, her mouth dry from thirst and fear.

'Soon. He's going to call CopperTone back in Estepona. I managed to wangle it for us to talk to Smale.'

Lost in their thoughts, they neglected to thank him.

The border was a bottleneck of lorries and day-trippers. They spent an hour on the baking tarmac before the barrier lifted to admit them into Gibraltar. At the base, they again showed their passports and were subjected to a body search. They were then directed to a series of squat buildings in a quadrangle where a young subaltern led them to an office. Metal filing cabinets lined the walls and a deep plan chest ate up most of the linoleum floor. The sun beamed through broken venetian blinds, making twisted rhomboids of light on the furniture. Tony Russell entered, guzzling a bottle of mineral water.

'Christ, it's hot,' he announced.

They murmured in agreement.

'So you're the infamous Mike and Sarah.'

Sarah took in the policeman's weary face and thinning hair. 'Can we talk to Smale?'

'Later. First, we'll need to have a chat.'

'But Drake hasn't told us anything,' interrupted Mike.

Tony glared at him and made assumptions about his class and background. He went for 'over-educated, lefty middle-class git'. 'Nevertheless—' he added firmly.

'Let's get on with it, then,' said Mike, folding his arms.

'When we *do* go in, you'd better leave most of the talking to me.' He turned to Sarah. 'Now, Miss . . . ?'

'Rutherford.'

'Miss Rutherford. Start from the beginning.'

Sarah was precise and impartial as she covered Lana's death, the doctored autopsy report and the evidence at Smale's villa. Russell asked if she knew whether Smale owned the place. She said she didn't, but that both Smale and Irish Sam had alluded to their presence at the crime. She moved on to her capture and outlined her conversations with Drake. Finally, their escape. Tony enquired whether she could pinpoint the exact location of Drake's villa. She said she could. Satisfied, Russell took a sheaf of papers from a nearby desk and, placing them in a beige binder, led them through peeling corridors to the cells.

'Look what the cat dragged in.'

They filed inside the tiny room. Smale lay on the bed picking idly at a scab. He was badly scarred and swathed in bandages.

'Morning, Barry. You know the girl,' said Tony indicating Sarah.

'Yeah. Crap actress,' he croaked.

Russell glanced at his papers. 'Tell us about this villa of yours.'

'Who says it's my place?'

He tapped the folder. 'Local land registry. The false name you used traces back to a bank account you opened a month before you bought the place.'

Smale wet his mouth with his tongue.

Tony swallowed his excitement. He was in fact, holding nothing more than the daily duty rosters. He decided to press home his advantage. 'We pulled the autopsy report out of Malaga. Makes interesting reading.'

'You can read, then?'

He ignored the comment. 'It isn't looking good for you, old son.'

'Bollocks. I weren't there.'

'Let's talk figures. Back home in Blighty you're looking at, what? Ten to twelve. Out here it's another story.'

'We ain't in Spain no more.'

Tony arched his eyebrows. 'I had a chat with the locals this morning.' He turned to the others and pulled a pained expression. 'Ever seen inside a Spanish prison? Medieval.'

'You ain't turning me over to the dagos.'

'Doesn't bother me. It's Drake I'm after, not you. Now, let's hear about this dead girl.'

'What's in it for me?'

Russell tweaked the skin at the bridge of his nose. 'I'll see to it you do your time back home. The rest depends on what you tell us. You can start with where Drake fits in to all this.'

Smale's eyelids fluttered.

'Come on, Barry. You don't owe him any favours.'

'I'll take that fucker down,' he rasped.

'That's the spirit,' said Mike, receiving a hard stare from Tony.

Smale demanded a cigarette and blew out a blue cloud, wincing as the smoke failed to emerge from his battered nostrils. 'Drake come to me a couple of months ago. Said he was looking for a little sideline. Could he borrow my equipment? He asked me to help him out so I got hold of the meat.'

Sarah fixed him with a disgusted frown. 'You mean Lana?'

Smale avoided her gaze. 'All I done was set up the camera.'

'Not very convincing,' said Tony.

Smale swung his legs off the bed and sat up. There was fire in his gimlet eyes. 'What's his game, anyway? Fuck's he doing, turning in his mates?'

The frog grin appeared. 'Haven't you sussed it yet?'

'I wanna hear it from you.'

'It's a squeal deal. You and Sam were the tickler.'

'Drake's going back to England,' said Clive.

'And getting away with it,' added Mike.

Smale's face hardened into a twisted mask. 'Fuckin' bastard!' He scrunched his feeble fists together. 'Fucking cunt bastard.'

He swept their faces with feverish eyes and his breath came in short, hard rasps. 'Drake done that film and snuffed them both. I gets a call to go up there and pack up the camera and he's there with Sam. I goes to the kitchen for a drink and the kid's dead on the floor, bleedin' claret everywhere. Drake saw me in there and fucked me off.'

Sarah fell back against the breeze block wall.

Mike and Clive rushed to her and propped her up as the guard was summoned to fetch some water. When it arrived, she drank a little and the colour returned to her face.

'You OK? Do you want to go?' Mike whispered to her.

She nodded limply. 'I have to hear this out.'

Tony faced Smale. 'Forget it, Smale. I don't buy Drake as a snuff-movie freak.'

'That's what happened.'

Mike butted in. 'How come you had the tape?'

Smale raised his eyes wearily. 'It was still inside the camera. Was you the cunt what nicked it off my cruiser?'

'That's me,' he replied gaily.

Smale put his hands to his face and winced at the pain. 'John never come and got it. I asked him why, once.' His rage reignited. 'Cunt made a joke about it. Said it was my fucking insurance in case he did me over!' He wiped flecks of spittle from his lips, shuddering as he grazed a scab. Tony tossed a paper tissue at Smale, who dabbed it crimson, then focused on Sarah with rheumy eyes. 'I had an idea something wasn't kosher. That film you fucked up was gonna break me in with the A-rabs. Reckoned they might sort out some protection in case John caused aggro. Never liked hanging on to that tape – specially with that Scottish psycho about.'

'Sam Calhoun,' stated Russell. 'Grade A psychopath.'

Mike blanched.

'We should talk to him,' said Clive.

'You do that,' rasped Smale. 'You got enough out of me.'

Tony knocked for the guard and they went back to the office. It was stiflingly hot. Mike tried to resuscitate a desk fan and failed. Sarah pulled herself up on the plan chest, resting her heels on the drawer handles.

'So what do we think?' asked Clive.

Tony wiped sweat from his neck. 'Bear in mind that he's a slippery bastard. All he wants to do right now is to shop Drake.'

'It could all be lies,' said Sarah. 'Maybe he stole the tape? Maybe he's the one who shot the film and killed them both?'

'What's on this film?' asked Tony.

'Lana and the Spanish boy.'

'How about this bloke Sam?' urged Clive. 'Couldn't we grill him and put his story together with Smale's?'

Without a word, Tony led them back to the cells. When Irish Sam saw them through the eyehole in the door, he heaved the bed at the wall and spewed a stream of invective at them. They beat a hasty retreat.

'Perhaps that wasn't a good time,' said Mike, visibly shaken.

They walked towards sunlight.

'What now?' asked Sarah.

Tony slipped off his jacket. 'Back to Estepona for me. Any chance of a lift?'

The tourists in the Avenida Jesús Santos Rein in Fuengirola took scant notice of the prowling white Rolls-Royce. It made frequent stops, disgorging a bald man and an economy-sized skinhead. They entered the cool gloom of the restaurants and bars, only to emerge some minutes later with bulging pockets. John had many friends in Fuengirola: friends with whom he had shared investments, friends who had been trustees of various 'funds' and friends who merely owed him favours.

Of the two, Kevin was enjoying himself the most. Not only had he recently expended a great deal of firepower, but now he was handling real laundered cash. To make his day perfect, he desired only two more things: to see his dog and to have sex with a woman – but not necessarily in that order.

Having dropped Russell at his hotel, Mike and Sarah went back to Clive's and ordered pizza. Half-way through their meal, Tony returned. He looked glum.

'What's up, guy?' Clive asked.

'Bloody Croucher. I was going to do a bit of detective work on Drake, so I checked it with him first. He went ballistic. God save us from brothers-in-law.'

'Ex-brothers-in-law,' corrected Clive, handing him a beer.

Russell's jowls sagged. 'He said that if I deviate in any way from the plan, then he'll be out here on the next plane.'

Sarah pushed her plate aside. 'Why did you get involved with this in the first place?'

Tony sat and chugged his beer. 'I was a desk jockey. Clockwatcher. Not cut out for the action or the politics.' He snorted in derision. 'My wife, being the ambitious sort, tried to do me a favour. Said Frank was a flyer and he'd help me out. I said to forget it, but she went ahead anyway. Cut a long story, we met up in a pub a couple of months ago. Frank said it was all lined up and he promised I'd come out of it smelling of roses.'

'And this is all officially sanctioned by the police?' Mike asked.

Tony gave him a look to curdle milk. 'I'm on leave,' he said darkly. 'No one knows except me and Frank and whoever he reports to.' He rammed his beer on the table. 'I wish the lads in Plumstead could have seen me in that cell. I was *good* in there with Smale!' He flushed, then fell silent and upended the bottle.

'So what was the outcome of your chat this evening?' asked Clive.

'No one interferes. That means you as well.'

'But we can't go to the Spanish police,' exhorted Sarah.

'. . . And I'd better have that tape,' added Tony.

Clive got up and hobbled around the room. 'This is crazy. Drake could be a double murderer and there's no evidence. The tape's useless and the police forces from two countries can't, or won't touch him. We've got *nada*, guys. Not even the autopsy report.'

Mike leaned towards Sarah. 'Is it possible to do another post-mortem?'

'Lana was cremated,' she replied darkly.

Russell toasted Clive with the empty bottle. 'Welcome to the world.'

'You're a policemen,' blurted out Mike. 'You're supposed to help.'

'It's my neck in the noose,' said Tony.

Clive pursed his lips. 'At least tell us about the money.'

'I let you see Smale. That's as far as I go.'

Sarah dragged her hands down her face. 'That's it, then,'

Mike looked at her, full of sympathy.

Clive paused by the window. 'It's shaken my faith in British justice.'

'What faith?' asked Mike.

Tony rolled out of his chair, fished out a packet of crumpled Fortuna and lit one with a match. He shook it dead.

'It's a million in cash. It's all Frank Croucher ever asks about.' He adopted a whiney tone. 'Where's the money? Where's the money?' He dragged deep. 'Know what I reckon? Drake's a liability. They're more interested in the dosh.'

Mike felt a sudden glimmer of hope. 'Maybe they intend to stitch him up when he gets home?'

'Don't ask me,' Tony said.

Clive's voice was distant. 'Does it have to be Drake who gives them the money?'

'What do you mean?'

'All I'm saying is, whoever has his money is in a position to bargain.'

'In what way?'

'Over what happens to Drake.'

Tony shrugged. 'It's a possibility.'

Clive went to the door. 'CopperTone, I need a bit of space, OK? Gotta think.'

Before Russell could protest, Clive had taken him by the arm and had bundled him outside. He closed the outer door and returned to Sarah's beaming face.

'Clive. You are brilliant!'

'Huh?' said Mike.

She stared at him as if they were half-way through a board game and he had just asked her for the rules.

'First of all, he's just saved us from losing our evidence. Tony was going to take the tape if Clive hadn't distracted him.'

'I got that part, yeah.'

'And now he's come up with a brilliant plan. We get hold of the money!'

Mike raised a tentative hand. 'Clive. I don't mean to pick holes, but how the hell do we get hold of Drake's money?'

'No idea, Doc,' he deadpanned.

The laundering of money on the Costa del Sol is a simple process, the coast having a cash-rich economy which benefits from those averse to keeping their funds in a bank account. Doubtful currency is filtered through cash-based businesses and many of the expats would not say no to a little windfall.

As they covered the Avenida San Lorenzo in Estepona, John Drake mused that this was probably the hardest day's work he'd ever done. Kevin, exhausted with all the legwork, paused by a fountain to remove his boots. After picking at his feet, he left behind a pair of aged tennis socks whose stench created a wide exclusion zone.

That evening, a thundering was heard in the back streets of Estepona. Fearing a sudden storm, the locals hurried their children inside and slammed their shutters. They were soon proved wrong when a drooling pack of dogs bounded past with Zoltan at the helm. Biting through the wire mesh at the pound, he'd scaled the wall in one inelegant bound – only to find he was being followed by the other inmates. Scattering them with random bites, his acute sense of smell now drew him straight to the rancid footwear. In one deft movement, he snapped up the socks and took off for the scrublands by the motorway.

'I think we should watch that tape again,' said Mike.

They were sprawled about on the furniture in a torpid gloom.

'Not me,' said Sarah. 'I'm going for a walk.'

'Shall I come with you?'

'No, I just want to be by myself for a bit.'

Once she had left, they played the tape. In the final scene, the boy ejaculated into Lana's anus and disappeared from the frame, leaving her trussed and helpless. They rewound and played it again, struggling to find a link with Drake. Growing restless, Clive went off to take a shower. He'd just smothered himself in lather when Mike burst into the bathroom.

'Quick. Get in here,' he barked, swiftly averting his eyes.

Clive grabbed a towel. His sodden cast left smears of chalky plaster as he clomped back into the room.

'This had better be good, Doc.'

The tape was frozen on the patio scene near the beginning.

'Let's run through this again,' said Mike, patronisingly. 'If we connect Drake to the tape then we've got the proof, right?'

'Spit it out, Sherlock.'

'It's right here in the first scene. Obvious.'

Clive looked. Mike had paused the tape at the point where the Spaniard's hands were on Lana's breasts. She was arching her back, her hands by her sides.

'I don't get it.'

Mike pressed rewind. 'Watch her left hand.'

Lana's sunglasses jumped into her hand and were instantly replaced on her face.

'Nope.'

He nudged forward a few frames. Clive looked, stared and let out a yelp of glee. They jumped and gave one another high-fives until Clive's towel fell away. When Sarah returned from her walk, Mike kissed her feverishly and pulled her to the screen. 'There's our evidence.'

She broke into a broad grin.

Drake's face, complete with goatee, moustache and shining bald pate were clearly reflected in the lenses of Lana's sunglasses.

Her smile disappeared as she realised the full implication. It was definite. Drake had either killed or had allowed her sister to die in that sordid, sweltering room.

'OK,' she rasped. 'What now? Spanish police?'

'Problem,' said Clive.

Mike slapped his forehead. 'But there it is. John Drake. That and Smale's evidence—'

'He's in jail in Gibraltar,' Clive broke in. 'He'd have to be extradited back here.'

Sarah moaned.

Mike began to pace. 'OK. Why aren't the police doing anything? Maybe Drake's paying them off?'

'That's possible,' said Sarah.

'Why don't we go to the newspapers?' Clive asked.

Mike threw his hands in the air. 'They can't print allegations. They'd have to check their facts and that takes weeks, months, years.'

'Shit, bloody shit!' spat Sarah. 'The tape's still useless. And if we gave it to Russell, he'd only bury it.'

Mike stared out of the window and spun mental tumblers in his head. There was something there; something in the pieces. All they needed was the combination. He lit a cigarette. The tip glowed against the dark glass, illuminating his face. 'Sarah?'

'Yes, Mike.'

He faced her. 'There has to be someone to whom this tape means something.'

'Right.'

'Someone with access to Drake's connections.'

'Who?' said Clive, exasperated. 'The police ain't bothered. Won't do Smale any good. Or the Scotsman.'

'Guess again.'

'His wife,' said Sarah bluntly.

'Exactly,' said Mike, a little peeved that she had guessed so quickly.

Sarah was enthused now. 'That's right. Jackie Drake told me her husband never gets involved in porn. She was absolutely certain about that. Drake risked leaving me with her knowing she wouldn't believe my suspicions. He had it pinned on Smale. It's all a huge smoke screen. He pulled the wool on all of us, including his wife.' She gave Mike a big kiss on the lips. Her eyes were bright with excitement. 'And what you're going to suggest now is that we go to *her* with it. Use her as leverage. You little genius!' She hugged him tight.

'Thanks,' said Mike, not having worked it out nearly that far.

Clive pulled solemnly on his lower lip. 'I thought she was killed in the attack at the villa.'

'Doubt it,' countered Sarah. 'You'd need more than bullets to get through her hairspray.'

The men miaowed like cats.

26 ♪

'John!'

Jackie stood in the hall and surveyed the damage. As per Sam's instructions, an emergency team had arrived. Builders were spading up the rubble and electricians scurried about with cables. A swathe of blue tarpaulin had been stretched across the roof, making the rooms appear as if they were under water. Outside, a bulldozer chugged up and down, carving deep welts in the lawn. Jackie had a fierce hangover from running Sam's bar in his absence and, behind her shades, her pupils were shrunken to hard ebony dots. The stress had caused her to increase her cocaine intake and her body was now vibrating gently as if battery-powered.

'John!' she called again. A swarthy workman poked his head out from a shattered balustrade.

'*No, Mi marido.*' She waved him away.

A moment later, John Drake ambled out and wove his way downstairs. There was something different about him. As he reached her, Jackie's head did a pigeon-jerk in surprise.

'You shaved off your beard and the tache.'

He turned his head from side to side. His cheeks were smooth, his forehead already shiny with morning sweat. 'Like it?'

'What d'you do that for?'

'Fancied a change.' He fanned an arm at the wreckage. 'Bit of a clean slate, all this.'

She removed her sunglasses. 'Kevin says you been going round collecting dosh. What's going on?'

Drake pursed his lips and strolled into the kitchen. She followed him.

'John.' Her tone breached the border between enquiry and warning.

'Not your problem,' he muttered, fishing a beer from the dripping fridge.

She knocked the can from his hand. 'It is my problem. What am I supposed to do – wear a suit of bleeding armour round here?'

Drake fixed her with a ponderous stare.

'Come on, then,' she said, full of Columbian righteousness.

'It's cancer, love.'

Her face tightened. 'What are you on about?'

'Prostate,' he whispered.

Her mouth fell open. 'Wh—? Hold up. That's curable, ain't it?'

He blew a long sigh. 'Yeah, but I might have to have the old bollocks off.'

'How long have you known?'

'Couple of months. Garcia told me.'

She released a banshee wail. 'Why didn't you tell *me*?'

'Didn't want to.'

She slammed her fists against her sides and her bangles became rattlesnakes. 'Jesus Christ, John. I'm your wife! Didn't you think I'd wanna know? What about treatment? Can't you get it sorted down the hospital in Marbella?'

He'd been putting off this moment, knowing that no matter which way he looked at it, fireworks were inevitable 'We're going home,' he said in resignation.

'What!?' she screamed.

'I'm gonna have it seen to. Clinic in London.'

'Are you stupid or what? You set foot in England and the law will have your bollocks, not the quacks.'

He shut her out as she ranted on, using the time to mentally enumerate his trials of the past few weeks. He felt control slipping away fast. 'We're fucking going home, Jacks,' he bellowed. 'I ain't having some dago see to my plumbing. I wanna be back home, not baking out here like some old turd. I wanna see me mates, buses, proper pubs. Footy on Sat'days. And fog. I ain't seen fog in fucking years.'

She matched him for volume. 'Well you ain't gonna see it from Brixton nick, are ya?'

He held up a hand. 'It's all sorted. I'm paying off the law and the tax. I ain't divvy, Jacks. I got assurances. I'll only do a year or so inside.'

She flung herself at him, flailing madly and battering him with her fists. 'What about me, you selfish sod?'

He fended her away and gripped her hands so tightly that she was unable to writhe free. 'Pack it in,' he barked. 'Stop it, Jacks.'

She went limp.

'You'll be all right, love. I put enough dosh in your account so's you can buy somewhere. What about Blackheath? You always fancied that.'

'When was you going to tell me all this? On the fucking plane?'

He folded his chins into rolls of fat. 'Soon as things were sorted.'

'Bastard.' She pulled away and slapped him hard across the face. 'You've done it again, ain't cha?' She spun on her heels and stomped out of the room. Drake winced as a laser of pain scythed across his pelvis. Doubling over, he clutched at himself, too weak to call out her name. In the distance, he heard the squealing of wheels as she sped off in her car. After that, there was only the hammering and the scooping of spades in the strange blue light.

The burned-out husk of the Solly Sombra Discoteca stood out like a rotten tooth amongst the pristine white houses. The insurance loss adjustor was at work inside; a neat, middle-aged Spaniard in a pale suit, he was taking punctilious notes on a pad fastened to a clipboard. He looked up only fractionally as John and Kevin entered. Drake nodded a greeting and gave his nephew a stage wink.

'Nasty blaze that, weren't it, Kev? Down to the Spanish electrics, I reckon.'

Kevin wondered if his uncle was referring to a football team.

Drake came closer to the man. 'When do I see the settlement?'

The loss adjustor continued writing long enough for him to feel unsettled.

'*Señor* . . . ?' he said, finally.

'Drake. I'm the owner.'

'*Señor* Drake. I am not clear if the fire began inside the building.'

A hard stare from John. 'Think you'll find it did. Place is gutted.'

'I have to be certain.'

Drake tried and failed to hide his impatience. 'How long before the claim's sorted?'

The man tapped his pen on his incisors. '*Dos meses*. Two months?'

'No good to me.'

'These things take time.'

Drake held him in his gaze. There were two ways this could go. He'd either play the game to get a bigger bribe or – a remote possibility – he might be honest.

'Any way of hurrying it along?' he asked, all innocence with a slight undercurrent of menace.

He received a blank stare. 'The kitchen smells of petrol. Unusual for a bar, do you not think?'

Drake rubbed a hand over his newly smooth chins. Kevin was clattering about near the gutted bar and was examining the beer bottles to see if they were still drinkable. 'Boy was tinkering with his bike out the back'. 'Could've been that.'

A smile played on the face of the loss adjustor. 'And he carried the petrol tank through the kitchens, yes?' The smile faded. 'No. I do not think this is the answer.'

Drake lit up a cigarette and the smoke ribboned in the empty carcass. 'Listen, sunshine. I need the cash.'

'We do not pay cash. It is policy.'

'Exceptions, being?'

'No exceptions.'

'Kevin!'

The loss adjustor took a half-step backwards.

Drake gave a shark grin and patted him hard on the shoulder. His hand became a claw and bunched up the material. 'If you can get a result a bit sharpish, then there'll be something in it for you.' Releasing the man, he stormed out. Kevin, holding two smoke-blackened beers, ambled out from behind his uncle.

When Drake reached the car, his temper snapped. 'Fucking arseholes. Only point in torching the place was getting hold of the readies.' He punched the wing of the Rolls and instantly clutched his stinging fist. 'That, and pinning it on Ozorio.'

'How much are we short by, Uncle John?'

'Twenty-five G's.'

'How about them Spanish bastards?'

'What about 'em?'

'We ought to do 'em over.'

He looked at his nephew as if Kevin had just uttered his first words. The boy grinned gormlessly.

'You might have a future in this game,' muttered Drake, sliding into the driving seat.

They were soon in heavy traffic. John squirmed in his seat and ruffled his damp shirt away from his armpits. 'Gonna pop down Puerto Banús later. Villa first though. Fuck them builders off.'

Kevin smiled. He'd been looking forward to getting back to the house to check whether the snooker table was undamaged. He longed for a rematch after performing the miraculous feat of losing to himself at pool.

'Okey-dokey,' said Clive, 'I'll stick by CopperTone.'

They were standing by Sarah's car. That morning, she'd contacted the hospital to discover if anyone matching Jackie's description had been admitted. They hadn't. After that, she'd bought a mobile phone so that she and Clive could maintain regular contact about Drake's progress.

'How are you going to find her?' Clive asked. 'Women's intuition?'

Sarah donned her shades. 'We'll hide out near their villa and see if she comes out.'

They clambered into the car. Clive saluted and bent to the window. 'Sorry I can't join you.'

'No, you're not,' said Mike.

'You're right. Not my scene, kidnapping.'

'What could go wrong?' Mike called as they drove off.

Sarah listed a number of possibilities. It took most of the drive to Fuengirola.

*   *   *

The *Khan II* was the largest yacht in Puerto Banús harbour. A sixty-footer, it had three decks and slept forty people including staff. A satellite dish was perched by the mast and twin speed-boats hung from hawsers either side of the craft. Its cabins were opulent enough to make Kashoggi seethe with envy. Louis XVI furniture sat on rare Persian carpets, Ming dynasty vases jostled with Grecian statuettes and the walls were decorated with genuine Poussins. It was as if the world had held a car-boot sale and the owner, Mohammed Khan, had bought a job lot.

Despite it being long past the hour for cocktails, John Drake had deferred to his host's teetotalism and was sitting with a tiny cup of Earl Grey. Occasionally, he leaned over to caution his nephew, for fear that one movement of Kevin's booted foot would cause untold damage. Mohammed Khan emerged from his private study. He was a diminutive Saudi Arabian with an olive complexion and pockmarked skin. His luxuriant moustache was as grey as his coiffured hair and his eyes sparkled with intelligence. He held a briefcase which was covered in a patchwork hide of endangered species. He placed it, unopened, on top of a thirteenth-century Persian jewel-chest.

'How's it going then, Mo?' asked Drake.

'Business is good,' replied the sheik.

Drake raised a hand to his moustache and, finding it gone, placed his fingertips together over his lips. 'Sorry about calling in the favour. Cash flow problem.' He almost added the phrase 'Know what I mean?' but realised that in present company the phrase would be redundant.

'No problem.' Mohammed bent to the case and spun the cylinders. The catches sprang open with a satisfying click. 'Twenty-five thousand, yes?'

Drake nodded and Khan reached inside the case. He removed a neatly wrapped package which was approximately the size of a bag of sugar. He placed it on top of the case.

'You must accept my hospitality,' he said. 'I shall arrange a party.'

Drake's eyes darted back and forth between the parcel and the Arab.

'Er, sorry Mo. I need cash.'

'I do not carry currency,' replied Mohammed bluntly.

'Thing is, this'll take too long to shift.'

Khan held up a palm. 'You do not wish to accept this gift? The potential profit is sizeable, I am told.'

Drake saw his opportunity evaporating. 'No, that's fine. If it's all you got,' he added, ruefully.

Khan's even tone masked any signs of irritation. 'It is very pure. It will fetch nearer thirty. This is not a sign of disrespect, I hope?'

John folded his arms. 'No, not a bit. It's very good of you.'

Mohammed produced a small silver snuff box. 'You must sample the merchandise. I think you will be surprised.'

Drake waved a dismissive hand.

'Go on, then.'

Eventually, they extricated themselves from the attentions of their host and left the ship. Drake told Kevin to slip the package into his bomber jacket and lit his first cigarette in an hour.

'Fucking, shitting, cunting, bollocks!' he spat. 'This is no good to me.' He stuck a thumb towards the yacht. 'Five to one, he's got pots of cash stashed away in there.'

'Can I sort him out?' pleaded Kevin. He liked the idea of taking on someone his own height.

'Bad idea, son. See any muscle on that tub?'

'No.'

'Exactly. He don't even need protection.' Drake inhaled smoke. 'Bleedin' cowson. We'll just have to shift what we can.'

He scanned the row of restaurants and clubs in the harbour, knowing he'd have little trouble in finding any customers. The aggravation was going to be in the lost time. Time wasted, weighing it out, bagging it up, chatting and refusing their gold Amex cards until they stumped up the cash.

Kevin was also looking up the jetty. There appeared to be a commotion on the quayside. A scream came from the crowd and suddenly people were diving into the water. A gap appeared at the end of the jetty. The harbour lights were so positioned that Kevin could see nothing but a dark shape on the planks.

It was moving towards them at speed. People shouted warnings as the amorphous mass barrelled forwards. He made out legs, teeth, a lolloping tongue spooling drool in a vortex of fur.

'Zoltan!'

The dog barked joyously and bounded upwards. As the ecstatic mutt hit him full in the chest, a cloud of white powder flew into the air and covered them in a fine patina of dust. John Drake stood stock still, paralysed with rage. 'Kevin, you stupid cunt! I told you to get rid of that fucking dog!'

He kicked the hound, sending him tumbling into the water. Kevin made to move but caught his uncle's dark expression. Trying to make amends, he patted the cocaine off his tunic, gathered it up and held out a pathetic handful. Drake slapped it out of his hands and strode away. Before he reached the shore, however, Zoltan scrambled up and tore a hunk of flesh from his calf.

They drove back in heavy silence. Arriving at the villa, John found the first aid kit and swabbed his calf with antiseptic. He then wrapped a stretch bandage around it and limped to the study to immerse himself in subterfuge, vodka and narcotics. Distraught at losing his best friend once again, Kevin slunk off to the basketball court and began to ram the ball hard against the house.

A hot breeze blew in from the coast and rattled the makeshift row of lights strung around the property. Insects described parabolas around them, making light trails in the humid air. Kevin pounded the ball, which kept hitting craters and veering off in odd directions. As he retrieved it for the twentieth time in as many minutes, he noticed Jackie at the rear door. She was dressed in a denim jacket over a silk blouse and suede jeans with knee-high, fringed boots. She supported herself with a hand on the wall.

'I'm off shopping, Kev. Wanna come along?'

She had spent the day with friends and their liquid lunch had quickly become a liquid tea. Her intention was to go on a late-night shopping frenzy and maim her husband's credit cards.

'No thanks, Auntie Jackie,' said Kevin, miserably.

She was in no mood to cheer him up. 'I'm off down Marbella. Tell his Highness I'll be back late.'

Kevin grunted acknowledgement and lobbed the ball into the night. It landed on the railings of the iron gate and deflated with a cancerous wheeze.

They were parked with their headlights out when the Shogun sped past and barrelled off down the road.

'That's her,' yelped Mike.

'Is she alone?' asked Sarah, peering at the tail lights.

'Looks like it.'

They tailed Jackie as she rode the switchbacks. Dropping down, she met the N340 and turned south.

'She's heading for Marbella,' said Sarah.

'Any good to us?' Mike had prepared himself for the kidnapping by buying a roll of gaffer tape and a cheap blanket. For further protection, he had borrowed a kitchen knife from Clive.

'Too crowded. Unless she's a sucker for the trinket shops in the back streets.'

'Well,' grinned Mike, 'shopping *is* her middle name.'

The Shogun indicated right to the *centro urbano* and came off on the slip road. Entering the town, it took a tight turn at the Plaza de Naranjas and vanished into an underground car park. They tailed her to the basement and pulled into a bay a few cars away from hers.

'This is perfect,' whispered Mike urgently. 'Let's do it here.'

The garage was deserted and the attendant in the booth was glued to the phone.

'OK. Let's go,' Sarah hissed.

They slunk across the ribbed concrete floor. Jackie had stepped out of the driver's seat and was reaching for her Prada bag when they struck. Mike threw the blanket over her head and gripped her waist. To his annoyance, the blanket wasn't large enough to cover her. Jackie let out a yelp and tried to wriggle free. He rucked it up over her head and tugged it tight. It was like trying to dress a recalcitrant child. 'Get the gaffer tape!' he growled.

'Hang on!' said Sarah, furiously picking at the end of the roll which was refusing to come free of the spool. She tore off a strip which promptly folded back in on itself. Mike pawed at Jackie, pulling her away from the car.

'Don't move or you're dead,' he said in what he hoped was a threatening tone. The blanket began to slide towards the oily floor.

'Sarah, quick!'

She ran the tape around the cloth. 'It won't stick to the bloody blanket.'

'Keep going. It'll stick to itself.'

She stretched it around their victim, but instead of parcelling her up, it clung to her clothes and to Mike's hands.

Jackie laughed and whistled the first notes to the 'Laurel and Hardy' theme.

Remembering the blade, Mike clawed it out of his pocket and held it up so that she could see it.

'I've got a knife,' he said.

'So you have,' she countered, unimpressed. 'You wanna get that blade reground. Won't cut butter, that.'

Sarah solved the problem by grabbing Jackie by the throat and holding her fist to her face. 'You're coming with us,' she warned, 'or I'll break your nose.'

'Oh for God's sake.' Jackie pushed her fist away and stepped neatly out of the tangle of cloth and tape.

'This isn't going too well,' muttered Mike, darkly.

Jackie fingered her hair back into place. 'What's the problem?'

'We want to show you something,' said Sarah.

'Funny way of going about it.'

They stared dumbly at her.

Jackie threw them her sweetest smile. 'How's about a drink first?'

They found a quiet bar in the myriad side streets. Confused by the compliance of their victim, they were hesitant about their best approach. Mike and Sarah were further dismayed when she insisted on buying the drinks.

'What's this all about, then?' asked Jackie, sipping at a syrupy cocktail.

'Your husband,' said Sarah.

'Never.'

'We've connected him to the death of my sister.'

'And?'

Sarah locked eyes with Jackie. 'I think you'd better get ready for a shock.'

'After today, I'm used to it. Go on then.'

'We have the pornographic film and you can see your husband in it.'

Her smile lifted only the corners of her lips. 'I don't think so.'

Mike butted in. 'He shot the film. We can prove it if you come with us.'

Jackie sighed and dropped her swizzle stick. 'Where?'

'Fuengirola,' said Sarah.

Rising to her feet, Jackie placed ten red talons on the rim of the table.

'For your sakes, this had better not be bullshit.'

They drove in convoy, Mike with Jackie in the Shogun, Sarah struggling to keep up in her Peugeot. As they neared the town, Jackie slowed and allowed her to overtake them. When Sarah drew up in Clive's street, she glanced at the clock. They had made the journey in under forty minutes.

His apartment was hollow and musty from lack of use. Jackie refused to sit on a beanbag and instead fetched a chair from the kitchen. Mike quickly produced the tape and slid it into the recorder. He played it, pressing pause to point out Drake's reflection. She squinted hard, then nodded at him to continue. When Lana and the Spanish youth went into the bedroom, Jackie raised an imperious hand. Mike stopped the tape and Jackie excused herself.

When she emerged from the bathroom, her nostrils were quivering and her face was set into a grimace. 'He's crossed the line,' she spat. 'He's crossed the bleeding line.' With that, she dissolved into tears.

Mike went to search out some alcohol and, finding only lemonade, brought her a glassful. She waved it away. A clutch of crow's feet had gathered around her hard cocaine eyes and her lips were pale, as if kissed by tragedy. She aimed her words at Sarah.

'Man and wife, they lays down their own rules. I don't mean the crap in the ceremony. I'm talking about the limits. Ones you make yourselves. Mine was porn and there's reasons for that.'

Sarah touched her hand. 'I'm sorry. We just didn't know where to turn.'

Jackie reached for her cigarettes and looked up at Mike. 'What's your name again?'

'Mike.'

She dug into her purse and produced a five-thousand peseta note. 'Get us something to drink, there's a good lad.'

He looked to Sarah for confirmation. Jackie caught the glance. 'Don't worry about your girlfriend. Girls' talk, all right?'

Mike left the apartment, pleased at her assumption that they were a couple.

Jackie lit up with a shaking hand. 'When you came up the villa, what did you think of me?'

'Well.' Sarah paused. 'Actually, I was more concerned about being threatened by your husband.'

She fluttered her fingers. 'Forget him. I liked you. Thought we could become mates.'

Sarah smiled with everything but her eyebrows.

Jackie looked away, nagging at her lower lip with her teeth. 'The thing about the porn goes way back, when I was a kid. Fifteen I was. I thought it was gonna be easy money, bit of a laugh.' She pursed her lips. 'Bloody wasn't though. Far from it.'

'Were you . . . scarred or something?'

'Can't have kids,' she mumbled. 'Always wanted kids.'

Sarah felt callous. She'd assumed Jackie to be little more than a trophy wife. They sat in silence. Jackie finally plucked her cigarette from the ashtray and a long cylinder of ash tumbled to the floor. She took a long breath, composing herself.

'John knows all about it, so don't think you got one up on me for that.'

'God, no. Of course not.'

'He's a good husband. Does all right by me . . . usually.'

'Usually?'

Before Jackie could reply, the door clattered back on its hinges and Mike entered with a bulging plastic bag. A stick of bread poked out from the top. 'I got something to eat as well,' he said cheerily. 'But I don't think I'll ever get the hang of this language. What's butter in Spanish?'

'*Mantequilla*,' chimed the women.

His mouth formed an 'O' as he pulled out a bottle of tequila. 'Well, I got vodka as well,' he added lamely.

Jackie made a large drink for herself and ordered Mike to fetch some ice. Sarah lit a cigarette, gaining confidence from the nicotine rush. Sensing they stood a chance now, she decided to tell Jackie what they knew.

'Jackie. There's quite a lot else.'

'Yeah, I know.'

'He arranged to have Sam Calhoun and Barry Smale arrested. They're both in custody in Gibraltar.'

'He what?'

Mike broke in. 'Your husband's done a deal with the Home Office. Part of it was to turn those two in.'

Jackie drained her glass. 'Jesus. Sam's a close family friend. We've known him for years.' She lit another cigarette then, noticing her fingers were shaking, dropped it and crushed it under her boot.

'And he's going back to England,' Mike added.

'He told me that last night. Sod him. Bloody sod him.'

'Are you going too?' Sarah asked.

Her voice brimmed with resentment. 'Not if I can help it. What's there for me now? Fuck all. Bloody know-your-place, don't-get-above-your-station shithole.' She poured herself another drink, slopping vodka on the table. 'I got money and friends out here. Bloody brilliant, Spain is. What do I want to go back to that dump for?'

'That's a "no", then,' said Mike.

She jabbed a finger in his direction. 'I'm staying right here, mate.'

Mike and Sarah exchanged glances.

'Will you help us?' asked Sarah.

Jackie drank some more, then stared at the ice cubes in her glass. Their rattling became the only sound in the room.

'I reckon he's been planning this for a while.' Her tone was flat, emotionless. 'Probably from when he got the diagnosis.'

'What diagnosis?' they said together.

'Prostate cancer. He's getting it seen to back home.'

'But he can get that treated here,' Sarah said.

'He don't trust foreign quacks.'

'Oh really?' replied Mike with as much sarcasm as he could muster.

Jackie poured another drink. 'I reckon that's only half the story. He's past it and he knows it. Things are changing out here now. Lot of Eastern Europeans working the casinos. Other firms muscling in.' She paused for a sip. 'What's this deal he's done with the filth?'

Mike said, 'It's a million in cash at least.'

Her face flushed with realisation. 'That explains a lot. He's been cashing in his chips all over the shop.'

'We . . . want to keep him in Spain,' said Sarah. 'And if you're as upset as I think you are, then you'll help us to do it.'

'Why here?'

'Because my sister died here. They can't arrest him for that in England, can they?'

Jackie arched her eyebrows. 'I wouldn't know, but I take your point.' She nodded, more to herself. 'OK. There's someone I can talk to, but it's gonna cost. You'll have to get your hands on John's money.'

They made fish-mouths.

'Come on, you got this far. You get me the bunce and I'll see what I can do.'

'Let me get this straight,' began Mike. 'You're saying we should walk up and steal a million pounds off someone who makes Saddam Hussein look like a contender for the Nobel peace prize?'

Her shoulders shrugged upwards. 'Why not? He's three men down. That only leaves Kevin and he's two parts stupid to one dangerous.'

'Where's he keeping it?' asked Sarah.

'Not in the Villa. Take a look at the *Golden Behind*.'

'Is that a strip club?'

'It's a boat. He bought it me a couple of years back. Named it after the two things he loved most. Drake's galleon and this.' She patted her rear. 'Never used it, though.'

'I hope you mean the ship,' said Mike, never one to miss an innuendo.

They shot him identical withering looks.

'And when we've got it?' asked Sarah.

'You'll have to get it to me. I'll tell you where and when. Got a mobile?'

Sarah nodded.

'I'll call.'

Mike raised a hand. 'Excuse me, but there are some big holes in this. For a start, we're going to get killed. Secondly, we don't even know what you're planning. And third – why should we trust you anyway?'

Jackie reached for her jacket. 'You can't, but since you came to me I reckon I'm your last chance.' She nodded at the video recorder. 'Tell you what. You can keep hold of that tape as insurance. Hang on to it, I might need it later.'

She pulled on her jacket and picked up her bag.

'Hang on. If we succeed, then how do you know that we won't run off with the money?'

'You won't,' she replied, her smile sending a shiver through them.

Irish Sam, thinking of how his friend had sold him out, had built up a towering rage with some impressively spiky parapets. Slipping back into old Barlinnie patterns, he'd spent his days shouting invective and punching the breezeblock walls until his knuckles bled. His record contained at least two counts of first-degree murder and if he were to get to trial, he'd certainly never see freedom again. He was determined this was not going to happen.

Sam ceased all forms of protest at six p.m. Turning down his meal as usual, he left it where it lay instead of smearing the food on the walls. As the guard changed for the evening watch, he removed a button from his shirt and blocked the spyhole in the door. He then went to work on the mattress, tearing off the fabric and laying it out in long strips. An hour of sustained work enabled him to fashion it into a usable rope. He then upended the frame, jamming it between the toilet and the ceiling. He unplugged the spyhole, stood on his chair and placed the noose around his neck. Sam Calhoun then let out a roar and stepped down from the seat.

The noise and frenzied kicking brought a staring eye to the door. Feet clattered off and two pairs returned. The keys shivered in the lock and two guards eased their way inside. The giant Scot hung a few inches from the ground, his body slack and his neck bent at an awkward angle. Approaching him, one prodded his gun into Sam's stomach. Invisible to him, was the additional rope which Sam had strung behind his back to bear his weight.

He struck with split-second timing and brute animal force. Gripping the muzzle of the gun, Sam sent the man flying backwards and swung a kick at the other guard. It caught him on the jaw, shattering it and severing the man's tongue. Sam threw off his contraption, leaped on top of the armed guard and beat him to oblivion. He spun round to the other guard, who lay jerking in a puddle of blood. He trod on his windpipe until the man stopped breathing and then locked them both in the cell.

At the outer door to the barracks, he shot another guard dead and sprinted across the tarmac, reaching the sentry in time to disarm the squaddie with a blow from his rifle butt. A second soldier appeared and fumbled for his gun. Sam felled him expertly, opened the gates and slipped away from the base.

Discarding his weapon on the grounds it would draw unnecessary attention, he came up to Line Wall Road and mingled with the jovial night crowds. He made for the border crossing. Reaching the open span of road and runway, he slunk along the cars until he came to the hard shadows cast by the container lorries. The post was staffed by five guards, all armed and alert. He scanned the rear of the nearest lorry. The doors were of tall dull metal and were securely fastened. He turned round. The cab behind him was empty and a knot of drivers were smoking and talking further down. Sam stepped up on to the footplate and gauged the distance to the roof. He leaped, missed and fell back on to concrete. Two more attempts gave him a finger grip on the rim. He hoisted himself up, spread himself flat and waited.

The vehicles moved forwards at a snail's pace. Sam felt the vibrations as the engine spluttered into life. The border guards lazily riffled papers and shone torches. A plane boomed out of the sky, heading for the runway at Gibraltar Airport. As it shrieked overhead, he saw every detail of the undercarriage. The air brakes beneath him hissed and they inched on to Spanish soil. He kept absolutely still, knowing that a casual glance from a border guard would reveal his position. The pitch of the gears then rose as they picked up speed. Sam permitted himself a small sigh of relief.

They passed through La Línea and on to San Roque. He knew the route. If the lorry took the north fork he would be able to stay on board all the way back to Fuengirola. To his annoyance, it turned left for Algeciras. He waited until they were in dark scrub, then slid to the edge and hung off the end of the truck. As it slowed for a bend, the lorry ground down through its gears. Sam threw himself off, hit the road and went into a roll. He tumbled over and over and came to rest in a dusty gully. Spitting dirt, Irish Sam picked himself up, smoothed a hand across his moonlit skull and turned towards Fuengirola.

28 ♩

The headlights of the Shogun frittered across the craters and grew large on the ruined portico. Jackie cut the engine and emerged from the car. Behind her, the damaged pineapple palms made splinted fingers against the sky. She scanned the dark garden, her gaze coming to rest on the pale expanse of the empty pool. Sighing, she turned away and tottered into the hall. There was movement in the lounge, a furtive scrambling on the torn leather sofa. She took a couple of steps towards it and Kevin's head popped up.

'Hello, Auntie Jackie,' he said, his face glowing red.

'Kev.'

She moved round to face him, searching for the cause of his embarrassment. He had positioned a cushion on his lap and one of her long suede boots lay crumpled on the floor beside him. She didn't want to think about it.

'Auntie? Any chance of you helping me find Zoltan?' he asked in a strained voice.

'We'll have a look tomorrow. Where's John?'

'Upstairs.'

'Kev. Want to ask you something. Did you come out here on your own?'

Kevin said nothing.

'So you didn't have a copper with you?'

Mike and Sarah had told her all about Tony Russell and she wanted to be one hundred per cent sure of their story. Kevin shook his head and his face flushed even more. She lifted a foot and grazed the toe of her boot against his thigh.

'You sure about that?'

'Yeah,' he replied, his little jaw jutting out further.

'It's written on your face, love.'

He gave her a puppy-dog stare.

She smiled now. 'Don't worry about it. Me and John had a talk and sorted it all out. Now, you get off to bed, there's a good lad.'

Kevin scampered away. She made herself a long drink and took it out on to the terrace. A light breeze ruffled the plastic sheeting, but this and the burr of cicadas were not enough to drown out her thoughts. She left her empty glass on the low wall and came back inside to John's study. The weapons chest was no longer locked. Reaching inside, she pulled out a revolver and checked the clip. She took off her boots and padded silently up to their bedroom.

John lay slumbering, his fat face squashed against the pillow. She studied the familiar lines of his forehead, the shiny pate, the crescents of his eyelids and nostrils, the shaven rolls of flab under his chin. She tried to see him as he saw others; as victims – or irritants. He murmured and rolled over in his sleep. She moved closer, raising the barrel and holding it an inch from his forehead. She focused on the distance between the gun and his head; a negative space in which death could blaze a fresh trail in a split second. The moonlight cast a silver line along the barrel of the gun. She gripped the butt in both hands and held it there for a good five minutes, almost wishing he would awaken. Drake remained oblivious.

Slowly, she lowered the gun to her side and left the room. She crept back downstairs, replaced the weapon in the chest and collapsed in a flood of silent tears.

At seven the following morning she rose, made a quick call on her mobile and took a shower. Even the buzz of her hair-dryer failed to awaken her husband. She dressed in her smartest suit, took the Shogun into town and met Juan Márquez in the reception area of the Marbella Club hotel. The Mayor kissed her on both cheeks and led her to a table on the bright terrace. He sat her down, then took his place opposite and unfurled a linen napkin. He was freshly shaven and his eyes were as blue as the calm morning sea.

'This is a great pleasure, *Señora* Jackie. You have a message from your husband?'

''Fraid not. This is personal.'

His eyebrows gathered about the bridge of his nose. He was about to speak when the waiter hovered towards them. Márquez waved away the menu and ordered fruit compote and *tostadas con miel*. She had a *café solo*, he a *cortado*. They made small talk, knowing that they would only be interrupted once more by the arrival of the food. When it came, Jackie stirred her coffee but did not drink. 'I been thinking, Juan. I don't know you that well, do I?'

The smile reached his eyes with ease. 'It is always good to make friends.'

'Yeah, it is. I was also thinking about a little bit of business.'

'I am not sure what you mean.'

She mock-frowned. 'I hope you're not one of those old-fashioned men who won't do business with a woman.'

'I believe you said this was personal?'

'It is.'

He held up his palms. '*¿Por favor?*'

She dipped a spoon in her compote and moved it around in the bowl. 'You've been dealing with my husband for quite a while now.'

'Several years.' He smiled at the memories.

She took a mouthful. 'John and I don't have any secrets, so you needn't hold back. One thing you had was a little arrangement concerning the death of a British girl.' She chewed thoughtfully. 'There was a Spaniard as well.'

'*Heroina.*' he said, defensively. 'The report was quite clear.'

'Except the facts were changed after they died.'

Márquez rested a manicured hand on the table. 'Jackie, you must understand the sensitive nature of the tourist industry. We attempt to keep such incidents in their proper proportions.'

She gave him one of her best and broadest smiles. 'Lovely car you got outside. Classic Mercedes convertible, isn't it?'

He flushed a little. 'It is an *estupendo* car, Señora Drake.'

'I know. I helped John choose it.'

'He is a very generous man.'

'And I'm a very generous woman,' she countered, adding, 'and John won't be around for ever.'

'But for some years, I think.'

She shook her head. 'He's leaving Spain.'

Márquez stroked his chin thoughtfully.

'He's done a deal with Scotland Yard. British Police are waiting to fly him home. That shouldn't bother you too much, but we'll come to that. What gives me grief, Juan, is he's got too much blood on his hands.'

The Mayor pulled at the skin under his chin.

Jackie took a deep breath. 'It ain't acceptable. That or the pornography.'

'¿Pornografía?'

'I think you know.'

Márquez' expression gave nothing away. 'Of course, I understand your position. But what do you want from me?'

'I want you to stop him going.'

He looked at the horizon and his gaze fell to the empty beach. Jackie promptly reached into her handbag for a pen and wrote a large number on a paper napkin. She folded it and slid it across to Márquez.

'And I'll give you this, in cash, if you'll do it for me.'

As he glimpsed the figure, his moustache formed a crescent of surprise. 'A most generous offer.'

'Ta, muchly,' she chirped.

He crumpled the paper and fixed her in a limpid gaze. 'You must allow me to extend you my hospitality sometime soon.'

'That'd be nice,' she smiled.

John Drake stood at the foot of Angel's hospital bed and downed a handful of painkillers he had purloined from a nurse's cupboard. Having been operated on, Angel's foot was bound in a tight bandage. Also, the bullet in his shoulder had been removed. Pleased to be visited by his new employer, he had decided that *Señor* Drake was a kind man.

'Get up, Ange. No more malingering.'

'But the doctor say two more days.'

'Bollocks to that. You're coming with me.'

As Angel struggled to his feet, John helped himself to a dish of grapes that belonged to another sleeping patient. He then strode to the lift with Angel hopping precariously behind him. They emerged in blistering heat. Kevin was waiting by the Rolls. 'Right, you two,' said Drake. 'Time we gave Ozorio a little slap.'

'Brilliant,' said Kevin.

'*Voy*,' echoed Angel.

'First, we're going up Torrie-town. Ange, I want you to suss out what the dope situation's like up there. Go see Pablo at the hotel. Kevin. You're coming with me.'

They clambered into the car and sped off. Drake dropped Angel at the MiraFlores, then raced back to Marbella, where he purchased two bland, brown suitcases. Kevin stared out of the window the whole way. Like a child fixated on a lost toy, he craved any sign of Zoltan and his heart beat fast when he saw a man with a limp. They took a light lunch of several pints of lager and returned to the villa.

Angel's call came through at four that afternoon and confirmed Drake's suspicions that supplies of *porro* were low. Pablo's intimate knowledge of the drug scene had also provided more vital information. A delivery was imminent. Drake, smiling for the first time that day, suggested a game of darts to his nephew. They played in the garage but Drake soon lost interest when Kevin's excellent aim proved unbeatable. He sent the boy out to play and went inside to consume three lines of coke and a tumblerful of neat vodka. Once he had risen to a sufficient chemical height, he went to his study and cradled the mobile to his neck. Tony Russell came on line after seven rings.

'Where you been?' Drake growled.

'I was on the bog. Spanish tummy.'

'Typical filth. Full of shit.'

Tony refused to rise to the bait. 'What's the news? Have you got the money?'

'As agreed,' said Drake.

Kevin ran past the window with a clutch of darts in his hand.

'Flight's tomorrow morning. Six a.m. Malaga airport. British Airways.'

'Naturally,' said Tony, sardonically.

'Meet me at the check-in, right?'

'Alone, I trust?'

'Just me and the wife.'

'You never said anything about your wife,' spurned Tony.

'Obviously she's coming as well, you prat.'

Tony sighed. 'We can't possibly cover her fare.'

'Don't be a cunt all your life. It's all taken care of.'

'Who gets the window seat?'

'I do.'

There was disappointment in Russell's tone. 'All right. But you're mine the moment we get to Gatwick. Clear?'

'Just be there.'

Drake hung up and turned to the window. A seagull plummeted to the terrace, its wing neatly speared by a dart.

Mike and Sarah woke late in the morning and fetched snacks from the local *supermercado*. The heat was oppressive and they soon found themselves snapping at one another for no concrete reason. At noon, Mike badgered Sarah into driving them to Puerto Banús to look for Drake's houseboat. Lost in their own thoughts, they strolled along the quay and found no sign of the *Golden Behind*. Feeling as if they were being watched, they abandoned their quest after half an hour and arrived back at Fuengirola in a funk of paranoia and suspicion.

'I just wish there was something we could do about Russell and the British end,' said Sarah, knotting up her long print skirt. 'I mean, they're our police after all.'

Mike slumped against the wall in the sun. 'Tony's just an errand boy. We've been over trying to bribe him.'

She undid the knot and smoothed the material on her knee. 'Wish we could just give him the money and tell him to get on the plane alone. Leave Drake stranded here.'

'He wouldn't do it. We'll have to rely on Jackie.'

She slapped her hands on the floor. 'How do we know we can trust her? We take all the risks and we can't even find his sodding boat.'

Mike closed his eyes. 'Sarah. We haven't got any choice.'

Her mobile chirruped and Mike flapped around her as she spoke into it.

'That was Clive,' she said, turning it off.

'What's happening?'

'Flight's tomorrow morning. Drake's meeting him at Malaga.'

'Shit, that doesn't give us much time.'

She shot him a worried frown. 'Are we really going to go through with this?'

Mike was firm. 'Drake's yacht has to be there somewhere. We didn't look at the smaller boats on the far side of the harbour, did we?'

'Well, I was scared,' said Sarah resentfully.

He lifted her to her feet and held her by the waist. 'Let's go with the plan. I've stolen things off boats before, you know.' He wiggled his eyebrows comically and a brief smile played across Sarah's lips. 'But I agree with Jackie. We should be . . .' his voice dropped to a South London growl, '. . . *tooled up* for this one.'

'Let's pick up a gun in the *supermercado*, shall we?'

He grinned smugly. 'I've got a better idea. Get your shoes on, we're going for a walk.'

It was early evening when they arrived at Angel's apartment. The outer iron-bar gate was locked from the inside. Mike scanned the geranium-strewn balcony. The shutters were closed and there was nothing parked nearby to help them up.

'Jackie said he's in hospital,' he said. 'We just need to break in.'

'How about I see if the landlord has a spare key?'

'And tell him what?'

'I could be an anxious relative.'

'But, you don't look Spanish.'

'You don't think so?' she said, fingering her mane of dark hair.

'Slim chance.'

'At least I speak the language,' she pouted, then went to the door and began pressing buzzers. On the third ring, a woman's voice answered in a gabble of Spanish. Sarah went into her act, complete with small sobs.

'*Lo siento molestaria Señora, pero mio he visto a uni primo Angel por varias semanas y pienso que puede estar enfermo.*'

There was a pause. She translated, explaining that she'd said she was Angel's cousin and was worried he was ill. The buzzer went and the door sprang open. As they entered the cool of the hall, a plump elderly woman appeared at the front door of a flat above them. She rattled off a stream of vowels and Sarah replied proficiently with a surfeit of hand gestures.

Mike could tell she was embellishing her story but the woman appeared to be going along with it. Perhaps she heard this kind of thing every day? Or perhaps she was just a lonely old woman who liked stories? The crone beckoned to them and Sarah began climbing the stairs. He followed her, hissing. 'Six. Angel's flat is number six.'

She ignored him as the woman ushered them inside. The dim, over-furnished living room was stuffed with old bulky furniture. There were framed pictures of relatives on every surface, far too many chairs and a sofa with a rainbow crocheted throw. A lime-green budgerigar twittered in a cage above the television which was tuned to the news on TVE.

The woman disappeared into the kitchen, returning shortly with a bottle of Tio Pepe and three fino glasses. She filled each one to the brim and handed them to her guests. Sipping the bitter drink, Mike felt as if he were in the home of a mad aunt; the kind you can't escape until you've consumed your body weight in cake and seen your career options ridiculed. Sarah appeared to be enjoying herself, nodding at the woman's comments and throwing her head back in laughter. Feeling like a mute, he tapped her on the arm.

'Tell her we need to fetch some guns from the flat down the hall. We have some a-killin' to do.'

The crone peered at him as if he were a specimen from a nature programme. She asked Sarah to translate and she spouted a gargle of words. The woman looked at him sadly and Mike assumed it had been a loose translation at best. He endured the polite chatter and glanced at his watch every now and then. It was soon past nine.

It was another hour before they were released. The woman pressed a key into Sarah's palm and exhorted them to return as soon as possible. Or so Mike gathered. She could have been describing crop rotation in arable pasture for all he knew.

'What the hell was she going on about?'

'We got the keys, didn't we?' she said, primly.

'We were in there for bloody hours.'

Sarah shrugged. 'She was a very interesting wo[man] me all about her affair with Franco.'

'The dictator?'

'No, the double-glazing salesman. Of course, F[ranco the dic]tator. Apparently he wasn't much of a dictator i[n...]

Mike pulled a face. If there was one thing wors[e than] having a fabulous sex life, it was hearing about old [people with] a fabulous sex life.

They came to the door and Mike put his ear to [it. There was] no discernible sound within. Sarah slipped the key [in the lock.] The door opened and they slipped into the dark[ness of] the hall.

29 ♪

Soft waves tickled the shore as Drake inhaled sea air and studied the horizon. They were parked near the beach a few kilometres east of San Roque. He knew the routine well, having himself shifted tons of Lebanese and Moroccan dope to similar shores. Gazing up at the sky, he noted with a little pleasure that a pulpy cloud had begun to obscure the moon. He went back to the car to ensure that it was invisible from the road before handing out the weapons. Angel was given a Kalashnikov rifle. He loaded it with glee and struck a number of combat poses before Kevin smacked him. John passed his nephew a revolver and saved the best for himself. The AK 47 automatic was heavy but effective and could cut down any number of men in seconds. He ordered the boys to lower their barrels to the sand.

'Ozorio's crew should be here soon. Angel, we're gonna wait here. Kevin. See that clump of rocks?'

As his eyes became accustomed to the night, Kevin made out a promontory at the far end of the cove. 'Yes, Uncle?'

'Get round there quick as you can. First thing they'll do is put a man up there with a beacon to guide the boat in. I want you to take him out. Don't shoot him. Smack him. Then use the light yourself. Once you see a speedboat, swing it round on the water and bring it in. Got it?'

Kevin nodded, peeved that he wasn't going to be in the centre of the action.

'Good boy. Once they make the drop, you flash the light on them. We'll take over from there. Off you go, then.' He clapped him on the back and Kevin bolted off like a spring hare.

'Angel, you and me wait here, ¿entiendes?'

'*Sí, Señor* Drake.'

They crouched on the cool sand, Angel copying his employer by smoking with his palm shrouding the glow. As he grew bored, he lay down his rifle and poured sand on to it.

Drake held up a finger. 'Hear that?' he croaked.

A distant throbbing came from the sea and a light appeared over on the promontory. It swayed out over the water, then flickered and disappeared behind the rocks. Kevin was doing his job. Drake held his breath and counted. On nine, the beam reappeared and wavered out across the water.

A car hissed on to the sand behind them and its engine stopped and began to cool. Doors swung open. Angel went for the rifle but John held his arm. Dancing cigarette fireflies pinpointed the men as they approached. The air was still enough for Angel to overhear their conversation: it was a debate about the relative merits of Melanie Griffith's mammaries.

Drake looked out to sea and saw the prow of the speedboat as it hit the cone of light. The boat swung parallel and remained six metres from shore to avoid grounding. It went into neutral and sculled forwards. There were quiet plops as the bales of hashish splashed overboard.

Drake tightened his grip on Angel's arm, feeling his own sinews tense up. The adrenalin/speed/coke buzz had frozen his jaw muscles and had turned his tongue to a lumpy dough. Blood coursed through his arteries as every muscle readied itself for action. Angel, at his side, vibrated like a dildo with fresh batteries.

The four men broke into a run and hit the water. Their splashes slowed to a fast wade as they manhandled the packages. Drake released Angel, clambered to his feet and centred his rifle. Kevin's beacon made the scene a frozen tableau of surprise. Drake released a hail of bullets and two men danced, their blood spouting a black arc as they hit the water. The others scrambled for their guns as Kevin doused the light. A shot erupted from the beach behind them. Drake spun round, taking out the driver and the radiator of the car. Angel screamed at the top of his lungs and let off a spurt of metal diarrhoea. His bullets spattered the sea and creased the sand and none of them hit any member of the rival hash gang. With his next round, the gun jammed. Drake sprayed the other two men with the nonchalance of someone watering his lawn. He made a mental body-count. Kevin had immobilised the lookout. Four down on the beach. The driver? He emptied another round into their car just to be on the safe side. The deafening noise abated and there was total silence, but for the angry speedboat as it sped away. Angel was still clicking his trigger in a rapid staccato. Drake took the gun off him.

'Nice one, Ange.'

'The gun jam, *Señor*.'

'Never mind. Job done. Let's go get that Bob Hope.'

Drake let Angel out on the Avenida Condes de San Isidrio in Fuengirola and sped away with Kevin. The young Spaniard practised his Schwarzenegger drawl all the way home, the pain in his foot superseded in the rush of adrenalin. He sauntered into the building and bounded up the stairs. Once inside the apartment, he failed to notice the lights were on as he fished a beer from the fridge. Overjoyed at having exacted vengeance for Ramón's death, he now considered himself a real soldier: he would shine in his *Mili*, the compulsory military service due to start on his next birthday. He strode to the bedroom, intent on commencing his night of triumph with a little light masturbation. Mike stood with a gun to his head.

'Me again,' he said. 'Sorry to trouble you.'

'*Mierda*.' Angel leaped on to his bed and saw Sarah huddled in the corner.

Mike took a step towards him. 'Stay still, you little sod.'

Angel dropped to the mattress, pulled out an identical pistol to the one Mike held and aimed it at his face. Stalemate.

'Shit, Mike,' barked Sarah. 'What now?'

'Drop the gun,' he shouted.

'*Jodete*. You drop the gun,' replied Angel, with equal force.

'Drop the gun.'

'You drop the gun,' mimicked Angel, enjoying the game.

Nobody moved. Sarah raked her eyes across the room, searching for a solution. Posters of naked women, some shod, others with gun-belts. Deodorant, but not the spray kind. A bong.

Nothing that could feasibly be used as a weapon. She remembered the party on Smale's cruiser. Slowly, she began to inch her hands up to her waist. Angel turned the gun on her.

'You kill me, your girlfriend die first.'

'Do that and I'll shoot you in the bollocks,' retorted Mike.

Sarah rolled her fingers around the hem of her T-shirt and freed it from her jeans. Angel looked at her, then at Mike. He glanced over.

'Sarah. What are you doing?'

It was over in an instant. Sarah lifted her T-shirt to her neck, exposing her bare breasts. Angel dropped his gun in surprise. Mike sprang forwards and clubbed Angel unconscious with the gun butt. It took only one blow this time. Sarah primly lowered her T-shirt.

'I do not *believe* you did that,' gasped Mike.

'Don't get jealous. I saved our lives, didn't I?'

He gave her a big hug. 'Exhibitionist.'

'Cheers, me dears.' She put her hands on her hips. 'What are we going to do with him?'

'Leave him here?'

'He'll find some way of getting straight back to Drake.'

'Good point.'

Mike stuck the gun in his belt and went off to clean the sweat from his hands. Sarah bent to pick up Angel's weapon and found it was unloaded. She was about to mention this to Mike when she heard a lorry pulling up outside. She watched from the window as the driver emerged and wandered off into a bar.

'Mike. Come here. I've got an idea.'

He liked it. They put Angel's arms over their shoulders and dragged him out into the street. The alley was silent, save for phlegmatic laughter of the patrons in the bar. The side of the van read Pescados Frescos Antonio.

'What's that mean?' asked Mike.

'I'll show you.'

The rear doors weren't locked and opening them up released the powerful odour of fish. The chiller compartment contained plastic trays of shellfish, squid and cuts of sole and tuna. They hoisted Angel up, set him down at the back and moved the stacks so that he was hidden. They padded out and closed up the rear doors. Sarah then went back to the flats and slipped the key under the old woman's door. As she emerged, she passed the fishmonger. They exchanged a friendly greeting as he climbed into his cab.

The fishmonger never heard the cries for help as he drove south for Algeciras. The van gained speed, took a bend too sharply and a mixture of calamari, tuna and sole battered Angel senseless once more.

John and Kevin were doing brisk business in the clubs around Fuengirola. They tore open the bales and shoved the slabs of hash into plastic carrier bags until the handles strained. Drake started with a general call to the numerous small-time dealers. The young Scandinavians, Germans and Brits marvelled at the deal he was offering and promptly turned over all the cash they could muster. The knock-on effect had their contacts and their contacts' contacts forging a steady stream to Brown's disco. John set up his stall. The owner was a friend who was only too happy to clear them a space at the back of the dance floor. Word spread. The disco quickly became a seething mass of ecstatic teenagers, many of whom had been at the beach for the 'burning bales' incident, and had already renamed the resort, 'FunRollin.'

Drake allowed Kevin to take over and counted up. Takings grew fast and their supply was easily replenished by trips to the boot of the Mercedes. He considered the ramifications of the evening. Not only had he wiped out Ozorio's operation but he had also flooded the market and crippled the price of cannabis. Only a severe drought would push the prices back up. He'd also brought with him an emergency stash of five thousand tabs of E. With gleeful malevolence, he instructed Kevin to punt these out like Smarties at a thousand pesetas each. He popped a couple himself as he bundled the crumpled notes into the suitcases. Satisfied, he shouted at Kevin over the relentless beat of Trip-hop and Jungle.

'I'm taking this lot to the boat. Once you sold the rest, meet me there.'

Kevin gave him a stoned grin, his gimlet eyes bloodshot in the haze.

'You can get a cab to Banús, all right?'

'Okey-dokey, Uncle John.'

'You got enough cash for that?' he asked, all innocence.

Kevin held up a fistful of notes.

Following Drake's call, Tony realised that he'd need a car to get him to Malaga. They hired a Seat and went on a practice drive with Clive covering his eyes and moaning as the policeman failed to get the hang of driving on the right. They returned, shaken, to Clive's Estepona flat. During the afternoon, Tony had showed no inclination to talk further about Drake or the plan. As the sun faded, Clive prepared them a light evening meal.

'CopperTone?' he said, munching on his omelette. 'When we get to Malaga, do you reckon Drake'll come up with the goods?'

'What d'you mean, when *we* get to Malaga?'

'I thought I was coming?'

Tony loaded his fork. 'I took you all to see Smale. What more do you want?'

Clive took a swig of beer. 'See it through, just like you.'

Tony manoeuvred egg into his mouth. 'It's my arse on the line.'

When they had spoken on the phone, Sarah had told Clive of Jackie's plan and had asked him not to reveal it to the policeman unless absolutely necessary. With Tony's current attitude, this was becoming a real possibility. Clive decided he'd best handle it carefully.

'CopperTone, you needn't worry about us. We all want the same thing.'

Tony lit a Fortuna. He'd got a taste for them now and was back up to thirty a day.

'Mike and Sarah went to see Drake's wife yesterday,' Clive said, with as much nonchalance as he could muster.

'They what?'

'It's cool. She's cooking something up.'

Tony puffed hard. 'I don't like that at all. If Drake gets a sniff of it he'll sodding disappear.'

'We'll have to risk that.'

'I can't.'

Clive fixed him with an inquisitive look. 'You're more worried about your own career, aren't you?' It had recently occurred to him that questions hold a great deal of power in themselves. There seemed to be something in the human psyche that, when faced with a request, makes us volunteer an answer. Clive's theory was confirmed when Tony replied, his voice tense with passion.

'The wife's left me. What else have I got?'

'Has she actually gone? Left the house?'

Russell smashed his palm flat on the table. 'Yes. She bloody told me.'

'Do you want her back?'

Tony considered it. Debbie had always said she'd be there for him, but now she'd gone off to explore her sexuality with someone who ate lentils. Clive, letting it hang, gathered up the plates and went off to wash up. A couple of minutes later, Tony appeared in the doorway and leaned his head against the dark wood. 'I need to talk something out. Need a springboard, OK?'

Clive's yellow rubber gloves were a stark contrast to his deep brown forearms.

'Sure. Go ahead.'

'It's the end of the line for me. If this deal doesn't come together I've got nothing. I've lost Debbie anyway. Something you'll learn one day, is that once they stray you can't get them back . . . Well, you can, but I've seen the result of that in the station. Too many times.'

Clive peeled off the gloves with a wet thwack. 'So what do you want out of this? Big headline? Copper Captures Con in Costa del Crime?'

Tony forced a grudging smile. 'Be nice.'

'But that's not going to happen, is it? They're trusting you to keep quiet. With all you know?'

'Frank made it seem plausible. I get upped a couple of ranks to a cushy number.'

'Not pushed out or pensioned off?'

Tony went back in to the living room and stared out of the window. After a while he returned, his face set in resignation.

'All right. Tell your mates I'm willing to listen to offers.'

Clive called Sarah and passed on the information. With hours to spare, Clive went and read a book on his bed. It was eleven by the kitchen clock when he put his head round the door of the living room. Tony was drinking beer and staring off into space.

'I was wondering who was going to drive later?' asked Clive.

'I am.'

'You're pissed now. You'll get us killed before we reach the end of the street.'

Tony waved the neck of the bottle at Clive's plastered leg. 'You can't. Not with that.'

Clive produced a bread knife, sawed off the remains of the cast and spent five minutes sighing and scratching at his fresh leg. When he had finished, Tony tossed him the keys.

Three men lay on the beach, washed ashore like wet driftwood. The fourth lay dying on the sand, his body riddled with metal. The sea soaked his shoes as the life oozed out of him. His left eye was buried in wet sand; his right gazed unmoving at the dark silk of the sky. It took an age for him to crook his left arm to his waist. His fingers crawled crab-like on to an oblong black object. He trembled it from its casing and, in a movement of searing agony, forced it to his ear. He massaged the buttons. The LED flickered on.

'*Felipe, es José.*' he croaked. 'Sabotage. Drake has the drugs. He heading for Fuengirola.'

'*¡Madre Mía! Dime algo más.* Tell me more.'

But there were no more words in the dying lieutenant's throat.

30

Drake parked on the quay at Puerto Banús, heaved the suitcase from the boot and strode along the front. Jackie was sitting sipping a spritzer on the terrace at Valli's bar. He gave her a cursory peck on the cheek.

'Busy night?' she asked.

'Yeah. Ready for the off, then?'

She glanced at the parade of tourists. 'My stuff's in the Shogun.'

He grunted. 'Gotta sort something on the boat. I'll be back in a bit. We'll have a last drink and say ta-da to Spain.'

'Whatever you say.'

He wiped fresh sweat from his forehead. 'You all right about all this now?'

She offered him a tart little smile.

'Good girl. You'll love it once you get home. And I'll be out the nick in two shakes.'

Jackie wiggled the bridge of her nose and sniffed hard.

'You wanna go easy on the Charlie. It's habit-forming.'

'Don't you worry about me.'

Acquitted by her words, Drake stood up, took hold of the case and waddled off. Jackie watched him disappear into the throng and then called Juan Márquez on her mobile. After that, she ordered another drink. When it arrived, she rang Sarah.

'Where are you?'

Sarah's voice was enthusiastic but tinged with fear. 'In the car. We're coming into Puerto Banús.'

'I'm at Valli's.' She tapped out a cigarette. 'John's got the goods in a brown suitcase. He's on the boat.'

'Where is this boat? We couldn't find it.'

'Round the back of the harbour. Do the business then meet us at the airport.'

'OK.'

'I've made the arrangements, so don't get carried away.'

There was a buzzing on the line. 'Is he armed?' asked Sarah.

'Does a bear shit in the woods? Just watch yourselves.'

Jackie rung off, slurped her drink and made another call. Moments later, Mike and Sarah came out of a side street and were swallowed up by the busy crowd.

'Did she tell you where it was berthed?' asked Mike.

'Yes. It's further up.'

They hurried past the shops. At the end of them, a short beach mushroomed with dark parasols. A long concrete spit led out past a tall boathouse, then turned at a right-angle to form the outer wall of the harbour. They jogged into the shadow of the high wooden building. Mike eased out his gun.

'I guess this is it.'

Sarah produced Angel's gun from the pocket of her denim jacket. She had loaded it from the box of ammunition under Ramón's bed.

'I didn't see you pick that up,' he said, surprised.

'It's just in case.'

He raised a finger in admonition, but thought better of it. 'Are we ready then?'

'As we'll ever be.'

He wrapped his arms around her waist and kissed her – a hard kiss full of passion. 'I could fall for you if I'm not careful.'

'Mike. This is hardly the time.'

'But we could be dead in five minutes.'

'That,' she said, frowning, 'is hardly encouraging.'

'I wanted you to know, that's all.'

She pulled away. 'Well now I know. Thanks.'

'How about you?' he ventured.

'Mike!' she hissed.

They crept to the edge of the boathouse. In the crook of the harbour and tucked away in dry dock, was a battered houseboat. A small square of waxy light shone from its cabin windows and illuminated a few planks of peeling paint on the hull. They stepped into the moonlight and felt the breeze which fluttered through the rusting hawsers. There was a movement behind an iron post. The attack was sudden as, bald, hungry and ragged, Irish Sam Calhoun leaped on them. Firing punches, he caught Sarah hard across the face and elbowed Mike in the throat. He jabbed her hard in the stomach and steam-hammered Mike to the ground with his fists.

'Fucken tourists,' he growled.

Leaving them dazed and sprawling on the concrete, he palmed Mike's gun and broke into a trot. He reached the boat in seconds and prowled on to the deck. Three steps led down to the cabin. Sam gripped the wooden lintel and splintered the door with a swift, hard kick. He swung inside and landed squarely on his feet. John Drake dropped the wad of notes in his hand.

'Fuck me.'

Sam thrust out the gun. 'Don't fucken move pal.'

Drake's eyes fell on the Scotsman's face.

'Explanations, is it, Sam?'

'Too fucken right.'

'How'd you break out that nick?'

'Fuck that, ya cunt. I want the truth out of you. Starting with that porn thing.'

Drake gave a weary sigh. 'I done it to set up Smale. You needed good reasons to have that piss-ant little turd. I gave 'em to you.'

Sam screeched. 'Fucken set me up and all. After all I done for you.'

Drake's hand inched towards his cigarettes. Sam kicked the desk into his flabby stomach. Drake folded over, struggling for breath.

'Told ye not to move,' barked Sam. 'Keep your hands onna table.'

Drake did so.

'Whassa deal you made with the filth?'

'I'm dying, Sam. I just wanna go home.'

'You're a toe-rag, you know that.'

'Fair point.'

'What you dying of? Being a cunt?'

'Cancer, as it goes.'

There wasn't a flicker of concern in Sam's livid face. He waved the pistol at the piles of wadded notes. 'What's this for?'

'Kick-backs. Gotta pay off the law back home.' His voice became placatory. 'Sam, I weren't gonna go through with it. Jacks was well cut up when Ozorio done us over. We was gonna bugger off up the Costa Brava. Benidorm. I just done Ozorio's mob down in San Roque. The folding's what we got shifting the puff ourselves. I got half a mill here Sam. Kevin's coming with the rest. Look, I'll cut you in for half – see you right.'

Irish Sam Calhoun contemplated it for a brief moment. It was enough time for Drake to slide a revolver from his lap and shoot him in the neck. The bullet severed Sam's jugular vein and blood sprayed the walls of the tiny cabin. The Scotsman's face twisted into shock. A second bullet plunged into his chest. He fell on top of Drake, shattering the flimsy desk. He clawed wildly as his fresh orifices spewed red. Drake writhed under him, pinioned to the floor. With the last of his strength, Sam closed a hairy hand around Drake's throat. The Scot gargled hot fluid as it filled his throat and mouth. A final curse died on his lips as his heart stopped and the life dribbled out of him.

His weight increased as the muscles began to slacken. Drake's right arm was crushed under his own body and his left flopped uselessly at his side. Panic took hold and his heart beat a speeding rhythm in his ears. Sam's giant hand was still welded to his larynx. Drake fought for breath. A sickly sweet smell filled the air. His forehead sprouted perspiration, rivulets of it pouring round his ears, dripping from his neck and mingling with the spreading pool of blood. He wriggled his stodgy hips, hoping to lever the dead man off him.

'Don't move.'

Mike's face appeared over the rim of Sam's bald head. He was holding a gun. Sarah bent down and plucked Drake's pistol from the sticky floor.

'I'm fuckin' dying here,' Drake wheezed.

'Good,' said Mike.

'Get him off of me.'

Sam's hand was a frozen claw around his neck.

'I'm going to free him enough, so he can talk,' said Sarah.
Mike kept his eyes on Drake. 'Let's just take the money
and go.'

'No. This is my only chance for the truth.'

She eased two of Sam's fingers off his windpipe and Drake
managed a few shallow breaths. As the colour returned to
his face, Sarah raised Drake's gun and pointed it at him. Her
tone was cold and measured. 'Tell me what really happened to
my sister.'

'It was an accident.'

'Bullshit!'

Seeing the rage in her eyes and knowing that this time, the
gun was loaded, Drake began to talk.

'I wanted Smale to think I was gonna be his partner. He picked
up the two of them in some club. We went up the villa. Those
kids had a good time.'

Pain swelled up in Sarah's heart. 'Did you send Smale away?'

'Yeah. Didn't like having that nonce about.'

'So you did all the filming?'

Drake blinked once.

'And then?'

'I got enough footage so's Smale would think it was kosher.
Spanish kid was out of it. I forgot about the girl. Time I got to
her, she'd pegged it. Like I said, it was an accident.'

Tears streamed unchecked down her face.

'So there's me with a stiff on me hands. The Spanish kid goes
ape-shit and can't handle it. I had to shut him up.' Drake's eyes
slid to the corpse. 'Got him to come up with some smack. He
was a good fixer, Sam. Get you anything.'

'So you fixed him,' sneered Mike.

Sarah lips shivered uncontrollably. 'Go on.'

'We wanted to make it easy for the local filth. Only trouble
was her being English. They started sniffing about.'

'So you made sure that the autopsy report was buried.'

'Yeah. They was known as druggies anyway,'

She drew back, her puzzle complete. Lana's death was a
tragic blend of complicity and circumstance. She had died as
she lived. And what now? How could she make reparation
for her sister? Drake had omitted his reasons for leaving her

trussed and gagged, but this hardly seemed to matter. He had never shown anything but callous indifference to anyone. Could she show him the same? She fought off a wave of dizziness. He must pay. Her thoughts coagulated as she swung her eyes over the bloodied mess. She dropped to her knees by the open suitcase. Slowly, she scooped up a handful of money and dropped it inside. Her hand searched out again and soon she was stuffing bundles into the case, cramming it to the brim.

Mike raised his gun. 'My turn.' he said, quietly.

'The fuck *are* you anyway?'

'Doesn't matter. Remember me telling you about a man you injured?'

'Some fucking hero.'

'He was my father. I want you to understand how he felt.'

Drake rolled his eyes. 'What you gonna do? Shoot me? Get banged up yourself? Come off it.'

The truth of it sliced him like a razor. 'But you destroyed his life.'

Drake struggled under the weight. 'If your old man couldn't pull himself out of it, then that was his tough shit. Face it son. You're both losers.'

Mike began to hyperventilate. Sarah rose and tugged at his arm.

'Let's go. We've got most of the money here.'

'I—'

'Come on. Stick to the arrangement. There's nothing more we can do.'

Mike pressed the barrel to the man's forehead. Drake sneered, but his eyes gave it away. Seeing the fear, Mike slowly removed the pistol.

Sarah let out a long juddering sigh and dragged the case outside. Mike followed her to the concrete jetty and took gulping breaths. His heart would not stop racing. 'Wait for me,' he croaked.

Mike bounded back into the cabin and faced his enemy once more. Without hesitation, he drew a bead and blasted a hole in John Drake's thigh.

He ran back outside, dropped the gun on to the stone and bent double. Drool poured from his lips as he began to retch. Nothing came. Mike spat and wiped away the spittle.

'No good.'

'We'd better move,' said Sarah, urgently. 'Someone's bound to have heard the shots.'

There were only a few stragglers on the quayside and a small knot of them were looking in their direction. Many of the restaurants had closed and the *discotecas* still boomed into the night. Sarah picked up the case and headed towards the shore.

'Jesus, Mike. Did you kill him?'

'Bullet in the leg. It should slow him down.'

'Bit Old Testament, isn't it?'

He stopped in his tracks. 'Oh shitting Christ,' he said.

Kevin, with the second case, was running full pelt towards them. A wiry mange-ball of fur lolloped at his side. Sarah spun on her heels, dashed to the gun and sprinted back with it. 'Hold it right there,' she shouted, raising the pistol.

Kevin stopped. Zoltan fell into a crumpled tangle around his ankles.

'Drop the case.'

He stared at her.

'We shot your uncle. If you don't do as I say then you're next.'

Kevin lowered the suitcase. Zoltan unknotted himself, lowered his body and prepared to pounce.

'Call the dog off,' she yelled.

Kevin grinned his crocodile smile. 'Zoltan. Fetch!'

The dog leaped high. Sarah swivelled and threw the gun out to sea. Zoltan, a flailing parabola of paws and fur, twisted in the air and plunged into the water after it. Simultaneously, Kevin darted forward and delivered a running kick to Mike's stomach. Mike promptly threw up all over him.

Stunned by the coating of half-digested food, Kevin tried to wipe it from his face as Mike grabbed the second case. Recovering, the skinhead tackled him to the ground and jumped on his back. Sarah dug her nails into Kevin's neck and he let out a strange, strangled cry. An arm snaked back and gripped a fistful of her hair. Kevin tossed her aside and scrambled to his feet. He delivered a tattoo of fast kicks to Mike's ribs. On the floor, Mike summoned his strength and grabbed Kevin's foot. He twisted hard and the skinhead bit concrete.

Zoltan doggy paddled to the rocks, tried to gain purchase and slipped back into the warm water. Sarah grabbed the other case. Kevin sat bolt upright and leered. Sarah hit him with it. He went down, his nose leaking blood. He rose up again with his jaw raised in defiance. Mike and Sarah whacked him either side of the head with the cases. Kevin fell back and his head bounced off the concrete. He came up again. His face met Mike's balled fist. Kevin went down and out.

'Run,' said Mike.

The dripping dog finally mounted the path and jerked his head in confusion. He took two halting paces towards Mike and Sarah, then backtracked and licked his master's face.

A shot rang out.

Sarah looked over her shoulder. John Drake had clambered on to the jetty and was firing haphazardly at them. They dived for cover behind the boathouse. The bullets chipped against stone and pecked at the walls. Then Drake ceased firing. Thinking he'd run out of ammunition, Mike peered cautiously around the corner.

Zoltan had Drake's gun-hand in his mouth.

31

Sarah white-knuckled the wheel as they sped out on to the motorway. The road was clear and the horizon was already beginning
to lighten above the Mediterranean. Mike lit a cigarette, wound
down his window and alternated gulps of air with smoke.

'God, we did it.'

'Is there anyone behind us? Is he chasing us?'

He squeezed her shoulder. 'It's OK, it's all clear.'

'I can't get over that bloody skinhead – and that monster of
a dog!'

'The Hound from Hell. What was he called in that film? . . .
Soltan?'

'That's a suntan cream.'

'Whatever.'

He flicked his butt out of the window. It showered orange
sparks on the road. Sarah then demanded a cigarette, lifting her
foot off the accelerator as the nicotine kicked in.

'Shit,' she said. 'We were doing eighty-five and I didn't even
know it.'

'Better slow up. Don't want to get stopped.'

She smiled thinly. 'Least of our worries.'

'Let's hope Jackie does her part.'

'Yeah.'

'Sarah? What if she doesn't?'

'Then we're buggered, aren't we?'

They watched the road as the resort of Calahonda flashed past.
A lone coach sped by on the other side of the road, its driver
visible through the windscreen. He wore tinted shades.

*   *   *

Twenty kilometres in front of them, Clive and Tony Russell were skirting round Torremolinos. Tony's silence indicated that he was in full accord with their plans; either that or Clive's singing had lulled him into a stupor.

'Think I might go back to England myself one of these days,' Clive said.

'How long you been out here?'

'Eight, nine months.'

'Bumming around, eh?' Tony frowned. 'You ought to do something with your life.'

'Ooh. A job with a mop and a paper hat.'

He ignored the sarcasm. 'What are you, twenty-two? Got your whole life ahead of you. Don't want to get to my age and realise it's been an utter balls-up.'

Clive ground his teeth. 'Stop playing dad or I'll put you out right here.'

Tony held up his hands.

'Anyway. What are you going to do when you get home?'

The policeman sighed. 'First thing is, I'm leaving the force. I've had enough.'

'Gonna sell this story to the press, CopperTone?'

'Not worth my while. Get into more trouble.'

'Chicken.'

'Oh sure, coming from you.'

Clive accelerated just enough to throw Tony back in his seat.

Having wrestled himself free of Zoltan's clutches, Drake limped back to the boat and made a makeshift tourniquet out of one of the curtains. He gave Sam's corpse a cursory kick before rejoining his nephew outside.

'Gi's a hand then,' he said, indicating his blood-drenched leg.

Kevin looped John's arm over his shoulder and guided him to the quay.

'Jackie's over at Valli's. Get her, will you.'

The boy left him leaning against the wall at the end of the shopping mall and rushed off. He returned quickly with Jackie.

'Jesus, John. What's happened?'

'Sam went fuckin' loopy. English bastard winged me in the leg and had it away with my dosh.'

'What happened to Sam?'

'He got his.'

She stared at him for a long moment.

'Jacks?'

A look of determination sparked in her eyes. 'Kevin. Help me out.'

They carried him to the Mercedes and eased him into the passenger seat.

'I'll drive,' she snapped. 'You can't with that leg.'

Drake gripped his thigh. 'It ain't gone through the bone. I'll be all right.'

'No you won't. Airport, right?'

Kevin and Zoltan jumped in the back.

'Get that fuckin' dog out of here,' barked Drake.

'But he saved my life, Uncle John.'

'What did I say?'

'Aww,' he whined. 'Uncle Jooohn.'

Jackie broke in. 'God's sake, let him.' Without waiting for a reply, she eased out to the main strip and nosed the Mercedes on to the N340.

'Little fuckers, the pair of them.' grumbled Drake. 'Reckon they had this scam set up all along. All that guff about her sister an' his dad—'

Jackie listened as her husband tried to rationalise. Given time, he'd ask himself just how Mike and Sarah knew he'd be on the *Golden Behind* with the money. Blood was soaking into the leather upholstery. John tightened his tourniquet and fished a small packet of coke from his shirt pocket. He stuffed it into his nostrils and lit up a Royal Crown.

'We got problems, Jacks.'

'You're telling me.'

'Gotta get those two before they reach the airport.'

'Right.'

'And we have to make that plane. Once they find Sam I'm in schtuck.'

'Thought you had the mayor in your pocket?'

Drake winced in pain. 'Not his jurisdiction. Nor's San Roque. Had a little tumble down there earlier. Five dead.'

Nobody said anything.

Zoltan scrabbled at the window and his paw hit the electric lock. The glass slid down and he thrust his head outside. His ears began to flap like windsocks. The car purred along, eating up the road.

'What about your little arrangement with the copper?' asked Jackie.

'All bets are off.'

On learning of the loss of his cannabis and the deaths of José and the others, Felipe Ozorio alerted his remaining cohorts to start an immediate search for Drake. He and three loyal men had scoured Fuengirola and were now waiting on a motorway bridge in an open-topped convertible. He stood by the car to receive updates on his mobile. None of the news was good. His dealers had been unable to stop the freefall in dope prices and word had subsequently leaked out to Torremolinos. The knock-on effect had forced him to authorise a massive cut in the prices of all drugs. Other messages followed. The skinhead had been seen selling off large quantities of hash. More recently, there was a report of shots fired in Puerto Banús. A croupier at the casino had investigated and had spotted the Drakes heading north. Ozorio turned to the car. His two cronies were vying with one another to conceive of the most creative death for the *bastardo inglés*. Ozorio broke in when one of them suggested a considerably unhygienic method of home surgery.

'*¡Maricon!* Drake dies. It does not matter how.'

They nodded sagely, then began to squabble once more.

'*¿Señor? ¿Un Mercedes blanco?*' said the driver, sharply.

'*¿Donde esta? ¡Hijo de puta!*'

'It just passed us, heading for Malaga.'

'Follow him.'

The powerful engine hit a hundred in under fifteen seconds. The Mercedes soon came into view in the sparse morning traffic.

'*Cuatro personas,*' called out one of the men.

'Load your weapons,' barked Ozorio.

The car was filled with the noise of clicking machinery as the driver pushed the accelerator to the floor and wove into the clear middle lane. The men leaned out and braced their automatic weapons against their shoulders. The first burst of fire took out the tyres of a removals lorry. It fish-tailed on to the hard shoulder and ploughed into the cliff-face with a sickening crunch. The second stream of metal threw spats off the tarmac. The third blew three holes in the boot of Drake's car and shattered its registration plate.

'Fire,' said Ozorio, shaking his head.

The vast caramel shed of Malaga airport stood silent at five in the morning. The straw between the runways was creased by a light morning breeze and the planes hugged their gates like slumbering animals. Squealing tyres scared away the birds as, on the raised causeway, a row of Jeeps juddered to a halt. Their headlights played across the tinted front of the terminal as the first team of *guardia civil* leaped down. They positioned themselves behind the stanchions in the car park. A back up team marched into the hangar and split off into two groups, one at either end of the check-in desks. The concourse was empty, save for a scattering of early travellers. A cleaner drove his cart across the polished floor, shunting the cigarette butts in front of him. The desks were closed, the indicator board mute.

A police car arrived and disgorged the airport chief of security, two detectives and Señor Juan Alberto Ruiz Márquez. Even at this hour, he was clean-shaven and smart in chino pants and a blazer. He strode across the concourse with the chief of security at his side. They disappeared into an office, where they briefed the security staff. They were to remain calm and merely observe until Marquez had the situation under control. The whole operation was to be effected without danger to staff or passengers.

Márquez emerged and slowly paced the entire length of the departure area. He paused by a drinks dispenser and used its reflection to straighten his tie. The indicator board clattered into life like a frightened rattlesnake. He watched as it spun through the destinations and came to a halt, white on black. **06.15 LONDRES. BA 724.**

He lit a small cheroot, took a pensive drag and settled down to wait.

Jackie threw the Merc in front of a lorry which contained a

consignment of tomatoes. Behind them, bullets played across the road and rang off the crash barriers with a metallic miaow. She held her speed, using the vehicle as cover. 'Good girl,' shouted Drake above the noise of Zoltan's furious barking. Bullets thudded into the tarpaulin of the lorry and severed the guy ropes. A shower of tomatoes flew into the air and speckled the roof and windscreen. Jackie hit the wipers, smearing juice across the screen.

'Use the spray,' barked Drake.

She did so and the red mist dissipated.

'It's gotta be Ozorio,' Drake bellowed.

'Bastard,' shouted Kevin. Zoltan echoed him with a fresh howl.

'Don't give a fuck who it is,' screamed Jackie. 'What are we gonna do?'

'Petrol station,' said Drake, pointing. 'Pull in sharpish.'

They were fast approaching a low service area on a flat bed of land beside the road. A tanker sat in the forecourt, its coiled innards snaking out as the petrol fed into a manhole cover. Jackie spun the wheel, slid behind the tanker and slewed to a shuddering halt, inches from the pumps. All three shot forward and were jerked breathless by their seat belts. Zoltan, a jumble of fur and paws, tumbled into the front and landed on Drake's lap. Jackie killed the engine. Drake peered out and saw Ozorio's car speed past and out of sight.

A fresh clump of traffic made it impossible for Ozorio to see Drake's car.

'Where the fuck they go?' he screamed.

'Behind us,' shouted one of the men.

Ozorio bellowed at the driver to take the next exit and come round.

The driver, who avoided low gears whenever possible, shot up the slip ramp at top speed and flattened the central plastic bollard. The car spun out of control, hit the crash barrier and sent a shower of sparks on to the road below. They rose up, held in check by the curved metal as they skidded over the bridge.

'*Mierda*. I still have two payments left,' cursed the driver.

The men grabbed the sides of the car and prayed they would not be thrown clear. Ozorio made a mental note to fire the driver. The convertible shot back down on to the opposite carriageway narrowly missing a group of nuns in a VW beetle. With a smile, the driver kicked back into fifth and floored it.

There was a moment of calm in the Mercedes as the Drakes rubbed their necks and checked their bodies for further damage. Drake took hold of Zoltan by the scruff of his neck, opened the door and threw him out.

'What now?' asked Jackie.

'Stay down. They'll be coming back this way.'

'We're behind a sodding petrol tanker. One bullet in that and we've had it.'

Kevin, his nose streaming blood, leaned forward. 'Uncle John?' He sounded as if he were asking for permission to go out and play.

'Yes, Kev?'

'Can I take them out?'

'Do what?'

'How?' asked Jackie.

'They'll prob'ly go back and come up here again. I can use the tanker to stop 'em while you get away.'

Drake clapped his hands together. 'Bloody brilliant,' he said, stunned by the logic, bravery and utter foolishness of the plan.

'But Kevin! You could be killed,' said Jackie.

The boy shrugged. 'Not me Auntie Jackie. I'm irreversible. Like Captain Crimson.'

'Scarlet,' muttered his uncle.

Jackie turned and took in Kevin's piggy, moronic features, the tufted eyebrows, the gimlet eyes and the crocodile jaw.

'Kevin,' she said, kissing him on the cheek. 'You're a brave boy.'

He blushed. 'Thanks, Auntie Jackie.'

'Go on my son! Off you go,' said Drake.

Kevin stepped out and petted his dog. Zoltan panted and ruffled up against his thigh, keen at the prospect of a new adventure. The skinhead looked at the bulky driver's cab. Its door was open, the keys hanging from the ignition. The dashboard was a swamp of used drink cartons, pendants and tissues. He turned to the kiosk. The driver was talking to the man inside.

'Kevin?' called out Drake.

He bent to the window. John had a set of keys in his hand.

'You're a diamond, son. Take these.' He dropped them in Kevin's paw. 'You get us out of this and the villa's yours. Bit buggered at the moment – but it's a start.'

'Pool as well? And the games room?'

'The lot.'

'Can I have Zoltan up there?'

'It's your place.'

Kevin gave him a double thumbs-up and turned to the tanker.

'Kev?'

'Yes, Uncle John?'

'You know how to drive that rig?'

'Nah.' He gave his uncle a toothy grin and sauntered off.

Zoltan bounded up alongside as he clambered up into the cabin. Twisting the ignition, the diesel engine throbbed into life. Kevin stared at the controls. The first one he pressed caused the wipers to fan at a furious rate. The second blew cool air into the cab and flapped Zoltan's ears. His third attempt was more successful. He dug down for the air brake and released a sighing hiss.

Ozorio's car came past on the other side of the carriageway. He gave them the finger.

Drake tooted the horn. Kevin waved. Jackie started up the Merc and prowled towards the road. Kevin scrabbled to the other side of the cab and watched his auntie and uncle disappear slowly into the dawn.

'Come here, boy,' he said.

Zoltan put a floppy paw on his lap. Kevin revved up the engine. It gave off a deep growl. Zoltan barked as if it were a rival hound.

'It's OK, Zolty.'

The driver, having heard the noise, began to sprint towards them. The juggernaut moved backwards and severed the cables, causing petrol to spurt out across the forecourt. Kevin slammed the cabin door shut and wrestled the gear into first. The driver, seeing the spreading pool, turned and ran off into the brush. Kevin pulled the tanker round and faced it in the direction of the oncoming traffic.

Spewing petrol, the lumbering behemoth moved forwards and picked up speed. Zoltan barked with joy and placed his front paws on the dashboard as they went up to fifty. A clump of cars approached, hooting at them like angry hornets, then slewing to a halt or screaming past. Kevin held the middle lane and twiddled the buttons on the dash. The cabin was filled with an insipid rendition of Bacharach & David's 'What the World needs now is Love'.

Kevin drove on.

The sky had shifted down from ultramarine to dusty eggshell blue. They were now heading along the coastal stretch of road, roughly half-way between Fuengirola and Torremolinos. To one side there were cliffs; to the other, a ten-metre drop to the sea below.

Ozorio and his men covered the distance back to the last intersection and made the turn. The men reloaded and propped themselves up, ready to fire. The driver suddenly let out a shout.

'*¿Qué cosa tan jodida es esa?* What the fuck is that?'

The shining juggernaut was bearing down on them with its air horn blaring.

In the driver's cabin, Kevin hugged Zoltan's hot body to his chest and pulled hard on the air brake. The tanker bucked and reared out of control. Zoltan howled. Kevin saw the petrified faces of the men in the car in front. He screamed at the top of his voice. 'Caaaaaants!' The radio segued into 'Do you know the way to San José?'

With a metallic banshee howl, the juggernaut jackknifed and Ozorio's car ploughed into its side. The remaining petrol in the tanker's belly ignited and sent a mushroom of flame twenty-five metres into the sky. The heat welded the vehicles together and melted the road into a slick of black tar. Ozorio and his men died instantly. The convertible and the tanker rammed through the crash barrier and spun out over the cliff edge. The blazing, twisted wreckage plummeted down and shattered the calm surface of the sea. The water sizzled and boiled and a plume of smoke choked up into the air.

Back on the road, the hole surrounding the crash barrier was marked by small fires. The carriageway was littered with glass and dented, scorched metal. The flames sniffed out the petrol trail which led back to the service station and, in seconds, a streak of orange and blue heat began to shoot along the motorway, faster than any vehicle.

With great presence of mind, Carlos Hernández, the attendant, had thrown the sand from the fire buckets across the slick at the entrance. As a result, the line of fire stopped shy of the building by just five metres.

Carlos eventually recovered from the shock, but later developed a compulsive disorder which caused him to snuff out combustible objects such as lighters or matches. This put a severe crick in his social life.

As Mike and Sarah drew into the raised carport at Malaga airport, they became aware of movement around them. Dark shapes lurked behind the stanchions, their presence given away by the crackling of transmitters. Sarah switched off the engine. It began to cool with a series of metallic clicks.

'What now?' asked Mike.

'Go to departures, I suppose.'

He tilted his head at the armed guards who were positioned at either side of the entrance. 'What about them?'

'They aren't to know we've got a million quid in stolen drug money, are they?'

'True, but I reckon we should leave the cases in the boot until we know what's going on.'

Sarah sighed. 'All right.'

She stepped out and stretched, pressing her thumbs into the small of her back to rotate her knotted muscles. Mike hitched up his jeans and closed his door with a satisfying slam. The *guardia civil* watched, but did not react.

They crossed to the entrance and moved inside. There was a dense police presence in the wide departure area. Three of the check-in desks were open and clumps of passengers were gathered around the flight information screens. Sarah scanned the concourse and spotted Clive and Tony nursing coffees by a drinks dispenser. Both looked haggard and drawn. Seeing them, Clive broke into a grin and trotted over. His cast was gone and he now moved with nothing more than a slight limp.

'Hey, guys. Looks like you made it,' he said, hugging Sarah.

Mike shrugged. 'Actually, we were killed in a shoot-out.'

Tony Russell joined them. He wore his usual irritated scowl. 'What's going on? The place is stuffed with security. You blown the whistle or what?'

Mike gave him a superior smile. 'It's all under control. We've got the money.'

He looked around. 'You, er. You told Clive you'd be willing to deal with us?'

'Mike!' hissed Sarah.

He ignored her. 'So how much would it take for you to leave Drake here?'

Sarah gripped Mike's arm and led him away. 'What are you doing?'

'Well, we don't know if Jackie's going to come through yet, do we?'

Her nostrils flared. 'That's no reason to go straight in and try to bribe him.'

'I thought it was worth a go.'

'Should've asked me first.'

'Sorry.'

'Better be.' She replied with a taut smile.

They rejoined Clive and the policeman.

'The money's no good to me,' said Tony, flatly. 'Where would I go with it? Bent ex-coppers aren't particularly high on anyone's popularity list.'

Mike broke in. 'I heard Buenos Aires is nice.'

Tony snorted. 'Too hot. I get sunburn standing by a radiator.'

A tall, elegant Spaniard approached them. He was flanked by two armed guardia civil.

'*Señoras y Señores*. My name is Márquez and I am in charge of this operation.' He turned to Sarah. 'You are the girl who had some trouble over her sister?' She nodded. He glanced at Mike, then at Clive.

'And you?'

'Clive Watson.'

'I'm Mike,' said Mike.

Márquez turned to Tony Russell. 'You must be the British policeman?'

'Detective Sergeant Russell. I'm here to take custody of John Drake.'

Márquez raised an eyebrow. 'You have the necessary papers?'

Tony blinked. 'I have the full authorisation of the Home Office.'

'And this is sanctioned by airport security? By the authorities at Malaga? By the Andalucian parliament?'

'No need. Drake's returning entirely of his own volition.'

Márquez drew himself to his full height and towered over Tony. 'A known criminal, possibly dangerous, on a commercial flight. With no form of restraint? This is highly irregular. Why were the authorities not consulted on this matter?'

Tony caved in. 'I don't know. I'm just the courier.'

'You realise you have no right to extradite one of our citizens without permission.'

The others watched the game of verbal ping-pong, torn between patriotism and their desire to see Márquez win out.

'It's not strictly an extradition,' said Tony, flushing. 'He . . . he's just coming home with me.'

Márquez cut him off. 'I cannot permit you to take this man.' He turned to the policemen flanking him. 'Llevenselos. Take them into custody.'

The *guardia civil* had marched them halfway across the concourse when Márquez' radio sparked into life. He halted the procession, absorbed the message and then issued another order to the men. They moved swiftly, bundling the four of them to the nearest wall and raising their machine guns to waist height.

The automatic doors hissed open and sent a blast of cool air into the hangar. The Drakes stumbled inside. Jackie's clothes were smeared in blood and her hair had collapsed. She had an arm around John's waist and was supporting him as he dragged his injured leg. His trousers were soaked red and his loafers left sticky imprints as he shuffled forwards. As they headed for the oasis of the check-in, Drake's eyes darted around, taking in the passengers and the armed men. His head jerked back in surprise when he saw Tony with Clive, Mike and Sarah.

'What's this? Surprise party?' he sneered.

Mike and Sarah gave Drake a little wave.

'Russell! What's going on, you ponce?'

Tony didn't have a chance to reply. The departure lounge became a blur of action as the combined team of police and *guardia civil* ringed the Drakes in an iron fence of weaponry.

'Oh, bollocks!' said Drake.

The soldiers hustled them into a bright, shadowless security office. The spartan room contained only a large metal desk and two plastic chairs. Drake was searched, handcuffed and forced to sit. Juan Márquez had a few quiet words with the chief of airport security and all but two of the guards left the room. 'Where to begin?' he said to no one in particular.

Drake banged his fists on the desk. 'Fuck you doin' here, Juan?'

The mayor eyed him like prey, then flicked his eyes up at Jackie. 'First. There is a matter of some money.'

'Too right,' spat Drake, staring murderously at Mike. 'What you done with it, you cunt?'

'Language,' said Sarah. 'Ladies present, remember?'

Jackie turned slightly towards her. 'You got it?'

'It's in the car, along with the film.'

Márquez' voice was like honey. 'If you would please fetch it for me? I shall arrange an escort.'

'I'll come too,' said Mike.

Flanked by guards, Mike and Sarah recrossed the concourse and went out to the car park. The air had warmed up by a few degrees and was now tinged with a faint odour of slurry. Mike lit a cigarette, pulled a face at the harshness of the tobacco and immediately stamped it out. Sarah took the tape from her handbag and opened up the boot. Mike was about to hoist out the cases when one of the guards took them off him.

'Bet he's after a tip,' muttered Mike.

When they returned, Drake was a ball of fury. 'You ain't got no right keeping me here,' he roared. 'Someone tell us what's bleedin' going on?'

The guards raised their weapons but Márquez waved them down. 'It was a surprise to me, John,' he began, 'when it came to my attention that you were planning to return to your country.' He placed his hands together, almost in prayer. 'Am I to gather that our business together is at an end?'

'Jackie. Call my brief.'

She said nothing and did not move as the guard placed the suitcases on the desk. Stroking his heavy moustache, Márquez slowly unzipped the cases, lifted a corner of each and peered inside. His expression remained stoical. 'I believe there was a videotape?'

Sarah handed it to him.

'*Gracias*. Now, if *Señora* Drake would care to come with me?'

Jackie stepped around her husband and moved to the door.

'The fuck you doing?' shouted Drake. 'Jackie. Answer me!'

She turned to Márquez and smiled sweetly. 'Have you got another room? I can't think in here.'

'Jacks? Jacks!'

Márquez closed the cases, pulled them off the desk and they left the room. Drake immediately rose to his feet, but was restrained by the guards. He sank into his seat and furrowed his brows.

The others watched him.

Clive spoke first. 'This is better than the telly.'

Tony shot him a weary look.

'I'll have you for this Russell,' growled Drake.

Tony Russell reached for his cigarettes and offered them round. No one accepted so he smoked alone in the tense silence.

Mike stared at the back of Drake's shining skull, thinking of how the man would never give in, no matter what. His home had been destroyed, his drug-running operations obliterated, his loyalties shredded. And yet, stripped of his power, he raged on, a deposed, demented king.

Sarah focused on a throbbing vein on Drake's thick neck. She sensed he was still scheming, readjusting the facts, planning his escape scenario.

Clive was wondering too. About the lies; the deceit, the complex web which Jackie was about to unravel. How, he wondered, how could she pacify all the parties concerned. What *was* her solution?

Tony Russell looked at the Spanish guards and decided that their uniforms were nicer than the English ones.

Márquez put his head around the door and beckoned to him. 'Detective Sergeant. If you would come this way, please?'

Tony left the room, shrugging for everyone's benefit.

Ten minutes later, he re-entered carrying a bulging airport security bag and wearing his wide amphibian grin.

'What you so happy about?' snarled Drake.

'We're going home,' said Tony. 'Just like you wanted.'

Sarah and Mike stared at one another, speechless with shock.

Jackie came in with Márquez and placed herself in front of her husband. Márquez shut the door, stood to one side and folded his arms.

There was a hairline crack of worry in Drake's voice. 'Jacks? What the fuck is this?'

She raked her eyes down his face, taking in the piercing stare, the fat nose, the leathery skin. Finally, his cruel lips which had been made more prominent by the removal of his facial hair. She spoke matter-of-factly, as if reading out a series of charges.

'Way I see it's this. You done everyone over, me included. Specially me. "Jackie don't need to know. Jackie ain't important." I never been consulted, John. Right from the start, when we come out here. You never asked if I wanted to live out here, didcha? You told me we was going and that was that.'

Drake shot a dismissive glance at Márquez.

'I ain't gonna go on about it John. It's the end of it, that's all. You can have your little deal with the filth.' She glanced at Tony Russell. 'I've sorted it so he's paid off. You can go home and do your time, only you do it solo. I ain't coming back.'

'What's his angle?' Drake murmured, flicking his eyes at Márquez once more.

She fumbled out a cigarette and the mayor lit it for her. Jackie took a drag and waved the tip at Mike and Sarah.

'These two wanted you to stay here, so's you could go down for her sister. I was going to go along with it. Have Juan put you away.' She took a quick little suck. 'Only I changed my mind. Talked him round to letting you go.'

'And it's my dosh you're using for this?'

Her smile was twisted and her eyes burned with hatred. 'Hurts does it? Come on John. You'll get your op. You'll do your time, then you'll get all the fog and footy you want. You'll be all right, won't you lover?'

Her husband gave her a solitary blink. 'Yeah,' he rasped in gravel tones. 'I'll be all right.'

She placed her hands on the desk and, with sudden ferocity, spat full in his face. 'You never fucking listened did you? I told you never to get involved with porn, you filthy toe-rag!' She slapped him hard. 'You didn't even have to make that film. All you had to do was let Smale think you was up for it, but you wanted to make your own dirty little movie, didn't you? Wanted to watch, was that it? That what turns you on these days?'

The spittle trailed down Drake's cheek.

'Bitch!'

She narrowed her eyes to slits. 'You think you're God Almighty, don't you? I got news for you John, you ain't. You're just another toss-pot second-rater who thinks he's got one up on everyone. Sitting up there on your fucking throne in your little British ghetto and hiring your little slaves to do your dirty work. You reckon this is the bleedin' British empire, don'tcha? I'll tell you, Spain's better off without you.'

'What's all this dago shit?' he growled.

'Twenty years I been here. This is my home, John. No one takes the piss out of me 'cos of where I come from. What would I be back in the smoke,? Just another tart with money. You get grief off of your mates and snotty looks out of them girls in the posh shops. Think I wanna put up with that? Bunch of upper class twats laughing at me 'cos I don't speak *raight*? It's all right for you, John. Money's power to a bloke, but to a woman, it's indulgence.'

She closed her eyes to recoup her strength.

'I love it here, John. I belong here. I speak the language.' As if to prove her point, Jackie spoke a few fluent sentences in Spanish to Márquez. He replied courteously and the guards suppressed their smiles.

'What'd she say?' asked Drake.

'It was not very . . . complimentary,' Márquez replied.

Jackie leaned in to her husband, her voice now a purr. 'What you done's unforgivable and I want you out my life.' She motioned for the tape. 'I'll do you one last favour and that's it.' She took it, flipped open the cartridge and pulled out a ream of shiny black film.

'No!' Sarah screamed and lunged out to stop her. A guard grabbed her and held her back. 'You promised!' she sobbed.

'Sorry, love. That's the end of it,' Jackie said.

They watched helplessly as she pulled snakes of plastic from the spool. Loops of it grew into a shimmering pool on the floor.

The public address system then began to mumble through the walls. Márquez unfolded his arms. 'I believe your flight is leaving, *Señor* Drake.'

Jackie swayed on her feet. 'We got time for a coffee, Juan? I'm knackered.'

The mayor glanced at his watch and nodded.

A medic gave John a shot of pethidine and dressed the wound with a fresh tourniquet. After swallowing a handful of pain-killers, Drake's handcuffs were removed and, flanked by the *guardia civil*, he left the room. Tony Russell went along with him, his bag held tightly to his side.

Sarah, Mike and Clive followed in a trance as they were ushered through the customs area. The vast departure lounge was bathed in fresh sunlight which streamed in through the tall cathedral windows. Outside, a plane taxied past against the lavender Sierra mountains. Groups of tired, sunburned passengers were lolling on the seats, too engrossed with thoughts of home to pay much attention to the blood-spattered prisoner and his entourage.

Juan Márquez led the procession, Drake limping a pace behind him with the guards. Jackie walked stiffly beside them, avoiding eye contact with her husband. The others followed as they rose up the escalator to the duty-free and restaurant area.

'Tell you what I think,' said Clive. 'She divvied it up. Probably a third each.'

'Russell, the mayor and who else?' asked Mike.

'A third for herself so she can carry on living out here.'

'Good for her,' muttered Sarah darkly.

They arrived on the mezzanine level and gathered in the fast food area. Families were wolfing down last-minute breakfasts or dealing with belligerent children. Márquez studied the flight indicator screens, saw that the plane was shortly to board and tapped his watch at Jackie.

'Think I'll go get a paper,' said Tony Russell.

Sarah planted herself in front of him.

'Don't you realise he's getting away with murder?'

Russell assumed an authoritarian tone. 'Look, miss. I'm sorry it didn't work out your way. But if it's any good to you, Drake's deal isn't going to happen now.'

'What do you mean?'

'There's a lot in here.' He patted the case. 'But it's not the full amount. Drake'll be doing the full stretch.'

Clive butted in. 'And you'll keep your job.'

Tony gave a taut smile.

'What about that contract you signed?' asked Mike.

'That's Croucher's problem.'

Márquez placed a hand on Tony's shoulder. 'It is time. You must go.'

'I didn't get my paper.'

Márquez hooded his eyes. 'We will send it on. *Venga.*'

Tony held out a hand and Mike and Sarah shook it in turn. Clive gave him a brother's shake.

'See you, CopperTone.'

'Good luck, son. Get yourself sorted, eh?'

'Maybe,' said Clive.

Drake faced his wife with lizard eyes. Jackie took a step away from him and was back-lit by a blazing sunbeam.

'Jacks. You know I'm a goner back home. They can sort out the cancer but I ain't going to last out a long stretch . . . Come on, love. It ain't too late. I still got assets out here. Let's do something.'

Jackie said nothing.

'Then fuck you, Jacks!' His voice rose to a bellow, drowning out the chatter and the muzak around them. 'Fuck the lot of you. You need me! I bring you work. Work and prosperity.' His face bloomed scarlet. 'Spain had nothing 'til I come along. Dope? It's your new industrial age. No barriers, no unions, no ruling class cunts. Fucking economy runs on it. And I'll tell you. Soon the whole world will run on it.' Every fibre of his body boiled with rage and hatred. 'I'm a fucking pioneer me. Just like my ancestor. Do me down? You should give me a fucking knighthood!' He swung an arm at the window. 'Look at it. Hotels, bars, clubs. My money built this place. My brains. My guts. My hard graft!' His voice lowered as his breath shortened and his pain inside ate him up. 'You need me, and you don't even know it. This what I get? Well, you can have it all back. I don't want it no more!'

With that, he swung his fists in the faces of the guards and grabbed Tony's bag. In a flash, he had tossed its contents into the air. Drake made to run but Márquez was in front of him and stopped him with a hard jab to the stomach. The guards held their weapons to Drake's head. Around them, an autumn of money cascaded on the tables, on the floor, on the passengers. They fingered, they grabbed, and they tussled for the fistfuls of currency.

Sarah sensed another danger.

A waiter had pushed aside his trolley-load of dirty plates. His hand was inside the cart and he was grasping something metallic.

He came up shooting.

Two ear-splitting explosions seared across the hall. The passengers screamed and scattered in all directions. Mike lunged at Sarah and threw her to the floor. Clive leaped to protect a child at a nearby table. Márquez barked an order and the guards released a flurry of shots into the waiter's body.

Time haemorrhaged into a clotted second. The assassin's bullets had smashed Drake's sternum, plunging deep into his heart. A rope of blood jerked out of his body and lassoed the air. Drake twitched in shock and spasm, emitting a plaintive gurgle as a mouthful of blood burst over his belly. His eyes rolled to the whites and he toppled over, hitting the ground with a slam. The screaming, shouted orders and running feet faded away and became a sharp, acid silence. John Drake's corpse was cradled by a spreading pool of blood. It glistened as red as a sunset.

The muscles around Jackie Drake's mouth began to twitch. She gazed at the body of her husband and slowly, very slowly, closed her eyes.

Most of the money was returned to Tony Russell. He was cautioned about international diplomacy and then allowed to leave on the next flight. Mike, Sarah and Clive were questioned and shortly afterwards released by the police. Using the airport facilities, Jackie Drake repaired herself as best she could and the four of them drove in convoy to Fuengirola. They went to Scoffer's bar on the front where Clive then excused himself to go off and get some sleep. Mike and Sarah ordered the full English breakfast and wolfed down eggs, bacon, sausage and beans. Jackie picked at a plain omelette.

'So?' said Mike between mouthfuls. 'Who shot your husband?'

Her dark sunglasses gave nothing away. 'An independent contractor,' said Jackie, eventually.

Sarah dropped her fork. 'You didn't hire him, did you?'

'The mayor reckons it was a hit by a rival hash firm. John wiped out four of theirs and the rest chased us on the way to the airport. Kevin nicked a petrol tanker and went to sort them out.'

'That explains the chaos on the motorway,' said Mike.

Two lanes of the *autovía* near Torremolinos had been cordoned off, creating a ten-mile tailback. It was a glowing testament to the destructiveness of the moronic midget and his best friend.

Jackie sighed. 'He was a brave kid.'

'You didn't answer my question,' said Sarah.

A terse little smile played across Jackie's lips.

'Well? Did you have anything to do with it?'

She removed her glasses. 'Listen. I trusted you with the money. You could have run off with it and I'd have been up shit creek. I relied on you and you came through. Let's leave it at that.'

Sarah nodded sympathetically. 'What are you going to do now?'

'Gotta get the villa sorted first. Reckon I'll sell it and get an apartment in Marbella. Might open a boutique. Always fancied being a fashion designer.'

Sarah bit her lip.

'I saw that,' chided Jackie. 'I know what people want, believe you me.'

'You certainly do,' said Mike.

'You two going to stay on the coast, then?'

Mike and Sarah exchanged glances.

'Well, if you come back, you're welcome anytime, all right?' She rose to her feet. 'Anyways, I got a lot to do. See you around.'

'And that's it?' asked Sarah, incredulously.

'That's it.'

She kissed Mike on the cheek and gave Sarah a big hug.

'Thanks Jackie,' she whispered. 'I haven't had time to figure out how I'm going to react to all this, but thanks anyway.'

John Drake's widow pulled away and held her by the shoulders. 'Sarah, you was way out your depth from the start. You two better get back to England and leave the gun-play to us peasants.'

She tossed down a few notes and then walked off into the heat, her heels beating a light staccato on the pavement.

'Tough lady,' said Mike.

Sarah smiled at Jackie's retreating back. 'You bet. Shall we go?'

'Where to?'

'My place. If the ants haven't eaten it.'

'What? To sleep?'

She faced him. 'I'm too wired up to sleep.'

'Me too. What shall we do?'

'I'm sure you'll think of something.'

* * *

They lay side by side, their bodies slippery with sweat. Afternoon sunlight slatted through the shutters and bathed them in gold.

'What now?' she asked.

'Sleep,' murmured Mike, already drifting off.

She prodded him awake. 'I mean, what about us?'

He stuck out a thoughtful lip and smoothed a hand across her belly. 'Is it "Us"? I did ask you before.'

She grinned, showing the slight gap between her front teeth. He began to toy with her dark ropes of hair and his quickening erection grazed against her thigh.

'Someone's double keen,' she said, clambering on top and straddling him.

'We going out, then?' he asked as bluntly as a seventeen-year-old.

She nodded like a pert puppy. He chuckled and rolled her off him.

'Aargh. Wet patch,' she yelped as the cool glue spread across her bottom.

'I made that,' said Mike.

'Don't sound so pleased with yourself.'

They kissed and he slipped smoothly inside her once more. She contracted her thighs to slow his pace and they ground together tightly until he came.

'Did you?' he asked, rolling off her.

'Not that time, no.'

'Oh . . . sorry.'

'Doesn't matter. There'll be plenty of other times.'

He sat cross-legged on the bed and traced a slow finger around her body.

'That's nice. What are you doing?'

'Drawing you.'

She struck a pose with a hand on her hip and the other on her head. Her hair tumbled over her face.

'I love your hair.'

'You won't on a bad-hair day. Of which there are many.'

'Would too . . . Sarey.'

'Sarey?'

'Doesn't work, does it? As a pet-name.'

She frowned. 'That's one rule. No puerile bunny snuggly names, OK?'

'Aww, just a few. We can make our friends sick.'

'Deal. I'm going to have a shower.'

She swung her legs off the bed and pulled on her robe. Mike lay back, watching her as he absently rearranged his sticky penis.

'What day is it today?' he asked.

'Thursday? No, the bins have gone from outside. Must be Friday.'

'Friday? . . . Shit.' He jumped up. 'Shit, my flight home. It's today.'

'You sure?'

'Course I'm sure. Two weeks. My holiday's over. The flight goes at six-forty.'

He struggled into his shorts, oblivious to everything except the need to pack and get moving. Sarah watched him as he tried to force his feet into his still laced trainers.

'Do you have to go?'

'If I miss the flight, I won't be able to afford to get home.'

'I could lend you the money.'

He bundled his clothes into his suitcase. 'Can't let you do that. We'll get together back at home.'

'You never asked me when I'm coming back.'

'When are you coming back?'

She folded her arms. 'I've got to sort out my job first.'

'That won't take long, will it?'

'That's not the—' She glared at him. 'Come on then. You'll miss your flight.'

They entered the busy caramel building for the second time that day, both feeling quite divorced from the beer-bellied Brits and their squalling children. Mike checked his bag at the desk and took his boarding pass from the smiling clerk. Sarah stood alone in the centre of the concourse, lost in thought. He came up and kissed her.

'It's on the board,' she said, hollowly. 'You've got twenty minutes.'

'We'll get together as soon as we can, yeah?'

She didn't reply.

'We're only, what, ten miles apart in London. Call me this evening?'

ır Juan Alberto **Ruiz Márquez** has spearheaded an effective
ti-drug programme in the area.

ın **Drake's** body was flown back to England and cremated.
cording to a stipulation in his will, his ashes were to be
ttered across Peckham High Street. This wish was found to
illegal but his brother went through with it all the same.
ing to an unfavourable wind on the day, Drake's final remains
porarily blinded a bus driver and caused a five-car pile-up.

kie **Drake** opened a highly successful series of boutiques
der the name of 'Jacqui's'. Her sixth store recently opened
ladrid and she has plans for expansion across Europe. She
been romantically linked in the pages of *Hola!* with a number
rominent businessmen and politicians.

in and **Zoltan's** bodies were never found. However, in a
nt report in Ibiza, a boy and dog answering their description
e seen exposing themselves to a group of Swedish nudists.

e **Trent** and **Sarah Rutherford** were reunited the next day
engirola. They returned to England and set up home. Sarah
back into travel management and Mike joined a prominent
hing company. They were married the following spring
ent their honeymoon in Hawaii. They have not, as yet,
ed to Spain.

He was already seeing his dingy flat above the shop in Tooting
High Street, imagining himself plonking down his luggage and
trawling through the bad post.

'Why don't you call me? On my mobile.'

'Sure.'

Her chin trembled. 'Look, who are we kidding? You'll forget
to call tonight, then tomorrow, you'll feel guilty so you won't
call then either.'

'I'll call you tonight. I promise.'

'Don't bother.'

'Sarah,' he pleaded. 'Please.'

'Mike, what have we got in common apart from sex, death
and carnage?'

He smiled weakly. 'Marriages are based on less.'

Her face was tight with tension. 'You'd better get going.'

'Sarah. I'm not letting you go. No way.'

'Stay, then.'

He hugged her and she buried her face in his neck.

'I love you,' he whispered.

She pulled back. 'Don't say that.'

Mike felt his eyes prickle and moisten and hot tears flowed
down his face. He clung to her again for a long moment
as the crowd bustled around them. The flight announcement separated them like a stern parent. Mike slowly let her
hands trail through his fingers. He then walked backwards,
away from her with his eyes still locked on hers. He tumbled
over a trolley and jumped up like a cat, pretending it had
never happened. Sarah broke into a tiny smile. Mike turned
and went through passport control and disappeared out of
her life.

She kept his image in her mind until the sounds of the airport
became a rush in her ears. Turning on her heels, she strode back
to her car. She held on to the tears until she was alone and safe
in the driver's seat.

The plane rose into the sky and the landscape became a patch-
work quilt of ochre and tan. The 737 arched over the city of
Malaga and turned northwards into the setting sun. Mike sat,
deep in thought. Drake was dead. He was free of the ghost that

had haunted his family for so long. He'd found an inner strength, a resilience and love. Finally, real love.

They climbed to their cruising altitude and the safety belt lights blinked out. The stewardesses began to work their way down the aisles, offering drinks and duty-frees. Why? Why didn't I stay with you, Sarah? He said her name aloud and moved his mouth in an imaginary kiss. He thought of her laugh, her smile, the way she ran her hands through her hair. Meeting her in the bar. The fire. The party on the yacht. Jimena, and making love under the fireworks. How could I let her go? How could I?

I can't.

The stewardess leaned over and smiled at him.

'Can I get you anything sir?'

'Yes. The next flight back to Malaga.'

EPI

In recognition of his work in extraditing Barry S Russell was promoted to Detective Inspector. Soon he divorced his wife Debbie and left the force with a He now owns a pub in Watford and has no cont former wife or brother-in-law.

Clive 'The Fonk' Watson returned to England tha now works as a housing benefits officer for Hack Council and is studying for the bar.

Nicola Sedgwick left *Sorted!* magazine and contin until the following summer when she met and m bar owner in Kos. They recently returned to Eng since separated.

Barry Smale is doing a fifteen-year sentence the distribution and sale of pornography. He from rectal conditions, in part due to his cell offender.

Angel Esteban renounced all connections trafficking and moved home to his native runs a souvenir shop with his wife, a lo Herrera. The wedding was consummated ceremony. He has developed an extrem seafood.

Neither **Ramón Esteban** nor **Felipe O** ifiable, even through dental records. isation is responsible for drug supp

He was already seeing his dingy flat above the shop in Tooting High Street, imagining himself plonking down his luggage and trawling through the bad post.

'Why don't you call me? On my mobile.'

'Sure.'

Her chin trembled. 'Look, who are we kidding? You'll forget to call tonight, then tomorrow, you'll feel guilty so you won't call then either.'

'I'll call you tonight. I promise.'

'Don't bother.'

'Sarah,' he pleaded. 'Please.'

'Mike, what have we got in common apart from sex, death and carnage?'

He smiled weakly. 'Marriages are based on less.'

Her face was tight with tension. 'You'd better get going.'

'Sarah. I'm not letting you go. No way.'

'Stay, then.'

He hugged her and she buried her face in his neck.

'I love you,' he whispered.

She pulled back. 'Don't say that.'

Mike felt his eyes prickle and moisten and hot tears flowed down his face. He clung to her again for a long moment as the crowd bustled around them. The flight announcement separated them like a stern parent. Mike slowly let her hands trail through his fingers. He then walked backwards, away from her with his eyes still locked on hers. He tumbled over a trolley and jumped up like a cat, pretending it had never happened. Sarah broke into a tiny smile. Mike turned and went through passport control and disappeared out of her life.

She kept his image in her mind until the sounds of the airport became a rush in her ears. Turning on her heels, she strode back to her car. She held on to the tears until she was alone and safe in the driver's seat.

The plane rose into the sky and the landscape became a patch-work quilt of ochre and tan. The 737 arched over the city of Malaga and turned northwards into the setting sun. Mike sat, deep in thought. Drake was dead. He was free of the ghost that had haunted his family for so long. He'd found an inner strength, a resilience and love. Finally, real love.

They climbed to their cruising altitude and the safety belt lights blinked out. The stewardesses began to work their way down the aisles, offering drinks and duty-frees. Why? Why didn't I stay with you, Sarah? He said her name aloud and moved his mouth in an imaginary kiss. He thought of her laugh, her smile, the way she ran her hands through her hair. Meeting her in the bar. The fire. The party on the yacht. Jimena, and making love under the fireworks. How could I let her go? How could I?

I can't.

The stewardess leaned over and smiled at him.

'Can I get you anything sir?'

'Yes. The next flight back to Malaga.'

EPILOGUE

In recognition of his work in extraditing Barry Smale, **Tony Russell** was promoted to Detective Inspector. Soon afterwards, he divorced his wife Debbie and left the force with a full pension. He now owns a pub in Watford and has no contact with his former wife or brother-in-law.

Clive 'The Fonk' Watson returned to England that autumn. He now works as a housing benefits officer for Hackney Borough Council and is studying for the bar.

Nicola Sedgwick left *Sorted!* magazine and continued to temp until the following summer when she met and married a beach bar owner in Kos. They recently returned to England and have since separated.

Barry Smale is doing a fifteen-year sentence in Parkhurst for the distribution and sale of pornography. He frequently suffers from rectal conditions, in part due to his cell mate, a violent sex offender.

Angel Esteban renounced all connections to violence and drug trafficking and moved home to his native village of Istan. He runs a souvenir shop with his wife, a local girl called Juanita Herrera. The wedding was consummated within an hour of the ceremony. He has developed an extreme allergy to all types of seafood.

Neither **Ramón Esteban** nor **Felipe Ozorio's** bodies were identifiable, even through dental records. At present, no sole organisation is responsible for drug supplies in the Costa Del Sol.

Snr Juan Alberto Ruiz Márquez has spearheaded an effective anti-drug programme in the area.

John Drake's body was flown back to England and cremated. According to a stipulation in his will, his ashes were to be scattered across Peckham High Street. This wish was found to be illegal but his brother went through with it all the same. Owing to an unfavourable wind on the day, Drake's final remains temporarily blinded a bus driver and caused a five-car pile-up.

Jackie Drake opened a highly successful series of boutiques under the name of 'Jacqui's'. Her sixth store recently opened in Madrid and she has plans for expansion across Europe. She has been romantically linked in the pages of *Hola!* with a number of prominent businessmen and politicians.

Kevin and **Zoltan's** bodies were never found. However, in a recent report in Ibiza, a boy and dog answering their description were seen exposing themselves to a group of Swedish nudists.

Mike Trent and **Sarah Rutherford** were reunited the next day in Fuengirola. They returned to England and set up home. Sarah went back into travel management and Mike joined a prominent publishing company. They were married the following spring and spent their honeymoon in Hawaii. They have not, as yet, returned to Spain.

PHIL ANDREWS

OWN GOALS

When City's star Italian footballer is had up for sexual assault by a glamorous model, the media has a field day; he's the second player to be facing a ban.

The Northern Premiership club secretary thinks they've been framed and employs Steve Strong to investigate.

As a film noir buff and Chandler expert with a tenuous connection to the model, Strong is hardly qualified as a PI. (And it's not likely to appease his high flying wife's dictate that he get a proper job.)

As he checks out the behind-the-stadium-scenes where directors' accessories include crocodile shoes and tipsy trophy-wives, Strong soon discovers that there is something far more sinister afoot than a sex scandal. City are about to be relegated and he's facing a penalty shoot-out. Can he avoid a permanent transfer before the final whistle blows?

A witty, topical thriller set in a gritty Yorkshire city, Own Goals offers an insiders' view of the popular world of big time soccer, the (corrupting) influence of television money on a Premiership club, its players and directors, and the seedy side of a modern British city, its clubs, pubs, good-time girls and shady businessmen.

HODDER AND STOUGHTON PAPERBACKS

A selection of bestsellers from Hodder and Stoughton

Own Goals   Phil Andrews   0 340 74821 4   £10.00 ☐

All Hodder & Stoughton books are available at your local bookshop or newsagent, or can be ordered direct from the publisher. Just tick the titles you want and fill in the form below. Prices and availability subject to change without notice.

Hodder & Stoughton Books, Cash Sales Department, Bookpoint, 39 Milton Park, Abingdon, OXON, OX14 4TD, UK. E-mail address: order@bookpoint.co.uk. If you have a credit card you may order by telephone – (01235) 400414.

Please enclose a cheque or postal order made payable to Bookpoint Ltd to the value of the cover price and allow the following for postage and packing:
UK & BFPO – £1.00 for the first book, 50p for the second book, and 30p for each additional book ordered up to a maximum charge of £3.00.
OVERSEAS & EIRE – £2.00 for the first book, £1.00 for the second book, and 50p for each additional book.

Name _____

Address_____

_____

_____

If you would prefer to pay by credit card, please complete:
Please debit my Visa/Access/Diner's Card/American Express (delete as applicable) card no:

Signature _____

Expiry Date _____

If you would NOT like to receive further information on our products please tick the box. ☐